NO PERFECT PRINCESS

SECRETS OF STONE: BOOK THREE

ANGEL PAYNE & VICTORIA BLUE

This book is an original publication of Angel Payne & Victoria Blue.

Cover Design by Emmy Ellis
Cover Photographs: 123RF

Paperback ISBN: 978-1-947222-64-9

NO PERFECT PRINCESS

SECRETS OF STONE: BOOK THREE

ANGEL PAYNE & VICTORIA BLUE

It takes an amazing family to live with, love,
and support a neurotic writer. I cannot thank
my beautiful husband and daughter enough.
You are both the world to me.

Victoria, you are more than my partner.
You are the awesome, OCD other half of me,
and I have no idea what I'd do without you.
Love you, amazing woman!

For the girls who put up with my drama when
I need it the most: Shannon Hunt, Zoey Derrick,
Dani Wade, Rachel Harper. Mwah!

John and Sue: Writing sibling love is easy
when one's experienced it firsthand.
I love you both so much.
Now go find my avocado, damn it.

—Angel

My dedications this time around
need to be split into three categories:

At home: My amazing, handsome, sexy, supportive, loving, superhero husband David, and his protégé (our son) Kadin. I love you both so very much, and I can't thank you enough for all the hours you spent listening to my ideas, my complaining, my weariness and fears, and the list goes on.
You two are amazing and I couldn't be your namesake without you. I love you dearly.
Of course, I can't leave out the Queen. Her love and happiness drive me to be a better human being. What's better than that?

At work: Miss Angel Payne, the most talented, driven, supportive, inspiring writing partner a girl could dream of having. Even on the days I can't imagine sitting down in front of the computer, you're there to cheer me on. You lift me up when I need it, and you've taught me so much about this craft, and about this 'game' we play. You've given me an invaluable gift I'll never be able to thank you enough for. I love you with all of my heart.

On the playground: Elisa, Anna, and Kim, my own personal cheering section. Who knew I'd deserve you? Each one of you brings such unique, beautiful, generous, loving and inspiring gifts into my daily life. You call me on my shit, and you hold me to the standard I set for myself. That, my friends, is exactly what true love is all about. I will always be here to return that favor for you. XOXOXO

—Victoria

CHAPTER ONE

Margaux

Fashion icon. It was a dirty job, but someone had to do it.

Even if all I saw outside the window of San Diego's most exclusive couture bridal shop was a parade of last year's jeans and ugly Christmas sweaters.

Ugh. The humanity.

I turned away from the horror show, sighing as I stopped in front of a mirror to readjust my beanie. It was a bold choice of accessory, running the risk of tumbling from damn-she's-fabulous to oh-no-she-didn't inside five seconds. The trick was the backside dangle. If that fell right, you were golden.

Perfect.

I sat on a couch and thumbed impatiently through a magazine. China patterns, honeymoon locales, reception favors, more china patterns...

I threw the thing down, pretty damn sure I felt a migraine coming on.

"Claire!"

For the love of Louboutin, how long did putting on one wedding dress take? Okay, so she was my sister. Sort of. Technically, my soon-to-be sister-in-law—even if only a handful of people on the planet knew that. I wasn't sure I wanted the news expanded past those boundaries either. It had been sheer hell working out the bullshit surrounding the family everyone did know about.

No. Today wasn't a day for moping about Mother. Or the way she'd used my birth like a bargaining chip. Or the fact that she'd kept that truth from me for twenty-six years—and not felt a moment of remorse once I did find out.

Christ almighty. What was Claire doing in there? Sewing the damn thing by herself? Since there were three attendants with her, that was the *mystère du jour*.

"Claire!" I repeated. "Honestly, I'm growing roots from standing in the same—"

My derision died as my doe-eyed stepsister stepped out of the small room, silk and lace trailing behind her in a wave of tulle and princess-bride splendor. If I were a weaker woman, which I most certainly was not, I would cop to a lump in my throat at the vision standing before me, eyes aglow, dimples bracketing a shy smile, red hair tumbling into the gown's regal neckline.

Holy hell. Wait until Killian saw this. He thought he was head over heels before? Brother of mine, prepare your gut for a real train collision.

"Claire Bear. Wow."

It was all I could manage. And no, the tightness at the base of my throat had nothing to do with it.

The sales bitches beamed like they'd just birthed the fucking Baby New Year. They had this one in the bag and knew it—the exact reason why I pulled a full ice princess, glaring just enough to let them know the real bitch would come next. In an instant, they rushed forward to fuss around Claire once more.

"This dress was made for you, Miss Montgomery."

"Mr. Stone's eyes are going to fall out of his head."

"Amazing. Simply amazing."

It went on for fifteen minutes, one blah blah blah after another. I tuned out, my stomach turning on the latte I'd subbed for breakfast this morning.

This would never be me.

Never.

I would never walk down the aisle into the controlling clutches of a man. Ha—I didn't even have a father to walk me down the aisle. Like it was even a big deal anymore. Until ten months ago, I'd written off the dad angle from my life, with no reason to disbelieve what Mother always asserted—that my father had run out on us and didn't deserve a moment more of my attention. That all changed in a Chicago hospital room, where Josiah Stone had confessed to something much different—before taking his last breath.

Never knowing that his death had also killed off one of the most enduring fantasies of my life.

That somehow, my father would realize what a huge mistake he'd made in running from me—and return to embrace me with tears of grateful reunion. He'd tell me he didn't care about my makeup or clothes, that he only wanted to know what I was really like, on the inside, before sweeping me off to his mountain cabin, where—

Like going any further down that road was going to help right now.

Thank you, Mommy Dearest.

I officially hated that woman.

No, you don't.

Hmmm. I was pretty sure I did. Though I was too damn afraid of her to ever say it to her face, which was...unnerving. At really deep levels.

"Margaux? Are you okay?"

Claire's enormous brown eyes were fixed on me through the mirror. This chick didn't miss a beat with her attention or her concern, which pounded the unnerving right down into disturbed.

Christ, I was a mess lately. And the kicker? I was actually aware of it. Puke. Life had been much simpler when all I thought about in the morning was digging into someone else's dirt—and how fabulous I'd look while helping them with it.

"Have you seen the back of this one, Claire?" I flashed more daggers at the bitches. "Did any of you think to show her the back? It's stunning, Bear. Truly."

My diversion tactic worked, at least on the sales flock. They flurried again, turning Claire so she could see, erupting into more gibberish about the gown and its perfect fit, flare, and hemline. But damn it if my sister didn't keep her eyes fixed on me, silently—and unashamedly—trying to probe. I finally rolled my eyes and gave her the Margaux salute, jabbing my middle finger when the attendants weren't looking. She suppressed a giggle, but that didn't fool me. She'd be all over me the minute we were alone—because that was simply the kind of girl she was. Observant. Intuitive. And caring to the point where it was her damn superpower.

Lucky, lucky me.

The morning from hell transitioned into afternoon. Dress after dress. Perfection upon perfection. Okay, some not so much. The lavender one had to go. Who the hell wore a lavender wedding dress? I suspected Claire tried that one on to see if I was still paying attention. Thank God I'd paused between emails, which had become my new obsession lately. Now that I was on the full-time roster with Stone Global, I needed to be serious about shining there.

The idea of continuing on with Mother—with Andrea—had seemed impossible when we returned from Chicago. After all her secrets had been unveiled, I couldn't even stand being in the same room with her. Even a simple explanation might have helped, though I never gave in to the illusion of receiving a full apology. That kind of thing happened in worlds where unicorns descended from heaven to save humanity from the zombie apocalypse.

She'd never come. Never called. Never said another word. And with her silence had wrecked whatever connection we'd had, however dysfunctional. I sent a formal letter declaring a leave of absence, but she and I both knew I was never coming back. Too many lies, too much deception. I was tired of Andrea Asher's games and refused to be a pawn in them anymore. Or so I told myself on the good days.

I'd barely had a chance to realize that woman of leisure wasn't a role I enjoyed playing, when Killian approached with the opportunity to stay on permanently with Stone Global's expanded PR department. It made perfect sense from a couple of angles. The Asher and Associates team had already been working exclusively with SGC, so everything already felt like my home turf. And as they say, blood is thicker than water. Or did it form the ties that bind? Or coagulate if you used hot honey? Whatever. It was irony at its best, however you phrased it. Killian, only a Stone by adoption, hired me, the real Stone, for the family business. To add a ha atop of that ha, Killian's lineage was now full public knowledge—and mine still a carefully guarded secret.

Because I demanded it that way.

I'd had a first-row seat for the media's last feeding frenzy about Stone family news. It had driven Killian Stone, one of the finest men I knew, into months of hiding. Well, last time I checked, my name wasn't Shark Chum. I'd be damned if I'd voluntarily splash into that same tank.

When Killian opened SGC's San Diego branch and brought me on, my friendship—and unique sisterhood—with Claire was forged deeper. Sure, we had less in common than most typical besties, but somehow it worked in our favor. With unanimous backing by the board, Killian named her the director of the new public relations department, with me as her tight wingwoman. She was the first to admit that she still had a lot to learn, so my experience had come into play in ways that made me feel, for the first time in a long time, like my contributions mattered.

So far, it had been a pretty cool gig.

So far.

It wasn't like we didn't keep tabs on what was happening over in Mother's realm. Talia, Chad, and Michael had stayed on with Asher and Associates, since there were only so many positions to fill at SGC without displacing the very capable people who already occupied them. So, the five of us got together on a regular basis to talk shop—in a fly-over, let's-not-mention-names kind of way—and to shoot the breeze or some darts, or often both.

Yes. I just said that. I now went to bars with dartboards. And even—wait for it—jukeboxes. Maybe I'd taken a sip or two of beer, as well. The designer shit only. Something handcrafted or microbrewed.

Still. Beer.

A girl was capable of crazy shit when given the throwdown by a lopsided grin and a pair of dazzling hazel eyes. Okay, fine—

and biceps the size of melons. And legs like a damn gladiator. Hey, Perry Ellis could only hide so much—especially when it was fitted over the fine, fine form of one Michael Adam Pearson...

I was yanked from my fantasy by Claire pointedly clearing her throat. I looked up, relieved to see her back in casual wear instead of another glob of cotton candy pretending to be a couture creation.

"Thank God," I blurted. "Is it over? Really, really over?"

Claire giggled, but I was sure karma chimed in with an echo. The bitch loved sticking it to me in fun little ways like this.

Especially when she could get in the last laugh.

As if knowing that was her cue, Claire's little wedding coordinator breezed out of the dressing room, smart pad in one hand and coffee in the other. I was stunned to see the cup, certain the woman had a caffeine dispenser lodged somewhere in her body.

Ginny.

Best said with a wince and an insulin shot—or an EpiPen, if one felt one's throat closing up at the first sign of perkiness.

Ginny.

Ugh.

The little woman grabbed Claire around the waist and twirled her around in a dance out of a bad Broadway musical. "You are going to be the most beautiful bride the world has ever seen. Isn't she going to be the most beautiful bride the world has ever seen, Maggie?"

"It's Margaux."

"Right. Sorry. Why can't I keep that straight? Oh, my goodness." She whirled and giggled to Claire. Again. Claire tamed her response to a polite smile—or was that a smirk?—as I fought the urge to dash into the bar across the street for something that'd make my eyes water and my head swim.

How could a woman who spoke every sentence twice and put together Lady Gaga-sized wedding spectacles not remember my name?

And just how many months were left until this event?

And how was I not going to take my own life before then?

A moment of weakness. It was the only explanation for why I'd agreed to be Claire's maid of honor. I wasn't cut out for this shit. I hated everything weddings stood for. Love, commitment, promises—

Yep, here came that latte again.

"Claire." I grabbed her arm.

"Hey," she answered. "You okay? You don't look so—"

"I need sustenance." I jogged my head toward the door. "Lunch break? I know a great sushi place right up the street."

Ginny let go long enough to clap her hands, giddy-cheerleader style. "Perfect. Yes, perfect. We can talk about the menu. Let's talk about the menu over lunch. You don't mind if I tag along, do you, Marge?"

"It's Margaux."

"Oh, God. There I go again. Watch me go, go, go!"

Oh, how I wished, wished, wished.

"We just have so much ground to cover. It'll be great to get the extra time. Right. Claire? So much ground to cover. My goodness."

"Of course, Ginny," Claire answered before I could invent a way to mix bitchy and polite into the same flat turn-down to the woman. "That sounds like a good plan."

Ice picks. My gaze. Two for one deal, right over the shorter woman's head, letting Claire know exactly that. In return, she gave me the doe-eyed treatment again. Not buying it, sister. Not this time. This one knew exactly what she was doing.

"I need to use the ladies' room before we leave," I snipped. "I'll meet you out at the car."

I retreated to the back of the store to do my business and freshen up. When I returned to the parking lot, Claire was leaning against her A8, absorbed in whatever message she'd received on her cell. She held up a finger, a wordless request that I wait before getting in the car. I parked my ass next to her, against the car's sleek hood, while glancing inside. Ginny was already in the back seat, belt buckled, hands folded in her lap, as prim as a toddler on a preschool field trip. This was not going to be the nice, peaceful, raw fish lunch I'd looked forward to.

Stowing her phone in her enormous bag, Claire looked up at me.

"Have you talked to your brother today? He hasn't picked up his phone for hours."

I swung out, landing my fist on her arm a little harder than I'd intended.

"Owww! Jesus, Margaux. What was that for?"

I—gasp—felt a little sorry for the punch. But only a little. "Ix-nay on the rother-bay, okay-kay?"

She stared. Then some more. How was this possible? The woman rocked the deer-in-the-headlights thing as easily as the cotton-candy-wedding dress thing. Not fair.

"M, what are you—"

"Just don't call him my"—time for the clenched whisper—"brother in public." I darted a glance around. "The last thing I need is to learn some gossip mag photog freak's been hiding in the bushes around here, waiting to scoop a lead for tonight's entertainment circuit."

She paled before joining me in the furtive three-sixty for said reporter. Any detail about the day she was going to take Kil off the market was media gold right now—meaning he and Claire and all the rest of us weren't enjoying much privacy anymore. We couldn't even assume a peaceful street like this was safe ground from the vultures.

"So...you think you'll ever be comfortable enough to go public with it?" Claire muttered.

"I don't know." I playfully knocked my shoulder to hers. "Tell you what... One thing at a time. Let's stress about you right now." A moment later, her snicker had me slanting a narrower glare. "What the hell does that mean?"

"You know effective diversion should be your middle name, right?"

"That's two words."

"Your point is...?"

"Shit." She was the girl preparing to marry the guy with two middle names. Fucking society wannabes, thinking they could be royals by giving their spawn a thousand names.

"It's okay, Margaux. I've been onto you for a while, you know." She looked at me sideways while digging through her monstrosity of a purse to find her keys.

I snorted good-naturedly. "I know, baby."

She winked. "Glad we're straight, then."

"But that's part of the problem now, isn't it?" I hooked an elbow through hers. "C'mon, honey. Let's ditch Miss Ginny Sunshine and hit a few bars instead of lunch. I've got the mother of all tension headaches coming on, and only alcohol or great sex is going to work it out. And since choice B doesn't seem to be in my immediate future..."

Her eyebrows shot up. "Wait. I thought things were on the right track with you and Michael. You know how he stares at you, right? Do not tell me he isn't pulling out every single move in his book when you two are alone."

I didn't say anything as we climbed into the car. Once I glanced back, confirming Ginny was engrossed in composing an email on her phone, I decided to throw my sister a bone. How's this for distraction, Claire Allyn Montgomery?

"Okay, so that's the problem," I muttered, leaning toward her. "Michael...I'm not sure if he has any moves." When her forehead furrowed, I rushed on, "He's not like any of the guys I'm used to dating." I threw air quotes around the last word. God forbid that I say fucking in front of Ginny. The fallout from her aneurysm wouldn't be pretty.

"What do you mean?" Claire pressed. "Are you sure? Mare, I've seen the man in action at bars and clubs. He's a panty charmer when he wants to be. There's definitely game there."

I let my head fall against the headrest. "That sure as hell doesn't help."

"Why?"

I shrugged and dropped my voice lower. "Meh. Forget it. Maybe I'm not the right quarter for his game."

She tempted the Botox gods again. "No. No. I refuse to believe—"

"Well, believe," I retorted. "Sorry, Bear, but I know what I know. The guy is so...polite...like all the time." Heavy sigh. "So polite."

"Define polite."

"He treats me like I'm made of china, right? One wrong

move and I'll shatter into a million pieces. It's...frustrating." Go for it. Just tell her. "I'm used to it—well, I like it—on the rougher side, you know? I'm not a hearts and flowers kind of girl. I need down and dirty, fuck me hard and bruise me fast, you know?"

"Guess I do now."

I rolled the back of my head against the leather cushion. "He may just be from the wrong side of town for me. Or me for him. I don't know. I...like him. I like him a lot. But he just never makes a move. Like I'm in a glass case...fifty feet over his head."

"So shatter the glass. You jump first."

"Uh-uh. Been there. And I'll be damned if I go there again. When a relationship starts there, I'm already bored. I love the hunt, sister—but only if it keeps me a little scared, you know?"

"Scared?" she echoed. "Are you serious?"

I enjoyed the chance to get back at her with the snicker. "Oh, c'mon, Claire. Killian still scares you a little...in the good ways. Don't tell me he doesn't still bring that little rush to your chest, that telltale pulse in your pussy—"

"Margaux!"

"He does, doesn't he?" I took her secretive grin as a yes. "I made myself a promise to not do the chasing anymore. I deserve better."

She nodded while starting the car and pulling out into traffic. "You're right. You do deserve better. You have so much to offer. I'm glad you've finally recognized that about yourself."

I slammed my eyes shut.

Uggghh. I didn't want this. I sure as hell didn't need it. Why was everyone so hot to lecture me about how glad they were that I'd turned some mystical corner in my life and how much better I was than before?

Better than what?

I wasn't better, damn it. I was the exact same coldhearted bitch my mother raised me to be. Different factor at the moment? I had a decent guy following me around like a sweet little puppy, when all I wanted from him was an hour or so of his doggie side, the harder the better. When the hell had it become so hard for a girl to find a good fuck in this town?

We'd missed the lunch rush so were seated immediately at the sushi joint. Less than five minutes after that, I was gratefully sucking down sake—and able to tune out Ginny a little.

Until she dropped the bomb heard around the world.

"So, Mary—tell me what you're hoping for in the maid of honor's dress."

Claire choked but pretended it was her iced tea. I wasn't so subtle about my reaction, an open glare at the woman who blithely bit into her ahi roll, unaware she'd just issued the one word I hated more than any.

Mary.

She should have just said bitch. It wouldn't have cut as deep, reminding me all over again that before Andrea Asher decided to use my Pampers-covered ass as a pawn in her chess match with the Chicago old-boys' club, I might have been loved for who I was and not the power I represented. I might have been wanted, even loved, by Josiah Stone and a woman I'd never known. Violet Tosca. That had been her name. Yes, had been, past tense—because thousands of dollars and two private dicks later, the only thing I knew besides her name was that she'd disappeared off the face of the earth about a year after I was born. No address. No bank accounts. Not even a death certificate. She'd simply...ceased to exist.

Damn good excuse to wave down the waitress for another tokkuri of booze. Tossing back more of the sweet rice wine realigned my head with the task at hand. I was going to be the best damn maid of honor the wedding world had ever seen, even if it killed me. And yes, even if this crazy woman couldn't remember my name if it was being tortured out of her.

"First things first, Ginny. Margaux. My name is Margaux. Secondly, I'll wear a burlap sack if it makes Claire happy. And for the record, I'd rock it."

I plastered on my best pageant smile, shocked at how easily its falseness slid back into place...masking the pain that clenched so deeply underneath.

Damn it. Not now.

I thought I was done with this agony, but with one stupid slip of a name, from a complete stranger, all the anger and betrayal churned my gut again.

Why couldn't I deal with this? How the hell did Mother keep me in her clutches, even now?

I was stronger than this. I was better than this.

Just not right now.

"I need the little girls' room."

My blurt blasted the mama-bear thing across Claire's face again. I winked at her, my wordless version of calm down or I will cut you, before slipping out and heading down the narrow hall to the restroom. The heels of my tall boots echoed on the slate floor as I marched—faster, faster—getting to the stall just in time to slam the door shut, drop over the toilet, and sacrifice my lunch to the porcelain god.

Crazily, I was almost thankful for the moment. At least my mind filled with things other than Andrea. *Thank God it's clean in here.* Damn it, what a waste of good food. Too much sake and too much drama do not make for a happy stomach.

The bathroom wasn't just clean but vacant—gratitude factor number two—making it possible to blot my face and rinse my mouth in privacy. By the time I returned to our table, no one should've been the wiser about my true purpose for the bio break, though Claire had clearly renewed her Nancy Drew Club card, shooting me the sideways detective stare all over again. Not *bueno*. The woman was getting to know me in unnerving detail. People were just so much easier at arm's length.

Thankfully, she was distracted by an incoming text. The Timberlake ringtone gave away the sender, though Claire's goofy grin would've done the job too. Killian.

One look at the expression on my sister's face and my belly cramped all over again. There was no food left in it to give me fits, so I was forced to admit the real source of the pangs. Claire Montgomery was a woman desperately, deeply in love... and I couldn't stomach watching it at this proximity.

Love was for fools.

And I was many things, but a fool wasn't one of them.

Claire's confused scowl caused my own. "What is it?"

"This doesn't add up," she mumbled, thumbs flying as she tapped out a reply text to Kil. "Not even a little bit."

"Still in the dark, girlfriend."

"It's my crazy fiancé. He says he's having car trouble and he needs me to pick him up at this address...all the way out in Rancho Santa Fe."

"Is he joking?" I held out my hand, palm up. "Let me see that thing."

Gawk. Then again. Sure enough, the address was out in the middle of San Diego's version of Beverly Hills, a neighborhood where even the housemaids drove BMWs. It wasn't far, but it wasn't close, either.

"This is strange," Claire said. "All of his cars are in excellent condition."

"Except for the truck," I pointed out.

She rolled her eyes. "He keeps the beater for sentimental reasons."

"You think?"

"And he only takes it out when he goes surfing. If he's in Rancho Santa Fe, then he must be there for business. Even so, why is he texting me instead of Alfred?"

"And why is he even texting you?" Revelation struck. A shudder ensued. "Unless the bastard can't even wait until tonight for a booty call. In which case, ew."

That didn't loosen even a tiny giggle from her. "He knows I'm still with you. But he's adamant. He wants me there."

"And you just jump every time he throws down a summons?"

"It's not a summons. It's a request. And I've already told him we'll be there in fifteen minutes."

"Of course you have."

"It's just a few exits north of here. I have to take Ginny back to the dress shop to get her car anyway."

"There's something to look forward to."

After saying goodbye to Ginny, Claire pulled onto I-5. We headed north and cut inland after the sparkling stretch of Solana Beach, on a quest to rescue her beau. The coastal views helped me relax again, along with the knowledge that I'd have fodder to hold over Kil's head for weeks. Running through one-liners to taunt him with, I didn't pay much attention to the increasing price tags on the homes—make that estates—we winded past until Claire started mumbling to herself again.

"This is ridiculous. If this is where his business meeting was, how is it this person couldn't give him a ride or help with his car?" She scowled deeper. "I smell a rat."

"Rat," I repeated. "Hmmm. That has possibilities for a good goad..."

"Huh?"

The car's disembodied GPS was my knight in shining armor.

"You have arrived at your destination."

But we were at the end of a street lined with lush trees, with nothing around except a set of iron gates that belonged on Wayne Manor. We couldn't see where the drive beyond led, but I guessed it was a private residence like the others in this neighborhood, containing a mansion and grounds that could easily house a medieval village.

"We're in the right place," Claire stated. "This is the address he gave me." As she tapped out a text, she gritted the same words beneath her breath. "Where...the...hell...are...we? And...where...the...hell...are...you?"

As if she'd spoken the open sesame for the gates, they parted slowly, perfectly framing a figure strolling down the drive. Sure as hell, it was my brother, definitely looking like a sexy Bruce Wayne update. His cocky grin was in place, and his thick black hair was a windblown contrast to his crisp white shirt and light-blue tie. He was jacketless, though the perfect cut of his black pants told me he'd gone for one of his favorite designers' looks today, customized Kiton. Damn, the man had great taste.

Didn't stop me from giggling at Claire as she watched him stride up. Poor, pathetic woman. She went to pieces every time she laid eyes on him, and this one was no different. She lasted two seconds before leaping out of the Audi, launching herself at Kil, and then sealing him in the most obscene lip lock I could ever gag about.

"As soon as you're finished extracting each other's tonsils," I finally drawled, "you'd better be ready for some fast talking, Kil. A minute ago, your bride was comparing you to large rodents." When he flashed a put-out glare, I rolled my eyes. "Still not selling it, brother."

"Because I'm barely trying." He buried his nose and lips against the skin beneath Claire's ear. "I can be very convincing when I need to be. Right, baby?"

Claire broke out in a crimson blush accompanied by a heavy sigh. My gag didn't stop her—or Killian. "I suppose get a room wouldn't be a reasonable demand of you two right now?"

To my shock, Killian pulled back. Slid another grin at me. Shit. If he added a muah-ha-ha to it, wicked glee would have its new poster boy. "Fascinating comment."

"What?" Claire interjected. "Why?"

"For God's sake, just spill it, Stone." I rolled my eyes again, though there was real ire behind it now. "And spare the bullshit about your car being broken. Where is your scrap metal, anyhow?"

I almost joined in Claire's laughter as he straightened, firming his face into a glare that had withered moguls, millionaires, and even royalty. I loved inciting it in him—because it scared me as much as a dust mite did a cat.

"Did you just call my Aston Martin...a piece of scrap metal?"

I preened. "Kudos, brother. At least you didn't name the damn thing." My last word was swallowed by Claire's laugh.

"Ohhh, hell. You did name it."

"Her," Killian muttered. "I did name her."

"Lulu?" I volleyed. "Betty Sue? Velma?"

"You know those are fightin' words, right, Mare Bear?"

"Save the bear endearments for doe eyes." I didn't hide my clenched teeth as I pointed at Claire with my chin. She giggled again, keeping the mood tolerably playful, but I flashed a look at my brother that spoke one message only. Thin ice, bro. More and more lately, he'd started slipping various forms of Mary into our exchanges—and getting away with it. I wasn't sure how I felt about that or if it would even matter. A year ago, Killian Stone might have been living out of a cardboard box at the beach, but now he was back to getting away with a lot of things most people couldn't.

Like the determined way he grabbed Claire's hand and began towing her up the flagstone driveway. And the grand way he swept a hand toward the castle-like Italianate home that peeked into view at the top. And the expectant stare he didn't yank from Claire's face. Not for one damn second.

I almost smacked her for the blank look she kept up in return. She wasn't getting this yet?

Killian finally stopped and scooped his other hand around hers. "Well?" he asked her softly.

Claire peered at him, a hopeless case of clueless still stamped across her face. "Well...what?"

"What do you think, Fairy Queen?"

"Think of what?"

"Of this place?"

Claire shrugged. Shrugged.

That was it. I went ahead and growled. "Shit, Claire. Really?"

Killian pointed a finger at me. "Enough."

"Ohhhh, no," I snapped. "You did not—"

"I don't know, Kil." Like always, our bickering flowed right past the woman. I loved her and hated her for it. "It's beautiful, of course. You know I love the Mediterranean look."

"Yeah...I do." His features softened. Yay, Claire. Nothing like a good case of pussy-whipped to get a guy over the pissies with his sister.

"I still don't understand," Claire went on. "Why are we here? Who does this belong to? Does one of your friends live here?"

He sucked in a deep breath. Oh, my God. This was a first. If I wasn't mistaken, my brother was...nervous. And I was a little nervous for him. It was sort of fun.

"Well...ummm..."

"Killian. Spit it out!"

He shifted a little. Cupped her hands tighter. Attempted a smile. "Actually...we live here."

Claire choked. Not a help-me-I-ate-too-many-fries choke. More like a help-me-I'm-going-into-shock choke.

"Claire?" he finally prompted.

"Yeah?"

"It looks like the ones you keep telling me you love."

"Y-Yes. It does...but—"

"So...happy wedding. A little early. I wanted to surprise you."

She laughed—like someone who'd just been admitted to the psych ward by accident. "Oh, I'm surprised."

"The Realtor will be showing up any minute. She was supposed to be here already, but you got here faster than I thought you would."

"We caught good traffic." Her voice still floated on a tone between dazzled and confused.

"Or you were speeding again."

"I wasn't speeding."

"I thought we talked about the speeding thing, Fairy."

I snickered. There was no restraining this one. Killian Stone, going all Mrs. Doubtfire on his fiancée... This scene just got better by the minute.

When my brother shot me a dirty look, I held up both hands in chuckling surrender. I'd never had the chance to catch him sneaking snacks at night or talking to a girlfriend past bedtime, but this sure as hell made up for part of the loss.

"Maybe I'll give you two a little space," I finally offered before turning back toward the road.

Killian steepled his hands and bowed a little in thanks. Claire was still too shell-shocked—or uptight—to notice. I shook my head at that. Damn. I loved the woman but couldn't figure her out sometimes. Killian bent over like a Cirque acrobat for her—in an act where he somersaulted through fire, dove with sharks, and descended down a two hundred-foot wall, landing in a worshiping heap at her feet—only to see her freeze when he spoiled her with that adoration. Most women would sear their panties off from his over-the-top gestures, but Claire bolted in the exact opposite direction.

The craziest part? From what I could see, Kil still lapped up every drop. The less his extravagance mattered to Claire, the more he found ways of drenching her in it.

Or was it just that the man was hopelessly in love?

There went my conscience again. Damn it, the thing's off switch had to be nearby...

I leaned against her car to lie in wait, hoping the wind

favored me and returned at least a few snippets of their discussion.

My phone buzzed in my back pocket. Then again.

Incoming text.

Shit.

But maybe...not so much. The window displayed Michael Pearson as the sender.

After ignoring the funny flip in my belly, I unlocked the screen.

Need to leave town for a little while. Can you meet me?

I stared at the screen. Swallowed hard. Rubbed a hand across my chest. Why did it ache? And why was the queasiness back in my stomach?

Was I...sad?

Bullshit.

No, no... I was probably coming down with something. That had to be it. First, the speed date with the toilet after lunch and now this yummy bile chaser... Lovely. Claire walked away from the day with a mansion, and I got to go home with the flu.

And now, no Michael to even pull a pouty plea for a soup stop with.

I responded, letting him know I was still with Claire and didn't have my car.

Text the address. I'll stop there.

My eyebrows jumped. He'd never been so aggressive about anything—ever. "Bring it on, Mr. Pearson," I laughed out, sending him the address—and denying how the acid in my belly had suddenly taken wing into butterflies.

Ohhh, no. Not a damn chance.

Butterflies were for tweens, twits, and...well...Claire.

I didn't do butterflies.

I proved the point by firing off replies to at least twenty emails, and that was before the real estate agent arrived to give Claire and Killian the full tour of the estate. I got out another ten before Michael's huge black Sierra Denali appeared around the corner.

And my stomach fizzed, popped, and somersaulted all over again.

The flu. I had the flu, not butterflies.

Which worsened in direct proportion to every foot of road his truck covered. Just the damn flu. And every degree of focus I gained on his cropped blond waves, his broad, chiseled shoulders, and his easy, anticipating smile.

Making me smile in return. Then smooth my hair. And bounce on my toes.

Oh, dear hell.

I was turning into Claire.

This was getting out of hand. And I was...

Going to have to stop seeing him.

I hated the resolution as thoroughly as I welcomed it. Feelings were becoming involved, and that just couldn't happen. Issues would be stirred. Emotions would start to be discussed. And when that happened, things always turned dirty and ugly...and painful.

I looked down at my phone, using his own words as fortitude. *Need to leave town for a little while.* Perhaps it was a crazy cosmic sign, giving the perfect timing for a break on this thing between us... Whatever this thing was. Keeping it clean was best. Surgical precision. The anesthetic of time. A pain-free solution for everyone.

He double-parked alongside Claire's car and swung down from the driver's side. He was dressed casually, jeans and a chest-hugging tee roughened by a slightly scuffed black leather jacket and boots—*so* not what I was used to seeing him in. But goddamn, did he rock the look. Out loud.

I sucked in a breath, wondering if my mouth was watering. Not a word of my normal cute and clever came to mind, so I was left to gawking as he strolled to where I leaned against the hood of Claire's Audi. Wind, wood, leather, cedar... He always smelled smoky yet misty, a perfect combination of forest and ocean, making me wonder if he was about to scoop me onto his back and fly me through the trees, spider monkey-style. *Hell. Now you're officially worse than Claire.*

He only made the torment worse by stepping closer, right up into my space, toe-to-toe. As I grinned a little, wondering what he'd do if I yanked him forward to make it hip-to-hip as well, he looked down, riveting me in place with his sparkling hazel eyes. After that, the adorable half smile came out...

Damn it.

I was going to be in the market for a butterfly net, wasn't I? Maybe even a cage to stow the little beasts in. I drew the line at letting him decorate it in lovesick little hearts with his initials in them, though.

He grinned a little deeper, showing off dimples that set my senses fluttering all over again, before murmuring, "Hey."

"Hey, yourself." I'd copped to the butterflies, so I might as well concede to the craving to gaze in his eyes all day too. I wouldn't call myself entranced...yet...but the afternoon sun, dancing with all those gorgeous green flecks... In a word, wow.

"So how was the dress shopping today? Looks like you survived, yeah?"

I rolled my eyes, resisting the urge to give my signature gag. He laughed anyway, able to complete my thought simply from the first gesture. Why not? Sometimes he read my thoughts from a lot less—which really should've scared me more.

He should've scared me more.

But he didn't.

And that scared me. To the point that I shivered.

Michael chuckled again. Thank God he just took it as an extension of my bridal-salon PTSD. "That bad, huh?"

I burrowed a little closer to him. "I'll spare you the gory details."

"Awww, you do care about me. Where are the love birds anyway?"

I relished the opportunity to grin. "I'd tell you to sit down for this, but even that won't help."

His eyebrows, just a shade darker than his hair, scrunched over his eyes. "Serious?"

I tapped at the phone jammed into his back right pocket. "Better store that addy I just gave you. That's where you'll need to address the Christmas cards to them from now on."

"Whaaaat?"

"I'm not kidding." I jabbed a thumb over my shoulder but watched Michael's face to catch his whole reaction. "Behold, the Killian Stone version of a wedding present."

I wasn't certain what to watch for in him—but his face-splitting grin was, admittedly, stunning. "Well, no kidding," he drawled. "Kil really does believe in being a tough act to follow. He's raised the bar for the rest of us chumps, hasn't he?"

"Wait, let me get this straight. You don't think it's too

much? Too over the top?"

"Why? Killian can afford it. And if Claire loves it too, then no, I don't. If a guy is lucky enough to find the woman of his dreams and is capable of bringing her the world on a platter, why does anything have to be over the top?"

Who the hell was this guy and what amazing planet did he come from? And where could I buy a ticket to get there?

Before those exact words tumbled out, I stopped them with a sardonic mutter and an arched brow. "Is that right?"

"Hmmm. Pretty much." He added a shrug but only for effect.

He totally owned his opinion, not making a single excuse for it. At times, like this one, his conviction was a bit sigh-worthy. He always meant what he said, no fancy tact just because of my bitch-on-wheels act, and then never backed down. He was honest. Authentic. My breath of fresh air in a damned irresistible package.

"So, hey, blondie, I have to go home for a bit. I always do this time of year, to help my mom out with year-end arrangements for bookkeeping and associated bullshit."

I popped out a little grin. "Of course you do, Captain America."

"Well, this year, things are a little more involved, so I'm not sure how long I'll be." He reached and brushed an errant strand of hair off my cheek. "So...I wanted to say goodbye in person."

Before I could stop myself, I flattened my hand over his. "Goodbye isn't a good thing for me, Pearson." I swallowed, hating to let him see even that, but it was either that or pushing the words out on a seesaw of tone. I picked the lesser damage. "Let's just do see you soon."

"Sooner...if you want to come visit." He kicked up one side of his mouth while biting down on the other. Damn. *I'll take* Effortless Hunks *for eight hundred please, Mr. Trebek.* "It's not far from here, just east, up in Julian. If you want to get away for a couple of days, it's pretty peaceful. Or maybe if you miss me or some shit like that."

"Or some shit like that?" I managed it past the strange twists of my stomach. Christ, maybe this was the flu—a virus he seemed to have sole control over. I tensed, fighting the urge to throw myself at him like a moony dimwit. "Well, is everything okay? Is your family all right? Can I do anything to help?" And when the hell did you turn me into Captain America too?

"I don't want to weigh you down with it all," he answered. "And if you want to do something nice, say you'll think about coming for a visit. Because...I think I'll miss you."

He lowered his hand to my waist, drawing me closer to him—and, despite how I'd longed for it, I was still surprised by my willingness to let him.

"Or some shit like that?" I murmured, attempting not to feel like a twelve-year-old at her first school dance.

"Yeah."

His voice was grittier than mine, vibrating through both of us—heightening the ache in my chest. What was going on? Was I...sad? What was the BFD if I was? He'd become my safe harbor, and I wasn't ashamed.

So, yeah...I would miss him.

I did it. Went ahead and wrapped my arms around his neck, securing his body tighter to mine. I turned my face into the warm, firm column of his neck—and for a moment, just one, surrendered all my tension into his unmistakable strength.

When would I be able to do this again?

I didn't like this. Not one damn bit.

"Are you sure...you have to go?"

"I'm sorry, sugar." His whisper blended with the wind. "I do." He cleared his throat and added volume again.

And why did I feel like that was only half the story?

"My place is prepaid for a while. Both my landlady and Andrea were cool about it, at least."

I bit back a retort to that. Of course Mother was fine with it. Chances were, she was chomping at the bit to abolish as many reminders as she could of the team who'd been in Chicago with us during that disastrous trip back in February. If she could fully fire Michael and Chad, she probably would.

"So I'm your last stop?"

"Best for last." He bent his head to directly meet my eyes. Then bit his lip again.

Hell.

"I'm—I'm glad," I stammered, before frantically modifying, "I mean, I'm glad you came to at least see me before you ditched me."

"Margaux."

"Teasing." Not really. "Will you...call and text and shit?"

And write my initials all over your notebook? And save me a spot in the cafeteria? Huh, huh, huh?

"Of course I will."

"I'll try my best to come see you."

"Uh-huh."

"I mean it! Julian isn't far. Besides, I've never been there. I hear the pie is killer."

I felt a little better. At least my best defense mechanism still worked. Making light out of a crappy situation, especially with the genius stroke of changing the subject to pie. No man could resist that one. He was putty in my—

Shit.

I dissolved to goo as his smile turned into an expression I'd never seen from him before. While his lips were still upturned, they'd gone...soft. Protective? Yeah, okay...that was it. His soft kiss on the top of my head was proof. He'd done it a thousand times before, a sweet and tender gesture that made me think of a father's affection for his daughter, not that I knew anything about that firsthand. But, like always, I smiled too. It made me feel...cherished, I guess. But not better about him going.

On that note, I pulled back.

But not far.

Michael slipped his arms tighter around me. And became oddly quiet.

I tilted my head to look up at him. His brilliant hazel stare was already waiting, alive with an unmistakable message. He was struggling with all this as much as I was.

"I'm going to do this."

The words were so soft, I almost wondered if he had said them. Then I realized they might have been more for himself than me.

Then I realized it didn't matter.

As he bent close enough to kiss me.

Then even closer.

My eyes slid closed. My senses opened up. I vowed to savor everything I could, remembering every nuance and scent and flavor and feel of this man...

The solid strength of his arms, wrapped around me so perfectly.

His smell, like he'd taken a bath in fresh mountain air and then flown over the ocean.

The scrape of his stubble on my face, rough with the urgency of his need, his possession.

This...was the kiss of a man. Not a groping poser, not a desperate boy—and yet, because of that, I knew it would be over too soon. For once, I wanted hours of making out. I wanted his hands all over me, his beard burn across my face, his imprint on every corner of my mind...not his lingering heat as he pulled away much, much too soon.

I stood, unwilling to open my eyes, still only aware of his harsh breaths matched in cadence to mine. Just when I thought my heart was slowing, he gripped the back of my head, slammed my face into his chest, and groaned into my hair.

"Why," I finally rasped, "does it always end?"

"Huh?"

"You heard me." I spat it, hoping he'd be enraged enough to kiss me again. Instead, he pulled back with that same playful grin tugging at his sinful lips.

Oh, yeah? Well, two can play that game, buddy.

"Nothing," I quipped. "Never mind. I was just thinking out loud, wondering when my damn bro—bestie—and her boy-toy will be done in there. I've been standing out here forever."

I jumped my gaze toward the gates of the house, determined not to give him the remotest chance of wondering about my half slip—or reading anything else in me right now. Maybe it was a good thing, him leaving for a while. Like Claire, Michael was getting too damn good at excavating little factoids out of me. Well, he could give up that quest right now.

"Why do you always do that?"

Give it up, Captain America.

"Do what?"

"Pull back like that...when you think you've said too

much."

"The hell I do."

"You totally do."

"Don't you have a trip to take? Up your big damn mountain?" I gave him a teasing shove toward his truck.

"Margaux?"

"Hmmm?"

"You won't always be able to run, you know."

"Maybe not. But for now, it's all I've got."

"That's not true. You have me."

"For the five remaining minutes before you leave?" I jammed both hands into the pockets of my puffer vest and kicked at the ground, able to effectively cloak my smirk when he pushed out a heavy breath. Good. I'd tapped into his guilt at last—deflecting his attention in all the right ways.

"It's not permanent."

"I know."

"I'll be back in a few weeks."

"I know."

"And we'll continue this conversation then."

"We'll see."

Angry exhale, the sequel. "I need to head out. I want to get there before sundown."

My victory ended all too quickly. The reality that he wouldn't be here, even for a few weeks...well, it sucked. Big, hard ones. And not in the good way.

"Text me when you get there?"

"I will."

He unlocked the door to his truck but only hitched one boot up to the step before I sprinted over, grabbed both sides of his face, and kissed him soundly one last time.

No help. This still sucked, worse than I thought it would—especially right after the man called me out on my shit. Again.

"Be safe, Michael."

He smiled that unique little smile. What the hell was that new look all about? I felt like asking him to freeze it so I could yank out my phone and snap a pic in order to indulge in some more conjecturing.

Instead, I watched him climb up, slam the door, and then drive away—

Taking a small but unmistakable piece of my heart with him.

I stared until he made the turn, leaving me to follow the paths of oak leaves and pine needles as they swirled across the road in the light afternoon wind. I almost begged them to take me with them. Maybe then I could focus on something other than the weirdness of standing alone in the middle of silence too huge to bear, a lump in my throat and my heart in my hand. I wasn't used to either feeling—and I sure as hell wasn't going to ask them to stick around for dinner.

CHAPTER TWO

Michael

"Damn it."

Spewing it for the fortieth time felt no better than the first. My go-tos for times like this, a bottle of full-sugar Coke and the best classic rock station on the radio, didn't help my mood for shit either.

Could've had something to do with the nonstop make-out session my cock was having with my jeans.

Fuck.

I had to go and think of making out again.

More specifically, making out with Margaux Asher. The taste of her lips, like strawberry candy. The smell of her hair, exotic and expensive. The feel of her skin, sleeker than satin sheets...

Damn. Satin sheets. Oh, yeah. The ones on the bed beneath us in my fantasies. A big one, for all kinds of fun games...

Come and get me, Mr. Pearson.

You're tempting the dragon, Miss Asher.

Dragon? What dragon? You're all the way over there.

Because if I come all the way over there, you won't be a safe woman.

Pfft. You expect me to believe that, when—ahhh!

You believe me now?

You ripped off my panties!

And you loved it.

I waited for her breathless yes—but her lips released a blare instead. A car horn. Then another.

I blinked.

Shit. Where had that stop sign come from? And why was I asking the question as I noticed the sign—in my rearview?

"Head outta your ass, idiot!"

I let the eloquent one speed by in his souped-up Camaro. Douche had probably blown through that intersection yesterday, but that didn't negate his accuracy now. Near accuracy. My head hadn't been in my ass, per se—though he had the neighborhood right.

I pulled over—safely this time—and hauled in a couple of deep breaths, crossing arms over the steering wheel. After a second, I peered over them. Another lazy day in Ramona. The town was a slice of Mayberry-meets-modern, vintage and antique stores vying with trendy taco joints and name-brand fast food. In the distance were the mountains I'd be driving into, taking me home.

Taking me home...or away from Margaux?

And there went another five minutes I wasn't able to get through without a thought of her.

So, yeah, maybe I'd exaggerated Mom's need for me, stretching a week into a month—not that Andrea had been listening when I approached her about taking the time. The woman uttered ten sentences to me during the three minutes she'd tolerated me in her office, granting the request with barely a snort. I wasn't about to pull a fucking John Mayer and write a song about it, but the behavior was not the norm for the woman who'd turned micromanagement into an art form.

Until ten months ago. Almost to the day that our biggest client, Stone Global, nearly went the way of Rome, Enron, and the Harlem Shake for grand declines. It had started with Trey Stone's dazzling backslide into debauchery. Two days after that, the family estate burned to the ground. A week later, Josiah Stone was six feet under. A month after that, Killian Stone was officially missing.

All of the Stones' drama should've added another gleam to Andrea's eyes. She needed PR crises like a leopard needed meat. Instead, she'd returned from Chicago as if she'd gone vegan. The glitch worsened when everyone wondered why Margaux hadn't returned with her.

Everyone except the person who'd noticed the anomaly first.

Me.

I'd never forget that instant as long as I lived. The weird confusion of watching Andrea walk in alone. The weirder experience of gaping at the empty space behind her, normally occupied by Margaux, and feeling like I'd eaten my brussels sprouts but didn't get dessert. Weirdest of all? Locking myself into my office, punching her number on my phone, and texting her for a reason other than work.

Where are you? Is all okay?

I'd parked at my desk like a pathetic ball sack, waiting for her to text back. Then grinned like a bigger sac when she did, ensuring she was "just sorting some things through." I'd burned to ask more, strangely glad when her sorting included fully stepping away from the company—for good. Conceding my jones for the boss's daughter had been one thing. Hiding it from everyone, especially Claire, Chad, and Talia, was different. Once upon a time, Margaux had been our little private joke, the easy-bitch oven we could blame for all our stresses. Her *isms*—narcissism, materialism, sarcasm—always made it easier to deal with hating on Andrea by hating on daughter dearest instead.

Especially for Margaux herself.

Once that revelation zapped me, work had gotten a lot more interesting.

The woman's humor, once grating, was now my gateway into her quicksilver mind. Her vanity? Blatant bid for common ground with her mother. Her sulks were easy to see as the nosedives into insecurity they really were. And her constant anger? Easiest one of all. Anger's bitch of a mother was fear.

But, as the schooling behind the new law degree on my wall attested, answers sometimes only led to lots more questions. What was Margaux Asher afraid of? And what had happened in Chicago to intensify it? And what would she be like if that terror was gone?

Now that she'd stepped out from Andrea's shadow, it was time for her to find out—to pull a phoenix and fly free from the ashes of her past. I'd been psyched for the transformation to begin.

As if connected to my thoughts, the late-afternoon sun fired the landscape around me in dark gold and yellow. Good thing Mother Nature was jiving with the message, because Margaux sure as hell hadn't. Phoenix from the flames? Not exactly. While she'd grown wings in some important ways, she insisted on folding them back in so many others—to the point nobody could even peek beneath.

Not true. She'd let me peek. A little.

And goddamn, I liked what I'd seen.

And tasted.

And felt.

I restarted the truck with a vicious grunt. Like that was going to banish the new highway my thoughts sped along...and the unnerving revelation they led to.

That I'd let her get a peek at me too.

Maybe more than a peek.

I gunned the engine. Not a lot. Enough to move the truck just over the speed limit as I passed Dudley's, normally my must-stop for a bear claw and the strongest coffee outside my kitchen. Not today. Not with a hard-on that would've had the hostesses gawking—and then dialing Mom the second I left.

I went for creative visualization instead. Pretended the tension in my balls surged down my leg and into the gas pedal. The Denali roared, appreciating the extra juice as I hooked a right to start the climb up the mountain. Couldn't say the same for my testicles—or the goddamn missile they were connected to, seemingly wired to only one guidance system on the planet.

The only signal they didn't dare respond to.

Connected to the one woman on the planet I couldn't keep desiring like this.

So tragic, so poetic. *Doesn't stop the fact that you're from a much different world than her, asswipe—as in, a different galaxy. Now get your ass up this mountain and out of your goddamn funk.*

"I'm not in a funk."

Which was why I growled aloud at the fucking voices in my head. And was on my way to voluntarily sleep in my old bed, on the Spiderman sheets Mom kept out of nostalgia, for weeks instead of days. And had taken a four-week-long checkout from my job, my condo, my friends, and the sun on

Mission Bay in favor of sketchy internet, sketchier plumbing, and likely a snow dusting or two.

Check, check, and check. Filled boxes backing the bigger truth—that if I cut a one-eighty right here and now, I'd use any excuse I could to be near Margaux again. And once I was there, I'd find reasons to put my hands on her. Then my lips. As far as where things went from there...

Fuck.

I had a goddamn healthy imagination when it came to that woman these days.

Well, whaddya know. Denali steering wheels made for decent punching bags.

Reversion to adolescence? No shit. But beating up the steering wheel was a better option than taking the road like I was Speed Racer in the Mach Five, the spiffy sexual frustration model.

Damn. I'd really tilted left of sideways—to worse degrees than I'd originally thought. What the hell? The view was not pleasant. Not one damn bit. Mom had worked, saved, and sacrificed for most of my life so I could be—

What? What are you, Michael Adam Pearson? Who are you?

Not this.

Not the guy who got tripped up about shit like this.

I was the one with my head screwed on right and tight. The first Pearson through college and then law school. The son who said he loved his mom and meant it. The guy with the easy smile and the come-cry-here shoulders. When that was done, I helped the old ladies cross the street before stopping at the coffee shop with the town elders, ready to give them a few chuckles about life in the big city.

And yeah, I liked being that guy. Sometimes, even needed it. More importantly, I knew Mom did too. I was her phoenix, the good rising out of a hell of a lot of bad, reminding us both that tough times didn't last but tough people did.

I just needed some wisdom about the other times. The moments when I didn't feel so goddamn golden. When I peeled back the layers and let the animal out. The passions, deep and dark and primeval, that didn't just ask for release but demanded it. Burned for it.

And, with alarming frequency, showed up to collect... every time my eyes locked into the gorgeous green seas of Margaux's. In those split seconds after we kissed...

When her eyes changed too.

As if she was calling my animal out to play.

Like she'd enjoy it.

Hell, no.

Delusions. That was all they were. Desperate delusions from a brain the woman had turned to mulch and the balls she'd turned into—

It keeps coming around to those bastards, doesn't it?

How had I done this? Turned the most fascinating window in my life into a pane I could barely look through anymore because of the smears of my depraved fantasies...triggered by the agony of continuing to get near her.

Not anymore.

The vow was an ice pick in the chest, but I forced the thing in. She was Margaux Corina Asher. The Princess of PR. And yeah...sometimes a bitch too. At other times, a girl barely grown. Then others, a cock-grabbing combo of the two, smart and sexy blended until a guy couldn't breathe for being stunned in her presence.

But she was always, always a princess.

Princesses weren't created for guys like me.

They were made to be spoiled and worshiped, wined and dined, pampered and romanced...

Not groped, fondled, and then fucked like a peasant in the hay.

Which had absolutely become my favorite fantasy lately.

Her nipples stiffened against my tongue and then flattened between my teeth. Her legs hiked around my waist. The imprints of my hands on her thighs, opening her wider for me, obeying my order to stay that way as I lined up my cock to her tight pink entrance and—

"Fuck."

Four weeks of sleeping on Spiderman sheets suddenly made perfect sense again.

And with the uncanny timing she always had, Mom called. I jabbed a shaking thumb on the green button, ending the Duran Duran ringtone.

"Hey, Mom."

"Greetings, beloved offspring."

I shook my head and rolled my eyes. Had I actually wondered why Margaux's sarcasm was so appealing? "What's up?"

"My question exactly. I expected you here a few hours ago."

I exhaled, our unwritten version of an apology. "I had a quick side trip to take first. I just passed Oasis Farms. And before you ask, they're closed. No camel milk chocolate for you tonight." She loved that stuff!

Her chuckle warmed the line. "I stocked up last week. Oh, and I learned both the farm's calves got sold."

"Thank God."

"Oh, come on."

"No comment."

"A couple of camels would've been fun to have around!"

"No comment."

She capitulated with a playfully huffed, "Fine. Just get your ass here safely. Good to know you're close. Dinner's almost ready."

"Yesssss." I could practically smell her fried chicken and homemade applesauce through the line. It was my favorite meal, always served the first night I came home to help with the yearly paperwork.

"See you soon, then."

"Mom?"

"Yeah?"

"Have I mentioned how much I love you?"

She laughed again, this time adding a little psshh. "That's your stomach talking."

I hung up without saying goodbye, with the full knowledge of fueling her laughter more. I grinned and cranked up the radio. Nothing like a little Simon and Garfunkel to add a touch of hipster-approved perfection to the moment.

Home, where my thought's escaping— home, where my music's playing...

The steering wheel turned into my drum. Felt a lot better than a punching bag. I let down the window, inviting air that added a brisk snare to my drum, pine and oak and the smoky undertones unique to nighttime in the mountains. Shock of shocks, I managed a full breath that wasn't mostly stress. And even a few more.

Left clicker on, along with the headlights, as afternoon

blended to twilight. I swung the truck through the still-open gate, its two halves splitting up one word welded into the wrought iron. *PEAR SON'S*

Just beyond the gates was the farm's first grove, many branches dipped low by brave off-season apples. Thirty feet in, a directional sign told delivery trucks to veer right for our supply barns and warehouses. Fifty feet later, another guided the public to the left for apple picking, hay rides, and the petting zoo. Just beyond that, I passed the darkened gift shop before turning down a smaller road through the groves, toward the house I grew up in.

Another deep breath. As slowly, surely, I began to feel normal again.

What was that famous expression, about conclusions belonging to the stupid? There wasn't one? It was about time someone changed that. They could use me as the world's first and best justification.

A grunt and growl combo made their way through my teeth as I slammed on the brakes. The asshole in the middle of the road didn't offer many more options. He didn't flinch as the truck screeched, continuing to scroll messages on his phone.

I shifted into park, shoved open the door, and slammed my left boot to the step, swinging upward. With one elbow braced to the roof and the other atop the open door, I gave myself a silent command.

Breathe.

Breathe.

Was I really doing just that, calmly and normally, a minute ago?

Calm wasn't a remote option now.

Calm and Declan Pearson would never belong in the

same thought for me. Ever.

He lifted his head, showing threads of gray through his trend-conscious hair and well-trimmed beard. I was almost surprised he'd decided to go natural, until realizing he'd likely figured a way to get traction out of the distinguished-guy vibe. Declan didn't make a move in his life without it serving one higher purpose. Himself.

"Welcome home, Michael." A quick sweep of his stare took in what he could see of me. "San Diego certainly suits you. Looking well, son."

"I'm not your son."

I gave myself an inward fist bump for straining the emotion from it. Probably could've performed brain surgery with less difficulty.

The little clicks of his tongue presented a different challenge. My senses went Pavlovian, heartrate spiking and stomach clenching as if I were twelve again, facedown on my bed after I'd threatened to call the cops on his ass if he didn't stop backhanding Mom—and he prepared to punish me double for it. Those tongue clicks. Then his deadly pacing. Then the thwack of the belt as he pulled it from the loops...

Breathe.

Breathe.

No pacing. Only crickets. The wind through the groves. A car passing up on the highway.

"Now, now. Is that any way to say hello to your one and only uncle? I thought your mother did better than that. Maybe I should've come around more to help."

"Hmmm. Yeah. Too bad about that. Restraining orders can be such fuckers."

Bull's-eye. His gaze tightened enough to confirm my hit.

"Your welfare was always my primary concern, my boy."

I'm not your goddamn boy, either. Nothing of mine is yours, you depraved bastard. "Since this conversation is already a waste of my time, let's just cut to the chase. What the fuck do you want, Dec?"

He spread his arms, going for the saint-on-stained-glass pose. I thought about telling him that shit didn't work when you were Lucifer incarnate, but why spoil the laugh? "Only what's best for you and Diana."

"Leave Mom out of this." *You're in dangerous territory now, fucker.*

"Then leave your little-girl emotions out too." He squared his shoulders and bounded forward. My grunt, shocking even me when it burst like a defensive elephant, stopped him short. "Talk some sense into her. You read the papers, listen to the news. The whole state is in a damn drought and—"

"I told you to leave her out of this." The words sliced at myself as much as him. I should've seen through him like crystal a full minute ago.

"So you think you're being a good son, letting her have her way about this? Being her sweet golden boy by allowing her keep the river a little secret from everyone?"

"If it was little, I doubt you—or your oil company buddies—would still be jizzing in your rompers about it." I glared before continuing. "A river on pristine private property, fed by a boundless underground spring—the perfect source to help out with the off-shore fracking they want to start down here. How convenient."

A heavy breath whooshed from him. Fuck, I hoped he hadn't done the jizzing in his pants thing. Yech. Could've lived without that visual. "Instead of phrasing it like we're about to rape puppies, why not think of it as keeping your mother financially comfortable for the rest of her life?"

"She's comfortable the way she is."

"Really, now? Hmmm. If you say so, then. Who would I be to tell a man he doesn't know the needs of his own mother?"

His tone, morning-lake-calm, was an insinuation of the opposite. I swore not to nibble his bait—but, shit, I already had. The new knot in my gut said as much.

Was that instinct wrong? Who was I to claim what Mom wanted now? She'd married into this life. Fallen head over heels for Dad when their paths had collided at the base in San Diego, he freshly returned from the Middle East, she a civilian contractor. The second he got out, they were married and moved up here. A couple of years later, I came along.

She'd known nothing but this farm for a very long time.

Did she want to?

The blank space my mind gave as answer only sharpened my angry retort. "Fuck off, Declan."

He chuckled. *Smug ass wart.* "Glad we had this chat, Michael." He stashed his phone and cocked his head. "By the way, a little birdie tells me you're planning on staying longer than a few days this time. I'll be around too. Give a holler if you want to shoot the shit about...things."

A holler. Right. I'd get right on that—especially if he guaranteed the meeting would conclude with his hacked-off dick in his filthy mouth.

The fantasy kept me company while I swung back into the truck and jammed it into drive. Once more ramming my tension into my pedal foot, I gunned the engine enough to create a lovely spray of dirt and leaves in my wake. Tonguing dust out of his teeth ought to keep the bastard uncomfortable for a while.

Uncomfortable?

I wanted the dildo to suffer. Badly. Especially now, as another moment of clarity hit—like lying in a pile of glass after falling through a window.

I'd worked hard. Left the farm. Made it big in the city. But in less than five minutes, Declan Pearson could turn me back into that trembling kid, taking my blows as Mom watched from the corner, covered in her own bruises.

We'd both covered our scars with tattoos.

But they were still scars.

No wonder I couldn't think about getting intimate with a woman unless raunch and dirt were involved. Maybe that was simply who I was now.

Maybe part of that fucker's depravity had rubbed off on me.

Maybe that was why I excelled at the friend zone—and nothing more.

Maybe this was a good time to remind myself of that—no matter how goddamn hard it got, even sixty miles from the woman I still couldn't stop thinking about.

"It'll get easier." I repeated it beneath my breath. Once. Twice. A third time. Eventually, I had to believe it—or drive myself insane trying to. Either was a better option than living with the day in, day out torment of dreaming about Margaux Asher—and the agony of knowing none of it would ever come true.

CHAPTER THREE

Margaux

I knew I should've sent a text to Michael before I went out for New Year's Eve. The drunk text message carnage on my phone the next morning was both endearing and mortifying. I would pay the next time we spoke, that much was obvious.

Happy New Year, blondie.

Same! OMG soooo dam dunk! Wish you were here to kiss me!

So do I—especially now that I see your dam dunk side.

You funning at me?

Probably.

Good. I like it when you're fun.

No driving like that, by the way.

Nope. Neber. Andre taking Taylor and me home.

Taylor?

Taylor GIRL not Taylor BOY, k? She works with me.

Oh. Well, okay. I guess I like Taylor, then.

I have to pee. Brb

You've been gone a while, you OK? Margaux? Answer, please.

Yep, yep. Fine, Daddy. Just texting Andre. Sorry.

Those weren't even the worst of it. The ones from after Taylor and I got back to my place...well, shit. He was never going to let me live those down.

Captain A! You still up? Oh, wait. You're always UP lol

Still being naughty, I see.

You like me naughty... Still here?

Yeah. I'm just glad you're okay. I was waiting

to hear you made it home.

Such a gentleman.

Not always.

Just when it counts. Ttyt k? So tried.

You mean so drunk?

Yeah, that too. Sleep well. XO

Better if you were here. Stop torturing me and say you'll come see me.

zzzzz zzzzzz

Brat

CHAPTER FOUR

Michael

I'd been waiting for her text all day.

Yo, Captain America.

Yes, beautiful?

Mack Daddy Teddy Bear has arrived safe and sound. Thought you'd want to know.

What the hell are you talking about?

Shut UP. This has YOU written all over it, Pearson. All eight fucking FEET of it.

All eight feet of what?

Fine. I'll just blame it on the cute guy at Starbuck's who keeps comping my latte. I'm sure he'd love to take credit for an eight-foot-tall teddy bear who came bearing six dozen black and red tulips.

The hell?

Thought you'd see it my way.

You win, sugar. You win.

Of course I do.

You do have your ways.

So can I ask a question?

Of course.

How'd you know black and red are my favorite colors?

I have MY ways too, beautiful. Now can I ask you a question?

Only seems fair.

Will you be my valentine?

Does the hideous bear have to stay at my house or yours?

Yours, of course.

Then I won't be your valentine.

Damn it.

CHAPTER FIVE

Margaux

In like a lion, out like a lamb—or some dumb poetry shit like that. Spring pulled into San Diego in all its glorious fashion, but my heart felt frozen in place. Not such a new feeling, really, but my self-imposed dry spell wasn't helping one damn bit.

Working day and night helped dull the pain, but even Killian started to notice—especially when I politely turned down a dinner invitation from his buddies, Fletcher Ford and Drake Newland, during their visit to SoCal for the year-end board meeting. Kil had gaped like I'd dyed my hair into a rainbow and then let the color sink into my brain. I'd almost agreed with him. More than a few times, I'd confessed about pining for that matched set of hotness and their idea of dinner, a special package deal that redefined the words best buddies share everything. Imagining the possibilities usually got me wet and tingly in all the right ways. The fantasy ranked high on my personal bucket list. But I couldn't muster the enthusiasm even to have drinks with the boys.

What the hell?

I'd gotten home that night and checked my temperature, convinced I was coming down with some virus that caused irrational behavior. Sadly, everything was normal, confirming my ailment couldn't be written off as a physical issue.

The real—and worse—diagnosis?

I had it bad for Michael Pearson.

And had no damn idea if he felt remotely the same way.

That wasn't true. There was that kiss before he'd left—and since then, a lot of those teasing, semisteamy texts. Okay, he'd also tried calling, all of two times—but on both, I'd been at the office on deadlines, meaning conversations didn't delve much deeper than the weather, Montgomery-Stone wedding updates and a few attempts at cutesy on his part, always starting the same way. Was I staying out of trouble? And if I wasn't, was I at least being safe?

Ugh. It was as comfortable as Charlie Brown and his cute little redheaded girl—only he didn't have a dancing dog for his comedy relief, and I wasn't sure cute and I shared the same universe. I vowed to give him hell about paying five cents for Lucy the Shrink the next time we talked.

Like I knew when the hell that would be.

Which laid the breadcrumbs back to our huge damn problem.

Would there be a next time to talk?

He'd said a month's absence. It was now closing in on three. And his begging invitations for me to join him in Podunk—err, I mean Julian—had almost stopped. Everything was still friendly between us, but it stopped right there, no more and no less. I had no right to pry, so I never did. I also had no right to expect calls and texts on a regular basis, so I never asked. We were locked in a *Peanuts* world. Pleasant, pretty, sometimes funny—and flat, flat, flat.

Exactly where I'd pressed my love life.

Good grief.

I phoned Taylor, Claire, and two other girls from sales,

talking them into hitting one of the gastropubs in the Gaslamp District. I so needed this. I wasn't the one who'd gone hermit crab in Sweet Apple Acres, and it was damn time to remind myself of that. I intended to live tonight, starting with a cosmo down my throat and—chemistry and karma willing—ending with a cock between my legs. I was done pining for a guy who'd dumped me before even knowing he wanted me.

Three hours, four cocktails, and eleven strikeouts later, I clacked back in to my building with my head low and spirits lower. I was half drunk and one hundred percent lonely. A little miserable and a lot confused.

I'd feel better after a good night's sleep, which couldn't come soon enough.

With the bad memories of the night washed away by my lavender shampoo and rosemary soap, I felt coherent again. After slipping into my favorite silk pajamas, I grabbed my phone for one more email scan while I settled into bed. Not giving in to the temptation of Michael-oriented thoughts wasn't as easy.

Shit. I'd done it. With his name back out in the universe, coupled now with my impaired judgment, I decided to put my liquid courage to use and send the recluse a text.

One text. One.

I nodded groggily. One wouldn't hurt. I deserved it, damn it. The miserable attempt at a night of fun and fornication had only led to a thousand more thoughts of him, nameless and all. Maybe touching base would scrub him off my mind too—at least for a little bit.

Thinking of you. Sleep well.

I blinked hard at the text that came back. Then swore like

a sailor.

Who is this?

I didn't know what to say. "Who the fuck is this?" Well, that was something. Just not the right something. Obviously.

What the hell was going on? While I fought back thoughts of him like a swoony girl half my age, was Adonis-on-the-mountain juggling so many girls, he couldn't keep track?

Fury blazed. I'd turned down a parade of himbos willing to come back here and service me with their young, nubile cocks—even it meant drawing them a guide for where things went—but rejected them all out of comparison to him. Had I used the wrong analysis data? Held up the wrong example? Broken my own rules and let myself walk out on a limb—for this return?

I hit the caps lock and started flicking my thumbs over the keys. *F-U-C-K Y-O—*

JK, sugar. Can't seem to stop thinking of you, either.

"Shit shit shit shit shit."

I couldn't slam the Backspace key fast enough, freaked he'd sense even the obscenities I hadn't gotten to yet.

After I finally allowed myself to breathe again, I also smiled. Well, well. He was thinking about me too.

As I flopped back into the pillows, my grin faded.

Now what?

"Your turn on the high dive, lady."

The self-encouragement was anything but that. But I couldn't just leave him hanging.

I hopped out of bed and paced to soothe my hammering

pulse—and racing brain. It had been weeks since I last heard from him— that alone ruled out a lot of plays except sweet or sour. The obvious choice was full throttle on the bitch wagon—but even if well justified, it'd crash the conversation before it started. More long weeks would pass before either of us screwed up the balls to reach out again.

Okay, so...I was doing sweet.

"No," I spat. "No, no, no. You're not Twilight Sparkle, for chrissake."

Say something, damn it.

"Something."

That one definitely sounded better on paper. Annnnd, I was wasting time. The time stamp on his text conveyed that four minutes had passed. An eternity in text time. *You're fucking this up.*

My phone vibrated again.

Did I lose you? Reception spotty here.

Shit. Shit. "Okay. Keep it casual. You can do that. Casual. Sure."

I'm here. Just got out of the shower.

I looked at the words and instantly wanted to hurl on them. What the hell was that? Had I caught the teeny-bop virus at the bar and brought it home with me?

I plopped into the window seat with a disgusted snort. "Say something else that lame, and I'll deny ever knowing you, Asher."

But...maybe it was sexy. Kind of. If the man thought creatively...or not.

What's done is done. Wait and see what he says. Or...not.

It was official. I was a fucking basket case—over words on a screen smaller than my damn lipstick case. A screen I now stared at like a bomb about to go off in my hands.

When it finally vibrated again, I jumped. Me. It was ridiculous, but I couldn't wait to read.

Wish I was there to dry the hard-to-reach spots.

My cheeks hurt from the width of my smile. Worth it. So worth it. As my woozy mind concocted a vision of him standing behind me, dressed in nothing but his own towel, wicking water from me with slow strokes of his big hands, my whole body prickled in sensual need. This was what I'd been seeking at the bar. This was what I'd been craving for weeks...months... ever since he'd left...

You and me both, Mr. P.

I gripped the phone with both hands, enduring the wait for his response. Attempting to ignore the ache of my nipples... the rush of my blood...the need between my legs...

Call him. Just call him, damn it. Explain you're still half drunk and need more creative imagery for stress relief. Yes—that's it. Phone sex could be the perfect ice breaker...

Five minutes.

This was unbearable. I shifted one of my hands, pinching my breast while thinking of Michael, hand wrapped around his cock as he fantasized about my freshly showered body. Torture? Maybe a little. Okay, more than a little. But I desperately needed to believe I'd gotten under his skin as he had mine.

Need to get some sleep, blondie. Talk soon.

"What?"

I hammered a finger at the phone.

What?

Was. He. Fucking. Kidding?

My jaw worked against the rekindled fire of rage before I just gave in, hurling the phone across the room. It skimmed the bed and clattered against the wall. I hoped the screen was shattered this time. It sure as hell beat flinging myself out of the window—like I'd give any person that power, let alone a man. But, within seconds, a breeze against the glass made me shiver. I turned and stumbled back to bed as a desolate chill took over, making me curl the covers tight.

Damn it. Damn it. I was running hot and cold about this bastard. Literally.

Well, I'd had it.

I kicked the covers off, stiff with resolution.

No one jerks Margaux Asher around like this and gets away with it.

Starting this minute, he wasn't getting away with it. Not any longer. I was done with Michael Pearson. He thought I'd been elusive and evasive before? Darling, you haven't seen anything yet. My walls were about to shrivel the balls of even skilled mountain climbers.

The next morning, I put on my take-no-shit Prada heels and hauled my ass to work, despite the third-degree hangover. It wasn't my worst by far and came in handy for ramping my bitch game, a gift I'd kept pitifully closeted for too long. Well, it was time to dust that girl off and let her strut—and it felt as wonderful as slipping into a well-worn pair of jeans. This was home. This I knew and understood.

By the end of the day, everyone else did too. I had my assistant crying by ten. The coffee cart girl hand-delivered my eleven o'clock latte, shaking as she did. I closed a major account Claire had been toying with for two weeks—with one phone call. As I walked out for my lunch appointment with Killian's top European clients, people stopped and stood back. Sometimes, old habits were worth returning to. It was refreshing to see how everyone agreed with me. Like they had any choice.

That's right, gang. Princess-zilla is back. Fuck with me, and you'll deal with my dragon breath. And it won't smell like Tic Tacs.

After celebrating the day's successes by clicking to my favorite online boutique and buying the slingbacks I'd been eyeing—being shipped overnight, of course, because I was good like that—I actually hummed a little while climbing into my car.

No more helplessness. No more wallowing. And no more pining away for a farm boy who wanted nothing to do with me.

I was back where I belonged, and it felt good.

Now if I could get the message to the ache right beneath my sternum, things would be even better.

CHAPTER SIX

Michael

The mountains had taken spring seriously this year. Everywhere was another view that should've been on a postcard or in a painting. A lot of people agreed with me, to the point that Mom opened up the back meadows for artists' clubs, bird-watching groups, even a few bridal showers.

She'd needed extra help. At least that was the excuse I was using this week to rationalize staying a while longer.

It had nothing to do with the text conversations that Margaux and I had been having.

Hi there, sugar.

Hi.

Just thought I'd say hi. Didn't know if I'd get you.

Well, you did. Congrats.

Haven't heard from you in a week.

Haven't seen you in four months.

Like I needed to be reminded.

It's been busy up here.

Sure. I get it. We're all busy these days.

So, what have you been up to? Anything interesting? Want to talk?

Can't talk. Busy, remember?

Maybe tonight, then. After work.

Busy then, too.

Yeah. Of course.

Your own bed, asshole. Now you lie in it.

Or maybe just take it off this fucking mountain, back to the land where she can be busy with you.

Well, being busy is good.

Quite.

Have a great day. I miss you.

Silence.

And a lot of unanswered questions.

Like when the hell was I going to get my head out of my ass, deal with this goddamn complex I had about her, and get the hell on with real life?

Silence. Imagine that. It was such a versatile theme for so many occasions. Especially when one pulled their head out of their ass and jammed it into the ground instead.

CHAPTER SEVEN

Margaux

Being the maid of honor sucked. Did somebody want to indicate where the honor in all of this was? I'd been schlepping shit around for the past week, making ridiculous requests of people I didn't know—and worst of all, I didn't even believe in the institution of marriage. Don't even get me started on love in general.

Fools. Every last one of them.

And on cue, my phone signaled an incoming text from places near but far. Very far.

Hey.

Hey.

Busy?

Pretty much. You?

Not really. Just hoping we could talk.

Need to be at appointment with Bridezilla in ten.

Will you be home later?

Pretty sure I have a date.

So what if he didn't know the "date" involved a mani-pedi and a facial. Like Ranger Rick would care. If he wanted to keep hiding in the wilderness, I was over it. Over. It.

Well, have fun. I guess...

What ev

Don't be like that.

Like what, Michael? Like we're BFFs now? Just let it go, k?

Let's talk later when you get home.

What if I don't come home?

Don't be like that!

Like what? Like the real me?

STOP.

Already have.

CHAPTER EIGHT

Michael

For the first time in my life, I understood why they called these things fucking monkey suits.

I was normally the guy who liked putting on a tux when the occasion called for it. I even listened when Andrea yakked at us about the newest men's trend, and I liked paying attention to shit like cut and fabric and lines. After growing up in muddy jeans, flannel shirts, and nails full of apple tree mulch, it was all a fun new world for me. Nothing I took too crazy-serious, of course, but investing enough energy that Chad had threatened to revoke my guy card on a few occasions.

He happily gave it back now. The jerk even smirked about it as he snickered at me through the gazebo we stood on either side of, occupying a strategic corner of the massive lawn in the back yard of Claire's "wedding present." The structure was fronted by fancy gold chairs seating two hundred guests in brand-new clothes. And yeah, I was sure about that. Nobody wore last year's fashions to the wedding of the year.

The gazebo was positioned behind the arch Claire and Killian would soon be standing under. Inside the shelter itself, there was a string quartet and eight urns brimming with a florist's shop full of red and white flowers. Poofs of white fabric were tucked, wrapped, and swagged around every other available surface. For Claire, everything had to be perfect.

If only my nervous system would get with that program. Though it was damn near six o'clock on the second day of June, I sweat like a hog in the middle of August. The sun was low, filtering through the trees in swaths of gold and amber, carrying a twilight breeze smelling of star jasmine and pine. None of it tamped my craving to rip myself clear of the tux and roll around naked in the grass.

Strange strain of the flu?

If only I could get so lucky.

At the moment, even a case of Ebola sounded better than the ordeal ahead. And I wasn't the guy about to step into the ball and chain.

The man with that task all but bounded up to the arch in the minister's wake. Happy? Killian transcended happy by about a thousand miles. He was the Gollum who'd found the ring. The Scarecrow who had his brain. The kid with triple chocolate and cherries on his sundae.

I was just going to put it out there.

Killian Stone was glowing.

So maybe I was glad I hadn't busted his face for nearly turning Claire—and Stone Global—into unfixable messes last summer. Thank fuck the guy had gotten a clue and come back to salvage both. Now, he stood prouder and stronger than ever, a man in love, at peace, and on top of his world. SGC's successes were only a small part of it. In the joy on his face and the smile on his lips, I saw how Killian would dump the cars, the mansions, and all the stuff if they ever threatened his relationship with Claire.

As long as the man maintained that world view, he and I would be copacetic.

If I could only lay claim to a shred of that peace.

Not if you keep carrying this goddamn torch for Margaux Asher.

Not if every ping from your phone makes your gut leap like it has for the last six months, hoping it's a message or picture from her.

Not if you don't grow a pair and realize what you have with her is nothing more than a long-distance—if flirty to the point of dangerous—relationship.

The time and distance I'd thought would save me? Backfired would be a kind assessment. Like an untended spark in dry brush, my thoughts of her burned more fiercely than before. To quote the worst cliché of them all, she was under my goddamn skin. I could no more fight it than I could explain it, only knowing that once my time in Julian hit the one-month mark, I'd been less ready to get back to normal than I was before. I wasn't sure I even knew what normal was anymore—only that if it meant rewinding life to the days when I didn't have her at all, then I was completely content being abnormal for another month more. Then another. And another. And three more after those.

And I still wasn't ready. After six goddamn months, a handful of phone calls and those let's-dance-around-the-truth texts...I was still wondering when my turn in the moving-on queue was coming.

Under my skin?

Who the hell was I kidding?

Somehow, this sorceress had burrowed into my spirit, my mind, and my body. Ohhh, shit, my body. I'd given up trying to reason it out, only knowing that even her texts were like butterfly kisses on my cock. And the phone calls, being subjected to the husky beauty of her voice? The wood between my thighs could've occupied an acre in the groves all by itself.

I'd quickly learned that the groves were a great place to be alone to take the edge off things.

Fuck.

Was there a twelve-step program for this shit somewhere?

Hi, I'm Michael, and I jack off in the apple groves to thoughts of Margaux Asher. It's been about five seconds since my last thought of her...

I had to get over this.

Like there was a this to get over. Six months had only driven the point in harder. We weren't a this and couldn't ever be. The woman was...

Smart. Snarky. Sexy.

Challenging. Charming. Sexy.

Wicked. Wild. Sexy.

And so fucking far out of my league...

She was the hottest girl in school. The beauty in the castle tower. And yeah, I cleaned up well, but under it all, I was still the geek at the back of class and the serf at the bottom of the hill...

The apple farmer's son, fallen for the girl who'd worn Prada onesies.

Nothing seared that truth deeper into me than the next moment...

When I actually saw her again.

She paused at the end of the aisle, addressing the crowd like a princess acknowledging her subjects. One arm was hooked gracefully beneath the elbow of Killian's brother, Lance.

As they started walking again, the term tunnel vision

became defined. Everything fell away except the awareness of her. The beauty of her.

Christ. My knees were literally weak.

Paralyzed.

Speechless.

Not that anyone was asking me to speak up at the moment. But this stall into inarticulate... It was more than the words refusing to form on my lips. It was the thoughts no longer bridging in my mind, rerouting down different paths, past the typical roadmaps I'd used to keep her far away, locked high in her tower, still safe from the valley of my fantasies.

As I stared...and stared...and stared...the valley fell away too.

Forget paralyzed. I was hypnotized. By everything about her...

The strong elegance of her steps.

The proud set of her head.

The perfect lift of her lips.

The ivory angles of her shoulders, rising from the strapless bodice of her dress—

Holy fuck, that dress.

Until now, I couldn't get enough of how the woman rocked T-shirts, jeans, and boots when we went out for beer and darts. Cancel that order, boss. I had a new Margaux fashion favorite. Red. The crimson material fit her in every perfect way I could imagine, hugging her breasts, waist, and hips before flaring into layers that were all romance and grace. Just enough ankle and leg showed with every step she took, along with a pair of strappy gold heels she was born to wear.

I locked my gaze on those shoes. Not like strappy pumps were my new fetish—it simply seemed the safest view for the moment, considering everything that slammed my brain when I fixated north of her waist. How much trouble could her feet get me into?

I had to ask.

Dumb shit.

First, I thought about how elegant her feet looked, no matter what she was doing—even bopping to the jukebox at the High Dive. Adorable, carefree girl. Then I thought about how she'd hike her cute ass on one of the bar stools and taunt me by dangling a shoe off one of her toes. Ruthless, seductive woman. Wasn't hard to make a jump from there, remembering how she'd slide off the seat for a trip to the ladies' room, imitating something she called the Olivia Pope strut. How the feisty sway of her ass made me drag her out to my truck instead.

Maddening, magnificent goddess.

Now all I could think about were her heels parked on my shoulders. Her ankles beneath my lips. Her legs locked around my neck as I surged my body into hers, over and over, harder and harder—

Shit.

Her feet weren't an option, either.

The plain and simple? I was doomed. Dazzled to the point of motionless, not daring to move for fear the chafe of my pants would turn my erection into a goddamn tent pole.

This was all so strange, looking at her but feeling like I'd never seen her until now. I suddenly realized that even after I'd come to those new opinions of her last summer, first impressions had hung around for a while. Ice princess. Bitch on wheels. Jacqueline Frost. Maybe I'd kept them around as a safety net against the inevitable—tumbling fast and hard like this. If that was so, I'd sure as hell misplaced the thing now.

Funny what could go missing during a six-month exile...

And what hung around, no matter how hard you tried to get rid of it.

As soon as she turned and looked toward me, I was as good as a dry pine in a brushfire.

Two seconds of a glance, maybe three—but I was in hopeless thrall. The sun gleamed across her whole face but concentrated in her eyes, transforming them to brilliant green stars, searing into me even deeper.

Paradise. Purgatory.

Thank God it was time to focus on the bride.

Claire was, to be cliché, fucking perfect. I was sure even the birds in the trees stopped as the quartet changed up their tune, breaking into a sweet version of "A Thousand Years" as she and her father, Colin, walked up the aisle. Her white gown was also strapless and adhered to the understated elegance she used in dressing for every occasion. A delicate diamond necklace hung to the hollow of her throat, leading the eye to tiny jewels embedded into the gown's neckline. The bodice was fitted to an empire waist before flowing down, Grecian-goddess fashion, in layers that billowed behind her in all the right ways. With her hair gathered beneath a double-stranded Grecian headpiece, she really did seem Aphrodite come to life. The woman seemed to possess extra superpowers tonight—if the permanent drop of Killian's jaw was any giveaway.

I traded a smirk with his best buddies, Drake Newland and Fletcher Ford, who were serving as ushers along with Chad and me. Their faces said it all. They didn't get chances to witness Kil as the spokesmodel for gobsmacked very often, so they relished every moment. Chad's lips quirked too, joining in Fletch and Drake's private party, but no way in hell was I jumping in. How could I bask in Killian's fight for composure when I related to so much of it?

Focus on Claire. Focus on Claire. Focus on Claire.

Stupidest call of my life.

Had I conveniently forgotten the maid of honor was the one who helped the bride—as in standing next to her? As in, all I had to do was click my vision one degree to the right in order to stare again at the eyes, the smile, even the damn feet of the lady in red who rapidly gave me balls of blue?

And now told me, with another glance my way, that her serenity was just an act for the cameras?

Damn it.

I locked my hands behind my back. Ordered them to stay there, subsidizing my battle not to rush to her and haul her into my arms, soothing that anxiety. As far back as Thanksgiving, she'd hinted about how hard today might be, having to see Andrea after their estrangement. She'd also changed the subject right after that—surprise, surprise—but I hadn't pushed.

But the stress was clearly taking its toll.

And you think your long-distance hot-and-cold game hasn't impacted the woman one bit, asshole?

"Pffft." The disclaimer was barely audible but useful. It was time to be honest with myself. The escape up the mountain was over. While it hadn't done shit for getting me over Margaux, I held no illusions that she'd ever taken the innuendos from our texts and calls out to the orchard. Moreover, she'd declined my invitations to come visit with increasing creativity—and contempt. Good thing I'd left Julian when I did, because I was pretty certain she'd be pulling the "I have to wash my hair" excuse next.

I had to face a disgusting truth. There was a good chance someone—maybe a few someones—were fueling that ingenuity.

A someone she might have even brought as her date to this gig.

The realization hit like a physical blow. I rocked on my heels from it. I swung a stare over the crowd. Until now I'd just skimmed over the sea of faces, not registering anyone except the key wedding party players and a few celebrities. Different story this time, at least for the guys. Which one of them gawked at Margaux as fiercely as me?

Not any help. That covered nearly every bastard in the crowd. Okay, which one of them did it with that I'm-tapping-that-tonight glint in his eyes? I was no Special Forces stud, but I knew how to disguise paranoia when I had to...

Except when it was interrupted by the start of Killian and Claire's vows...

And was hit by the gleam of sun, shimmering through tears...

On Margaux's face.

Keep your jaw off the lawn, man.

Much easier said than done.

Kil and Claire had opted for traditional vows, every syllable in its rusty but mushy place, which doubled my shock at Margaux's reaction. The woman didn't do rusty. She certainly didn't do mushy. But I couldn't deny what I witnessed beneath the stubborn jut of her chin, the tiny wobble of her lips, the heavy gulps down her throat.

Once more, with four times the intensity, I battled the craving to go to her.

Get a fucking grip.

It was a wedding, for chrissake. Girls cried for each other at weddings. It was no secret how she and Claire had grown closer over the last year. She was just happy for...

So why did her waterworks get worse as Killian started his half of the vows?

The answers in my gut weren't encouraging. At all.

When she and I had first started hanging out, after whatever shit had hit the fan in Chicago, she'd gone straight-shooter with me about her history with Killian. I'd appreciated the honesty, having been in the limo the day she'd declared the man her next meal in front of us all. Very few knew the story of what happened after that, though—about the night a few months later, when she'd gone totally boiled bunny on the guy. After surprising Kil in his condo in a blatant bid at seduction, all she'd gotten was her ass handed to her on a platter of humiliation, confronted by the reality of how rock-solid he was about Claire.

When I'd sucked it up and asked her if any of her feelings for the guy lingered, her reaction had been surprising—and vehement. Appearing like my suggestion had shoved a lemon in her mouth, she'd declared that Killian was now more brother to her than lover.

I'd thoroughly believed her—until now.

Were those tears of happiness...or sorrow?

Was Margaux's discomfort due entirely to Andrea, or was another layer at play here? Had she been deceiving herself—and me, along for that ride—when reassigning Killian to the like-a-brother zone? Had her feelings been rekindled by spending so much time near the man during the wedding preparations? Was that the reason she'd concocted so many reasons not to come up for a visit?

Bashing my head into the gazebo was feeling like a better option by the second.

★★★★

My head—and the gazebo—made it through the ceremony in one piece.

I'd done the smart thing. Concentrated anew on Claire and Killian, taking encouragement from their love, certain the space station was picking up its brightness on radar. They exchanged rings and then lit a unity candle, almost breaking the rules by macking down on each other then and there.

If there was a single dry eye left in the place after that, Kil handled it by revealing a surprise he'd been saving for his bride—a duet performance of "My Heart Is Open," sung live by Adam Levine and Gwen Stefani. Until then, Claire had been impressively reining her composure to a few dewy tears. The song turned those tethers to dust, especially when the minister used the bridge to officially proclaim her as Mrs. Killian Stone. She sobbed so hard that she crumpled into Killian, giving the guy a perfect excuse to scoop her up and just carry her back down the aisle, surrounded by the wild applause of the crowd.

I had to admit, the moment dissolved even my black cloud a little. For the next half hour, the usher-ly duties were a decent distraction too. It also helped to offer a helping hand to the six-piece party band, freshly arrived to take the string quartet's place in the gazebo. I killed another half hour at the bar with Chad, Drake, and Fletcher, probably learning more than I wanted about Killian's two friends. They'd had quite an adventure last night at an interesting private club beneath one of downtown's most famous—and supposedly respectable—

dinner clubs. It was one of Andrea's favorite places to take clients for dinner. Now I began to wonder why.

Damn.

Had Margaux discovered something along those lines about her mother? Was that the reason for their sudden estrangement last summer?

And where the fuck did that leave Colin Montgomery?

Poor, pussy-whipped man.

You calling it like you see it or just welcoming the dude into your boat?

I rewarded the thought with a chest-deep snarl while sinking into an empty chair at an abandoned party table. A dinner buffet, catered by Wolfgang Puck's team, had long ago been cleared. Many reception guests were lingering over their slices of red velvet wedding cake. Looked like Killian might still have a speck of it on his nose, but it also looked like Claire didn't care.

Laughter. Music. Lights. Cake. Even the mist I'd predicted gave respect to the joy in the air, lingering at the edges of the party, afraid to ruin the night.

Talk about your perfect romance movie scenes. And yes, I had authority to make the ruling, considering how many of the damn things Margaux had made me sit through last summer.

Last summer.

When things had been simpler.

Bullshit. You only remember them that way.

Simple wasn't ever a luxury when it came to Margaux Asher.

And that's just the way you like it.

Chest snarl number two. And another vow to never spend more than a month at a time back at home again. Clean air, fresh farm food, and no night life? Points for the clear lungs, the solid sleep patterns, and the body fat drop even with pie every night for dessert. Major minus for the solitude. Too damn much of it. No wonder I dove into my head too much now.

Mom had tried to be a gentle sounding board—and I appreciated her efforts—but between her book club, wine-tasting group, kick boxing, and time on the shooting range, she also had city council duties, as well as making sure the PD kept the restraining order on Declan active. And oh yeah, running one of the mountain's hugest orchards. That little thing.

In short, my worries about her had been pointless, which cleared a swath through my brain for what-the-hell-do-I-do-now.

But I wasn't the fucking Dalai Lama. Aligning my chi was not the goal tonight.

Finding a tactful and respectful way to get my ass out of here? A worthy goal. Hadn't I seen an ad for a weekend marathon of *Ice Road Truckers* when thumbing through SI while shoveling my oatmeal this morning? Boxers, beer, and sixteen-wheelers on frozen lakes were sounding damn good.

"Care to dance?"

I visibly exhaled.

Karma did know how to send angels.

Especially ones in you-know-you-want-this red dresses, who had the girl cojones to walk right up to a guy and ask for a twirl. Who also had the guts to go Scarlett Johansson-dominatrix with her tone to said guy, infusing her request with enough badass Black Widow to emphasize that it wasn't a request.

It was time like this I didn't know whether I adored her

or feared her. No way was I tempting fate's wrath by going for the trite answer of a little of each. Margaux Asher deserved so much more than trite. So much more than easy. So the answer to that? Yeah, I adored her and feared her.

And revered her.

And wanted her—now more than ever.

And had no fucking idea how I was going to get through this entire song without fully mauling her.

Holy shit, how I'd missed this. All of it.

Her spine beneath my fingers. Her body pressed against mine. Her fingers, soft and slender. Her gaze, huge and mesmerizing. Her hair, a mist-kissed halo.

Diamond captured.

Moonbeam pinned.

Princess come to life.

And I thought I'd be able to just get over this?

"I've missed you, blondie."

Cheeks still stained, she looked down and then back up. Her eyes were just as incredible, thick lashes framing the luminescent green depths—an accurate description, given the extra fires now burning their way up to me.

Uh-oh.

That extra heat usually meant the princess was pissed—and though I couldn't figure how my sincerity could've sparked it, I braced myself for impact.

"Missed me?" She canted her head. "Well, I'm glad you cleared that up—because it felt more like being avoided."

My feet jammed us to a stop this time. I squeezed her extra close to counteract the shock to her balance, though instantly wondered if I could get away with doing it all over again. The feel of her leaning completely into me, her body soft and pliant... I was Zeus harnessing the lightning, ready to scale Olympus in a single bound.

If only there wasn't the not-so-small issue of her voice to deal with. And the ire in it—acting as a thin disguise for the hurt.

I kept her locked in the standstill, despite her effort to return to the rhythm of the song. Pushing a tiny huff through her nose, she glanced back up. Glanced. Giving me just enough let-it-drop-buddy impatience to communicate she'd meant that as the last and only word.

In another world—like, say, the one of six months ago—I'd have rolled with that. When Margaux raised her walls, especially with those strange lines of loneliness etched across her face, my MO had typically been to respect the boundary. But where the hell had that gotten us? Six stupid months of separation. Texts so awkward, teenagers would likely laugh in derision. A handful of phone calls that hardly made it past talk of the weather—the fucking weather—so that now, I'd driven myself crazy about wondering who she'd brought as a date to this thing, only to get my first up-close of the night and see the exact same solitude haunting her beautiful eyes.

Isolation I now related a little more to.

Maybe more than a little.

"Guilty as charged," I finally murmured. The upsweep of her gaze nearly unraveled my resolve to blurt the rest. "I was... avoiding...things. But not because of..."

"Of what?"

Not because of you.

The lie pounded at my lips, threatening to charge through the gates of my control. But what would that say about the respect I'd just admitted for her? And all the things I'd come to feel beyond that...which had, without a doubt, only strengthened over the last six months...

But the truth sure as hell wasn't an option, either.

No. Fucking. Way.

"Dude?"

I couldn't help but laugh when she waved a hand in front of my face. Though she stopped short of adding "Earth to Michael," her single syllable handled the syntax pretty damn well.

"Sorry. I'm here." I pressed one of my thumbs into the base of her spine, the other into the middle of her hand, cupped in mine. "I'm...all here."

Fuck. Guarding the truth like one of the hounds of Cerebus, eh, man? Because that won't tip her off at all...

Her quirky little smile told me nothing—except that her quirky little smiles could still turn me into something close to a real dog. Dear fuck, I hoped I didn't drool. "And I'm damn glad you are, mister."

Translation—let me fondle your crotch here and now. It was exactly what her words did anyway, making me suck in tight air, clench my jaw, and force my body a few inches away from her—when all it yearned to do was the opposite.

"You're not going back up there, are you?"

"What? Back up where?"

"To Julian." Her forehead V'ed. "Pearson, are you all right?"

Besides trying to keep up the semblance of dancing with you—while not getting everything else up in the process? "Yeah, yeah. I'm sorry, princess. I'm just—"

"Princess?"

I scowled. Shit, it wasn't like I'd called her the b word, or some other girl's name. "What's wrong with princess?"

Her eyes bugged. "What's wrong with princess?"

I shrugged. "Okay, scratch it. I'll just graduate you to queen." I prayed like hell that one would stick—and not like the crap pile I'd apparently stepped into. For insurance, I added a little tug, bringing her close again. Surely I could keep the monster in my crotch under control for a few lousy seconds. "No. Fuck that too. You're beautiful enough tonight to be the empress." I hated that I'd miffed her, but the way her angry flush worked with the tint of that dress... Damn. More than a few guys here were glaring daggers at me right now, I was certain of it. And I smirked a little because of it.

Wrong. Move.

Margaux stopped again. Stepped back. Revision—jerked away. "Are you trying to dig yourself in deeper?"

I reached for her again—a second too late. She'd already begun her march off the dance floor. I followed her out to the grass, where the light was dimmer—which only enhanced every aspect of her beauty. Fuck. I wasn't going to win the hypnosis-by-Margaux battle tonight.

"I'm not trying for anything, prin—" Hell. "Margaux. We haven't seen each other in half a year—"

"And whose choice was that?"

My teeth jammed together. "You had a standing invitation to visit and never used it."

Air rushed out of her in a mirthless laugh. "Me? In frontier land? You've been breathing thin air for too long, Davey Crockett."

I dropped my hands. "So choices were made on both sides."

Her head slid back as if on a horizontal rail. The new

distance didn't lessen the shock in her gaze. "Wait. You think I didn't want to see you?" When I maintained deliberate neutrality, her head slid back—and she didn't stop there. After revving the move into a gorgeous, gold-stilletoed stomp, she fired, "How the hell do you get off, arriving at that kind of a conclusion?"

Because believing alternate answers isn't an option, princess. That number one, somebody was keeping you too busy to make the trip to frontier land, or number two...you were just as scared to get together as I was.

Deep breath in. Equal effort on the exhale. Pick. Words. Carefully. "Probably the same way you got off making yours."

Her lips pursed. "Except that mine was right." She jutted her chin. "You left, Michael. I don't give a damn that you were only sixty miles away. You told me you'd be gone for a few weeks—not six months." She pushed out another breath. Not a note of surface mirth this time. The dark-green sheen in her eyes confirmed it—despite how flippant she tried to be with her next rasp. "Did you...meet someone...up there?"

"What?" I stopped to unglue my eyebrows from their crash landings over my eyes. "Holy fuck. No."

Was I dreaming this? Was this woman, the hottest reboot of Aphrodite that ever lived, standing here with pooled eyes and shaking breaths because of imagining me with someone up on the mountain? I almost laughed. Christ, if she knew. Five days out of each week I'd been in Julian, the only females I'd seen were Mom, the knitting club ladies, and a camel named Bertha.

I went ahead and laughed. Not loud, not hard, but enough to land my foot into the ca-ca mound again.

"Okay, then." Margaux tossed her head up, even turning

the pissed filly thing into something entirely new and sexy. "Glad to know I could amuse you tonight, Mr. Pearson."

"Fuck," I growled. "That didn't come out right."

"You think?"

"Margaux. Shit. Work with me here."

"I work with people who work with me, Pearson." No more tears now, either, hardening her eyes to emerald crystals. "And right now, I don't feel worked with. I only feel...worked."

My teeth tangoed again. My lungs lurched, pulling in heavy air. Her accusation screamed for a fire-and-brimstone comeback.

I stayed on the mountain because I was trying to get over you, princess.

Amazing, antagonizing, gorgeous, gutsy, smart-assed, sexy...you.

And I kept on trying—and trying. And failing. So I just stayed longer. Time. Distance. I prayed they'd be my keys out of the straitjacket of you—but they only locked me in tighter. Thinking of you. Craving you. Touching myself because of those cravings...

And the more time I spent inside that prison...the more I liked it.

And after those words were out? Then what?

I'd imagined how the moment would play out, more than just a few times. Run all the possible scenarios of what she'd look like, what she'd say, what she'd do. Odds were on it ending pretty damn great, at least for a few hours. The sexual spark between us had never been an issue or a secret. From the moment I'd first kissed her—and fuck, I'd never forget it—in front of the lions at the San Diego Zoo, we'd known about the combustion of our mouths and the chemistry of our bodies.

We'd been holding ice cream bars. By the time we finished that kiss, we were both covered in smeared lipstick and melted ice cream.

So yeah, I'd likely get lucky—if I kept the confession restrained. If all I told her about were the hot fantasies and the trips to the orchard to whack off because of them. If I could hold back on all the other parts, like how I missed the room lighting up from her smile, or my chest bursting from her laugh, or my face splitting when that laugh turned into snorts...

Yeah.

Only all the shit like that.

Because I'd mentally run the scenario of that little reveal too. Not such a pretty picture. Telling Margaux Asher that you dreamed of playing house with her... The carnage from there wasn't tough to envision. Expecting different was stupidity. The woman had been raised by the love child of Alexis Carrington and Betty Draper, turning the concepts of home, family, and traditions into a joke, if not a horror show, for her. Earlier, when I'd forced myself to make nicey-nice with Andrea and assure her I'd be returning to the office Monday, I'd wondered what Colin Montgomery got out of his marriage to the woman. For all I could see, the man was nothing more than her purse holder and her drink fetcher. Maybe their roles got reversed when they were behind closed doors...

Wasn't going there for all the sand in the Sahara.

Talk about an instant yank back to reality—though Margaux's glower spoke enough about my tardiness to the party and the sulk she clearly thought I was indulging.

Ohhh, princess, if you only knew what was really going on.

But she couldn't. She wouldn't.

My silence had put a few pounds on my psyche—and that

was just fine by me. Maybe it was time to haul ass out of here, salvaging whatever relationship she and I could have now.

I had hope, a lot of it. We'd started with less than this in the beginning. We could be good friends, I believed it—once I got my shit together and controlled my rampaging dick.

But tonight wasn't the time to start. She was right. I'd stayed away too long. And she looked so damn good. Smelled so perfect and sweet. Even glared at me with such perfect fire. If we kept talking...I'd nuke the whole thing. My truth would be out. And our relationship would be toast.

Ice Road Truckers was the way better choice.

How the hell I'd muttered that aloud, I had no idea. But I sure as hell had.

"Ice road what?" Margaux charged. "Pearson, are you even here right now?"

Cloud, meet your silver lining. She made my next move damn easy. All I had to do was mutter something sounding stranger than that and then shove on out of here and call her tomorrow, blaming my bullshit on a bad shrimp reaction or something equally lame. My ticket out of the party was also my way to push the Restart button on things with her. So simple, it was beautiful...

And went unused.

Because I was an idiot.

An idiot who was nuts about her. Especially now, folding her arms as she shot one foot out from under that dress, seductress gone to sassy, pissy, and hurt—ensuring my senses were blasted equally by arousal and guilt.

The former told me to get the fuck out of here now. But the latter tied me to her, unwilling to let things be like this, even for one night. It forced me forward to once more flatten the space between us to nothing, one hand snaring her waist, the other slipping up to her neck. Her little gasp was surely just an involuntary burst of surprise, but it was so goddamn sexy, I pretended it was more—at least for one moment.

One moment that made the world go away.

One moment where everything was just me...and her...and the way we'd been in front of the lions at the zoo.

I tightened my fingers along her scalp. Tugged her head back, as if preparing to inspect her. Let our breaths tangle, our heartbeats blend...our lusts crash.

It's not too late to cash in the carnality card, man. To drag her off to one of Kil and Claire's twelve bedrooms, bend her over the bed, and show her exactly what kind of damage she wreaks on your cock. Make her bite the bedspread so everyone won't hear her scream as you stroke her to a climax.

Then another.

And another.

Before you detonate deep inside her...

And shattered the remaining foundations of our friendship.

"Okay...you are here." It stumbled out of her on another one of those raspy little breaths—which might as well have been a caress that covered everything south of my waist. *Fuck, princess. Please stop doing that...*

Please don't ever stop doing that...

After juicing the fortitude from every muscle in my body, I answered, "Not...for much longer."

Her face darkened. "So...you are going back?"

The longing to kiss away the stress from her lips... Excruciating received a world of new meaning. "Just to my place in town," I said instead.

Her shadows remained. Even deepened a little. "Now?"

I teeter-tottered my head a little. "As they say, ma'am, my job here is done." I wasn't surprised when she didn't rise to that one. I wouldn't have, either. "You know how this shit goes, blondie. It just gets messy and drunk from here. Pretty soon, people will be making out in the bushes, skinny-dipping in the pool..."

"I'm with you so far."

Damn, damn, damn. "I'm going to go."

Dear God, I needed to go.

Her shadows gave way to full darkness. With her lips slanted tight, she jerked free from my hold. "Fine. Then go."

I stepped back too. "I'll call you tomorrow. Maybe we can grab some coffee."

Margaux had already grabbed a full glass of champagne from a passing waiter's tray, polishing it off while waving at me with the other.

As I turned and started toward the house, she'd already downed a second.

I glanced back, just once, to catch the gleam of the party lights on the third glass she tipped up—which might as well have been jammed down my throat and then shattered there.

Changing the subject again in your own unique way, eh, Margaux?

The assessment didn't smooth over the shards still tearing my gut. Leaving her here like this, determined to become the new It Girl for Cristal, felt wrong on thousands of levels. But would staying help? The footing on our "reunion" tonight... Shit. It was a round of fucking Frogger. Take one step, breathe in relief, pray like hell not to get slammed while deliberating the next move...

If I stayed, the carnage would only get worse.

I grimaced while crossing the polished Italian marble of Claire's palatial foyer. If she kept up the pace on the Cris, Margaux was going to wake up in the morning feeling like she'd swan dived off the second-floor landing onto this slab. What the hell? Slamming down the bubbles, or even the shit without bubbles, wasn't like her. Sometimes we'd hung out for hours after work, and I'd rarely seen her go for anything other than water after her second round. But in the last five minutes, she'd killed off three whole glasses of champagne.

Holy fuck, I hoped she hadn't driven herself to this thing.

My first step out the front door brought a reassuring answer to that.

Her on-call 750i was parked near the front of the luxury car traffic jam in the expansive driveway. Her regular driver, Andre, was leaning against the hood while chatting with another driver. When he noticed me, the big man grinned and waved.

"Mr. Michael Pearson," the man said in his musical Jamaican accent. The guy pulled me in for a shoulder bump that felt like colliding with a bank vault. Andre was at least three inches taller than me, with a chest like the bow of a cruise ship and a laugh like an island Santa Claus. "It has been much too long, my friend."

I smiled. "Yeah, Andre. It has."

"I understand you have been"—his mouth pursed as if holding in a laugh—"an apple-plucking, nonshowering hermit as of late?"

I obliged with a chuckle, all the better to hide the new—and strange—torque to my senses. Andre had all but recorded Margaux's words and played them back for me, but why the hell had the woman even cared to issue them?

"Apple season doesn't start for another three months," I answered Andre, "so technically, there was nothing to pick. And I can attest that showering occurred...hmmm, at least once a week."

The driver flashed a huge white grin as he chortled. "And it shows." He poked the trio of baby red roses in my lapel. "My, my, Michael Pearson. You clean up well."

"Pssshh. You've seen me in suits plenty of times, man."

"Not before Miss Margaux has...rearranged them."

"Errr, right."

He laughed once more, the sound reverberating even deeper through that cavernous chest. There wasn't much choice but to endure it. He was right. Andre usually only saw me after Margaux and I had gotten in a solid kiss or three—or four, or five—meaning I probably looked like a mugging victim by the time he rolled up, always ready to take over with a protectiveness toward Margaux that I appreciated.

Right now, the man canted his head toward me with a subtle glint in his eyes. "Will you be joining Miss Margaux for the trip back to her building?"

Awkward kick at the gravel. "No, Andre. I don't think so. I'm leaving now, but she'll be staying a little while longer." I cocked my own head to the side, staring back at Claire's huge house, wishing I could X-ray vision my sights through the damn walls of the place. "She's...really enjoying the reception."

"Oh." Its framework, from front to back, was silence.

"Yeah," I muttered. "Oh. So take good care of her, you got it?"

"Most certainly, sir."

★ ★ ★ ★

Driving into the city yesterday, I'd gotten a weird hair up my ass and stopped at the grocery, stocking up on essentials for the fridge—beer, cheese sticks, chips and salsa. Yeah, yeah... I knew the chips didn't go in the fridge. It beat shuttling them to the pantry, where they'd be doomed to keeping company with three soup cans, four expired CLIF Bars, and an alphabetized spice rack that had been used twice. Wasn't like anyone was going to call me out on the shit—except for my mountain-babe-girlfriend-in-hiding, who, according to the entire world, had been waiting naked in my bed all day.

I grunted at the thought while popping my second beer and shucking my pants. I had time before the ice road truckers resumed their adventures. The extended commercial break between the episodes, wedging fast-food ads between pitches for motor oil and chili, gave me time to consider putting something on in their place.

"Pssshh."

I picked up the pants with a toe and dunked them into the dry-cleaning bag on top of my shirt, which I'd stripped off the second I walked in the door. I took two steps toward the dresser to retrieve a pair of sweats but ditched the idea, slinking back to the couch in my skivs. The pretend mountain babe liked me better that way.

Screw the fact that I didn't. Or that part of me—the part even the beer couldn't seem to drown—that wouldn't stop clawing at my psyche like a starving cat at the back door.

Call her. Tell her you're sitting here halfway to naked, dreaming about her. Command her to put her champagne down, get into her goddamn oversize car, and get her incredible ass over here so you both can scratch this itch once and for all. If you're going to declare the woman off-limits, then give her something to remember you by other than lame texts and that ridiculous fight at the wedding.

I grunted again. Harder. Longer.

Fuck it. I was growling. At myself. In a dark apartment. On a Saturday night. In my goddamn underwear. Surrounded by tortilla chip crumbs.

On the TV, an eighteen-wheeler plummeted through a sheet of jagged ice. I dragged on my beer, scratched my balls, and mumbled, "Just give it up, man. The fight isn't worth—"

The doorbell interrupted me.

Then the demanding pounding at my door.

Then the doorbell again.

I growled again. Cleared the distance to the door in three furious stomps. Flipped the dead bolt free and locked down my shittiest glower.

"Lerner, you dick. No means no, okay? I already told you—"

Jaw full of rug burn. What a crazy new experience.

But not half as crazy as the inferno through my brain—and body—as I processed it sure as hell wasn't Chad standing there, looking like my fucking fantasies come to life, less than three feet away—in a red dress that took my breath away as much as the first time I'd seen her in it.

"What...the...?"

CHAPTER NINE

Margaux

"Take me to Michael's." I heaved myself into the back seat of the 750i and turned the seat warmer on. Yeah, yeah... It was June in California, but fitted satin did shit for keeping a girl warm.

"Ma'am?"

"Ma'am? Since when do you call me fucking *ma'am*? I'm not *ma'am*. I am not my mother, Andre. Okay?"

"Yeah. Okay. So—"

"You know what I am, Andre? I'm sick of champagne, that's what I am. So please—please, already—just fucking—just drive me to Michael's. Or not. I can always call a cab and just fire your ass tomorrow when I'm sober."

"Ma'am—Margaux—I am happy to take you. I simply don't know which Michael's you are talking about. The club downtown? The wine bar in Del Mar?" He grunted and grimaced. "That scary little pool hall in North Park, the one you insisted on going to with Mr. Pearson that night—"

I stabbed a finger up. "That's it!"

"The pool hall?"

"No, no. That's it. That's him. Uggghh. How much clearer do I need to be? Michael. Michael, Andre. As in Pearson?"

"Mr. Pearson's house." A smile took over his voice, deep

and sure. I met his eyes in the rearview, daring him to try it again. "Right away. Of course."

I slumped over onto the seat. "Hey, and Andre? Sweetie?"

"Yes?"

"Wake me up when we get there if I fall asleep, 'kay?" A huge hiccup escaped before I could help it.

A baritone chuckle filled the car. "You sure you're tired of champagne?"

"Fuck off."

Another laugh from the front. I felt too good to retaliate anymore. Oh God, the leather felt nice against my cheek. Smooth. Cool. Peaceful. The car rocked as we accelerated onto the freeway, bearing south toward La Jolla.

★ ★ ★ ★

"And we're here."

"Mmmfff?" I mumbled to the voice crashing into my lovely little nap. And, damn it, I meant little. Hadn't I only just shut my eyes? How had we gotten anywhere in three seconds?

"Miss Margaux?" Andre tugged open the back door and leaned in, gently nudging my shoulder. "Ma'am?" He grunted. "Goddamnit. I don't get paid enough for this."

I hitched my head up. "I heard that, asshole." After rising fully back up, I moaned. Clutched my head. Somebody seriously needed to take the world off the spin setting.

"How much did you really have?"

The twinge of concern in his voice made me pry my eyes open. He was a good guy. Handsome too, in a Momoa-meets-God kind of way. His dark dreads were pulled back with a satin tie that matched his elegant suit. "Enough," I finally mumbled.

"I think the bartender at the reception wanted some action."

"No shit." Irony had become an art form for him. He picked up a business card from the car's floor. "Gave you his card too? With numbers, Instagram, and Snapchat?"

"How should I know? I thought I threw that in the trash." I peered at the card. "Didn't I?"

Minor road bump. Time to focus on the current situation. Standing—well, swaying—outside my not-boyfriend's bungalow, in the very late hours of the night, in a bridesmaid's dress...ready to do what, exactly? Wait. Yes. It all came back to me. I was here to kick his ass for the dance floor double whammy earlier. Caginess and condescension, just what I'd needed—not—especially tonight. I'd all but confined myself to a nunnery because of him for six damn months, and then he treated me like that at my own brother's wedding? Not that he knew—or ever would know—about that last part or that it should've mattered at all. He'd been a douche. Margaux Asher didn't put up with douches. It was about time he heard that straight from Ms. Asher's lips. Right here, right now.

I pressed the yellow button next to his front door.

Bing-bong-bong.

I snickered. "Really?" Pushed again.

Bing-bong-bong.

Well, twice was more than enough for that. But not enough to get him to open.

Pound, pound, pound.

I rubbed my aching fist while tapping my foot. Not even the sight of my sparkly Jimmy Choos eased my temper now. "That's right, Pearson," I muttered. "I'm pissed off, and I'm not going away. Answer the damn door, and take what's coming to you."

The entryway light flicked on, inviting moths to join the one-girl party I was having on his doorstep. The dead bolt clicked back then the door swung open.

"Lerner, you dick. No means no, okay? I already told you—"

He'd definitely not been expecting to see me. And while I had the jump on this whole situation, it totally didn't prepare me for seeing him. Not like this.

"What...the...?"

I couldn't not look at him. The dilemma was, where to look first? His tuxedo was gone. Like, gone. The only shred of clothing covering any part of the man were blood-red boxer briefs that appeared as if custom-tailored for his rock-hard hips—and other parts—by Ralph Lauren himself.

Thank you, Jesus, for Ralph fucking Lauren.

"Margaux?"

"You expecting Pizza Hut?" Because I got nothing for you except the Jell-O in my knees.

"What're you—?"

"You have an old-man doorbell."

"Huh?"

"Your doorbell. It belongs to an old man. You should change it."

He canted one eyebrow. Shit, I loved that look, even when he wasn't standing in front of me in his underwear, letting me stare my fill of a body that was better than my wildest imaginings.

Wildest.

Muscles. He had muscles everywhere. Rippled, sculpted, beautiful, godlike. And they were covered in tattoos. Tattoos. Sure, I knew about the exotic aqua seascape wrapped around his right biceps but never realized it continued up over his shoulder and then turned into shooting stars down his right pec, guiding one's vision across the ridges of his abs, to where a flock of seagulls in silhouette were gathered. Around both his wrists were double bands of indigo, making me long to grab his hands simply for the pleasure of tracing them. Christ, even his wrists had muscles. How had I never noticed that before? I'd rubbed against him like a kitty in heat plenty of times and always thought I had a good understanding of the lay of the land, but it never prepared me for the feast my eyes were treated to now.

Shivers. And not from the misty night air.

Wow. From irate to aroused in ten seconds. That had to be a record. With Michael, it didn't surprise me. The man made me break rules I didn't know I had.

And still, all I could do was stare—though my fingertips tingled to life, screaming at me for a bigger piece of the action.

Soon.

It was all I could hope for.

Soon.

I pushed my way in. No sense letting the neighbors in on the miracle living right next door to them. He was my little secret, and I planned on keeping it that way—at least for right now.

I closed the door behind me. Fiddled with sliding the lock home again. It took me a few tries. Number one, I was still good and toasted. Number two, no way was I taking my eyes off Michael.

He crossed to the couch, grabbed a T-shirt off the back of the sofa, and rolled it up to sling it on—right before I ripped it away.

"Oh, hell, no. Not after letting me see all this, mister. It's a crime to destroy natural wonders, Mr. P. The universe would never forgive me."

I expected him to laugh. His reaction swung the opposite way, his eyes glowing intense with copper and gold, his chest rising and falling along with the cadence of mine.

"What are you doing here, Margaux?"

He was still tense. I'd probably be too, if not for the wholly illegal number of my blood-alcohol level. Liquid courage was a perfect wingman for my inhibitions tonight. Well, what remained of them.

"Goddamn. The rest of your ink, Michael... It's mesmerizing."

"You came here to talk about my tattoos?"

Left, right. Left, right. I shook my head in its fullest range of motion though managed to keep every inch of him in focus. That was how beautiful he was. How captivating. How completely, mouthwateringly, perfect.

Full sentences, on the other hand, were proving a bit of a challenge. "No. Not—not really. But as long as we're covering said—said subject"—I made the universal twirl-around motion with my finger—"is there more? On the back? Need to see, pretty please."

He gusted out a long sigh but obliged with heavy steps. I was almost tempted to stop him, unsure I could take a back view. I'd always had a thing for asses. His was pure perfection, even in a pair of pants. Covered only by the briefs, forming the dot on an exclamation point of inked dark blue circles running the length of his spine, it was—

"Holy. Shit."

He pivoted back around, finally splitting his lips into a

cocky grin. "Just scoping out the ink, huh?"

I'd always scoffed at women who talked about men turning them to putty before sex. On one hand, I could count the number of men who'd done it to me after the nasty, let alone before...

Until now.

"Michael." Miss Eloquent. That was me tonight. But maybe we just needed to forget "talking." I took a step toward him—

Only to be held back by his upstretched hands. "Is that wise, sugar? You hit the bar pretty hard after I left, hmmm?" His face darkened as if he remembered a pot roast burning in the oven or something. "But Andre drove you here, right?" When I didn't respond except by wringing his shirt harder, he prodded, "You going to tie-dye that or give it back?"

I clutched the cotton to my chest. Blurted out, "Yes. Of course, Andre drove me."

He exhaled. "Good. That's good. It would kill me if anything ever happened to you."

My head fell to the side. It was the default when my bullshit meter hit red. And while the center of my chest and the pit of my belly wanted to believe him, my mind wasn't even in the station for that train. "Seriously?"

"You don't believe me?"

"After you spoke to me at the reception like I'd become something the cat dragged in, before leaving without so much as a goodbye?"

His gaze narrowed. "Would you have heard it if I'd said one? You were approaching double digits on the champagne chugs by the time I looked back, princess."

"You were an ass, Pearson. If I drowned my rage in a little

bubbly, it was none of your business."

He folded his arms over the bulging planes of his chest. "I received that point. Loud and clear."

"Did you want to see anyone else's point? Have you wanted to, for six damn months?" I wadded the shirt and hurled it at him. "Yeah. Forgive the hell out of me for not buying the *it would kill me if you died* line."

He let the shirt fall. Whooshed out a heavy sigh. "You don't make anything easy, do you?"

"What's that supposed to mean? Did you– Are you saying this is my fault?" I barked a bitter laugh. "Wow. This keeps getting better and better."

He was quiet for a long moment. "Did you come all the way here to fight with me some more?"

I didn't know how to answer that. "You know what?" I finally rasped. "You're right." I put my flat palms up in supplication. "No, you really are. What the hell was I thinking?"

It was a legitimate question. I didn't want to answer it, either. I spun on my heel, pissed at myself and at him and at the world–

Only to feel the world spinning as he caught me by the elbow, yanking me back toward him. Against him.

I crashed back into the wall of his chest at full speed. We should've careened back onto the couch, but he locked his knees, absorbing me and the impact.

"Whoa!" I grabbed his arm, now braced solidly around my waist.

"Margaux," he growled into my ear. God, that sound. Protecting me with raw power. "I won't let you fall. Ever."

For a moment, I sagged against him some more. Perhaps I wanted to put the theory to the test right away.

Oh hell, how I longed to give in to it, surrender to him, if only for a little bit. Yearned to let my senses take over instead of shoving them away like I always did. Ached to experience the chaos that had struck so many times today alone, churning inside every time I laid eyes on him. Such chaos...

My head swam with the intensity of each and every memory. The ache of each and every longing...

So much.

Too much.

Not enough.

His nearness eroded what little resistance the alcohol had left for me to cling to. I couldn't fight it anymore. I needed more of him. Now.

"Michael."

"Yeah, sugar?" The words were hot on my neck...his body huge behind mine...

Shit. Shit.

"Please..." Instincts, urgent and primal, took over. I slid my ass against his crotch, a wordless plea for him to understand... to read the thoughts, the needs, that pitched to overwhelming intensity.

His breath, now ragged, skated along the back of my neck. "Please what, beautiful girl?" When I only moaned and pressed and writhed, he gripped my hair with his other hand, jerking my head in the other direction so he could access the opposite side of my neck. "Just say it, Margaux. I need to hear it."

Shivers. Then heat. So much more heat. Blissful, hot, stabbing blades of torturous, torrid fire, through every damn inch of me. "C-Can't you...tell?"

"Give me the words." He snarled it into my ear, as merciless with the order as he was with his hold. The hand around my waist fanned against my stomach. Began to trail lower. Lower... "Anything I have is yours...but I want the words."

Beautiful, bold man. He knew exactly what he was doing. Making it all right by throwing down the ultimatum. Making me put all the noise in my head aside for nothing but the needs of my body. "I— I want to be with you. Now. Here. Tonight. And I don't want to fight anymore. I just—"

"Okay," he soothed to my needy whimper. "Okay, okay. Ssshhh, I've got you, remember?" He tilted my head against his shoulder and pressed his lips to my forehead. "Why don't you tell Andre you're staying for a while? I can drive you home when you're ready to leave."

I pushed up but only to turn around, meeting his gaze directly. Lines of pure desire gave new definition to his hewn features. I longed to run my fingers through his dark-gold scruff, to explore every chiseled crevice in adoring detail.

"What if I don't want to leave at all?" I pulled off sultry with the tone, but the champagne made it tough to gauge if I looked convincing or just stupid. I felt so gawky, unsure. It was scary—and thrilling.

"That's fine too." He eased the moment with a slow wink and a lusty half smile, finally letting me free to dig my phone from my bag and let Andre know he could clock out for the night.

I expected a shitload of gloating chortles from Andre, but he simply answered with a firm "Be safe," inciting a soft smile as I slipped the phone away again.

"Aha," Michael said, watching me drop the red Gucci to the coffee table.

"Aha?"

"There it is."

"There what is?"

"Your smile. I was beginning to think I'd lost it forever."

"Very funny, Pearson."

"I'm not joking."

He clearly wasn't. But he sure as hell was sexy, standing there like an idol carved of gold, the devil's own henchman sent out to seduce a woman into the most wicked of sins. Well, it was past time to dance with the devil, if I had anything to do with it.

"My smile has been right here all along," I finally whispered. "Waiting for you. Like the rest of me."

He stepped toward me again—though there was an air of wariness to his approach. Slowly, he lifted a finger up to my lips. Then another. Traced along the curves of them with careful, feathering strokes. "I was a goddamn fool, wasn't I?"

I parted my lips—only enough to return his caress with the brush of my breath. "It doesn't matter anymore."

His eyes slid briefly shut. He didn't have to do more. I heard his gratitude louder than as if he'd voiced it. "So what now?"

I tilted my head again. No bullshit monitor this time, only a guide to help the turnaround for the rest of me. Once my back was to him again, I lifted my hair up and softly requested, "Unzip me first, maybe?"

Showtime.

With the lighting from the living room as a backdrop, I dropped my hold on the fabric. Swish. The dress fell away, leaving me exposed in the underthings I'd taken care in selecting this morning—a scarlet corset, matching satin panties and coordinated garter belt, finished off with nude thigh highs.

He got rid of the uneasy kid right away. Fully embraced his man-beast side again, his jaw constricting, his briefs tightening, his lips moving with heavy, grated words.

"Holy...fuck."

This all couldn't have worked out better. I reveled in where I had him now—nibbling out of the palm of my hand—though every other second there were two of him, thanks to the bubbles still battling each other in my blood like bitches at a Prada clearance sale. At least the buzz lent more bravado for this saucy little strip act I'd started, yet another first in the name of pursuing Mr. Pearson. I was a tie-me-up-and-do-me-hard girl, not a see-anything-you-like-big-boy girl.

"See anything you like?"

Oh, that had to have sounded as ludicrous as it felt.

"I see a whole lot of things I like."

Or not.

"Then I'm all yours," I told him. "And I want to make every single second count."

He raised a finger. "I'll second every word of...that."

The last of it was nothing but a strangle from him, as I turned and pressed my back to the jamb. The move forced my breasts out in a pose that dropped his jaw—and then brought him sidling close. Closer. Ohhhh, yes. That was it...

He pressed in, hovering just inches away, staring down with those fantastic eyes of his. When his nostrils flared and his lips parted, the demon turned all man again. All desire. All need and hunger he couldn't restrain any longer. Thank God. Thank God. Finally. Finally.

He pressed in more. Our hips formed to each other. The heat beneath his underwear pressed into the wetness beneath mine. He curved one hand to my waist. Raised the other to the jamb over my head. Leaned in. Kissed me. Again. *Ohhh, again.*

He began softly, flicking in only the tip of his tongue, rocking gently against me. Pulled back, just out of reach, when I reached for him. Let out the devil's own chuckle. "So impatient, little one."

"Impatient?" I shot both brows up. "Who you working that line on, mister? I've waited six damn months. I should be suing you for torture."

His eyes glittered—right before he surged back in again, with one word spilling off his lips in a growl. "Torture."

No more teasing. Forget about gentle. He slammed our mouths together, opening me up, filling me. It was invasion more than kiss, mind-bending with passion and force. Skyrockets. Explosions in my blood and beyond.

Oh Christ, could this man kiss.

But I still needed more. If he was simply using this as the precursor for more making out and dry humping, he'd have a full riot on his hands, proudly sponsored by my libido. One flick of my hand and the man would be naked, anyway—but no, too easy, too simple. I wanted to unspool him. Unglue him as thoroughly as he pried off all my moorings. Make him feel every pounding, exploding, hot, horny degree of desire tormenting the River Styx now doubling as my bloodstream...

I moaned softly into his mouth as our tongues continued to duel. He was winning, but only because I let him. And yes, damn it, I loved letting him. I never—never—let a man take the lead on this end of things. As if any of them knew what the hell they were doing, anyway.

But Michael Adam Pearson...

Was different. So beautifully, magnificently different.

Decisive.

Powerful.

Passionate.

And God, so arrogant. But self-aware of it. And so openly, brazenly sexy about his promise to deliver on that arrogance. Yeah, his golden gaze declared, you're going to sample my sinful side tonight, sugar—and you're going to fucking love it.

It was a bold promise, and not many had fulfilled it with me. But hell, I wanted to let him try. Craved a thorough, brutal unraveling at his magical hands. Needed him to solve my puzzle, piece by complicated piece...

He was off to an amazing start. He kissed across my jaw, under my ear and then against it, suffusing me with the heat of his heavy breaths, his open-mouthed caresses.

"You want me to do filthy things to you tonight, don't you?" he snarled at a volume meant only for me...and my throbbing body. "You want me to take this cock out, fit it into your aching pussy, and then ram it over and over until it hurts? Tell me, Margaux. Yes or no. Now."

"Y-Yes. Oh hell—yes!" I gasped for air, rocking my head back. Wow. Wow. I'd always known the guy had a wicked side to him, but this was...good. So damn good. Beyond anything I'd dared to dream.

He scraped his teeth along my jaw again, marking my skin with his stubble as he pulled my head to the other side, clearing my other ear for his dirty, delicious words. "I was holding back, thinking a woman like you needed to be handled like fine china...but you're the china that likes to be shattered, aren't you? Splintered into a thousand tiny pieces...and then ground up again until you dissolve into dust."

I nodded but realized that wouldn't be good enough. Swallowing to get enough air into my throat, I rasped, "Yes.

Break me. Hard. Hard." I'd waited so long to hear these words—from him. Had damn near given up that I ever would.

No more waiting. This was happening. My head whirled with desire. My body sizzled with awareness. I couldn't predict his next words...the next naughty thing my ears could translate went straight to my clit, now grinding against his thigh in open, wanton need.

"I want you on my bed, Margaux."

"Yeah," I rasped. "Bed. Good...idea."

"Go there now." Incredibly, his voice dove deeper with command. "In the center. On your knees. Waiting for me." He rocked back, scouring his gaze over every inch of me, rubbing his forefingers against his thumbs as if warming his fingers for what he wanted to do to me next. "And keep those shoes on. They're fucking hot."

At first, I didn't move. Process. Process. Did he really just say...?

I lifted my head to meet his stare. He'd just questioned if I was an apparition from a dream, but now I wondered if he'd invaded mine—especially since I cocked a glare of open sass, expecting to back him down with it, only to make his eyes narrow and his stance stiffen.

"What are you waiting for? Do it."

Forget the Jell-O knees. Everything south of my navel turned to soup. I attempted recovery by tossing my head and pushing a finger into the middle of his chest. God, how I wanted to just slide it down, between the twin ladders of his abs, following that incredible V of muscle...

Soon.

"Fine, fine. Just don't expect me to call you Sir and all that shit."

His laugh was warm and full. “Not a chance, sugar. I don’t do all that shit either. But putting you in your place every now and then will be my thorough pleasure. And yours.”

“Hmmm. That so?”

“Yeah.” Without skipping a beat, he turned me, guiding me backward until my knees hit the side of the bed. “That is so. Sooner you learn who leads and follows around here, the sooner we’ll get to the fun parts.”

I hummed again. Longer. Silkier. “Oh, I like the fun parts.” Now this was familiar ground. Or, as it were, mattress. No matter what the surface, I could do this—and I did. Like a self-sure cat, I crawled across the bed, swaying my barely covered ass, feeling the lusty weight of his stare on every inch of my movements.

When I finally got to the center, I kneeled as he instructed, though not without a slinky glimpse over my shoulder.

“Having fun yet, Mr. P.?”

He paced to the foot of the bed, eyes hooded. “Wow. You can play nice.”

“When I’m rewarded.” My gaze dipped to the swell in his briefs. Holy shit. “And it looks like I’m going to be very well rewarded.”

So there I was in my full Agent Provocateur glory, in the middle of the bed, in the hottest stare-down of my life, with Mr. July himself. His ink. Those muscles. That bulge. And his eyes, brilliant and feral, taking me in like I was his next meal. Ohhh, the planets were finally aligning, and I was going to enjoy every last drop of their spectral kindness.

I wriggled a little, unable to help myself, but I was already missing his huge, hard heat pressed up against me. I decided to try crooking a finger at him, but damn it if Michael wasn’t onto my game. He slipped around the bed, graceful as the demon-god he was, shaking his head at me with every perfect, smooth step.

"Patience, sugar. Let's make this right. If I get near you now, I won't be responsible for what happens next."

"Responsibility is overrated." I chuckled as he did, arching and then bowing my back, damn near clawing the comforter in my growing need.

He didn't budge. Instead he said, "I love it when you laugh. When you really laugh. It always makes me harder."

"Always? You mean it's happened before?"

"All the damn time." He had the nerve to stand there and stroke himself through the Ralph Laurens. I let my knees drop and sat up, licking my lips, yearning that they could join his fingers. He must've activated his special mind-meld thing, because his cock surged against the fabric in direct response to my thoughts. "But if I started listing everything about you that makes me hard, we'd be here until dawn."

I slid my gaze up to his face. "And I have other ideas about what we can do until dawn."

"You are the most beautiful woman I've ever laid eyes on." He finally hiked one knee up on the bed, his thigh sliding a few inches outside mine. I vacillated between scooting closer to get more of his addictive heat or diving for the ravine of self-consciousness his compliments always opened inside me.

Without thinking, I started twirling the delicate gold ring that never left my right pinkie. The habit only reared when I was nervous and even then, only when I trusted someone. Except for Mother. She didn't just know about the pattern but every painful incentive behind it.

Pain that strangely lessened at once as Michael wrapped

his hands around both of mine. He stilled my fingers by intertwining his with them.

"Tell me about this," he prompted, caressing the ring himself.

I shook my head. I'd signed on tonight for mind-numbing sex, not heart-ripping psychotherapy. "It's...just a thing. Just jewelry. Good-luck charm, maybe."

"No kidding. You never take it off." He kissed my little finger, followed by each one in turn while I watched, mesmerized by his lips on my skin.

His adoration...his patience...they wrenched at me. Clawed my chest open.

Unspooled me.

Exactly what I'd asked for.

Damn it.

"It—it was a gift when I was a little girl," I croaked out. "That's why it only fits on my pinkie now."

"From who?"

He rubbed his cheek from my knuckles to my wrist, still clasped together with his. Every rasp from his beard shot lightning bolts up my arms, through my breasts, even along the sensitive ends of my nipples. I knew my core would feel the effect next, and it wouldn't be so subtle. How could his prying questions be turning me on so deeply?

You know why.

Because he hadn't automatically assumed the ring was from Andrea. Because he knows you that well. Because it feels damn good to have someone know you that well.

But it was damn terrifying too.

"Why are we going into this now?" I grimaced and tried to pull away. No-go on that front, with Michael enforcing uber-talon grip with the hold. Okay, different tack. I leaned forward a little, weighing down my gaze with lust. "Can't we just kiss some more? That was some good shit, Michael."

"Couldn't agree more. But it's also good shit to know more things about you. And now that I know there's a real story behind this ring, I'll guess that whoever gave it to you must be very special."

"She was." And just like that, he opened the tap on my tears. And all the memories, good and bad and joyous and sad, behind them. Damn alcohol. My desire dissolved beneath a flood of feelings I hadn't visited in a long, long time...and the beautiful woman's face that always accompanied them. "Yeah...she was."

The bed trembled as he climbed fully on. He pressed my forehead to his chest as he disentangled our hands and then wrapped his arms completely around me. "Hey, hey...I didn't mean to upset you." His biceps flexed as he hauled me right into his lap. My first reflexes urged me to struggle away—shit this good could never be trusted—but I decided to give him a second. Then maybe another.

This was...really good. Warm. Secure.

Sort of what I'd imagined home should always feel like.

Danger zone. Danger zone.

I had too many fronts exposed. Too much *real* busting out at the seams. But I let the alarms peal on, surrendering to an embrace so full and protective, fight or flight became nothing more than funny words. I sank against him, sniffling like a child while he rocked gently, stroked my hair, and ordered my sadness away with the power in his soft shushes.

"Tell me," he finally prodded. "Please."

Panic heaved up again. I couldn't even consider the

request. No, no, no. What had Mother always exhorted into me? Tears for the past are tears for the mud. Wasted weakness, darling. Wasted weakness.

And look where trusting her had gotten me. Alone. Afraid. Hated by most. Feared by everyone.

Not everyone.

Not this man, who'd been courageous enough to see through it all. To believe in someone different. To call her the most beautiful thing he'd ever seen...

I didn't dare believe that it would last. But as long as Michael was offering, maybe it would be nice to cave in. To buy into the fantasy for a while longer.

"When I was a little girl, I had a full-time nanny," I began tentatively. This sharing myself shit was so new...and kind of weird. "Her name was Caroline. She...we did everything together. She was the one who took care of all the little stuff, you know?" I smiled a little. "Potty training. ABCs. Tying my shoes..."

"You wore shoes that tied?"

I whapped him before going on. "We were pretty inseparable. I loved her dearly. And she loved me. I always felt like she loved me more than my own mother did. I know that probably sounds horrible, but it's true."

Michael cupped my cheek. "Not horrible. I know your mother just a little, remember?"

I gave him a watery laugh. It was irreverent and probably wrong, but was I picking now to feel crappy about that? Because he was wonderful that way, Michael laughed with me—until my mirth gave way to a shiver. *Shit.* My emotions were tearing down my buzz faster than I wanted, bringing on a pirate-boot kick of a headache, along with a few crazy sweeps of the spins.

Without a word, Michael pulled the comforter up around us both. Urged me to lie down, cushioned by his arm and a couple of the pillows, with him spooning perfectly into me. His linens smelled divine, like they'd been washed in a concoction of cinnamon, cardamom, and cloves. I was officially surrounded by him on all sides, and it was heaven.

"Tell me the rest," he encouraged then.

Despite everything, tension snuck back in. I sniffled again. Good God, what was wrong with me? I hadn't lost it like this since—well, since the last time I'd been able to bawl in Caroline's arms. Definitely nothing wrong with the waterworks tonight. It was getting to be embarrassing. Freaking champagne. I bet if I checked the MyPeriod app, that would be right around the corner too.

"So you were saying?" he urged. "About loving Caroline?"

"Sheez. You're like a dog with a bone, Pearson. Has anyone ever told you that?"

"Once or twice." There was a smile in his tone. "Was the ring from her?" He wrapped his arm around me and rubbed a thumb over the jewelry again.

"Yes. It was my birthday gift. I think I was nine. We saw it together in a boutique in Paris when Mother dragged our asses over there for Fashion Week. Caroline gave it to me, but it wasn't just about the ring. I realized how much work she'd put in to calling the boutique after our trip, ensuring it was the exact ring I'd liked in the window that day and then having it shipped to San Diego. She did all that despite the grueling schedule Andrea kept her to. The effort she put in... It meant more than what the ring cost or whatever extravagance Mother came up with that year..." I trailed off into a timid snort. "God.

That probably all sounds so stupid."

"No. Not at all. Stop interrupting your own story."

The man had a point. While I told him the story, he kept soothing my hair and back, lulling me into a calmer place. I was so relaxed now. The tears stopped. I felt myself drifting closer to sleep.

"One day, I came home from school...and Caroline was gone."

"Huh?"

I nodded. "All of her things were gone from her bedroom, her bathroom. Her car wasn't in the garage." I swallowed hard, burrowing deeper into the softness of the blanket and the firmness of his embrace, gaining strength to face memories I hadn't visited in years. "I went to ask Mother about it, of course. She—she responded in a horrible, cold voice...nearly as awful as her silences, but not quite."

I felt Michael force down a hard gulp. "What did she say?" he whispered.

"That she had gotten rid of Caroline. Fired her. She told me she refused to keep someone around who possessed more of my heart than she did." I wouldn't forget the day as long as I lived. For the first time in my life, I'd known full, awful grief. "She told me I'd get beaten if I cried. That if I shed one tear for Caroline, she'd take away the *trashy ring* too." My fingers returned to the ring, twisting it quickly. "I held it to protect it. Probably, in some weird way, to guard my heart too. Ever since then, when shit goes down, I go to the ring for my center."

"Okay." He murmured it with respect. But no pity or fawning sympathy. Just the continued warmth and support of his arms, his presence. "That makes sense."

"Sense?" I retorted. "I'm sure a therapist would beg to

differ."

"Why? I don't think it would take a therapist to understand why it means so much to you."

I sighed. "All right. Maybe not."

My voice sounded so far away now. Vaguely, I realized it was due to almost being asleep. Being here with Michael...his warmth, his assurance, his acceptance... I felt safer than I had in a very long time. On so many levels.

Insanely enough, all thoughts of naughty sex were now trampled by the sleep sheep. I was absolutely positive I'd fleece a few of them in the morning in retaliation, but for the moment, I was so relaxed, a seven on the Richter wouldn't budge me.

★ ★ ★ ★

Jesus Christ!

What was that noise?

Was I dreaming?

If so, it was a nightmare—about that disaster of a client meeting at the Rainforest Café. They were VIP guests of SGC and insisted on going, and since it was right up the street from the El Cortez, I'd thought it would be fun too—until I was seated next to a mechanical toucan who made the squawkers in the Tiki Room seem like social outcasts.

I had to pee. So damn it, I was definitely awake. No culinary torture trip. But I still heard birds. What the hell?

Oh. Oh. Wait a minute. This wasn't my bed. The pillow was way too soft. The sheets and blankets were just as decadent as mine but smelled really, really masculine...

"Shit!"

I jolted to my elbows. Had I gone home with the bartender

after all?

Time for inventory. I wasn't sore in any interesting places. A quick look under the sheets...okay, wow...I was still wearing every piece of my lingerie.

All of it.

And a T-shirt too?

"What...the...?"

My tongue practically stuck to the roof of my mouth. Fuck, I needed some water. Thank you, Madame Cristal, for the worst hangover ever. My head throbbed like a midnight club scene, and my stomach felt like the alley behind it.

Aspirin. Liquid. Now.

I sat up carefully, in case my bedmate was a light sleeper. I was a master at the morning-after sneak-out, and the biggest secret to my success were the two Qs—quick and quiet.

A quick scan of the room, and the night came flooding back.

Michael.

Ohhh, shit, I was at Michael's.

I jerked my head toward the space next to me. Empty—thank God.

This was good. Really good.

Now to quietly find my dress and quickly get the hell out of there.

I swung out of bed and scanned the bedroom, only to come up empty on finding a stitch of clothing anywhere, his or mine.

This was bad. Really bad.

I could not get into the back of my car in a T-shirt and garter belt. Andre and I had shared a lot of interesting things over the years, but some lines just shouldn't be crossed. That dilemma was eclipsed by a second problem. Where the hell was my purse? But both those challenges were the cart before the horse—or, in this case, the getaway before the pee stop.

I tiptoed to the master bathroom, relieved myself as noiselessly as possible, and prayed Michael was as huge a control freak about his bathroom fixtures as the rest of his magazine-ready home. Yesssss—his uber-modern toilet flushed more quickly and quietly than mine.

I turned the faucet high enough to generate a trickle in order to wash my hands and then strip the last dregs of makeup off my face. At the same time, I borrowed a little blob of his toothpaste, swishing it over my teeth with a finger. I turned to look for a towel—

And wound up pumping a fist in silent victory. On the back of the bathroom door, my dress was hung on a lovely padded hanger, with my purse and shoes lined up on the floor nearby. I smiled, running a hand down the dress, practically feeling the care he'd taken with hanging it there. How was it possible that the sweet, caring, and adorable best-guy-friend-alive existed inside the same rippled, tattooed body as the illicit lover who'd turned me totally liquid last night?

That questions would have to remain unanswered. There was a higher mission at hand—getting the hell out of there before Michael discovered me. Enough snippets from last night had started coming back to me, enough that I knew a rehash was not in anyone's best interests right now. My stomach lurched from the remembrance of telling him about Caroline. I'd never told that story to anyone. Claire didn't even know that one, and she was the closest thing to—well, to anything—that I had.

I needed to get home. Shower. Prep for my day at work—

because that was how I rolled when the boss was going to be out for two weeks—and then call him from the office sometime this afternoon to hash things out, when the hangover was a dim memory and I had the familiarity of my own turf for strength.

Because, damn it, I needed every ounce of strength when it came to talking about anything past holding hands with that man.

I took one more second to dash off a text to Andre, directing him to pick me up a few blocks away from Michael's house. That, of course, earned me a yes, ma'am—punctuated by half a dozen snarky emoticons. I let him have the brazen chain yank, choosing to focus efforts on more important tasks for now. There'd be plenty of time for bitch slapping the man later.

Now...what to do about the...interesting...second half of my attire? Panties, garters, and hose weren't what any self-respecting hooker wore in La Jolla, let alone a woman used to greeting Sundays in Roxy and Vans.

Fist bump number two. There was a pair of track pants on the counter. After stashing my thigh highs, I yanked on the pants. Okay, this was good, despite the fact I had to roll the waist over twice and peg the bottoms so I wouldn't trip. I could make it a few blocks barefoot like this, carrying my dress and shoes.

I peeked out from the bathroom. The bedroom was still empty, the house strangely quiet. Michael's side of the bed wasn't disturbed at all. He must have slept on the sofa. Guess I needed to add flawless gentleman to his friendship, sex god, and dress-care skills.

Focus, damn it!

I was going to need the extra effort. The last stage of my

escape would be tricky. Heading out the front door wasn't an option. The path would lead me right past the living room—and the sofa where he'd undoubtedly slept. But this was a classic bungalow. It had to have a back door. And back doors were usually near laundry rooms. So if I just found the washer and dryer...

Back on ballet feet, dress and shoes and purse tucked under my arms, I turned and headed the opposite direction from the living room and kitchen. Morning sun streamed through a window, casting light into a hall and—

Bingo.

At the end of the hall there was a door set with a window pane covered by a sheer curtain. Through that covering, I made out the familiar shapes of a quaint laundry space. Lo and behold, there was a security alarm panel next to the washing equipment, all lights green. Home free.

Strangely, the back door was unlocked. Either Michael had forgotten to lock it last night after the party I brought to the door, or he'd already been up and was just keeping his peace, waiting for me to stir. I hoped for the former but took cautions for the latter, turning the knob and slipping out of the door like a church mouse wearing ballet slippers.

Mission accomplished. I hadn't made so much as a creak.

"Morning, beautiful."

"Blahhhhhh!" The scream erupted before I could think—and the blame lay thoroughly on the shoulders of the man who sat there with coffee cup in hand, the breeze in his hair and sexy scruff on his jaw, soaking up the morning sun like the freaking Greek god he was. "Seriously?" I snapped, frantic that he viewed my devouring stare as nothing more than anger. "Is this your fun morning routine for all your sleepover guests,

Pearson? Scaring the crap out of them for a giggle?"

A smile teased his lips. Damn it if that didn't double the palpitations now rocking my whole chest—tripled when he riffed on a Southern drawl, "Well, I do believe in hospitality, ma'am. This boy's mama raised him right."

I forced myself not to bolt past him and tear down the street—which was more like an alley, extending behind a shockingly big backyard—to find Andre. While the size was a stunner, the treatment wasn't. The area was just as photogenic as the rest of his place, plants mingling with landscaping touches to evoke tamed ruggedness. The inviting feel of it only enforced my resolve to be free of it. I couldn't allow myself any more threads of attachment to this place—or its owner.

Still, my mother had managed to shove a few manners in too. Michael wasn't the creepy bartender. He deserved a few words of conversation.

"So...why are you out here?"

He swung a hand out. "Beautiful day. But even on the not-so-beautiful ones, I usually sit out here with my coffee. Good thinking time. I like listening to the birds in the trees. It's a miniature symphony. Reminds me of home."

I canted a frown. "Gee. Put that way, birds are positively poetic."

"Aren't they?"

No. Comment. I slid a toe along the patio grout.

"I had an ulterior motive this morning, though," he went on. "Had a good hunch you would try to sneak away."

It nudged at accusation. My defenses prickled. "Is that so?" And if I had, why did he care?

"That is so. And you know I couldn't just let you do that."

And just like that, he blew my barricades apart by having

the nerve to finish it off with a cocky wink and a wicked grin—conveniently oblivious to how he tilted the axis of my senses with that one look alone. As dizziness flooded, my stomach roiled harder, alerting me of the possibility I'd be revisiting all that champagne. The three bites of dinner I'd enjoyed gleefully proclaimed they wanted in on the action too. My whole body fought back, breaking out in a sheen of sweat. I squirmed inside his pants I was wearing, barely fighting off the urge to tear off the T-shirt too.

"I— I have to go, okay? I'm not feeling well."

"No shit. That's an impressive shade of green, sugar."

"I'm...just going to leave..."

"Margaux. Sit."

I went ahead and let him yank me into the chair next to him. Validation? He offered the one thing better than an easy escape. A huge glass of water. Though I greedily gulped the stuff down, it didn't stop the horizon from teeter-tottering in my vision.

Shit.

I'd emptied my head—and maybe a little of my heart—to him in embarrassing detail last night. Now, I was going to empty my stomach on his patio. I begged heaven to wake me up from this nightmare—and to make it snappy.

CHAPTER TEN

Michael

"Thanks."

She rasped it after polishing off her second glass of water. Instead of saying anything, I chose to estimate how much Cristal she'd really put away last night—and then decided it was best I didn't know.

"Okay," she muttered. "That's better. I really do have to—"

I cut her short by yanking on her hand. Good move, following instinct to keep our fingers linked after I'd pulled her down. It had simply felt natural—and outright amazing when she didn't fight it.

"Michael—"

"Sshhh. Listen to the birds."

"Michael—"

"Am I going to have to tie you down?"

She snorted. "You're not into that shit, remember?"

"I like trying new things." *And damn, sugar, I'm not opposed to trying anything new with you...*

She let go of the water glass to scrape back her hair, closing her eyes and wincing against the sun. I took full advantage of the opportunity to just stare...despite how it aggravated the hugest erection I'd ever had in my life.

She took my breath away.

Sure, there'd been other moments when she'd done the same—but all of them had been shitty preparation for this. Screw the goddess in the red gown from the wedding. And the sassy trendsetter from the months before that. And the attitude-infused businesswoman from before that. I could barely remember those personas, let alone prefer them to the tousled, tentative woman curled up here now, clutching her clothes...but covered in mine.

Mine.

The word slammed, tempting me to drag her over, right into my lap. Or beat on my chest. Maybe both. I dragged a finger around the rim of my coffee cup instead, battling not to remember what she hid beneath the T-shirt and sweats.

My T-shirt and sweats.

That corset. Those panties. Those naughty, gorgeous garters...

Fuck. Closing my eyes only made it worse, joining her in cursing the sun as it blazed through my lids, bringing back the memory like a flame searing through rice paper.

Her dress beneath my fingers, falling away as I slid down the zipper.

The swish of the fabric, flowing down her ivory curves.

The sight of her in that lingerie, stopping my heart and seizing my dick like I'd reverted to fourteen again, searching the internet for whack-off-worthy lingerie ads...that in the stroke of three seconds, she officially put to shame.

Turned out to be the ideal metaphor—since the evening yielded the same results. Not that I'd planned it that way, after she'd detonated every cell of nobility in me before the dress came off. Maybe I'd simply been too damn tired to fight her beauty—and our chemistry—any longer.

And maybe you gazed into her eyes, stripped of their defenses by the booze, and saw that Neanderthal Michael wasn't going to scare her in the least. Yeah?

Ohhhh, yeah...

But then she'd taken down yet another barrier. A secret wall, buried so deep inside her that I'd never expected it...

And rocked me to equally deep levels.

Levels that I fantasized about giving her, while escaping into the shower after she'd passed out. The levels I would have given her if that hadn't happened. The levels I gave her in my mind as I fisted myself, pumping faster and harder until I exploded in thick, hot streams beneath the spray.

Groaning her name over and over again.

I took a long, hard drag from my coffee. The motion gave me the chance to strategically hide the tent in my sweats. The pair she wasn't wearing.

Holy fuck, my shit looked cute on her. Was she still wearing those panties and garters underneath?

Her soft laugh broke me out of that musing none too soon. "What?" I prompted.

She shook her head as if freeing it from private thoughts of her own. "I was just thinking..."

"Dangerous, huh?"

"No shit." Such drowsy relaxation. Instantly, I imagined her speaking those words from one of my pillows instead, stretching and arching tighter against me, winding the sheets around us...

So much for getting rescued from the gutter of my own thoughts.

"You were thinking...?"

"That this should feel more awkward."

"I'm glad it doesn't." I twisted my hand a little, rearranging it so our palms fit together, letting the warmth in my chest soak into my response. "But we should probably talk."

"Okay, now things are awkward."

"They don't have to be. Margaux...come on. It's me."

"And I *talked* enough with you last night," she snapped. "Don't you think?"

"Funny you bring that up."

"Annnnd, here we go."

Buh-bye, tooth enamel. I ground off a few layers, refusing the temptation—and fuck, was I tempted—to just give her what she wanted—her freedom. But letting that happen felt like three giant steps back, right after the forward we'd finally had last night.

"Hmmm," I finally murmured. "That's an interesting way of putting it. Are we, Margaux? Going anywhere?"

She squirmed.

I didn't relent my focus.

She yanked a knee up to her chest. Traced a circle over the top of it, making a groove in my sweats with the pressure.

I didn't yield.

"Why don't I push the pass button and let you take this one, Professor Pearson? You seem to know the answer already."

"Snark isn't the key to this either, sugar."

I used the endearment to soften my mandate. But only a little. She was fixating on the weak flank she'd unintentionally exposed to me last night—but I saw the whole picture, including the thing she'd wanted me to see—that sometimes she not only welcomed being led but needed it. Real leadership, not the messed-up shit she'd endured in the Gucci Gestapo of her mother. Strict words tempered with genuine care, rules given with boundaries that made sense...and rewards that made compliance worth it. She'd likely not had anything of the sort since childhood and the nanny who'd been more a mother to her than Andrea had. The theory made so much sense, I'd be willing to bet my left testicle on it, especially as she slanted her head and flashed a new gaze full of defiant green light. Pushing at boundaries again—but not because she wanted to bust them. Because she needed to know how safe they'd keep her.

"But snark is so much fun, Michael."

I tilted my own head—enough to make her see the skeptical tic of my lips.

"And if I keep it up, at least we have someplace to go. Up is a direction, right?"

I let my expression grow to a full but slow smile. "Hmmm. Clever girl."

She straightened. Make that preened. "Well, you keep me around for a reason."

Part of me screamed to just jump on her banter-mobile and go. Mentally sparring was our specialty, and no one else on earth gave me a higher rush from it than her. But it was also another squirrel she knew—*knew*—I would eagerly follow, given half the chance.

So I didn't let that chance through.

Not an inch's worth.

I told her the same thing by swinging my chair around until I faced her directly. Yanked her knee down and pulled her forward until my thighs trapped hers—and my stare pinned hers. "I don't keep you around, princess." I deliberately used the word to prick her, soothing the wound the very next second. "I...want you around." My throat constricted. "As a matter of fact, life was pretty fucking miserable without you around."

Her legs shifted against mine. Not fighting me but not flirting either. They almost emulated the unnerving pitch of my gut.

"But, dude...pie every day. Just how miserable was it?"

She had a lot of squirrels in that bag.

I had a lot of squirrel darts in mine.

"Keep dancing around the bush, Margaux. I'm not chopping it down. And I've got all day."

Her fingers fidgeted. Her eyes darted across the yard again. "Well, how lovely for you," she said, smile purposely pretentious. "Some of us aren't so lucky. My boss starts her honeymoon today. That makes Yours Truly now the head lunatic at the asylum—"

"Margaux."

"—and as we both know, asylums don't run themselves, so—"

"Margaux."

"What?"

Note to self—in the right circumstances, the take-no-prisoners approach really was the perfect spear into this woman. Her glare rivalled the northern lights for spectral intensity. Her nose pulled in hard breaths. And her body... Oh hell, the beautiful lines of her body... She was still tense, but her energy was so different, all different.

Fuck, it was good. Really good.

"We're going to have a talk, sugar. Now."

"Talk about what, Michael? I had too much to drink. End of story. I hit the champagne too hard and did something stupid because of it."

"Something stupid," I echoed from behind tight teeth.

"Like order Andre to drive you here?"

"No," she rushed out. "No. I'm not sorry for that." Her free hand slipped around the outside of my knee. "The way we ended things at the wedding...well, it sucked. I didn't want you to think I'm not happy you're back." My tight silence had her stammering on, "I even liked...a lot of what happened...after I got here." She peeked up through her lashes. "A lot of it."

Damn good thing I still had no shoes on. Digging my toes against the flagstones provided at least a little traction to fight the mother of all hard-ons.

Irony of ironies, very little of this was due to her premeditation. Un-fucking-believable. A thousand and one times, I'd weathered the oh-so-practiced skill this woman could use to derail a subject she didn't want to touch, only to now discover she'd been hoarding her most effective method of all—stripping the snark and baring the honesty. She'd peeled away more than makeup for me, giving me layers of herself that were so damn invigorating, inviting—and goddamn distracting.

Timing. When it was right, nobody noticed. But when it was wrong...

You ended up insisting on a talk with the only woman you now craved beneath you, around you...climaxing with you.

Without a doubt, that thought made its way to my face. Margaux's sharp little breath, along with her pursed lips, bore out the confirmation. I pulled in air deeply myself before murmuring, "A lot of it..."

"Yes," she answered quickly. Frantically?

"But not all of it."

The words themselves weren't great. I wasn't as good as she was at taking subjects by subterfuge. When a guy grew up on a farm, a tree was a tree and a spade, a spade. Despite all its big words, corporate law was a lot of the same thing—black words, white paper, sign-on-the-dotted-line-and-now-we're-done. But what I'd lacked in syntax, I'd made up in a neutral tone—

Big, hairy, wroooonnng conclusion.

She huffed. Snatched her knee back up, using it as a prop for her anxious glower. Did she take a bite at her thumbnail too? "Damn it, Michael. You know what I mean."

"Only if I've become a mind reader." I dared pressing in on her by another inch, covering that fortress of a knee with my free hand. "In which case, I wouldn't still be dying to know if you're wearing that corset or not."

"Who's trying to boogie around the bush now?"

"No dancing here. Just my own honesty." I rested my chin on my hand, unwilling to give up the privilege of gazing at her some more. "We crossed some significant bridges last night, Margaux—and I still have no idea which ones you'd like to keep and paint or which ones to trash and burn."

A discernible stillness fell over her. And, once again, across the whole yard. "Which ones do you want to paint?"

All of them.

"That's not important right now."

"Bullshit."

"Answer the question."

A hard swallow vibrated in her throat. She pulled in air and then released it in jagged spurts. Her conflict split me in half too. Her darts-and-beer buddy was a damn wreck, begging me to crack a couple of jokes and just flip everything back to the way things were before Christmas—the easy, clear boundaries of the friend zone. But the man who'd kissed her, undressed her, commanded her, caressed her? He wasn't about to give up. He'd finally shown up last night, refusing to let six months of pathetic wallowing stop him—and, damn it, I liked him. No. More than that. I needed him. He was good for Margaux. He was good with her. So things were a little messy right now. But sometimes—and yeah, this time—messes were worth fighting for.

"What if...I can't?"

She finally stopped fidgeting enough to utter it—though it was a good thing I was still close enough to hear. The wind kicked up, bringing ocean brine along with the lingering florals of her perfume. I threaded a couple of fingers through the hair that blew into her face and tucked it behind her ear. Perfect excuse to let my touch spread to the line where her hair met her nape, caressing the sweet spot that always relaxed her most—at least on most days. Right now, she remained a coil of tension.

"Can't what?" I murmured.

"Talk about the bridges?" She gave me two seconds of a nervous glance. "I— I just can't, Michael. Not here, not now. Please."

She winced on the last word. Wasn't like she never used it—the circumstances were usually just vastly different from these. "Please" became a different word when designer makeup, crystal-crusted heels, and model-perfect hair were part of the picture. But that arsenal was bare. Her only missile left was sincerity.

Not the only thing.

The allure of my clothes swaddled around her incredible little body... Yeah, there was that...

Not that she needed to know it. Especially now. She'd strung me across a damn barrel. This wasn't some work issue

I was happy to let her have space with. But I had no illusions about the risk of pushing her for communication either. She might have resurrected the tower, but its foundation was rickety at best. Storming it without toppling it—and crushing her beneath—was going to take more than just my Dom game from last night. Boldness won battles, but patience won wars.

She shifted a little, uncomfortable with my silence. "I just feel weird about everything right now. Is that okay?"

"Weirder than usual?" My smirk loosened one from her too. I seized the opportunity to try another gentle prod, asking a question I could practically predict the answer to. "Is it because I got bossy with you?" I slid my hand forward, slipping fingers around her shoulder, thankful for the baggy fit of my shirt on her. "And asked you to kneel on my bed?"

Her face changed to are-you-fucking-kidding-me mode. "Dork," she muttered, slapping my hand—but then leaving her fingers on top of mine. "You really think that's what I'm stressing about?"

"Not a mind reader," I countered, "remember? That's why I wanted to talk."

She bent her head toward our hands, using the angle to gaze over the yard again. And again, I held back from fantasizing about her and that look against the backdrop of my sheets and pillows. "You like to talk too much, Captain America." She sighed but pushed it out with determination. I had trouble decoding the move until she slipped her eyes closed, now looking like a woman about to get up and make her way to the executioner's block. "Shit," she whispered. "I can't believe I spewed all that about Caroline. Damn good way to slaughter your beautifully nasty start to things, stud."

I couldn't help chuckling. She popped her eyes back open,

looking a little surprised, which only widened my stupid grin. Stud. It was certainly something new, though a perfect weave of the camaraderie we'd had in the old days too. In the end, the blend felt...nice. And really right.

Was she actually meeting me halfway down the tower?

Didn't look like she wanted me considering the answer to that. She tensed, constricting back in on herself again. Uh-uh. No way. Without a second thought other than that, I wrapped both hands around her thighs. Yanked hard until I slid the hold around her ass. Kept pulling until I'd parted her legs to wrap them around mine, forcing her to straddle me in my chair instead.

When her mouth popped open to protest, I acted on instinct—lunging mine to silence her.

It wasn't a kiss for the movies—not a shred of Tatum or Dornan or any of the Hemsworths—but I wasn't about to stop for ratings cards. If sloppy, graceless, hard, and urgent were what it took to get her attention, then the world could color me the new Pigpen. I wouldn't mind one damn bit if it meant I could spend even another minute savoring her...tasting her.

Because, damn, she tasted...amazing. Fresh toothpaste and the magic that was solely her sweet, hot mouth...screw the coffee, I could wake up and rev through every day on this elixir alone. The wild rush of her heartbeat, now slammed over mine, confirmed I wasn't the only one here reaching the conclusion.

We finally dragged apart, sucking air past the mingled thickness of our breaths. When she dropped her forehead to mine, everything around us spun out of focus, only to seem amplified at the same time. I closed my eyes, hoping to regroup, but that only increased how perfect she felt, how good she smelled, how right this seemed.

Beautiful heaven. Exquisite hell. And everything in between.

Why the fuck had I spent six months running from this?

Instead of searching for the impossible answer to that, I forced in enough air to form words. "Does this...feel like... you wrecked anything?" I would've punctuated by sliding the bulge in my sweats against the sweet cleft in hers, but nature was already taking care of the task nicely, thank you very much.

Unexpected twist? The little cry that emanated from Margaux. It was pitchy and high but not aroused. More like... tormented. I pulled back a little more, needing to question it with a direct lock of gazes, but her eyes were squeezed shut again.

"Not a thing, huh?" she finally rasped. "So why do I still feel like throwing up?"

"Because you're vulnerable. And that's scary." I wrapped my hands around to her back. Ran them up and down her spine in assuring strokes. "What you told me last night...who else knows all that, besides your mother?"

The second I referred to Andrea, grooves of sadness etched into her face. No...deeper than that. It was sorrow, palpable gobs of the stuff. "Nobody," she finally answered.

I'd expected as much. But the grief that lingered on her face, in her eyes... It plowed into me and then enraged me. And confused me. All the heel clacking, snark talking, and bitch maneuvering this woman had made her name on was a grand illusion to hide this dark heartache, of that I was sure—but understanding the scope of it, even the complete reasoning for it, was like sanding down a layer of paint on a rare piece of art, only to learn eight more existed beneath.

Tearing someone's throat out sounded really good right

now, but I had no damn idea where to focus the shit—so I dealt in the best way I could. Pulled in a lot of calming air and tightened my hold on her even more.

"It's safe with me, Margaux." I raised a hand to her nape, compressing fingers in just enough that she felt my resolve. "Okay? You're safe with me. I won't ever let you fall, sugar."

She quietly took that in. Maybe too quietly. Damn it. If past experience bore out accurately on this, it'd only be a matter of seconds before she—

"Psssshhh."

Rolled her eyes and said exactly that.

"I was still conscious when you said it the first time, buddy."

She batted at my chest. I didn't match the playful groove. "I'm more than aware of that. But sometimes, you need to have things spanked into you a few times."

Then, sometimes life brought shit a guy didn't expect. Out of his own mouth. As I debated whether to go for a retraction or pray she let it go, the beauty in my arms went for Door Number Three—breaking into a shit-eating grin at my expense.

"Well, okay then. You offering that reinforcement now, stud?"

Stud. Why the hell did I like that so much when she drawled it? With every inch of my fucking body?

Breathe it down before it punches a hole through your pants, man.

"No," I finally got out. And, shock of shocks, sounded halfway sane about it too. "No reinforcements today, sugar."

She pouted. And, hell's goddamn bells, must have practiced that shit in the mirror. Nobody did adorably put-out like Margaux Asher. "But why? I mean...under the right circumstances..."

"No." I repeated it while bringing my hands back in to stop hers, skimming down my abdomen with saucy determination. Once I'd captured her wrists in my grip, I held them halfway between my body and hers, securing a lock on her stare again because of it.

She scowled. "Why?"

"Because"—I smiled into my exhalation—"this is good, Margaux. We're good, together. I think we both realized it a while ago, but fear got in our way. And now, we're probably both still picking our way through that a little. Only now, we can do that together. I mean, I'd like to...if you would—"

She cut me off with a hard kiss. "You're such a dork."

"I like stud better."

"Don't change the subject."

"Because that's your job?"

I yanked her hands around my neck and sealed our lips back together. This time, I gave no quarter to any inch of her delectable mouth. I claimed her, consumed her, devoured her, vowing that when she took her next breath, she'd also inhale the knowledge that I meant business here. That I wanted her—but that meant all of her. That I'd ask things from her—in a bunch of uncomfortable ways.

"Wow," she breathed. Not a note of discomfort yet—but double-checking that fact wasn't a chore I turned down. Holy hell, she was beautiful, with the sun glinting in her eyes and her lips stung by our passion to the shade of ripe cherries. I felt a small smile curling at my own, as I indulged a round of internal chest thumping. The thought of anyone else making her look like this...

Wasn't even going there. Not a fucking chance.

"There's a lot more of that coming, sugar."

She grinned until her dimples were deep and adorable. "Okay."

"But it comes with conditions."

The dimples disappeared. "Oh, here we go."

"Yeah." I grabbed the side of her face, curling fingers into her hairline. "Here we go. And, sugar, it's going to be good, damn good. But you have to show up for this. For us. I can't do this if you're going to check nothing but your body in for the flight."

She undulated a little, making me clench back a groan. "But my body can be fun. Seems your body agrees, mister."

"Not arguing that—but it's not the point here. Not right now." I braced my hands again at her hips, purposely setting her back a little. Did I really think that'd ease the pressure throbbing between my legs? Idiot. I pushed on. "No more dancing, no more evasions, no more hiding...not from me, Margaux. Last night...everything you gave me, including your confession about Caroline—hell, especially that...it was all the best gift you've ever given me." I jerked on her again, hard enough to make her look back into my eyes. "It was one of the best gifts anyone's ever given me."

She tilted her head, activating that intense ESP I loved and hated about her, before prompting, "But...?"

No use fighting it. Not that I wanted to. "But I want more," I stated. "A lot more. And...I think you do too." Pulling her close for another soft kiss was another lesson in masochism. Tasting her... It always felt like a sip of the season's first cider press. I instantly craved another. And another. "Say you'll try. Say you want to try."

She twisted fingertips into the hairs along my nape.

Her eyes were the Marianas Trench of uncertainty. "I'm still scared."

"I know," I assured. "I know." I slipped my hand up to her head, gently smoothing over her hair. "But you're going to let me worry about the falling part right now, okay?"

Because God knows, I'm halfway there already.

She surrendered a tentative nod but little else beyond that, including any indication that she comprehended the extra layer of my declaration. Still, from the way she curled her clutch on me a little tighter, lowered her head a little closer, and stared into me with unrelenting intensity, I guessed the ESP might still be twinging and now prodded her to double-check the facts.

Check away, princess. I could sit here and stare back at you all day—and find a thousand new things to adore about your face.

A car's horn stabbed into the morning's peace. Birds burst from the trees. The neighbor's dog woofed. And the woman on my lap hissed a sharp "Shit!"

I cocked a brow, pretty certain I hit the right combo of casual and piqued. I was tempted to go for a blasé smirk—before a head of dark, dreadlocked hair appeared over the back gate, attached to linebacker-sized shoulders. "Uhhh, blondie? Why is Andre in my back alley?" A troubling thought pierced. "Has he been there all night?"

Margaux smacked my shoulder. "Even I'm not that big of a bitch. I texted him twenty minutes ago to help with the getaway."

"You mean the thwarted getaway." Now I smirked. She countered with an eye roll, though her hand, still on my shoulder, bunched into my shirt to assist her new descent against me. After capturing my lips beneath her kittenish pout, she lifted the hand to tangle in my hair. Fuck, it felt good. And right. So right.

"Yes, officer," she purred, "you busted me, fair and square. So...is it time to take me to the slammer yet?"

She added nothing to the words but a little sigh against my neck, though my cock didn't know the difference. Everything from my sack to my crown swelled as if she'd reached down and gripped it all. I managed to growl past my moan, "Do you really have to go to work?"

She winced and rose up a little. "Damn it. Yeah, I do."

"Then let's bookmark this for tonight."

She wetted her lips and smiled. "Mmmm. I like your idea of bookmarks."

"Pick you up around seven?"

"Seven's good. But no picking up." At my deepened growl—I tolerated the car-and-driver act for business only and she knew it—she drew out a teasing giggle. "I meant...why don't we just make it a sleepover?"

Well, that did it for any prayer of subduing the pressure between my thighs. Accepting the torment made it a little easier to beam her a wicked grin. "Now *that* I like the sound of." As her hair fell and curtained our faces in, I whispered, "You going to wear footsie pajamas and tell me scary stories?"

Her gaze darkened in all the right ways. "I'm going to wear something you can take off with your teeth and let you remind me why 'scary' isn't part of our conversations anymore."

I kissed her hard, glad for the excuse to disguise how her trusting words blasted open more doors inside me. Doors I hadn't opened in a long damn time...

"You have a deal, sugar," I whispered against her lips. "I'll bring dinner."

"I'll handle dinner." She bit into my lower lip. "You just bring your teeth. And your lips. And...other useful body parts."

A moan echoed through me, and I swore it started from my balls. At the same moment, her phone binged. Saved by the bing. Or doomed. I wasn't sure which.

She laughed, opening the device to display Andre's text for me too.

Should I come back later?

I chuckled and then called out, "Miss Asher is on her way." After lifting her off by her waist and making sure her footing was steady, I rose as well. She didn't let me get very far, already popping on tiptoes to get in another kiss. Though I allowed her the clinch, I ended it with a firm smack on her gorgeous bottom. "Be good, damn it. Go work hard."

"So I can play hard later?"

Jesus Christ. The woman could flip any statement into verbal sex. And I fucking worshipped her for it.

"Something like that," I laughed out.

"And what's on Mr. Pearson's calendar for the day?" She wrapped her arms around my waist, gazing up with sincere interest.

"Long, cold shower. Workout. Lunch. Another cold shower. A few rounds with the bloodiest game I can find on my gaming system. Probably another cold shower."

She laughed louder before untangling herself, turning, and dashing down the path toward the gate. I watched every move, letting her believe I'd been joking about the words. But every syllable was true, along with a few others I hadn't thrown in. No coping mechanism was off the table today. Nothing.

Anything was a possibility if it helped me forget the endless countdown to tonight—and finally getting to speak the truth I'd kept shoved in my shadows for too damn long.

Margaux Asher, you have invaded every other thought in my head, every cell beneath my skin, every dream in my nights.

No more dreams. Tonight, she'd be reality.

Maybe I'd just spend the whole damn day in that cold shower.

CHAPTER ELEVEN

Margaux

Stop. Do not pass Go. Do not collect two hundred dollars.

Michael Pearson was invading every single cell in my body.

And I loved it.

Which meant this whole mess needed to stop.

But it felt so right. So amazingly, incredibly...right. And I had no freaking idea how to handle it.

When the upper hand slipped from me in a relationship, Starship Margaux hit the red emergency button. Mission aborted... Pop the parachute and dive beneath the hard deck. But right now, all I wanted to do was hit the thrusters and scream to Mach five with Captain America—even after spewing all that shit about Caroline last night.

As I walked toward the car, I fingered my ring and twirled it. Fast.

I could keep blaming everything on the alcohol, but deep inside, I knew why I'd spilled. Michael was more than my safe haven. He was, in so many ways, a match for my soul, confirmed when he'd revealed the decadent, nasty mind behind that boxer-straining bulge. Just the recall of what he'd done last night...how he'd commanded me...the words he'd done it with...

Wow.

Inner goddess? Screw that. I had an inner fuck bunny, and that man had blazed right into her garden. Once he'd burned away all the bullshit, I'd been eager to run in and play, letting one of my deepest secrets tumble out during the sprint. I hadn't regretted it. Still didn't. I trusted him without question, a truth my heart bestowed on someone for the very first time in my life.

So, yeah...maybe it was time to let the freak-out begin.

Andre seemed to sense as much as well. As he held the car door open, he stared at me with open curiosity. I flashed up my hand—do not even go there—before climbing in. He reached in after me to take the dress and the rest of my shit, stowing it in the trunk before lumbering in behind the wheel.

He didn't speak until we were cruising down the freeway toward downtown.

"You know that boy has it bad for you."

I glanced up in time to confront his soulful eyes, examining me from the rearview mirror.

"Concentrate on the road, big guy. Especially in heavy traffic."

"Right. Because I'm so busy fighting off all these church ladies. And the other early morning escapees."

Ugh! "Quit while you're ahead."

"Yes, ma'am." His gaze betrayed his cheeky grin. Damn it. Wanker with dreadlocks. He took advantage of limits I'd let slide for too damn long, though he was smart enough to remain quiet for now, leaving me to navel gaze for the rest of the ride.

With my wince-worthy second thoughts.

And my too-damn-deep-for-a-Sunday contemplations.

Like the universe cared.

As it tormented me with more memories of the best guy

I'd met in a long...long...time.

Shit on a shattered platter.

So what now? Ten minutes into the ride home, and I already missed Michael. Intensely. But the secrets in my head alone would blow his off its oh-so-amazing shoulders. In what world would it be fair to tangle him in them? My family shit alone was insane. Okay, Andrea and I had played nice in the sandbox for Kil and Claire's big day, but that healed nothing for me—and she showed no signs of wanting to reach out in understanding either. That didn't even touch the bigger issue. What the hell would Michael Pearson, as upfront and real as they came, think about suddenly calling me Mary Stone—with all the drama, notoriety, and closet skeletons that came with? The man knew skeletons. Had helped hide them, reshape them, even turn them into something else. He knew their time, their trouble, their legal ramifications, and their damage to people.

Michael Pearson didn't need or deserve a woman with skeletons.

Trouble was, his magical hands—and lips—didn't know that part yet. The man could...work things...out of me without even trying. Okay, so he wasn't intentionally trying to find out anything about me, let alone the complicated drama about my birth father and mother, but simply being with him made me crave to tell him.

What would happen...if I did? If I had a weak moment and unloaded everything to him? On him?

All of it?

I let out a long sigh. Andre impaled me again with his stare. I chose to ignore him, still battling to work things out in my mind.

Damn it, why did it have to be so hard?

I'd finally found someone I enjoyed being with. Enjoyed? Well, that was phrasing it all nice and Miss Manners-like, wasn't it? Being near him, with him...I fucking reveled in it. In some ways, he was more than safety. He was home.

Hold up, Laura Ingalls Wilder. Like you even know the meaning of the word.

Evoking it brought more memories of Caroline. If she were still around, she'd have pulled out several of her favorite colloquialisms by now, calling Michael something like "quite a catch" or "yummiest dish in town." And she'd be right. He was smart, sexy as hell, and funny. He adored me but didn't take my crap. Respected me as a person but made me feel every inch a sensual, desirable creature. He turned my pussy to mush like the world's hugest Galahad but was the most decent, dependable man—hell, human being—I'd ever met.

Which made it even worse to think of dragging him into my mess of a life. Because even if he hated the tangle, he'd stick around just to try to help fix it. And, damn it, I didn't need fixing. I just needed...time. Space. A chance to figure out who the hell I was now and what to do with that knowledge once I was solid with it.

If Michael stuck, I'd get stuck right back. I wasn't sure we hadn't already slathered a little sample packet of glue on each other already.

Not good. So not good.

If he'd been any other guy, I would've screwed him and left him a long, long time ago.

His checkout time was way overdue. The front desk of this joint was getting antsy about the issue.

Maybe after tonight.

Yes. Good plan. Just one last sampling. One taste of the candy to satisfy the sweet tooth and then cut him loose. A night of decadence I could remember him by forever.

The one who got away...

Andre dropped me off at the front entrance of the El Cortez, promising to get my dress to the dry cleaners on Monday morning, saving me the humiliation of carrying it under my arm as I crossed the lobby to the elevators. Fine, fine, so I was irony's bitch anyway, being noticed by a couple of church-bound neighbors while in sweatpants and a T-shirt that had clearly been pilfered from someone twice my size. Go ahead and wonder, bitches—but FYI, he was worth it. Not that I had ever cared what they or anyone else thought, so why start now? I pumped my head up and jutted my chin out as I waved the key fob to unlock the elevator for my floor.

With a long sigh, I stepped off on the top floor and made my way toward my little piece of San Diego's skyline. The El Cortez was an icon, constructed in 1927, though the historic charm ended at my front door, giving way to the modern lines of my two-floor unit. Instantly, the cathedral ceilings and bright-on-white color scheme were a mini-vacay on the chaos of my thoughts. Once I added a long soak beneath the rainforest spout of my enormous shower, I'd be even better.

I frowned when I opened the door and wasn't greeted by my security alarm, which normally begged me to enter my code to silence it. Maybe I forgot to set it yesterday morning when I left for the bridal salon. Claire—correction, little Ginny Foo-Foo—had insisted on hitting the road early, meaning I'd only had one cup of coffee before Andre called up to order my ass to get into gear.

A glance to the entryway table provided another

explanation. Sorrelle had clearly been by, because my mail sat on the surface, neatly sorted into three priority piles.

Urgent

Peruse Me Later

Bitch, Please—Circular File or Bust

His categories, not mine—though I adored the hell out of that handsome boy and had been thrilled when he started dropping hints about staying on with me after he'd been of service in Chicago. Good PAs were hard as hell to find. I'd even paid his moving expenses.

I turned for the kitchen. After grabbing a bottle of water, I'd hit the shower. I could feel the heaven of it already...

Until hell took over my world anew.

Revision. It sat on a stool next to my kitchen island, grinning like a hound of hell turned into one of earth's shittiest human beings. In case I didn't get the message from the bloodshot eyes, rusty-blade shave, and greasy skin, there was a fashion note too—last year's jeans and a threadbare polo were the perfect touches of dystopian chic.

I stopped so hard my bare feet squeaked against the floor. "How the hell did you get in here?"

His soft chortle bounced off the walls—and then hit my stomach like bullets. Shit.

"Now is that any sort of greeting for your brother?"

"Fuck off, Trey. How's that for a greeting?"

"Tsk, tsk...Mary."

"Shut up."

"But Mary is such a pretty—"

"I suggest you stop before I cut off your balls, drizzle them in expired tartar sauce, and then feed them back to you, asshole."

The bastard snickered. "Tartar sauce. How perfectly bourgeois of you, m'lady."

"I'm calling security."

"Good luck with that too." His words stopped me halfway down the hall to the VIP service phone. As I whirled back around, he laughed before flipping everything on a one-eighty, snarling with bared teeth. "Ridiculous bitch. Who do you think let me in here? Guess it's true what they say, about blondes and the gray matter. Or lack of it."

God, how I longed to park my fingernails in his eyes. But maiming him wouldn't lead to the information I needed. "What the hell do you want? Why are you here—aside from that adorable little stalker fantasy you keep entertaining?"

It wasn't that impossible. Not where Trey Stone was concerned. I was starting to get nervous, but predators like Trey fed on fear. Having the man as an on-again, off-again client for a year had proved at least that much.

At one time, the guy had been okay as a client. Just okay. He'd tried cleaning up his act but had taken a dive back into the filth right before the shit about Killian's true identity had hit the fan last year. In the end, nobody had cared whether Kil was a biological Stone or not—but that was after Trey had had time to swoop in and damn near destroy the company from within.

After Killian had reassumed the SGC helm, Trey had disappeared. We all assumed he'd slithered under his favorite rock for good, never to surface again.

Assumptions. This moment sure as hell proved what dangerous shit they could be.

I silently swore at my hammering heart and locked my legs, holding my ground—even after he rose from the stool and prowled toward my position. Okay, screw the locked legs. An instinctual step back. Another. But then, damn it, my back slammed the wall. There was literally nowhere to run or hide.

"Uh-oh, Mary-Mary-quite-contrary. Looks like I have you...right where I want you." He pressed in, trapping me with his huge frame. Killian may have been taller, but Trey was the width of a linebacker.

"Back off." I steeled my jaw but had to force out the next word. "P-Please. Whatever you want—I'm sure we can discuss it like rational adults." Keep the bad guys talking. Wasn't that what the experts always said? Damn it, I'd never paid much attention. In my world, bad guys were nothing worse than dumbass paparazzi and journalists who tossed out the talking points during interviews. Nothing like a washed-up rich boy with a brilliant mind that had gone to waste thanks to his entitlement issues and victim complex.

In short, a semipsychopath with a shiny new plan.

I think that qualified as the bad guy.

Damn it. Damn it. Damn it.

The asshole slanted toward me by another inch. Ran a finger down my nose and over my lips. "Where's that strut and sass now, hmmm? All that big talk and badass temper?"

Show no fear. It was a tougher mantra as he continued going with the finger, dipping it along the neckline of Michael's T-shirt in slow, almost sensual, assessment.

I swallowed hard against my gag reflex.

"Well. Looks like someone had a sleepover last night. Naughty little kitten. You really need to stop sleeping around so much, sister. You could give our family a bad name."

I glared. "But you've done so beautifully in that department already, *kitten*."

Pushed too hard. The explosion of pain through my skull verified it as he reared back and then backhanded me across the face. As my head snapped from the impact, instinct drove a hand up to cover my cheek. My fear had been justified—a fact that did nothing for my horror from the moisture welling in my eyes. *Weak. You're so goddamn weak. Why the hell didn't you see that coming? You deserved what you got, baby girl. Pain and humiliation.*

I knew what was coming next. The reaction Andrea Asher had programmed in me to be next. *You don't like being embarrassed and hurt, darling? Then take back your dignity. Fight for it!*

"Bastard!" I swung out, catching the edge of his jaw, trailing a thin red line beneath the grunge of his stubble. "You think you'll get away with this?"

He curled a gloating smile. "Ohhhh, sweet sister, I will indeed get away with it—and will be happy to tell you why."

"What. The. Fuck. Do. You. Want?"

His lips twisted again—back to the same sinister look he'd worn when I walked in. With equal menace, he seized my upper arm and dragged me into the living room before hurling me onto the large turquoise couch. "Listen to me very carefully, bitch. I don't like repeating myself. As you can probably guess—or maybe not, knowing your mental capacity—I've had a bit of time on my hands lately. Time to do some very careful research on a few things."

I pushed back against the cushions. Carefully. "Things... like what?"

"Like you."

"Like—" I huffed to disguise the fresh frisson of fear along my spine. There was a damn good chance he had nothing. This was classic bait-the-bear. "Me? Why?"

He exploded again. Scooped up a custom Venetian glass figurine and flung it against the wall. "Cut the crap, Margaux. You know damn well why! Granted, you had some very creative help with burying the bones, baby cakes, but money talks... This you know."

"Ahhh," I muttered. "Does that explain the fact that you look and smell like a sewer?"

He stalked back over. Loomed over as if I were the next Venetian glass under consideration. *Shit.* I wasn't in a boardroom with him anymore, surrounded by lots of witnesses to his temper. "Being cut off from what's mine explains that," he finally seethed.

"Guess it does," I said softly. "But Killian had no choice after discovering what a naughty boy you'd been with Papa Josiah's money." I dared a smile now. A tiny one. "The golden gates of Stone don't get opened for inside traders, Trey."

"Yeah? You don't say. That's cute, sis—real cute. Well, how's this for more cuteness—what can be buried can be dug up. And guess what appeared in my shovel about my very own sister dearest?"

I clamped up and simply glared. His taunt still didn't prove he'd learned anything significant. At least not the most significant secret I could think of. Nobody knew the whole truth about that except Andrea, and she'd paid lots of people to keep their mouths—and their files—shut.

Trey rocked on his heels. "So it seems someone once had a swoony love affair with a well-known Major League Baseball player."

Damn it. That landed closer to the mark. Much closer. But not right on the money.

Fortunately, I was a master of the nonchalant blow-off. "Not classified, asshole. Anyone who thumbed gossip magazines for those eight months knew about Doug and me." His silence spurred me on. "Are you kidding me? That's what this is all about? What you broke in here for?" I surged to my feet, marching toward the front door. "You're going to leave now. And if you don't, I'm going to find you in whatever hovel you're calling a home and sue you out of every box of ramen you're stashing in the place. Breaking and entering's just going to be the st—"

He flipped me around and slammed me against the entrance foyer wall. This time, I saw stars from the force. In a haze, I watched my mail tumble to the floor, victim to the backdraft of his assault.

Time to scream.

But, as I sucked in air, he clamped a ruthless hand over my mouth.

"I wasn't done, bitch. And if you think this is my bad side, just try interrupting me again. Are we clear?"

I nodded in frantic agreement. Tears stung once more, and this time I let them, blinking fast in an effort to keep my vision clear. My heart thrummed in my throat. My whole head pounded, but I had no choice. With Trey's hand locked over my mouth, I was pinned. Forced to hear out the rest of his tirade.

No. Not a tirade.

The darkest nightmare of my life—put into words.

"So, it was rough when Dougie broke up with your sad little ass, hmmm? Maybe a little more than rough?" He cocked both brows, officially making me hate him more than I ever thought possible. "Amazing what the right people in the right places will do for enough bribe money these days. My little friend at the hospital gave me some very interesting reading material for a few nights, dearest. Now let me try to remember all this correctly. Margaux Corina Asher, admitted for—what was it?—oh, that's right. In the papers, they called it 'exhaustion.'" He threw back his head, laughing loudly. "Right. Oh God, that's original. Exhaustion."

I squeezed my eyes shut, unable to stomach anymore. Maybe the floor would be merciful and break open times fifteen stories, allowing the earth to swallow me. My evil half brother was still laughing, not caring that the sound had turned cartoonish in its cackle factor. He was so proud of his little coup, unearthing my worst secret—and now clearly intent on destroying me with it.

But why me? Had this become the new Stone family initiation rite, watching your world go up in flames while Trey held the matchstick? Yes, he was the spawn of the devil, and yes, he still jonesed to crush Killian by any means possible, but where did I figure into either situation? I'd never, not in a million years, thought he would turn his hate on me.

What was his angle? Other than the fact that he obviously knew the true bomb to be dropped here—and couldn't wait to detonate it?

"We both know it wasn't exhaustion...right, sweetie? Let me try to see if I can remember all the details correctly. Oh, but wait. Silly me. How does one forget words like attempted suicide? I mean, wow, Margaux. That's something I'll bet the world would love knowing about you. 'Step right up, folks! Read it here. Perfect, polished Margaux Asher, really not the put-together diva you all know and revere.' No? Guess

Mommy Dearest thought so too. She took care of everything, didn't she? Had everything sealed up, nice and proper and sold a different story altogether to the media. Won't they be supremely interested to know they were utterly lied to, along with the rest of the world?"

With a flourish of smug satisfaction, he stepped back. As his hand popped free of my face, I heaved in a huge breath. Another. I hadn't exactly been suffocated, but pure fury required a lot of pure air.

I dragged my hand through my hair, openly glowering. "What the hell do you want, Trey? Or, should I say, how much do you want?"

He smacked his hands together so hard, the claps pinged audibly off the stucco walls. "Brava! See? You aren't really that dumb, after all! Hmmm. Hey"—he drew the word out, waggling brows over his dark, evil eyes—"maybe you aren't really a blonde, after all. I don't know, Margaux. Does the carpet match the drapes? That might be fun to find out."

I shuddered but managed to cloak it. Why the hell was all this happening? Why now?

From my purse on the table across the foyer, my cell phone started blaring.

"Apple Bottom Jeans."

I swallowed to combat the leap of my heart. Michael—likely just calling to make sure I'd survived the trip home without puking. The trip? Yes. The homecoming? Maybe not.

The ringing stopped but instantly started again. I wavered between laughter and tears. Michael hated that ring. I'd kept it to torment him, proclaiming he'd never have to hear it. I made a silent, desperate promise to God and every saint I'd change the ring if I could only blink my eyes and learn the last half hour had been a disgusting nightmare.

At least the song yanked Trey out of his obsession with my carpet—FYI, asshole, I am a real blonde, but you'll never get the proof—but there was a downside too. My sidesteps across the foyer weren't escaping his focus anymore.

"Ohhh, babe. Don't even think it. We haven't finished our little chat yet."

"Fine." I managed a curt shrug. "Whatever you say, brother—but I'll tell you right now, if he calls back and I don't answer, he'll have San Diego SWAT here in less than five minutes."

"More than enough time," Trey crooned. "I mean, we've finally gotten to the good part."

"Of course." Shit. Where were my Jimmy five-inchers when I needed them to elaborate on my bitch hip pose? "I've already asked, in case you don't remember. How much?"

Trey smirked. "Five million."

"Dollars?"

"No," he snapped. "Fucking gumballs."

He wasn't shocked by my gape. Like I expected him to be? "I just...don't have—"

"Of course you do, Mary Poppins. You think I walked in here ill-informed about that? You're at least there by half."

"Half," I growled. "But not all. And certainly not liquid!"

"Tsk tsk," he repeated. "And here I was just beginning to think you had an actual brain in your head." In one motion, he scooped an envelope off the floor and then shoved it into my hand. It was my SGC electronic paycheck stub. "You're playing in the big kids' playground now, Margaux. Fortune 500. And hey, isn't accounting right up the hall from you now?"

I wrenched free. "You're out of your mind. I'm not going

to steal from Killian!"

"Killian," he spat. "Who never stole a thing in his whole life—except my goddamn birthright."

"Which you had your chance to claim, Trey! Only you didn't just screw the pooch, brother. You fucked over the whole pack."

"Stop!" He stomped at me, pushing me against the wall again. "Stop it right now!" Just as fast, he pushed away as if I'd burned him. "You know the drill here, Margaux. Five million in three days, or I go public about everything. Your true identity. Your trip to the psych ward with all those pills in your system. Even the little fling you're having right now with Mr. Pearson." He grinned as I gasped, softening his grip because he knew he could. "Carefully done, I might even be able to get it all into one tweet. Wouldn't that make for a nice little internet implosion?"

"Shut up." Shut up? How lame could I be? But letting his threats fall to silence wasn't acceptable either. Not in any reality I chose to take part in. Though I desperately clung to the hope this was all a damn dream...

"Gladly," Trey drawled. "But remember this, sugar. I may stink like a sewer, but I've got the balls lined up here, nice and tight. If you don't want to find yourself behind number eight, then shift your adorable little ass in gear—and get me my money."

He reached down to pat my backside, openly admiring the view as he did.

My teeth locked. "Take your fucking hands off me." I bared them directly at the asshole. "And stay the hell away from Michael."

"Power's in your hands now, Mary. Don't disappointment

me."

He pivoted and strode out the door without looking at me again.

As soon as the door closed, I crumpled to the floor, dropped my face into my hands, and dissolved into pieces. Time seemed to freeze as I sat there shaking and sobbing, though the joke was on me... Nothing had stopped at all.

How the hell was this happening? An hour ago, my hugest concern was the changing dynamic between Michael and me, but issues—make that *large* issues—had found their way to my front door. Literally.

And I wasn't easing a single damn one of them by wallowing in this pity party.

I needed to get up, take action, and attempt to move ahead. That was how survivors behaved. Survivors made it through. They didn't sit on the floor swimming in their tears, still clad in their boyfriend's sweatpants from the night before.

There was the second slab of the large issues in the room right now. Michael wasn't my boyfriend—and even thinking of going there now with him was completely out of the question. The sooner my head—and my heart—grabbed that one as reality, the better. This was probably for the best. Michael took me to places that were...amazing. Places that could become addicting—or worse.

No more. For my protection and especially for his, I couldn't—I *wouldn't*—let him be caught in Trey's filthy crosshairs.

There was only one way to successfully accomplish that.

It was time to put on the bitch heels again and ice this place over. No getting in, no getting out. I was a solo act, and I was destined to stay that way.

Trey's visit just happened to be the very ugly reminder I needed.

CHAPTER TWELVE

Michael

Enough.

It had always been Killian Stone's go-to for the situations where "damn it" was too specific and "fuck" too broad. While I'd always jabbed a firm thumbs-up at his warrior spin on the word, I never imagined letting a woman drag me to a place furious enough that I'd be yanking it up for myself.

With an embellishment.

"This is enough, princess."

I bit out every word, though, hardly worried about anyone acknowledging them. Standing at the corner of Ash and Seventh, close to sundown on the third of July, was a crash course in noise levels of every kind. The crowds were thick, everybody from hipsters in bowlers and families with strollers to loudmouthed frat boys and off-duty military out to enjoy the festive feel of the approaching holiday. The air itself was already on board with the party, a tangle of terrace barbecue, ocean breeze, sidewalk vendor tamales and, yeah, beer. Lots and lots of beer.

The go-with-the-flow vibe did shit for mellowing my impatience—this after I was so damn certain I'd secured a handle on the stuff this morning. Of course, waking up and instantly feeling like an eighty-year-old had a tendency to realign certain thoughts. Yeah, yeah, I had only myself to blame—nobody had forced me to ring Keir and ask if he felt like playing Navy physical training torture master a couple of times a week with an old college buddy. And nobody had jammed a gun to my head when I ordered him not to give me any special sissy treatment either. Dude was just being a good friend. Wasn't his fault I couldn't move this morning.

Sometime in the ten minutes it took for me to shuffle into the shower, the mental lightbulb blared on. I had a choice. Continue to let Keir turn me into hamburger twice a week or face the goddamn piper and confront the real source of my agony.

Hamburger wasn't cutting it anymore.

Which was why I stood here now, staring up at all fifteen stories of her ivory tower, screwing up the courage to finally step into her domain.

A domain I'd been invited to a month ago—and then turned away from just as quickly.

I summoned new courage by scrolling up the window on my phone to arrive at the exact text message.

Still not feeling great. Tonight won't be good after all. M

I'd told her it didn't matter. That I'd bring soup and TLC instead of condoms and lube.

There'd never been an answer.

Not until two days later, when I'd gone half out of my mind with worry, hitting send on my fifty-first text.

Margaux, if you don't confirm you're still breathing, I'm calling the cops.

She'd said she was sorry. Pleaded for time. Said she needed space, that everything was moving too fast. But even that wasn't the most cryptic shit. She'd waited three more days to wind up that curve ball, treating my inbox with the news this time.

Dear Michael,

I know you're not a fan of personal emails, considering all the professional ones you have to write. But this isn't something I can communicate in a text, and talking to you in person will only unhinge my resolve, so we'll both have to deal with things this way.

Two sentences in, and I'd already been growling back at her. Unhinge her resolve? About what?

Here's the thing. My life is...complicated right now. I can't go into details, which might be part of the problem already. You're an an amazing guy, Michael. You deserve a woman without complications. Somebody who can give you everything you deserve...

I'd stopped again but not to growl. To grunt. In confusion. She'd missed a typo. Correction—a T-Y-P-O. The woman didn't miss lint on someone's suit, let alone a botch like that. And when the hell did she use words like amazing guy? That was the kind of trite shit they spewed on reality dating shows—the ones we'd laughed at together at the High Dive.

The rest of the email was more of the same and not worth reviewing—then yearning to puke on—again. Can't be sure of anything right now...blah, blah, blah... Probably jumped too fast...blah, blah, blah... The day just overwhelmed me...

Was she serious? Jumped too fast? After the day overwhelmed her? After she busted my balls at Kil and Claire's wedding about my mountaintop insanity only to show up at my place two hours later—begging me to help her get out of her gown?

If she'd written this in a sober, sane state of mind—if she'd even written it—I'd donate my right testicle for medical research.

Like I—or my testicle—had gotten a clear answer from her on that. Or any answer at all. After the text to assure she was at least alive and breathing, the woman had dropped off the grid on me once more. She'd even cut the string of what we'd once called the tin can telephone—her direct line at work, no switchboard necessary—always letting me sit through three dozen rings before she pushed poor Sorrelle to pick the damn thing up, always with a new and better excuse. When the boy finally realized I wasn't going for the regular lines of trips to the powder room, trapped on a conference call, or two-hour traffic jams after three-hour lunches, his creativity really kicked in. One day, it was a doctor's appointment. Then a nail appointment. Then a couple of out-of-town SGC responsibilities, since Claire and Killian had decided they needed to fuck their way across the second half of the globe, therefore extending their honeymoon. Then there was the DMV appointment—seriously?—followed by jury duty, a leg waxing, and a visit to her mother—

Which was as believable as the DMV thing.

Which had led to me calling Keir again. And becoming a nice hunk of ground round for him again.

And realizing nothing was going to take care of this

strange chasm between Margaux and me—except Margaux and me.

I wasn't letting her off the hook that easily, damn it.

The mental rehash incited me into motion. The light turned green, and I skirted my way through the throngs with sure-footed precision. On the other side of the street, I didn't stop. Pushed through the glass doors ahead of me, into the El Cortez's elegant Spain-influenced lobby. Gunned it to the buzzer box for the VIP condos.

The button for her unit was, as usual, unlabeled. I jammed on it. Two quicks, one long, two quicks again—the secret code that, to the best of my knowledge, belonged only to me.

Unless...it didn't anymore.

Don't go there.

Too late. My heartbeat crushed the crap out of my windpipe. I grimaced against the similar hunk of cement in my gut, counting every goddamn second that passed. Waiting.

Waiting.

Waiting.

Beneath my breath, I beat on myself. "Should've called first, shithead." What if she was out of town again? Worse, what if she wasn't? All too easily, the rock in my stomach gave up a nightmare image to my head. Margaux, standing there in her ivory and cream foyer, touching those perfect strawberry lips to another glass of champagne, perusing the callbox on her end with a smooth, secretive smile. But that wasn't the worst one. That came when the vision grew, including a faceless stranger sidling behind her, dipping his dark head to her neck, urging her away from my impotent buzzes...back to the bedroom.

"Fuck." My exhalation broke it into two syllables instead of one. As I stepped backward, my footsteps were heavy echoes across the lobby's terracotta tiles. My back finally collided with the wall—I snapped my head back to punch the same surface, grateful for the painful collision of my teeth.

I refused to punch that goddamn button again.

But turning and leaving? It was like playing a role in *Night of the Living Dead*—shot for being a zombie when everything inside was still human. And feeling just as bullet-in-the-head shitty.

What did you expect, dipwad? That she'd magically throw open the door after avoiding you like a virus the last four weeks? That you'd just walk in off the street and she'd be so stunned that she—

Her buzzer blared.

The elevator doors opened.

Three bounds later, I was inside the lift.

Fifteen floors later, my heartbeat started in on my lungs. The feet I'd compared to bricks downstairs now felt like bars of lead. Like that had any bearing on my pace the second the doors slid back and emptied me into the polished silence of the hall leading to her place.

I doubted a ninja could've successfully sneaked up on her door in the modern-day echo chamber, so I wasn't surprised when it opened as I neared. Her hand, wrapped around the edge of the wood, was the only indication she'd come to receive me instead of sending Sorrelle, who'd all but grown fur as her self-appointed guard bitch.

Hmmm. That was a pretty good one. I contemplated weaving it into my opening line but decided to play the moment straight until she steered things otherwise. Four weeks. Just a fraction of the time I'd closeted myself up in Julian, but every day, minute, and hour had felt like more. Like that was surprising, after what had happened since the last time we stood face-to-face?

I paused on the threshold. Opening the door didn't equal inviting me in, and assumptions were a really bad idea right now.

From behind the towering wood portal, I finally heard a soft, "Hey."

Did that mean come in or get lost? "Hey." Huge inhalation. "Thanks for letting me up."

She didn't move, but a new smile tinted her voice. "You were just going to come back if I didn't. Right?"

"Yeah. No. Maybe. Probably."

In usual circumstances, she'd have laughed at that. But we were a long way off from usual. "Come in, Michael."

Michael. Not mister or buddy or Captain America.

And definitely not stud.

Clamping back an unnerved grunt, I stepped into her condo.

Screw the grunt. Tough to make that happen when one's jaw was headed toward the floor.

No smirking berry lips. Or gloating gaze. Or even one of the cute little casual outfits she usually wore at home that drove me nuts because they left little of her incredible curves to the imagination. Her usual rock band tee was now an oversize USD sweatshirt, and her legs, normally encased in bright things that seemed like glorified pantyhose, were replaced by cotton shorts that barely covered the essentials. At the bottom, her feet were swallowed by bunched-up socks, one of the things I loved best about visiting her here. The look was such a glorious change-up from her designer platforms, it grabbed me in the cock at every new sighting.

Now was no exception.

Goddamnit.

I swung my gaze back up to her face. And said a silent farewell to every inch of my erection. Tendrils of her hair, falling loose from the messy ponytail atop her head, framed cheeks that seemed drawn in by exhaustion despite the light makeup she wore. The cosmetics did nothing to cover the shadows beneath her eyes either. I blinked hard, trying to recall how I'd ever imagined her up here as some preening *Gone Girl.* The tired woman—scratch that—the exhausted girl in front of me was a full one-eighty from the impression.

My frustration and fury of ten minutes ago? Now officially left behind in the lobby, where they belonged. Beyond that, I didn't know what to think, let alone fathom the words to express it, as she closed the door with a gentle click—

But not before rushing a furtive stare down the hallway.

Like she expected someone else?

No. Like she was afraid of something getting in. Or someone?

But that made no sense either. Did it?

My life is...complicated right now...

I scowled at the thought—along with the puzzlement at watching her fingers tremble while sliding the dead bolt home, before she swiveled back toward me. She studied me for a long moment. I stared back, definitely not studying. Unless an obsession with how she wetted and rewetted her lips counted as studying.

She flowed a toe over the floor in a little arc. "You—you look good."

"Thanks. You too." And gee willikers, great fucking weather we've been having, eh?

She stepped past me toward the living room. At the last second she stopped, turned, and sidestepped into the space-age-meets-Mission-chic kitchen instead.

"You want something to drink?" She tugged on the fridge's stainless-steel handle.

"Said the convict to her executioner?" I followed by a few steps and folded my arms.

"Huh?"

"Trying to delay the head roll?"

She glowered. "Trying to be nice. Just give it a go and see how it fits, okay, big guy?"

"Sure." I stepped over and leaned forward, elbows on the marble-topped center island. "As soon as you tell me how good a fit that refrigerator is—since you aren't able to get your head out of it."

Her snort pitched slightly toward soprano. "Not a crime to look in the fridge."

"Except for someone who labels three bowls of bar mix and a martini as dinner."

"I could so completely make you dinner."

I took advantage of the chance at an unmonitored smirk. "Let's not push it. Veg and dip?" A tub of sour cream dip sailed over the door. I caught it easily. "Way to go, Joe Namath."

"Who?"

"Tom Brady?"

"Oh, yeah. Giselle's husband."

Good thing we hadn't gotten to the drink part yet. Nothing to snort out my nose. "Uh, yeah. Him."

"Shit. I don't think Sorrelle got any vegetables."

"Did you check the crisper?"

"The what?"

Face, meet palm. “Forget about it.”

“No. Hey! I can do—”

By the time she got there, I’d skirted the island and grabbed her hand. “Come on.”

“But—”

“Margaux, I didn’t come here to eat.” I pulled her up, kicked the door shut, and led her back out to the living room.

“But I’m sure I can find the damn veg—”

“Come. Now.”

I freed her once we stood in front of her custom couch, a bright-blue monstrosity that looked strange but was comfortable as hell. All too quickly, I wished this was another night when we’d just polished off a Soleluna pizza and were about to settle in to order up a movie. But that would have meant we’d time-traveled back eight months—when I was still in the fucking friend zone. AKA a relationship coma.

I couldn’t settle for coma anymore. I wanted to be her wake-up climax. Her good night one too. And a lot of the good stuff in between... As much of it as I could seize...

Only now, she didn’t even look like she wanted me in front of her.

Wait. Assumptions again—and their dangers. That wasn’t it at all. It was the conclusion she wanted me to grab—before she was forced to give in to my persistent stance, finally returning my stare—

And showing me the lights of her real thoughts, brilliant and beautiful in her eyes.

Awareness sliced through me—just as it had when I’d first seen those glints, reflecting the morning sun on my patio. Tonight, their green was joined by the kaleidoscope of the city lights, all twinkling to life below... Different hues but the exact same magic. The precise same truth.

That she was just as confused now as she had been that morning.

"Damn," I rasped. Pledges I'd made during the elevator ride up, about being patient and taking this slow, were as insignificant as the headlights on the cars below. This was either really good or really bad. My body didn't stop to discern the difference. Every inch of my dick leapt again, straining at my jeans like the prisoner it had been for too long.

Until I realized my growl had made her jump. Not in a good-shivers way either. More like a cat springing at its own shadow.

"What?" she demanded, voice climbing again. "What is it, Michael?"

"Whoa," I countered. Lifted my hands to her shoulders, starting soothing rolls with my thumbs. "Whoa, princess. Sshhh."

"Don't call me that." She jerked away, wrapping her arms around herself as if rubbing off my touch.

My touch—or whatever trigger I'd hit with my words?

The glance I'd gotten in before she turned, betraying her unguarded alarm, shoved me toward the latter.

"Why?" I punched the insistence into the stomps I took to follow her toward the terrace. Her hunched posture galvanized my own apprehension. Shit. Had I interpreted things all wrong? Had I thought desire when she meant fear? If so, of what? Me? Then why had she even buzzed me up? Invited me in? Tossed vegetable dip at me?

"Margaux, what's going on?"

No answer. She unlocked the door, shoved it open, and rushed out to the Spanish tiles outside.

What the hell was going on?

I had zilch right now. With nothing but a load of vague texts, the cagey tone of her voice mail, and that email to go on—

Wait.

That email.

My life is...complicated...

Instincts detonated inside. The explosion was so huge, I stopped. When it faded, I kept my feet locked. If I lunged for her now, stopping wouldn't be an option. A fifteen-story freefall wouldn't be fun.

Complicated.

I'd thought she meant shit at work. Or issues with her mom. Or, damn it, even problems with the invisible guy I kept imagining her with while I was being a dumb fuck in Julian.

No. You'd thought it was a lie, was what you'd thought. An excuse in place of having to face you, to tell you she'd had a chance to think and the relationship thing just wasn't going to work...

Words I didn't read in her now. In any form. The only thing I observed was a girl wavering between flippant and fearful, unable to decide on which. Not surprising, since she was clearly preoccupied with peering into every corner like it was about to sprout Krueger, Pinhead, and Jason at the same time.

Assumptions. And their agonizing consequences.

What the hell was going on? And what words were going to unlock the answer from her?

"Margaux." I stepped onto the terrace too. The air was definitely different up here, a crisp breeze of sea salt and summer flowers, romance-novel perfection to accompany the sunset forming over the bay waters in the distance. Not that I'd be paying attention to it. "Margaux."

She whipped an unseeing stare at me. I almost jumped back myself. I liked disorienting the woman by seducing her, not scaring her.

"Margaux?"

"Huh?" A wave of a hand, a shake of her head, and suddenly, the lost princess had been dismissed. The PR princess took over again with a camera-ready pose, hand on her hip, practiced grin on her lips. "Hey! Sorry, babe." She tapped at her head. "With Claire still out, there's a party going on in here all the time these days."

I jogged up an eyebrow.

Babe?

Why did I suddenly crave a shower? And why from that one and not stud?

Because she meant it about as much as a red-carpet air kiss?

"Okay, what's really going on?" I approached her again, though her cheeky mien remained unchanged. So I stepped closer, getting near enough that I could smell her—expensive soap and favorite perfume—and observe the subtle trembles she was hiding so well beneath that attempt at a polished façade. "Margaux." I lifted a hand, gliding it over the one she still gripped to her hip. "Sugar. It's me." I meshed my fingers between hers. "It's me."

She wet her lips again—just as she tried to yank free, hiding the deeper shivers beneath those few inches of skin pressed against mine. "Nothing's going on." It was better than babe, despite the toothpaste-commercial mask she threw down yet again. "Nothing that's any of your business, Michael."

"You know I believe you like I'd believe Trey Stone in

rehab, right?"

The commercial grin suddenly took on a shit ton of plaque—with enough to spare for the newest crap turn of her composure. "Why the hell are you mentioning him?"

"Why the hell are you reacting like I just told you to wear white after Labor Day?"

"Cut the jokes."

"Then cut the entertainment-show cheese."

Her eyes narrowed, perhaps a lame attempt to make me think PR princess was about to wield her scepter of doom on my ass. But I was onto her game now and we both knew it, a recognition that swirled like thick incense between us before she snapped it in half, whirling and marching back inside. During the trip, she dashed out a retort that was classic, acidic her.

"Say what you came to say, big boy, and then get the hell out."

Shit. Why hadn't I let her pour me a drink when I'd had the chance? "I didn't come to say anything to you." I skirted around the couch to stake a position at the foot of the stairs to her second floor—obeying my instinct that she was ready to bolt any second. "I came to talk with you."

"Said the executioner to the convict?"

I shook my head. And let a soft laugh spill out. Should've seen that one coming but didn't—just like every other page of this chapter of my life with this woman's name on it. I'd been perfectly content in a world where my only deep wounds bore the name Laci and the sole source of fun at work was a scapegoat named Princess-zilla. But this astounding, confounding, bewildering, bewitching person had changed it all—and now I didn't want the chapter to end. Ever.

One minor hitch to that plan.

We'd written ourselves into a corner. An impasse overlooking a daunting blank page. Stood staring each other down in an ivory tower above a sea of lights, with walls of silence closing in on us more by the minute. Walls fortified by four fucking weeks of the same stuff.

But what were walls made of? Bricks.

And what did serfs at the base of the tower know how to do better than anything?

Lay bricks.

Which meant they could tear them down too.

I couldn't give up. I wouldn't. Not if it meant clawing out the mortar of this fucker with my bare hands.

Or taking advantage of the fact that she rushed back over to shut the door to the terrace—making it damn easy to pin her against the thing. She yipped as I flattened my hands on either side of her head—and refused to budge.

"Michael, this isn't—"

"Talk to me."

Her nostrils flared. "I'm not trashed tonight, Pearson. The Neanderthal thing isn't going to—"

"Talk to me. Damn it, Margaux, I think I deserve an explanation."

She raised her hands, almost pressing them to my chest—hell yeah, go there, sugar, please—but then whimpered as if ordering herself away from a chocolate bar, dropping them. "I sent you an email. I know you read it. Can't you just accept that and—"

"I accept job offers, babe. I accept global warming. I accept cash back at the grocery store. I do not accept complicated. What the fuck is complicated?" I didn't grant her any mercy, tracking her head's slow back-and-forth with equal arcs of my own. "And if you wet your lips like that one more time, I swear I'm just going to kiss the answer out of you."

As if loaded on springs, her hands did fly to my chest—

And shoved.

Wasn't caught with my pants down, though I was damn certain my cock would've preferred it that way, swelling into a distraction so significant, I stumbled back without a fight. Inside three seconds, I stood gaping at the smears I'd left behind on the glass...

And her new sprint across the room, as far away as she could get.

"I can't do this, Michael. Not now!" She got to the stairs, raced halfway up, and then whirled on the landing, reaching for the rail with a hand that visibly shook. "Things just...are what they are, okay? I let you come up because I figured you needed this—"

"I needed this? Needed what?"

"—so let's get it all said like the grown-ups we supposedly are. I do realize that getting closure can be important—"

"Closure?" Disbelief choked me from voicing anything original. Outrage prevented me from doing anything but advancing at those stairs like a SEAL tracking Bin Laden. Though she watched every step I took, she still started when I pounded a foot on the bottom step.

"Don't get surly," she snipped. "I'm attempting to be nice."

"Nice?"

"I can do that from time to time. And...well..."

"Well what?"

"You're—you're important to me."

Well, shit.

One little whisper, and she'd led my SEAL to an empty cave. Then ordered him to sit and chew on his nails just like she did now. With her feet on the next step down, she curled in both arms, baffling the crap out of me. Did I stand down against the insecure girl she evoked with the pose or surge up toward the minx who now had to steal glances at me through those thick, gorgeous lashes?

I sneaked a foot onto the next step. Let out a resigned sigh. "And you're important to me."

She sat a little straighter but left her hands curled in, posture still guarded. "I know that too. But if you need to... move on...and stuff, I understand, okay? I do."

"Is that what you want?"

My growl made her jump. Good.

I enjoyed that glory for two seconds before hating the fuck out of myself for it. Damn it, this was a mess, but I was not giving up. My new creed sent an invisible grappling hook into the rail behind her head, pulling me up the five stairs remaining between us. I knelt on the step below her feet, stare still locked, resolve still firm. "I don't think it's what you want, Margaux."

Another averted gaze. She was entranced with her kneecaps tonight. Like she needed an excuse. To me, every inch of her was entrancing on any night, but the woman was on a mission of her own—to keep her reactions hidden from me, in any way she could. Her rickety reply bore that truth out. "What I want doesn't matter right now, Michael. Not that it ever did." She twisted her fingers together. "My mistake was thinking it would ever be any different."

Hell. My body was perched on a step, but my mind stood at a crossroads. It had been the MO since I'd gotten here, hadn't it? She'd let me come up with the purpose of cutting me free—even when that option was torturing the crap out of both of us and even when she had no damn intention of explaining why. Complicated didn't qualify as explanation—not on this planet or any other.

But unlike all the other intersections she'd parked me at tonight, I had a very different outlook on this one. And smiled.

Because I already knew what direction I was headed for next.

Because she was coming with me.

The ju-ju from my grin finally altered the air between us. It tugged Margaux's head up. She jolted—again. In the years I'd known her, the woman had never done the scared-kitty twitch as many times as tonight. The observation lent new strength to my decision.

"Pearson? What are you—?"

I cut her off by yanking her to her feet. Without pause, kissed her. Though my body screamed for more, I kept it to a commanding smack. "No more questions," I decreed. "Not mine, not yours."

Her face crunched ten different ways. She was goddamn adorable when struggling to figure something out—or maybe I just thought so because the expression was rare. "So we're done?" Her voice pitched up and then down, a mixture of relief and then sorrow, the convict finally being given an execution date—still totally clueless she was about to be sprung from prison altogether.

"Not by a long shot, beautiful." I let myself laugh it. I cupped a hand around her nape, pulling down so her gaze was compelled back up. Our kiss had ignited new emerald specks in her eyes, splitting my grin even wider.

"I don't understand," she finally uttered.

"Of course you don't." I wound my fingers deeper into her hair. "Because you can't see past the demons you keep seeking in every corner of this place." Which was pretty funny, once I thought about it. Between the spotless white walls and the polished concrete floors, I doubted the tiniest dust bunny could successfully hide here.

One thing I didn't doubt—somehow, I'd sliced open a nerve.

"Michael," she snapped, "cut the games."

"Great idea," I returned. "Perfect idea, actually."

"You're making no sense."

"Another good point." I swept my gaze away long enough to take in all the nouveau-industrial décor—and then dismiss it in one grunt. "Not a lot of sense going on in here at all."

She cocked her head. "Which means...?"

"You need to get the hell out of here. So that's what's going to happen."

She stiffened. "Ummm, negative. It's a damn freak show down there, with the holiday crowds and the guys from the base. Besides, I thought you weren't interested in..." Her voice trailed as her stare narrowed, hooking into the steady intent of mine. "Shit. You don't mean dinner."

I curled my grin wider. And yeah, it probably made me a bit of a pig, but watching her fidget in expectation of my next words...instant wood sprung again between my thighs. Sometimes one had to leash a tigress for her own good. Didn't mean it had to all be work.

"You have ten minutes, Miss Asher," I charged. "Pack a bag. You'll need to bring shit for five days. Casual shit—got it? That means denim. And cotton. And a warm jacket. And comfortable shoes."

She glowered. "Heels are comfortable."

I lifted an eyebrow at my watch. "Nine minutes, thirty seconds."

"Michael, I'm not just packing a bag and leaving with you."

"Good enough." I folded my arms. "That means you're ready to tell me, right now, why you're as skittish as a virgin in an HBO script."

She grimaced. "I don't know whether to applaud you or smack you for that."

"Go for either, but you'll be eating deeper into your allowance. Which, by the way, is down to eight minutes, forty-five seconds."

Her glare weakened. The convict-in-conflict thing rushed over her face again, though this time, her eyes were brighter, almost hopeful, before diving under their shadows again. "No," she asserted. "No. Come on. I can't."

I gave my eyebrow another workout. "Or won't?"

"Can't. How the hell do I explain this? Claire's still not settled in after the honeymoon. She also has a bad case of the flu and—"

"Don't worry about Claire." I backed that up by pulling out my phone and flipping to my friend's number. "I'd be stressing more about the seven minutes you now have left to pack a full bag and change your clothes. Or not. Your choice as well. I do like those shorts..."

"Or what?" She persisted with a defiant stance, bunching fists to her waist, but now it felt like watching a poodle taunt a Great Dane. Everyone in the room could smile about it, knowing exactly which dog would end up on top in the end. "You going to just throw me over your shoulder and—ahhhh!"

I opened a smile into the luscious curve of her ass—now

taking up most of the view on my right side. "Thanks for the suggestion," I drawled. "One of your best ideas, sugar. Really."

She groaned but ended it in a giggle as she took advantage of my distraction to snatch my phone from my hand. "You get this back when you put me down. And add ten minutes back to the timer."

I reached up and landed a firm spank on her cheeks. When she squealed, I chuckled. "You want to play the negotiation game with a lawyer, Miss Asher?"

"And are you really tossing that one out for a slice-and-dice under my Louboutins, Mr. Pearson?"

"For the next five days, your Louboutins will be useless."

"And your law degree will be any different?"

At the top of the stairs, I followed the hall to the end, where a king-size production of a bed was centered in a room evoking the rest of the condo's minimalist chic. The whole place was clearly some overpaid designer's idea of what Margaux Asher stood for.

Idiot.

Everything in here would be so much different if he saw the woman I set down on the mattress, hair tumbling into her face, mouth parted in impish delight, eyes shining with joy. The sight of her...consumed me. Overjoyed me. Already made me feel like a goddamn firework.

I wanted to tell her just that. Managed to stop myself by kissing her instead—this time turning the union of our lips into a thorough, passionate exploration. She moaned to me in welcome, meeting every sweep of my tongue with her own, but pulled back when I tried to press in even deeper.

"I'd...I'd...better get packing. Tick-tock, right?"

I snorted. "Touché, Miss A."

"What? You don't want to look at me in this for the next five days, do you?"

I groaned while rising up, now standing in front of her—and battling back all the urges to join her again, tangling her six-hundred-thread-count sheets. "You want the real answer to that?"

She pushed at my stomach with a finger. "Get lost. Knowing you, I only have thirty seconds left."

With phone back in hand, I jogged downstairs and out to the terrace again. The smile hadn't left my face. The sky was on fire now, a blaze of red, purple, and orange left behind by the sun—though even the colors consuming the sky paled against the detonations now defining my spirit.

Want some tongs for that fucking corn, man?

I snorted. If that was the best my ego could come up with, I was sticking to the early fireworks show in my chest. Made it easier to concentrate on the business at hand anyway. Two calls, fast and fun, if a little loud. Claire shrieked with joy when I told her she'd have to make do without her wingwoman for a few days. Mom did the same when I told her I was returning home for another visit, starting tonight—with a special guest in tow.

★ ★ ★ ★

Mom's excitement only grew during the wait, a little over an hour long. She texted three times to ask what part of the journey we'd hit, something she'd never do if I was driving up alone but taking shameless advantage of Margaux's presence to be...well...Mom.

Not that the sixty-eight minutes weren't interesting

otherwise. On one hand, I was just as exhilarated as Mom, though everything was tempered by a sense of the surreal. I'd driven every curve, dip, and switchback of this mountain a hundred times in my life, but it was a trip into brand-new when accompanied by Margaux's commentary. Her touristy squee when we passed the Safari Park. Her bigger yelp when the headlights caught a family of squirrels, dashing out of the way just in time. Her fascinated gasps at the blanket of stars above, becoming astonished cries as we climbed to higher elevations.

She captivated me in equal measure. I had no damn doubt it would've been more if the road didn't demand my attention. Her delight, authentic and unguarded, flung open yet another window I never imagined her having, let alone allowing me a look into. A year ago, had anyone told me I'd have a finger hooked into the belt loop on Margaux Asher's jeans as she hung out of the window of my truck counting stars, I would've asked what crack they were smoking. Now, I grinned like a fool at the breathtaking creature next to me, wondering how her light had been purposely snuffed for so many years.

"Michael!"

"What?"

"There's millions of them!"

We'd reached the straight stretch before home. I took advantage of that to grab a longer stare at her. "From where I'm sitting, sugar, there's only one."

Screw the tongs. You've popped the fucking corn off the cob. How about some butter with that?

Sanity came with a sobering thought. It wouldn't last. No way. Undoubtedly she was on a little natural high after my ballsy Luke Skywalker move, crashing into her cell and freeing her from her invisible Darth Vader. Besides, it was after dark, providing an added rush of romantic adrenaline for our secret adventure.

But that was psycho-babble for tomorrow morning. Right now, I greedily sucked up the little look she flashed, lips jutted in a silent *I'm impressed*, as we turned in at the farm. I gave in to a little pride as she eagerly took in everything, deliberately driving more slowly to stretch the moment. If showing her my place in town was like showing off the winning science project, this was nabbing the fucking prom king crown.

All too soon, I had to pull up to the house. As soon as I braked next to the kitchen door, the screen door was punched open hard enough to slam the side of the house. Mom appeared, no less a force of nature, an effect aided by the bright lights from behind. I smiled as she forced herself to remain there while I circled around to help Margaux down from the truck. As soon as Margaux was safe on the ground, I chuckled and gestured to Mom.

"Okay, come on. Hit me with all you got."

Mom didn't need a second invitation. With Margaux watching, she damn near took a flying leap at me—in short, the usual—before mushing me with a cheek kiss and then rubbing my jaw scruff. "Well, hello there."

"Hi. Whoa, you look nice. Why the makeup?"

"City council photos."

I chuckled. "That time again already?"

"It's a dirty job, but someone's got to do it. Besides, I am the one with the hotshot son now." She ruffled my hair. "My beautiful boy."

Margaux giggled.

I growled. "Mom...sheez."

"Shut up. I'm due. This is the carrot God dangled while I

wiped your ass for two years."

"You've washed up since then, yeah?" I glanced toward Margaux. "I am so, so sorry about—"

I wasn't sure what snatched the rest of the words from me. The wistful smile on her face...or the pooling tears in her eyes.

Instant promise to the Guy Upstairs. I will never apologize for my mother's affection again.

To ensure I remembered it thoroughly, the woman herself stepped forward to salvage the moment, extending a hand like Margaux's tears were no more than the interference of summer bugs. "Welcome to Pearson's," she greeted. "I'm Diana Pearson, but nobody calls me that. Just go for Di, and we'll be good."

Margaux dipped her head. I almost wondered if she was going to bow next. "Okay then, Di. Nice to meet you. I'm—"

"Oh, I know who you are." Mom dashed off a little wink. "And it is very nice to meet you too, Margaux Asher. You're every bit as lovely as I expected."

Enough light spilled out from the house to pick up the flush in Margaux's cheeks. Whap. Another window to the woman flew open—a huge, fascinating one. I'd seen her flummoxed, furious, flirty, and haughty as all hell, but never—what was this, anyway? Bashful? Embarrassed? Cautious?

"Well," she laughed out, "I guess you keep an eye on the gossip magazines."

"I keep an eye on my son." Mom's warmth eclipsed the words of anything except love and pride. "Including how he talks about the important people in his life."

That didn't go unnoticed. With gaze flicking to me, Margaux quipped, "And...I'm important?"

"Do bees crap honey?" The two of them shared a giggle,

which Mom interpreted as permission to link arms like they'd been girlfriends for years. I watched in shock as Margaux squeezed back.

This wasn't good. At all. "It's getting chilly," I interceded. "Let me get Margaux's bags, and we can all go—"

"Great idea, honey. We'll see you inside." As Mom pulled Margaux toward the door, she went on, "So I already know some of the important stuff. You like chocolate, French movies, girl pop, and my son's humor. I'm sure there are a few things still missing from that list..."

I didn't know whether to laugh or cry as I paced around to retrieve the two suitcases, garment bag, and makeup satchel from the truck. After lugging them up the back stairs and parking them in the girlier of the two guest bedrooms—still wondering what the hell she could've been capable of with ten minutes to pack—I followed the sound of more giggling down to the den.

Two hours ago, I'd seriously wondered if zombies were going to materialize from the walls of Margaux's place. Now, I realized fate was holding back on the true horror scene of the night.

"I think he was about five or six in these." Mom swiped the screen of the electronic photo album I'd given her for Mother's Day. "God, he loved that little cape I made for him."

Heat claimed my face. I scrubbed at my jaw, glad I hadn't shaved. Thick scruff made for good ground cover in a pinch.

And gave me an excuse to pause, still unnoticed, to watch a soft smile breach Margaux's lips. "Captain America," she murmured, "even back then."

Mom popped her head up. "His favorite. How'd you know?"

"We're talking Michael, right? How could anyone not know?"

"Many don't." Mom tried to be light and fluffy about it—but the woman clearly didn't know who she was dealing with. Margaux I-See-Through-People-Like-Cellophane Asher.

Sure enough, Margaux forgot about the picture, swinging up her stare, intent on drilling through Mom's pretense. "I don't follow. Your son's pretty amazing, you know. No secret behind that."

Mom's face dipped into the same conflict punching my chest.

Oh, princess...if you only knew.

But she couldn't know. And wouldn't. I'd all but absconded her ass all the way up here because of the escape I wanted it to be for her, not the complication. Cleaning out her mind was the goal, not clogging it more with bullshit from my past—and the demon from it who thought he could terrorize his way into our future.

Fuck.

An image of Declan and his smirk invaded my mind, a blockade to getting into the den to run the interference Mom desperately needed. I fought back with a grunt, mentally punching into his features like cartoon clay. It was easier to shove the mess aside and then escalate my grunt to a growl that sounded peeved at discovering my childhood on twelve-inch display for the first woman I'd brought home since Laci.

"Well...shit," I grumbled, bursting them both into laughter. I picked up the monitor and snorted again before arching an eyebrow at Mom. "Now do you wonder why I wouldn't load the one of me doing this in my underwear?"

Margaux straightened. "There's an underwear one?"

"Don't. You. Dare," I barked before Mom could take a breath.

She laughed and then stood. "I think that's my cue to go rustle up some dinner."

A couple of hours later, after we'd stuffed ourselves full of lasagna, Caesar salad, pie, and more mortifying stories about my five-year-old superhero antics, Mom rose from the kitchen table with an exaggerated yawn. On her way out, she doused the fluorescents that illuminated the room like a surgi-center. The perimeter track lights took over, softening everything to shades of peach and gold. The hues played perfectly over the top of Margaux's head, turning her hair into a little cloud. Entrancing as it was, I fought the craving to pull down her ponytail, wondering if her strands felt as silken as they looked... and how they'd feel in my fist if I yanked her into my lap, kissing her without mercy...

She didn't help anything by tilting her head, throwing a stare over in open question.

"All right, I'm going to bite. What the hell's up, Pearson?"

Up? Except what the thoughts of your hair are doing to the wood between my thighs?

"Just enjoying the evening, Miss Asher." And thinking about how I never wanted it to end.

Surreal. I returned again to the descriptor, though I'd never really stopped. And why not? It was so fucking appropriate for all this, forcing me to confront a significant truth about why I'd insisted on the stunt to begin with. Sure, I'd sensed this might be exactly what she needed—what complicated life didn't benefit from fresh air and a sky full of stars?—but there was no denying the second half anymore. I'd done it for me too. Inviting her up here was one thing. Damn near forcing the event was another, especially when the scenario had disaster all but spelled out for it.

Her—square peg. Julian—round hole. Annihilated edges—distinct possibility.

A trap set on purpose?

If I denied it, I'd be lying.

But, damn it, if her life was so complicated that she was willing to douse us for it, then I needed a reason to let go too. A legitimate one. Six months away hadn't surrendered that reason for me. The last month sure as hell hadn't. So, maybe now I needed to detonate my own C-4 on the situation. Watch the princess curl up her nose at my home turf for a while, reinforcing the theory I'd tried to prove from the start. Our worlds had collided by accident, not fate. Bogie and Bergman without Sam and the piano. Tony and Maria without the fire escape. Bella and Edward without the sparkles. But maybe the blood. Yeah, maybe a little of the blood—namely my own, all self-inflicted—before this was through.

Because, God help me, it seemed like she'd belonged here all along.

Mom adored her. The house was brighter with her in it. Shit, she even sat here at the table we'd had since I was a kid, tracing over its nicks and grooves with scary familiarity.

Was the rat about to be snapped in his own trap?

And, if so...what the hell did that mean for his sanity now?

How the hell did I confront the concept of giving her up after this?

Thwack. She ordered me back to reality by snapping a fingernail against my thigh. I chuckled. She glowered.

"Enjoying the evening?" she shot back. "That's all?"

I quirked one side of my mouth. "Does there have to be

more?"

She yanked a knee up to her chest. Rested her cheek against it. But while the pose was casual, her stare wasn't. Her sass had flipped to serious—and the piercing attention she'd given to Mom earlier was now my fate. "I just supposed you'd be...distracted by now."

"Huh?" I was genuinely confused. And irked. Though the latter made no sense. "Why? With what?"

Her head lifted. Brow furrowed. "Come on, Michael. Don't tell me you didn't notice."

"Notice what?"

Only now, she looked like she had just seen a ghost. Her lips parted, and I wasn't sure if she'd speak or puke. "The... bruise," she finally stated.

"The bruise?" I scowled. "What the hell are you—what bruise? Where?"

She blinked. Again. "On your mom, Michael."

"On my—what?"

"Don't tell me you didn't see through all that makeup."

"She had city council pictures." Now I was totally lost. Disbelief took the spoon of my reality and twisted it into a pretzel. "Right? She said she had to—" I hurled my gaze back up at her. "And then I just thought she was tired."

I stabbed a hand through my hair. On its way down, Margaux grabbed it. "Sometimes we see what we want to see." There was no sympathy in it. Or pity. Just a lot of basic understanding. Thank fuck. "I was going to ask if she might have just fallen or something, but that isn't the case, is it?"

My chest constricted. My gut heaved. My chair snarled against the floor as I pulled back and surged to my feet.

Then drove my fist into the countertop.

A couple of spoons jangled in the sink. Some glasses clanged inside the cupboard. Blood trickled down my knuckles onto the granite surface as the night wind and the crickets took back over.

How Margaux knew not to say a word was both comforting and troubling.

"Let me...show you to your room," I finally grated.

"I think I can find the way." When I growled at that, she gave back as good as she got. "For chrissake, Michael. Go to her."

I didn't—maybe couldn't—argue with her. Hearing the words out loud made the action permissible.

I knocked three times on Mom's bedroom door—like she needed the code to know it was me. Still, I called, "I'm counting to ten and then coming in. Get decent now if you have to."

She answered just before I hit nine—

With cold cream covering everything from her chin to her temples.

"Who do you think I'm in here being indecent with?"

I let the quip fall into beat one of my steely silence. Beat two, the stomp I took into the room. Beat three, the kick I gave to close the door behind me.

Before reaching up and swiping the white shit out from beneath both her eyes—

"Michael! Hey!"

—exposing the black and blue palette defining the crest of her left cheekbone.

I still didn't speak a word. Stalked into her bathroom, scooped up a towel, and jabbed it toward her. "You going to wipe that shit off so I can see everything, or shall I?"

She let out air hard through her nostrils. "You're not too

old to spank."

"You sure about that? Maybe I've regressed somehow. You haven't lied to me since I was five. Guess I have gotten old enough for that."

"Stop it. Right now." Her eyes darkened to the sienna of her purest fury. Growing up, I did everything I could to avoid that color. Now, I squared off to meet it more fully. "I'm still your mother. I deserve your respect."

"Though it's clear I don't deserve yours."

It was over the line. I knew it right away and thanked God that Margaux wasn't here to whack the side of my head for it. But I wasn't about to take it back. I'd inherited my pigheaded side from someone, and it sure as hell wasn't "Diplomatic" Roark Pearson. That left the woman standing in front of me, still glaring through her cold cream.

"I won't talk to you when you're like this, Michael."

"And I'm not throwing a tantrum about a toy you refuse to buy." I kept the words firm but took a page out of Dad's book on the approach. A step back. A kinder tone. "I'm mad about this, Mom, because I'm scared. Were you ever going to tell me about this? What if I hadn't come up tonight?"

She started swiping at the cream. I steeled myself for what she'd expose. "The guys at the PD know. I was going to have them call you after they decided what they could legally do—"

"So it was Declan." My teeth grinded on the words as my gut roiled on the truth. Part of me had clung to a hope she'd call me a paranoid nut job, look me in the eye and swear on Grandma's Bible that she'd simply run into a wall the wrong way. "He violated the restraining order. How much more *legal* do they need?"

Mom winced. Fuck. Not good. "It happened in town."

"In town?" I jacked my head back against the wall, hoping to knock free the confusion. "That's even better. This is a holiday week. You probably had a dozen witnesses."

She lifted her head. The damage from Dec's blow wasn't as grisly as I'd expected. The remorse in her eyes was another story. "I had to park a few blocks off Main because of the crowds. When I returned to the car—"

"That asshole moved right in."

"Michael!"

I jerked my head up, realizing at least a minute had passed. Sixty seconds of a fury so deafening and violent, it had driven me across the room in blind, floor-eating strides, fighting back the craving to tear the goddamn furniture apart with my bare hands. Her shout jerked my glare around to her again. Seeing her again. Wanting to vomit from the sight of what that sick fuck had done to her. No. That was too kind. Declan Pearson was a coward and a bully, plain and simple, waiting until he figured I wouldn't be in town for a while to make his move on Mom when she was alone and defenseless.

"I'm going to kill him." I didn't recognize the snarl coming out of me, but I liked it. Right now, I liked that bloodthirsty beast...a lot. "You and Dad will have to find a way to forgive me. I'm going to kill him and—"

"No." Her hand fastened to the center of my chest and pushed. "No, damn it. We're not going to handle this by swimming in his gutter!"

"Even if he drowns you in it—again?" I shoved back, stomping forward. "You're not a weak widow anymore. And I'm not a scrawny kid who won't fight back."

"No, you're not." She whispered it, raising a hand to my face as a tearful smile overcame hers. "You're a miracle of a man, Michael. My successful, smart, wonderful lawyer." She jutted her chin up with that—snagging my goddamn heart in the doing. Even with the damage wrought by Dec, she'd never been more beautiful to me. *Because of her pride in you. Her faith in you to do this like a man in the right, not a kid in a superhero cape.*

Step back. Another. Deep breath. Another. Unbelievably, I found myself pretending I was at the office, purposely distancing myself in the name of professional effectiveness. "So you filed a full report with the police?"

She nodded. "At the same time I was checked out at the medical center. Everything was documented in full, with pictures and details. But they have to proceed carefully, Michael. You know this. Half the town is under his spell. Many think selling the water down the hill is the best idea since hybrid apples. They only see the dollar signs."

"But not what that animal is willing to do for them. Or who he's willing to hurt."

I watched her battling the urge to say more. In the end, it would all be words we'd spoken before. The road we'd traveled together after Dad's death definitely hadn't been Richie and Marian Cunningham. Protecting her from Declan's drunk rages with a steak knife and a trashcan lid definitely wasn't the same as wondering whether we'd be having pot pie or pizza for dinner—but it had also fast-tracked me past the my-mom-sucks bullshit of normal teens. Angst had always been a waste of time I couldn't afford—at least until I'd met Laci. Though I'd vowed to keep that shit out of the emotional budget after she left, Margaux taught me that some bottom lines were simply meant to be blown. If you cared for people, the shitty times came along with the good ones, and loving them meant you wouldn't want it any other way. Easy enough with Mom—but what about the woman who'd brought the lesson for me?

I did not love Margaux Asher.

No way. Not even close. Approach a different runway, man. You are not that stupid.

Was I?

The question shot a king-size gulp down my throat as Mom stepped over again, pulling me into one of her love-you-till-the-end-of-time hugs. As her arms roped my shoulders and she gripped the back of my head, I thought of her once again as she'd been downstairs, after Margaux and I first arrived. Laughing. Connecting. Seeing every awesome, adorable thing that I saw about the woman—as I knew she would. As I knew she still did.

As if reading my mind, Mom murmured, "Let's talk about it some more in the morning. I want to remember this day as a good one—and especially this night. And getting to hang out with your Margaux for the first time."

"Mom," I growled.

"What?"

"You know what." I leaned back, delivering my rebuke of a glower head-on. "She's not my Margaux." Though, holy fuck, it felt good to simply say the words.

"Right." She might as well have been telling my six-year-old self that Steve Rogers really did survive for years on ice and returned to the world a superhero.

"She just needed to get out of the city for a while, and—"

"Mmm-hmm."

"—I figured she'd enjoy all the fun tomorrow. We'll go into town for the parade and—"

"I only ask that you keep it down, okay? Remember, the

bed in the guest room squeaks."

"Mother!"

"Good night, my son."

She pushed me back out into the hall and quietly shut the door—no doubt so I could hear her giggling through it.

Or was that the sound of fate, laughing in my face as I once again told myself that nothing I felt for Margaux remotely approached the fucking L word?

CHAPTER THIRTEEN

Margaux

And they called us the Apple Dumpling Gang...

Close, but not quite right.

Fish out of water, party of one?

Warmer, yes. Both were appropriate in this situation, though I wondered if there was anything the fine people of Julian, along with a few thousand of their closest friends, considered inappropriate on this fine national holiday. Here, the Fourth of July carried an invisible subheading—Everything but the Kitchen Sink Day—and they sure as hell meant it, in every grand, bunting-and-stars-draped meaning of the word.

Michael and I dropped Di off at the high school so she could help with staging for the grand production of a parade, kicking off in a few hours. She was accompanied by Pearson's orchard foreman, Carlo, who listened patiently to Michael's strict instructions not to let her out of his sight. While waiting for him to finish, it was impossible not to hear the more vehement parts of Michael's speech.

"That asshole isn't allowed...copy of the restraining order...if Declan thinks he can make his point like this..."

I didn't want to admit how much his fury made me a little gooey. Nothing about restraining orders and guys who punched women was remotely hot. But a man who protected his mom that way? Color me a bowl of rice pudding—sugar-free and dairy-free, please. Besides, I already adored the hell out of Di. She shared so much of the grace, class, and exuberance of her British royalty namesake, with whom I'd been obsessed as a child in my princess-themed bedroom. The world had already lost that beloved Di, and while it wasn't my place to know all the details about her bruise, I cared as much as Michael and Carlo about keeping this one safe and protected.

We decided to leave the truck at the high school and walk the half mile into town. I especially enjoyed the experience, teasing Michael about all the possible places he'd likely made out with girls during his years there—though, having enjoyed the man's moves firsthand, I was certain he'd done more than neck in these-here parts.

It was a crisp morning that would give way to a steamy summer afternoon. The mountain wind rustled through the trees, barely noticed by the people bustling below like carpenter ants around the carcass of a hornet. Michael's grin grew as we walked along, meshing his fingers into mine to guide me through the crowds.

He'd promised me the best breakfast of my life with such a sexy gleam in his eyes, I'd follow him into a pit of snakes if he asked. I'd thrown on a pair of shorts and a tank top and worked a quick messy bun, assured he'd return me back to the house for a tidy-up after we ate in town, as he called it.

"So this is your idea of a town?" I asked it as we skirted the chaos on Main Street by strolling up a side road.

He nodded, suddenly looking way too sober for a day devoted to fireworks and ice cream, while guiding me to a picturesque bench beneath a sprawling oak. "Can I see your phone real quick?"

I handed the device over, but not without a question in my gaze.

"Things will get much busier here within the next few hours," he explained. "I'm installing Find My Phone for you. If we get separated, you'll be able to see where I am."

"And you can see where I am?"

"Only if you let me."

I narrowed my gaze, toying with him a little before quipping, "Hmmm. I think I'll let you."

He chuckled while tapping in the settings but, before returning my phone, swiveled to snap a picture of me. After I made him do the same and then scooted next to him to review the shots, he reached over and squeezed my knee, inciting an instant little-girl squeal.

"How the hell do you land that every time on the first try?" I was only ticklish in one spot. He'd found it several months ago during one of my unguarded moments at happy hour.

"I'm good that way." He winked, flip-flopping my chest again.

"It's still no fair," I groused. "You know mine, but I still don't know yours. I'm beginning to think you don't even have one."

"Oh, I have one."

"Uh-huh." I batted his hand back, but he snaked it over once more, wrapping around both my calves and pulling my legs over his lap. And yeah...I let him. Because it felt damn good to. Because just giving in for a change, not worrying about hiding everything that brewed inside...that was nice too.

I took a chance on glancing up at him through my lashes. When he looked over at the same time, I quickly averted my eyes.

A low chuckle rumbled out of him. "You're so busted."

"Whaaaat?"

"I caught you checking me out."

"You wish." Once more I batted at him, but he caught my arm, this time pulling me all the way into his lap. Like a lovestruck high school girl, I slid right across the bench, surrendering to his strength.

When his lips came down on mine, I heard a tiny whimper come from somewhere...before realizing it was me. Unreal. I was desperate and horny from a kiss, like the teenagers we'd just been making fun of. But damn it, my need was reaching a critical level, and Michael Pearson was playing with fire. His kisses drove me insane as no other ever had. How the hell did he do it? He was a dichotomy, so much divergence in one incredible package. He was powerful and gentle, sweet and dirty, kind and cruel...in all the best ways.

In all the scariest ways.

If I ever did let him in my bed, he'd seep right into other things too. Hard lines would be crossed. Not a chance my psyche would emerge unscathed.

I forced myself to face the facts. Even here, locked in a desperate make-out, sorely tempted to let him drag me into the trees for wild monkey sex, I had to keep the walls up. Had to tread carefully. Had to keep his game plan in mind. And oh yeah, he had one. Come on, everyone did. Relationships were always giant chess games, everyone waiting for their opponent to make their next move. Knights and ladies did it down back halls with passed notes... These days the match was waged over coffee, via text messages.

But even with that knowledge, I was in dangerous waters with Michael Pearson—because for one of the few times in my life, I had an opponent I wanted to lose to. With every beat of my galloping heart, I longed for it. Take my white flag, Captain America. Please.

When we finally parted, panting and dazed, I blinked and looked away, left in a haze.

"I'm wishing for a lot of things right now, sugar." His voice had descended lower, a husky, yummy after-effect of our kiss. His crotch, pressing at the undersides of my thighs, was discernibly tighter too.

"Huh?" Damn it. A serious opportunity for full sexy snark, and that was all my brain could muster.

A low, sensual rumble vibrated from his throat. "Fuck me," he growled. "You're so gorgeous, all dazed and sex-struck like this."

"I am?" Opportunity number two, blown like a Yugo gasket.

He toyed with a wisp of hair gone AWOL from my bun. "Makes me want to skip breakfast altogether, if I'm being honest."

I reached up, rolling fingers over his wrist while letting out a long sigh. "You are not fighting fair, mister."

His gaze narrowed, crinkling the corners of his eyes. "Why are we fighting this at all, Margaux?"

"It's complicated, remember?" I flattened his hand against my face, savoring the warm security of his skin next to mine, if only for a moment.

Taking one minute to feel truly safe.

There was no way Trey would find me here. A former mining camp in the Cayamacas was the last place anyone would think to look for me. That made everything about this moment, small as it was, utterly mine.

It was like my pinkie ring from childhood. Andrea may have bought me every trendy outfit of the season and every perfect toy for my bedroom, but no material possession would ever mean as much as that ring.

Guess it was true what they said, about the smallest things being the best. Since I had few of them, I guarded mine with vengeance so my enemies wouldn't know how much they truly meant to me. These few minutes in the sun with this amazing man... Yeah, definitely added to the list. If Trey found out how much Michael meant to me, he would set out to destroy him too.

Resolve surged through me. I had to make the most of all the days I had here. I needed to fill my heart and head with memories now—for when we returned, everything would be stuffed away, pushed as far back from my head and my heart as I could get them. It was the only way to ensure they'd be safe from Trey and his filthy touch.

And yeah, I had to confront the possibility of the mandate including Michael himself.

Not yet. Now's for embracing the happy stuff only.

"Okay, let's eat." I pushed at him and righted myself. "Feed me, stud. I'm starving. After that, you can tour me through the rest of this happenin' hamlet."

Michael stood. But not without gaping like I'd sprouted a second head.

"What?"

"That was the strangest one-eighty I've ever witnessed, even from you. And God knows I've seen you pull some crazy shit, blondie."

I smacked him in the arm as I nudged at him to get going down the sidewalk. He obliged but yanked me close again, towering over me more than he usually did due to my thong-sandals in lieu of my usual heels. For once, I didn't pull away or make even one snarky excuse about needing to get something out of my bag, my pocket, or my trunk. I breathed deep, reveling in his great outdoorsy scent, though being up here brought out the foresty part of it more. His unique musk still tingled through my senses in all the best ways, inspiring me to wrap my arm around his waist and hook my thumb into his back pocket. I relished the little growl I received for the boldness.

We took a left on B Street and immediately came upon the wooden steps to a place called Buffalo Bill's. Lots of people were milling around outside, chatting and enjoying the sun.

"Wait here, and I'll put our name in." Michael was off in a flash before I could protest. Weirdly, I seemed to be the new subject of attention for half the people in the crowd. *Anyone have a venti latte I can hide behind, please?* Just as fast, I tried to laugh at myself. *Even fish out of water can embrace the scenery, girlfriend. Screw them if they've never seen a pair of Jimmy Choo flip-flops.*

The restaurant was decorated for the holiday with red, white, and blue bunting on the outdoor patio. Homemade flower boxes along the railing had matching flowers in them. It was quaint and pretty—and definitely not like any place I'd ever stepped foot in before. We waited for a few minutes before a voice called overhead.

"Michael! Party of two!"

"Lead the way, stud."

Michael was all mountain-boy charm once more, leading me by the small of my back toward the restaurant's entrance.

After Michael had eaten enough food for a small village, we walked back to the truck and then headed to his mom's to pick up the pies she'd made for the mayor's hospitality social after the parade. The farm was a lot busier now. Several crew members were loading up the petting zoo animals to take to the park for the kids to enjoy. In the same neighborhood—what wasn't in the same neighborhood in town?—was the Women's Club building, home of the annual quilting competition. During our first drive in, Di had confessed she had an entry this year but was nervous about her chances. She hadn't said that in so many words, but my ability to read people like a book had come in handy yet again. I'd grabbed her hand and told her I already knew hers was the best quilt in the contest. Her grateful smile was worth every drop of sunshine in the sky.

If she'd already crawled into my heart like this, I couldn't imagine the scope of Michael's love for the woman. Maybe I'd already sensed it last night, which had led me to ask about her face. I felt horrible for upsetting him but would've never forgiven myself for remaining silent either. Kind of crazy, all the things I unequivocally knew about this guy-who-wasn't-my-boyfriend. At the top of the list, his fierce protectiveness of the people he cared deeply about. Whoever had hurt his mother needed to be watching their six damn closely right now—because I sure as hell wasn't standing in the way of Hurricane Michael.

Just like that, Trey's snarling face flashed in my mind. I froze in the middle of changing my clothes for the parade. Epiphany time. As violent as Michael had been about shielding his mom from another attack was exactly how I felt about thwarting Trey from ever touching him. Put in that context, I was reassured about my vow to keep everything between us—passions, feelings, connections—held to the confines of this weekend alone.

It was simply the way things had to be.

I took a few minutes to freshen up, apply some sunscreen, and change into a little sundress, pale pink and delicate, that I often wore to functions down by the beach. Given the way the day was rapidly heating up, it seemed like an excellent choice. I combed through my hair and braided it off to the side, finishing up with a little pink lip gloss. Nothing was worse than a melting face of full makeup, so the natural look was it. I wondered what Michael would think about my freckles, which would certainly be coaxed out in force by the sun. It would probably be another thing for him to rib me about, which had lately been followed by a lot of kissing, so...win-win for everyone! I slipped into my perfect final touch, a great pair of worn-looking, low-cut cowboy boots—not bad at all.

Michael's voice drifted up the stairs as I came down. He was in the kitchen, giving final instructions to the staff members who'd be handling the petting zoo in town for the day—or at least he was until I cleared the bottom of the stairwell. As soon as I stepped off, his voice trailed, his jaw dropped, and he stood, staring. I quickly looked down, making sure my dress wasn't tucked into my panties or something just as mortifying. My attention snapped back up at the distinct spurts of stifled snickers. All three of the farm hands were now gawking at Michael and then at me. Back to Michael. Back to me.

I certainly wasn't going to turn down this opportunity. Preen.

"Mr. Pearson, you are busted."

"Indeed I am, sugar."

We both chuckled softly, though his sounded more like an opossum being strangled and mine had returned to the land of giggly tween. The moment wasn't that funny, but right now, everything was amplified, more vibrant. Funnier. Better.

"So is this okay?" I looked down at what I was wearing, suddenly feeling overdressed. "I brought other things."

"I know." He flashed a grin, but when it didn't budge my scowl, he leaned in and kissed me for several long minutes. Hell. Even without tongue, his kisses were matches on the panties. After he pulled away, keeping one hand on my face, he murmured, "You look stunning, as always—and quite perfect."

"You always tell me I'm perfect," I groused.

"Because you always are."

Oh, Michael...if you knew only half of it...

"Come on," he mumbled around one last kiss. "You might need something warmer for tonight, but we can always hop back over and you can change again. Sound good?"

I grinned and popped up to give him another kiss. The animal guys had left as soon as we started bantering, so right then, it was just us. "Sounds perfect."

Outside was the quietest I had seen the farm since arriving. With all the animals gone, a hush had fallen over the entire place. Except for a few chickens in the pen across the lot and Carlo's basset hound sleeping under the pepper tree, everyone had migrated to town for the day's celebrations.

It was almost showtime!

★ ★ ★ ★

The next three hours were more fun than I had during three-week vacations in Bali, Belize, and the south of France. The parade was an hour-long promenade of people passionate about their kids, their businesses, and their Wild West roots, complete with town members participating in a mock bank robbery before the sheriff rode in and rustled 'em up. I laughed until my stomach hurt at the purposeful overacting, followed by a gun fight and stunt show that was pretty damn good.

"They should hit up Hollywood!" I whispered as two of the bad guys tumbled into a hay wagon from the roof of the old bank building.

"Nah," he murmured back. "Their mamas usually encourage them to take up more noble professions." A smirk tempted his lips. "Like law."

That prompted my fast double take. "Wait. What? You—"

"Was Scoundrel Number Three. When I was in high school."

I punched his shoulder. "You were not." The dork was making the whole thing up to impress me. If he only knew how thoroughly impressed I already was...

But then he started reciting the last lines of the play along with the performers. I held back from my eager applause, damn glad I did, because the entire audience joined the actors for the very last line, apparently a huge tradition of the play. After their recitation, everyone instantly stood and joined the cast for a flag salute and rousing rendition of the national anthem. There was no curtain call or ovation for the actors themselves. Michael explained that there never was. The flag always got first billing.

Well, damn it. The people of this silly little town were starting to get to me. One of them just a wee bit more than the others...

Michael pulled me up from the shaded grass where we'd been watching the parade, and we walked hand in hand to see the exhibits in the park. Finally, we got to the Women's Center, where Di's quilt hung proudly with the others. If I could've paid someone to ensure she won, I would've done it in a heartbeat. Hers was the most beautiful entry. I wanted her to have that victory more than anything, and I told her so. I could tell the ribbon meant a lot to her, perhaps because of whatever had been going down behind the scenes with mysterious-restraining-order-man. But none of it was my business, though it all sat heavy in my heart.

Whoa. Back up the damn apple cart.

Did I just reference my heart in a sentence?

Christ. Maybe I'd been taking all the esoteric bullshit a little too seriously. Escaping? Capturing memories? Ohhh, no, no, no. These fucking hicks would not worm their way into my subconscious after one damn day. I couldn't let them do it. I couldn't let anyone do it.

Panic prowled up my throat, so hard and fast that I stopped. Michael didn't miss a second of it. He roped an arm around me, instantly steering me beneath a tree. "Easy, princess."

"Don't call me princess."

He shook his head, blowing me off. "What's the problem? Talk to me. Is it the heat? You're pale as a ghost all of a sudden."

"The heat," I echoed. "Yeah, that's—that's good."

"That's good?"

"I mean that's it." I forced out a smile, the one I knew would make him forget his own name, let alone my little slip. "I don't think I've had enough water. Don't worry about it, okay?"

He cocked his head like I was speaking another language. I should've known better than to use those words with this one.

"Come on. I'm taking you back to the house. We can cool you down in the AC."

"I'll be fine, Michael. I don't want to spoil your day."

"Blondie, if you pass out in the heat, I guarantee you my day will be spoiled."

I whacked his chest. "Dork."

"You want to know something else? I've done this every Fourth of July since the day I could walk. It hasn't changed a bit. I'm not missing anything."

He leaned over so we were eye-to-eye. God and all his angels, the man was gorgeous in me-Tarzan-you-Jane mode. Maybe it wouldn't hurt to let him think the heat had affected me instead of a freaking panic attack about discovering that some of my emotions had gotten shifted in flight.

"Let's go," I finally relented.

He kept turning back to check on me while tugging me through the crowd. About the fifth time he did, I openly girl-growled.

"What's wrong? Are you going to faint?"

"No!" I snapped. "But if you don't stop hauling me through this crowd like a naughty child about to be spanked—"

Take foot. Insert in mouth. Or, in this case, take libido and insert into brain. Since our gazes were already locked, I watched the same hotter-than-hot imagery sink into his mind too. My bare ass beneath his disciplining hand. My skin blooming for his touch. My body arched and ready to take his in...

Every hard, erect inch of it.

I looked down. Twisted my toe in the dusty earth. Looked back up to meet his burning gaze and flaring nostrils, making him look like some primeval beast on the trail of something tasty.

"Shit." I held up my hands. "Rephrase time."

"Too late. It's in there." He tapped on his temple.

"Yeah." I sighed.

"Yeah." His half-bark was gruff.

"Please, let's just go. Only without the dirty caveman approach, okay?"

I called that a better rephrase? He obviously didn't agree either. His eyes widened before hunkering down in a glower.

"I need a cold shower."

Clearly, he thought I wouldn't hear the mumble. I didn't tell him I did. When he reached back with his open hand, I took it in willing silence.

The ride back to the farm was quick—and quiet. Excellent, the two Qs were present and accounted for. Problem was, we were nowhere near the morning after—and the sexual tension between us thickened with every mile we covered. It didn't help that a couple of cats darted out of the road right after we swung onto the farm again—interrupted in the middle of their afternoon delight. Shit. The whole countryside was out to remind us that it was not only Independence Day but a Wednesday.

Hump Day.

He'd barely cut the engine before turning, one hand still on the wheel, to demand, "You okay?"

I rolled my eyes, pushed open the door, and jumped down to the ground on my own. "Yes, Florence Nightingale, I'm fine. I was a good little girl, drank all the water you shoved at me. I had a moment, I'm over it, I feel better. This has just been a lot of"—I waved my hand around—"ruggedness."

"Guess that smart mouth of yours has recovered just fine."

My smart mouth? What the hell was up with his? Okay, so I'd gotten out of his big, bad truckie-wuckie all by myself instead of letting him help. That didn't justify his accusatory tone. Unfair label? I didn't think so. He usually liked my snark. Why the sensitive Air Supply synths now?

I dialed it all back a couple of notches, taking the bees-with-honey approach. "Well, I appreciate you bringing me back, nevertheless. Thank you."

He huffed a little but stepped toward the house. "You're welcome. Come on."

I folded my arms and angled a playful grin. "Before I get my big farm tour?"

He stopped. Stared. "Now?"

"Now."

Huge method to my madness. We were literally the only humans on the grounds right now. If he and I were alone in the house, with no parental supervision...well, God only knew where the visions in our minds would take our bodies. And right now, I wasn't sure my body could handle what my mind had conjured doing with him—during every minute of every hour of this day.

I jutted my lower lip and adopted my pouty anime gaze. "You promised me a tour, Pearson-san. This morning, yes? You remember?"

The corners of his mouth quirked. "After you rest a little."

"I'm done resting. Come on, show me." I skipped across the dirt, pointing at a bunch of big tractor-looking things. "What's that?"

"Blast sprayer."

"And that?"

"Compost spreader."

"And that?"

He snickered. "Tractor."

"Really?"

"Yeah."

"Can I have a ride on it tomorrow?"

"Sure."

"Yesssss."

He rolled his eyes, but my excitement swayed him to relent about the tour. Looping his arm around my neck, he guided me through the main buildings of the farm's operational core, pointing out the harvesting sheds, cider mill, and butter and candle making shops, along with a couple of smaller buildings that handled the non-apple products—lemons, oranges, and even some exotic varieties of olives. By the time we were done, I was beyond impressed—and, much to my dismay, even more smitten with him. The pride in his eyes and voice were unmistakable.

"This is a different side to you," I finally said, stopping to rest a hand on his chest.

"Yeah?" He bussed my forehead on his way to gazing toward the orchards, contemplating the words. "And? Penny for your thoughts..."

"And...I like it." A lot more than I should have. Which made this spot, right now, the damn crossroads of discomfort. But no way in hell was I leaving. The shelter of his arms, the timbre of his heartbeat, the closeness of this moment, felt too damn good. Maybe just a few more memories. "So what made you choose law instead of all this?"

His deep laugh rumbled through his chest, against my cheek. "You had the big town experience today. That was as exciting as it gets up here, sugar. Would you want to stay?"

"Well, you and I were raised very differently."

"Yeah. We were."

Shit. I'd hit a nerve. "Hey." I pushed back a little, grabbing his gaze. "That's not such a bad thing, Pearson. You pretty much know the shit storm that was my childhood."

His gaze started to flash with fierce fire again. "What the hell does that mean?"

"Easy!" I retorted. "It means nothing but the obvious."

"Which is?"

I stepped away. His mysterious anger was back in full force, and I didn't feel like playing detective right now. "Just the fact that I'm a fish out of water here, right? It shows how—stunted I am. You deserve better than me, Michael. You really—"

Like a firestorm raging up the side of this damn mountain, he was back on me. The big barn's outside wall became my new posture corrector, hard and rough, as he slammed me against it. His full frame sandwiched me from the front.

"Don't talk about yourself that way. Ever. Again. Especially not while you're with me. Are we clear?"

My breaths were a staccato mess, escaping any way they could. "Yeah. Yes," I stammered. "Now back off!"

I didn't believe it possible, but he pressed in harder, his eyes still aflame...mesmerizing me now, like a sick pyromaniac. "I don't think so," he snarled—and stole the rest of my breath, my senses, and all coherent thought with the most mind-bending kiss I'd ever experienced.

Before I could stop it, a moan broke free. Another. I scratched both hands up his chest and over his rippling shoulders, locking them around his neck—never wanting to let go.

So much for keeping the fucking distance.

Like I could think about caring.

"Don't stop, Michael. Please don't stop!" Oh, hell. I'd never sounded more needy or desperate with a lover—but never had I been on fire like this for a man. Quench it, my senses begged his. Quench me. So thirsty. So hot.

So needing you. Now.

This was it. What we'd both fantasized and feared. Desired and dreaded. Craved yet run from, both in our stupid ways. Why? Why? With this kiss, more raw and real than any other we'd ever shared, the truth blazed at me as sure as the gravity beneath our feet, the blue of the sky above. Every other attempt we'd made, so illogical and ill-fated, flashed through my mind like a movie short, a gorgeous but fleeting preview of the real thing.

This man.

This fire.

This need.

Of course.

"Fuck," he rasped, pressing his forehead to mine. "Fuck, Margaux. I'm burning up."

I laughed against his lips and then whispered, "Me too. You're the fever, you know. It's you. It always has been you."

He pulled back far enough that I was consumed again by the full intensity of his gaze. "And it's always been you—for me. You know that, right?"

I nodded but still scrutinized the darkest parts of his stare. I needed to see where he was with all this. Not that I couldn't feel it already. His chest rose and fell against mine, breaths rapid and urgent and ferocious. His hands dug through the silk of my dress, keeping his erection fitted to my crotch with demanding force. He was power and sinew and passion, almost another man completely, though with all the best things still intact.

Now, he was going to be my lover.

God, yes. I wanted him. Needed him. Over me. Inside me...

All I needed was one nod. Just one affirmative nod from him and all bets—along with a hell of a lot of other things—would be off. I didn't even care if we fucked standing here up against this barn. This mission was a blaring, green light go, the second he said the word.

"Margaux—"

"Don't you dare say no to me, Pearson. I swear, if—"

"Not no sugar, just not here." He stumbled back from me a couple of steps, a little hobbled from the huge ridge demanding exit from his cargo shorts, but regained his footing and tugged at my hand. "Come."

I would've crawled over a bed of hot coals if he asked, but thankfully, he just towed me through the giant sliding wooden doors of the barn.

As we stepped inside, the sweet earthy smell of hay surrounded me. "Tell me there's a bedroom in here."

I turned, lifting both eyebrows, to find him coming at me again, sin and lust and dirty promises agleam in his topaz eyes.

"Nope. No bedroom. But if you're good, I'll let you stay standing while my cock's inside you. How's that?"

A laugh dropped out—while my pussy melted. "I'm not sure where Nice Michael goes when Filthy Michael comes out to play, but tell him to stay there a while."

He almost smiled—before the devil's own wickedness coated his gorgeous features again. "On it."

I had nothing for that. How could I, when he rolled out the big guns—literally. I watched, speechless and awed, as he whipped his T-shirt over his head, once more revealing the masculine perfection that haunted so many of my fantasies.

God—those tattoos. Those bulges. Even the begging-to-be-licked trails of the veins along his muscles. Wow was getting cliché, but damn, did it fit.

He taunted me even more by spreading his arms wide in order to slide the barn's heavy bolt into place. My body was overheating again, but this time the warmth started between my legs and bloomed out, trembling my legs, filling my belly, crawling up my neck, and making my vision cloud over. I swallowed hard and closed my eyes, trying to gather myself for a moment.

Impossible.

It was just damned impossible to fight it. To fight him and all these insane things he did to me. I'd always known things would be good with Michael if they got to this point, but this was good on steroids. Never had a man affected me like this... made me feel so utterly but deliciously powerless.

Me. Powerless because of a man. Heady, even. And glad for every fucking minute of it.

Maybe those hard thumps through my whole body were echoes of the flying pigs hitting the side of the barn.

Or maybe it was the magic of Michael Pearson.

From the day I'd started noticing boys, Andrea had drilled another of her mantras into me: *Fun that you control, darling—never the other way around.* But with Michael, everything was different. I didn't just like his leadership. I craved it. Was dizzy with the need for it. Whatever something Andrea had never received from a man...Michael had it. Into giant, Julian-sized barrels—my senses had just dived, headfirst. My equilibrium spun...and I liked it. My heartbeat careened...and I liked it. The need in my sex spiked to an all-time high...and I liked it. Would I ever get enough of him? Did I have the courage to even try?

Damn it.

More fear.

For a person more used to instilling the shit in other people, I'd taken a massive payback in the last month—though this version was one of the suckiest of all. It made me turn from him, wrapping arms around myself, once more struggling to pull my crap together.

But then once more feeling him press in...literally having my back.

I smelled him first, a mix of sunscreen and wind and pine, before shivering in all the best ways as he skated hands up my arms, over my shoulders, and then in at my nape before gently pulling the tie from my braid and letting my hair fall loose. He hummed in appreciation as he ran his fingers through it, fanning the strands over my shoulders. My head fell to one side as his lips danced up my neck on the other, goosebumping my skin even in the heat of the summer day. Incredible bliss... climbing need...

His lips slid up, grazing the shell of my ear. He used soft, tantalizing nips at first but ramped his aggression in response to my deep moans, biting and then licking, kissing and then sucking. Like a lion claiming his mate, he was a passionate force, now barely leashed. My breaths punched out, harsh and high, as I met his surges with long thrusts, rubbing against him in a pure animal show of need.

"Are you sure about this?"

I reached back to mold my hand around the erection pushing out from his cargo shorts. Oh...my. The ridge filled my hand and then some. My eyes grew heavy as my throat thickened, turning my voice into a sexy rasp. "I'm sure that I want you to fuck me. Give it to me until I can't walk straight.

Until I can't remember my own name. Until I—"

His large hand suddenly clamped over my mouth. "You trying to make me come right now, wicked girl?"

Beneath his hand, I grinned. Couldn't help it. Not only was his growl twelve kinds of a turn-on, but knowing he was suffering now as I'd been for months... Oh, sweet victory, you taste so good.

But payback, as they said, was a bitch.

He pulled back his hand, only to spin me around and replace it with his mouth. Much better than his hand, even if it did come with a crazy set of challenges—like the realization that I'd likely never be kissed this perfectly again in my life. Warm, delicious strokes of his tongue, wetting my bottom lip before he sank his teeth in, stinging just enough before he reverted to licks once more...all before he plunged all the way in, tangling our mouths with deep, ever-demanding passion.

It was a crash course in patience for me, not calling a single damn shot. Suddenly, my mind and body were free for other pursuits, such as learning what pleased him when I touched him. And learning what pleased me too. I reveled in the feel of his torso beneath my hands, so hard and honed and fascinating. The man had muscles where I didn't know any existed. It wasn't long before I entertained the thought of dropping to my knees, flipping open his fly, and—

Ground already covered. I was pretty certain I'd be on my knees when Michael said I would and not before. For a moment, just one, I considered testing the theory. A punishment from him might be fun...

I pushed the thought away when he peeled the straps of my sundress down my arms, making the built-in cups fall away from my breasts. I had gone braless today, knowing the heat would be too stifling for tight underthings, so he got the full VIP treatment, courtesy of my 36Bs, as I stood in a slice of sunlight streaming through the loft's high cut-out window.

"Damn." He breathed it more than anything, shaking his head, his eyes still fixated on my nipples. "You look like an angel in this light."

I basked in his lusty fixation. I wasn't one of these women's lib girls who screamed about being objectified. Sometimes, it was damn nice to be revered as a thing of beauty. It was also cleaner that way, and everyone knew where they stood.

"Angel?" I chuckled a little. "Pssshh. We both know that's the furthest thing from reality. So come put that mouth to better use." Yeah, so old habits died hard. I bounced off the saucy tone with an equally cheeky grin.

Michael didn't go there. Something definitely changed in his stare, and it wasn't his desire level.

"Hiding."

"What?" I was suddenly very conscious of my nudity. I stepped back, yanking at the dress straps.

"Don't," he growled. "Don't cover yourself from me. The inside or the outside."

Snark had become my bestie again. "Holy Sigmund Freud, Batman. You want a psych eval or a good fuck?"

"Oh, we're going to fuck. And it's going to be amazing." He stepped toward me again. Prowling was more like it. Holy shit, I wanted to cover up again. "But when it's all over, we will talk—about what you're always trying to hide from me."

I rolled my eyes. That was it. But it was apparently the right it, because his sexual energy exploded through the building like a damn Highlander quickening. I saw starbursts if not lightning bolts as he grabbed me again, spinning my back to his front once more. Ohhhh hell, yes. He held my arm behind my back like a criminal, and it was so hot, I wouldn't have fought him off for all the Louboutins in Paris.

By the time he leaned over and sank his teeth into my shoulder, shoving his knee between my legs at the same time, I was officially past thoughts, let alone any sense of shame. I ground my crotch on his thigh, pretty certain I'd be at orgasm in record time, if I could keep my pussy hard against him like—

"Naughty girl." He chuckled while pulling his leg back, hauling me harder against him with brutal force. "So used to doing everything for yourself, I see. That changes now, princess." He glided a hand around to my front, hiking my dress out of the way and swooping fingers into my panties in a move that was damned impressive. "Fuck," he grated. "Yes. Ohhhh, yes. This is...incredible. Feel how soaked your panties are, sugar. Was your naughty little pussy dripping all over them? Because you were thinking about me?" He curled two of those fingers in, flicking in firm strokes at the lips cushioning my core...and then spreading them. "Cream some more for me, beautiful." Flick, flick. "I want to smell it now." Spread. "Fill this fucking barn with the scent of your delicious cunt."

And I'd thought his mouth was talented? His fingers needed to have their own insurance policy. He added to his play on my pussy with strong, skillful strokes on my clit, inciting moans from deep within, echoing up through my mouth until I was whining into the crook of the arm he practically held me up by. The man still didn't relent, turning everything down there into a hot, wet tangle, dipping into my tunnel for extra moisture, which he worked back up over my clit again.

"Fuck, Michael! Please! I'm begging you. Is that what you want to hear? I'm begging now. I need to be fucked!"

He answered with another harsh growl against my ear before pulling me forward a few steps. I dragged my eyes open far enough to watch him plant both my hands atop a pair of stacked hay bales.

"See those binding straps?" He said it against the distinct crinkle of unwrapping foil. "Grab those and hang on tight, Margaux. I can't guarantee gentle this time around."

"Do you hear a single complaint?" I retorted—for which I got a reprimanding smack on both ass cheeks as soon as he lifted my skirt from the back. I held to my word. Not a syllable of complaint—especially when he delivered on what I'd been pleading for. One motion. Firm and forceful. He was ruthless and dominating, plunging until his hips hit my ass.

"Yes!" I screamed.

"Yesssss," Michael hissed. He'd gone still for a long moment, all his muscles trembling. "God damn, woman. You feel so good. Let me...just...regroup here."

I smiled. The ultimate compliment. He was on the verge of coming himself and needed a pause for self-control. Perfectly fine by me. This moment had been nearly a year in the making, and I knew he was going to make it good—and messy and brutal and incredible—with a fucking I'd never forget.

Who was I kidding? I already knew I'd never forget him.

"Beyond my wildest dreams," Michael murmured, raking his hands to my hips. He began moving inside me, his thrusts deep but gentle.

"Damn it," I countered. I agreed with him—this was fantasy-worthy stuff—but I needed...

"More. Please, please...more."

"How can I refuse my princess?"

We'd discuss his persistence with that princess shit during

the talk he insisted on later. Right now, there was only the pleasure. My God, the pleasure. Before long, Michael proved true to his word. His cock swelled as his lunges grew longer, harder, just the way I craved them. I followed his direction and gripped the hay bindings, partly for balance and partly so I wouldn't rub myself to a fast orgasm. I wanted everything about this union to last, knowing it wouldn't ever happen again.

I steadied my breath and fought to focus on how Michael felt inside me, around me, behind me. He was everywhere! *Don't let this end. Don't let this end.*

He was steady and thorough, thrusting at a nice pace but never amping it to full power. He teased me more by leaning to pluck at my nipples, driving in the burn by twisting them with knowing pressure. At the same time, with each inward stroke, his tight sack smacked against my swollen clit, adding to the pleasurable sensations on that end of my body too.

As he pinched my left nipple to the point that I cried out, he queried, "Feel good, baby?"

"Bastard," I groused. "You know it does." I shuddered. The squeezes he gave my breasts rained pure star fire down to my pussy, where the sensitive ridge he'd toyed with was still exposed, erect and crying for stimulation. "I need to come," I whimpered. "Please..."

"There's no hurry, sugar. Nobody will be back for hours. We have all afternoon."

"All afternoon?" I snapped. "For you, maybe."

That generated another spank, stinging deeper than the first. Fuck, it was...nice. When a moan tumbled out, shocking me with its keen desperation, I got a matching smack on the other side.

"You like that too?"

"I— I do," I admitted. First and last time for those words on my lips. "Michael...let's just...please!"

"Easy, beautiful. Try to let it build. I promise it will be worth it."

"Is that your point? Because I'm pretty convinced it's going to be worth it."

I couldn't take any more. Redistributing my weight to my left hand, I reached between my legs with my right. Christ, it felt good to take even a second of the edge off—which was about what Michael gave me before lunging back on me.

"No fucking way, blondie." He laughed. "Christ, you're a bad girl."

"Said the pot to the kettle?"

"You don't know the half of it."

No other elaboration came except the tight hold he enforced on me, pinning my arm at the small of my back again. Pearson bondage, revisited. I was a damn goner. Thank God he got the message about what it would take to end this for me. With his other hand, he reached around, starting slow circles on my clit that were timed perfectly with his thrusts. As his fucking increased, so did the rubbing.

Pure pressure. Pure heat. Pure heaven.

"Michael! So...close! Fuck me. Fuck me harder. Do it!"

I succeeded, at last, in breaking past his composure again. This time, he exploded at me in fire instead of frustration. So much better. Oh hell...so much!

He started slamming into me, rocking my entire body forward with each ferocious sweep. It was...fucking...awesome.

I was wound so tightly, ready to detonate. A fast look over my shoulder revealed Michael with his head thrown back, mouth hanging open, so damn sexy. Well, that did it. Seeing the desire I'd incited in him...I was lost.

And tumbled headlong into the ecstasy he gave me in return.

"Michael!"

"Margaux!"

"So good!" We yelled it in unison as the fire finally swept us, tearing through our bodies with searing synchronization. As my sex clenched and gripped, his throbbed and pumped. I was stunned to glance up and see the roof and walls intact, not ablaze from the combustion of our passion. As Michael continued emptying himself, groaning harder from the release, one word insisted on resonating through my head.

Finally.

We'd really gone there. Really done this. And it was as explosive, extraordinary, and astonishing as I'd hoped...and feared.

Sensations I couldn't even come close to processing yet.

Many minutes and a lot of shuddering thrusts later, we panted together in sweaty, shaky, wordless wonder. Sometimes, moments couldn't be made any better by talking. The afterglow from mind-bending hay-barn sex was definitely one of those ideals.

He fell away from me, peeled off the condom in an efficient *thwick*, and paced away, likely in search of a trash can. When he returned, I had righted my clothes. He'd managed to zip up, but his shirt was still lying on the ground where he'd tossed it. I didn't have a problem with that at all.

I'd started plucking hay from my hair, making him chuckle softly. He wrapped his arms around me, drawing me tight and close once more, before planting the kiss to end all kisses on my lips. He was gentle yet commanding— tender but absolutely demanding.

How did he do it? Manage to be so many things in one scarily perfect package? It wasn't fair. I found myself ruminating on the possibility of—shit—keeping him around. Even smiled a little from the idea, giving him a peek at my dimples, imagining what it would be like to have this kind of magic around all the time. Now that was a nice thought...

Except that it was impossible.

No way, no how.

Time to call in the guards. Erect the walls and get out of Dodge while I could.

Except there was a problem with that plan too. Michael saw right through it.

"Damn it, Margaux. Don't do it."

I huffed to buy time. "Do what?"

"Slam those walls up. Then distract me from them with some snarky remark. Some clever little that-was-good-for-a-beginner zinger. It's not going to work anymore."

I smirked—and meant it. "Did it ever work with you? Really, I mean?"

"Nah. But I played along for a while like a good sport, didn't I?"

"Yeah." I couldn't help but grow the smile to a chuckle. "You did."

He tightened his embrace while his mien sobered. "I wasn't kidding before. I'm not now. I want to talk to you about what's going on here—between us. There's no one here to interrupt us, no one to run interference for you like usual." He dipped his head, seeming to know exactly what angle was best for the light to capture the piercing gold glints in his eyes. "Let's do this, Margaux. Lay our cards on the table, once and for all."

He tried pulling me to sit beside him on the hay bales, and I instantly wrinkled my nose. "Can we move this to the house? That stuff is animal dinner, you know."

He shook his head. "Nope. Here. Now." And, I swore, purposely kept his shirt off to emphasize the force of his assertion. "You'll get in the house and throw up a thousand distractions."

Shit.

Busted. Again.

My chivalrous not-boyfriend retrieved his shirt and laid it out flat so I could sit on the stinky animal food beside him. I had no escape. Like the sex, this was going to happen too—but if that was what he wanted, he could start first.

And he did.

"I'm just going to say it," he stated, reaching for my hand. "I'm falling for you, Margaux Asher. I think I did a long time ago, actually. I think maybe it was that time you chewed my ass for getting you a mocha instead of a latte from the coffee cart at the office..." He let that trail into his boyish-gone-sexy grin on me—not a fair move in the slightest, though I admired him for it.

I had nothing in return for him.

My mind was too busy with alarms.

Red Alert.

Red Alert.

Red Alert.

All women went through the same thing when a man laid himself at her feet.

Right?

While I waged that inner battle, the man sat there in bare-chested, hopeful-grinned beauty...and expectancy. If I said nothing, he'd finally get the correct gist—that I simply didn't have the emotional tools for this—and all that brilliance in his gaze would mist over to disappointment. Better now than later, I guess.

No.

Shit.

Say something.

Do something.

"Okay." He finally broke the silence. "So am I off-base? I wasn't the only one engaged here, yeah? Because that was fucking amazing, right?"

"Yes. Yes," I blurted. "You're right, Michael. It was amazing. Thank you, stud."

His smile could have lighted the whole highway back to San Diego. I took a relieved breath. At least I could give him that. Shit, he wasn't asking me to marry him or wear his letterman's jacket. He simply wanted to know if my socks had just been rocked off. I'd given a thoroughly honest answer.

God. How low had the princess been brought? It was unbelievable but true. I'd found a man in this world I didn't want to lie to. Thank God he didn't press for anything more, because I had no idea if I'd be able to resist. Even now, I yearned to fall to my knees in front of him, stare up into his breathtaking gaze, and proclaim that I was falling for him too.

Most ridiculous idea ever.

That was before factoring in the danger of it as well. All the shit in my life that neither he nor Di deserved to have dragged up to this paradise. I could never expose them to that risk—and would never forgive myself if they were collateral damage of Trey's demented schemes. God only knew what he had cooked up next for a demand, but I'd give the bastard a kidney if it meant keeping Michael and his mom out of it all.

My resolve from the morning was newly cemented. I'd spend the next few days here, savor and enjoy everything I could, and then leave it all safely behind when I returned to San Diego. My heart would be torn out in the process, but there was no other choice.

And for the second time in one day, I'd referenced my goddamn heart in a sentence.

Damn you, Michael Pearson, for showing me things better left undiscovered.

CHAPTER FOURTEEN

Michael

I woke up with a smile on my face.

Yeah, a real one. Not the left-over-from-the-sex-dream kind. Not the oh-yeah-it's-Saturday kind either.

It wasn't Saturday. But I almost wondered if the dream thing was a factor. Maybe all the scenes in my head were just that and not the memories I'd tagged them as.

If that was the case, I didn't care. Not one fucking bit.

Margaux in that incredible little dress. Her sassy ankle boots. Her messy, take-me-to-Nashville braid. The way she'd delighted in the parade like it was a multimillion-dollar Broadway spectacle. The way she'd become Mom's cheerleader for the quilt competition. Even the way she'd gone all possessive alpha bitch at the diner, climbing into my lap with the surety of a minx.

I'd liked that part a lot. Almost as much as what we'd done in the barn after getting back here...

If it had been a dream, then I was left with only one choice of action. Take hammer. Pound self in head. Pass out again, for the chance of reliving the best fucking Fourth of July I'd ever had—with the exception of worrying like hell about Mom until Carlo came and took over.

I shifted a little, gazing out at the sunshine filtering

through the trees, smiling at a mountain jay that landed on a branch outside the window. I grinned and murmured, "Yo, buddy. How's it hanging?"

And now I was talking to birds. Add a tiara and a catchy tune, and I'd be ready to take the act up the freeway to Disneyland.

I still didn't care. Another shift of my knee later, it was clear my cock didn't either. I hissed as the movement dragged the sheet across everything, moistening the fabric with arousal that was very real, even if its inspiration hadn't been.

I exhaled hard but quietly. Fuck. This boner wasn't going away on its own.

Was there time to do something about it?

I slid a hand toward my groin. My dick jerked in anticipation, but I stopped short of getting down to business. Another glance out of the window. It wasn't long after sunrise. No way Mom wasn't awake yet, though I didn't hear her downstairs. Good chance she was already up and out of the door, maybe touring part of the orchard with Carlo.

And Margaux?

The guest room was next door. I didn't hear her moving around in it. If she was still asleep...

You can just sneak in, slide under the covers with her...

And be paranoid about every damn squeak the bed made.

I palmed my balls. And clenched back a moan. Already tight and ready. Dream Margaux had gotten me worked up like a hopeless sex addict. But was it addiction when only one woman filled me with this kind of craving? Made my shaft spurt even more as I pulled the sheet away from it...

The jay watched in curiosity as I slid my fist up my length. I looked away, closing my eyes, retreating to the haven of my mind.

The barn there. The woman inside that barn.

Her lips locked beneath mine.

Her skin, so pliant beneath my fingers.

Her body, arching to me. Against me. Around me...

Humming for me?

I froze.

No. She'd made lots of sweet music for me in the barn, but none of it had been...hummed.

"Shit."

She was awake.

I bolted upright. Winced as my head whacked the headboard. Hissed while jerking the sheet up to my waist, as if she was going to walk in on me any second. Right. Go ahead and work that virginal-Victorian thing, Mr. Modesty—especially after what your squeaky-clean mind just conjured.

I growled before Zen-breathing my way to my feet. I didn't dare glance down, though ignoring the issue sure as hell wasn't going to diminish it—especially as she injected some singing between the humming. Shit. The husky threads in her speaking voice wove through her singing too. A little Bonnie Raitt, a little Karen Carpenter, a lot of sweet, sexy woman...

I stifled a moan as her little tune seeped through the walls—and zapped straight between my thighs. Think about root rot. And aphids. The pile of work on your desk. Bill O'Reilly.

Uh-uh. Nothing worked. No damn way this thing was going away on its own now.

I needed a better plan.

Time for cleaning up my act—in an ice-cold shower.

Wincing with every move, I wrapped the sheet around

my waist and crossed the room to the dresser. Inside were the standby clothes I always kept here for impromptu visits. With underwear, khakis, and a T-shirt in hand, I turned for the door. The bathroom was just three steps across the hall—

Where the shower now spurted into action.

"Damn it."

Again whispering, I pressed my forehead to the doorjamb. She'd beaten me to the punch. Worse, she hit the volume button on her singing to combat the din of the water.

Options to weigh. Stand here and listen, using the magic of her voice and the fantasy of her body to finish off—or tell Mr. Modesty to go hang in the wind and get my ass in there on a fact-finding mission? If yesterday was just a dream, this was a damn good excuse to find out. I'd either be screamed out of the bathroom or welcomed into heaven. One way or the other, I'd be able to put on my clothes without fear of breaking off something vital.

I took ten additional seconds to glance out of the window at the end of the hall. The trip was worth it. Mom's car was gone. Thumbs-up number one from karma. I hoped she'd be on board for the second as well.

A testing turn of the bathroom doorknob gave me that answer quickly enough.

Hell, yes.

Once I entered, I let the sheet drop with my clothes on top of it. Better for a fast getaway, if all this shit hit the massive fan.

Wasn't like I could get any other drop on her. Mom had remodeled the bathroom last year, taking out a wall and two closets to clear space for a fireplace, a massive tub, and a stall shower with glass walls on three sides.

And thank God for her extravagant design choices,

because I sure as hell never thought I'd behold a sight as incredible as this.

The water on her skin. Shimmering on her shoulders. Cascading down her thighs. Beading on the curls between those thighs. Dripping off her perfect coral nipples.

Something finally tipped her off that she was no longer alone. Margaux whirled, alarm claiming her face, but the second her gaze dropped over my nudity, she shoved it aside for an impish grin.

Backtrack. Impish, my ass. The woman went straight for seduction mode, care of the shameless water siren she so totally resembled.

"Good morning, Captain America."

That loosened me up enough to smile. "And hello there, Aquawoman."

She cocked her head. "I'm not sure they ever made an Aquawoman."

"Oh, they did." I took a step, never looking away from her. "And she was hot."

"Okay." She shrugged, starting at imp but ending at vixen. "Then I'll be her." As I approached by another step, she pivoted, letting the water pour along her front again. "She's got a kick-ass costume, right? Think I could fill it out okay?"

Christ. She could talk superhero while looking like a goddamn sex kitten. *Michael Pearson, you are the luckiest fucker alive.* "Hmmm," I murmured, running a finger along the glass still separating us. "I think I may need to collect some... research data...just to be sure."

She nodded with mock gravity. "Of course, Captain. I understand completely. I mean, if we're going to fight bad guys to...geth..."

Her voice gave way to a gasp as I whipped open the door and lunged next to her in one motion. With the next, I pinned her into the corner of the stall, diving my lips against hers, groaning at the erotic perfection of her slicked, gleaming body. Without breaking the kiss, I shoved shampoo and liquid soap bottles off the built-in, waist-high ledge before hiking her bottom up onto it.

Fuck. Yes.

This was just where I needed her—and would even say I'd dreamed of her, except this surpassed even my most incredible fantasies. With her breasts smashed to my chest, her hands gripping my hair, and the water sluicing between our bodies, I questioned the reality of it all—and once more told my brain to shut the hell up. *Dreams don't get better than this, asshole. You want to prep a fucking brief about it, or just show some gratitude and enjoy it?*

Steam. Skin. Wild, wonderful wetness...flowing with her whimpers of growing passion...

Gratitude, here I come. Damn near literally...

I forced my lips away from hers, sucking down air, trying to give my cock some room to regain control. "Damn. Damn." Much easier said than done. My dick was hard as a fucking tree limb, pulsing against her stomach, the head twitching as the water continued to tease it. The press of our bodies ensured the perfect fit of my balls against the slick lips at her core—but I wasn't moving them even if the Big One hit the state right now and brought the house down around us.

Margaux's forehead crunched. "Hey. You okay?"

It took a long second to process the underline of her voice. I'd never heard her get pitchy like that. It was different than arousal and difficult to—

Holy shit. Was she...worried? About me?

"Fine," I managed. "I'm fine." My shock about her concern was instantly obscured by my need to ease it. "It's fine. It's..." I shuddered as she lowered one of her arms, changing the water streams so they taunted more of my crotch. "Uh, yeah. It's—it's fine."

Her gaze flicked down. A smirk twisted her mouth. "Fine is just the start."

I smiled through my torment. God, I dug it when she masked her nervousness with sarcasm. The trait used to drive me insane with curiosity, always knowing there was more behind it than a need to be the funniest girl in the room, but when I finally figured it out, my file of obsession for her thickened by a good inch. There she was, assuming herself to be cloaked in her snarky little shell, when she was never more exposed to me. Or beautiful to me.

Or ripe for me to swoop in again, kissing her deeply, deeper still—but never deep enough. Never down as far as she'd affected me. But hell, I could sure try. And I did. Pulling her close again, I spread her mouth with the force of mine. Plunged in, taking her hot depths with urgent strokes and a hungry growl. She whimpered. Again. The sound intensified as she locked her legs around my waist and started rocking, using the press of our bodies to knead my erection to a new level of need.

God damn. I'd never use a regular shower massager and be satisfied ever again.

"Fuck!" It exploded from my lips onto hers. Blood pounded to dangerous levels up my dick. "Sugar, if we don't stop—"

My hiss ripped the rest of it away as she dug her nails into both my ass cheeks. "That's the general idea here."

I broke into another grin, shaking my head while kissing over the droplets on her chin, nose, and forehead. I dipped my head to her neck, pulled by the hypnotizing sheen of the water on her skin. Yesterday's passion in the barn had been one of the best experiences of my life but hadn't included the chance to fully take in her beauty like this. Taste her skin like this. Openly lick and suck and brand her with my mouth like this...

I trailed my kisses lower. Lower. Then bit down into her breast, letting her know I'd only just begun the assault.

"Shit!" Her cry bounced off the glass walls around us as I pulled her nipple between my teeth. "Oh, Michael..." As I skimmed toward her other peak, she grabbed my head, stopping me hard. "No! If you bite that one, I'm going to scream. And your mom—"

"Is already gone." I grinned. Rolled my tongue over her erect tip. Then dug my teeth in on that side. Harder.

And ohhhh yeah, did she scream.

My bloodstream did the same. I turned into a goddamn inferno, muscles bunching, nerves ablaze, heartbeat roaring through my ears. The rest of her breast slid easily into my mouth, filling me with the clean, feminine taste of her, mixed with a little of the vanilla soap she'd been using before my intrusion. As I suckled and scraped at her flesh, more delicious moans spilled from her, vibrating through her chest, chiming through my senses. Every few licks, I pulled away to let the water in, lifting her nipple for its watery tease. I kept it up simply for the joy of hearing her moan be interrupted by an aroused little laugh, until she couldn't take it any longer and tried squirming away. Not that it worked for her, especially after I grabbed her thighs and pulled them farther apart, exposing the dark-pink layers of her pussy to my hungry gaze.

"Oh, my God," she finally spurted on a little giggle. "You!"

"Yes?" I angled my gaze, communicating it wasn't rhetorical.

"You're a fucking scoundrel!"

"Mmmmm." I ran my thumbs along the inner flesh of her legs. "That sounds about right." So very right. Holy shit, what this woman did to me...the things she brought out in me...all the dirty, wicked things she made me long to explore...

Sure, I'd been naughty with women before. Yeah, even ventured to the nastier nuances of the meaning—but had always stopped myself short of letting the real animal all the way out of the carefully guarded cage within.

Margaux Asher saw every inch of my animal.

She didn't just see my animal, she understood him. Knew him. And, best of all, could more than handle him.

And he was crazy about her for it.

He prowled up from deep inside, newly unleashed, teething her from shoulder to shoulder with his possession, savoring every sweet snarl, rasp, and bite she gave him in return.

Her head thrown back, both hands now tangled in my hair, she blurted, "Holy shit. The scoundrels are out, and Mama's not home. Maybe I should fire up the bat signal."

I slid my head down, taking her other nipple into my mouth. "I think I have a good power source right here."

Her husky laugh steamed up the air even more. "I'm not sure about that. I mean, you're an awfully...big...threat, Mr. Scoundrel. All of Gotham is likely in peril from you."

I sucked her in a little deeper. "Unless a hot dame sacrifices herself for the cause and distracts the bad guys long enough..."

"There is that plan." She hissed and arched as I nipped at her again. Her nipple was swollen and red, the flesh surrounding it abraded from the burn of my stubble. Gazing at my marks on her skin...it was goddamn amazing. My cock jerked with such brutal need the veins stood out like a topographical map. More blood pounded up my length, making it stiffer, longer, harder.

I sucked her deeper. God damn, she tasted good—a taunting made no easier when an image flashed to mind, spiked by wondering what her juices would taste like if I added her pussy to the blend. As I imagined my tongue winding its way through her soaked heat, my teeth tightened on her breast, making her scream again. She finished the cry with a desperate, demanding little buck of her hips.

"Shameless temptress," I growled. "You sure Gotham PD didn't send you as a distraction?"

She blinked up at me, droplets collecting like beads of gold on the tips of her amber lashes. "You're the one who kidnapped me, honey."

I cocked my head and grinned. "Oh, yeah. Shit. I am a scoundrel."

Her eyes grew heavy. "The worst kind." Then the edges of her lips curled up. "In short, my dream man."

"Funny you mention that."

"What?"

"Dreaming." I swept upward, capturing her mouth again, kissing her so hard our teeth clashed. With our gazes still locked after, I grated, "Because I'm still unsure that I'm not."

She swallowed hard. Then rasped, "Then let me help convince you otherwise."

It only took another tug of her hand to bring my lips down on hers again. We fused, open-mouthed and devouring, passionate and greedy, sliding against each other like a pair of soaked, horny beasts. She moaned. I snarled. She whimpered. I growled. Between it all, our panting breaths threaded through the shower's rain, forming a fog of thicker lust on the glass walls.

Her hands dropped from my scalp to my shoulders. I pushed harder into her mouth as her nails scored my skin.

Fuck, yes.

I repeated it aloud when tearing away from her lips to bite at her jaw, ear, and neck, needing to imprint her body just as she had embedded herself into me...and not just those hot little scratches on my skin. Margaux Asher was my newest tattoo, inked permanently into the worse space I could have asked for—my psyche. She was going to change me. She already had. But in how many ways?

And did I even want to know the answer to that right now?

I stepped back from her again but only to reach out of the shower to the counter. Raincoats had never made my "favorite things" list, but just the thought of getting inside Margaux, even with a condom, was number one with a bullet on the countdown now.

She made the roll-on even better with her fixated stare, puckered areolas—and constricting pussy. Fuck. Fuck. The gates of heaven, bracketed by the thighs of an angel.

She added to the real-life fantasy by sliding a couple of fingers between her legs, stroking into the glistening depths. I caved to a surge of Tarzan, lunging once more against her, jerking her hand out of the way just in time. "That's mine to play with right now, sugar. And mine to please."

I swept her other arm up too. Captured them both beneath one hand while spreading her wider with the other. She was open as far as she could go, legs flattened at right angles against the stall's walls.

"Scoundrel."

"Temptress."

Her lips curled higher. "You going to fuck me, bad guy, or give the wind the satisfaction?"

Finally, I laughed. "You're asking for it...you know that, right?"

"Whatever."

With a grunt, I reached for the shower's other shelf, snatching a bottle of scented baby oil. Thank God for Mom and her weakness for shit like this. I didn't like using baby oil as a general rule, but in this pinch, I'd take it. There were several choices, but I lucked out, getting a container that smelled like oranges and lemons—an ideal match to the natural tang of her arousal, thickening the air by the minute.

As I trailed a path of oil from her navel to her pussy, a high, feline cry spilled from her. "Michael!" She gasped, wriggling hard, working the oil over the sensitive inches of her pouting cunt. "Oh damn...that's so...ahhhh!"

I trickled a little more. Then teased back her hood, uncovering the beautiful strip of nerves beneath and poured on a little more.

"Shit! Scoundrel! If you don't fuck me n—"

Making her interrupt herself with a scream was even better when accomplished by smacking her mound. I did it lightly at first, using the tip of the baby oil bottle, but her outcry was so perfect, I threw the oil down and used my palm for a second spank, making her shriek even louder, writhe even harder—

And tempt me even more to come right there.

Wouldn't the little minx love the hell out of that?

Time for some control. The kind both of us would get something out of.

"Orders, temptress? Does someone need another reminder of who's in charge when we're naked?"

"Are you kidding m—" She jerked, swinging her head, trying to glare. "Wait. Are—are you laughing?"

I answered that by unraveling a gloating chuckle in her ear. And sliding my thumb along both her wrist pulse points. And pressing my other thumb against her erect, wet clit.

"Michael!"

I replaced my thumb with my cock. Holy Christ, she felt good. Her tissues quivered beneath my head, now taking a dip in my own precome. I clenched my jaw and my ass, holding back the arousal from swelling my dick any further. I had no damn idea how I injected a new smile into my voice but managed to pull it off, taunting, "Who's in charge, beautiful?"

She spewed a sound between a sneer and a growl. "Bastard!"

"Not exactly the delivery I was looking for."

"Fine. Mister Bastard."

"Keep it up, beautiful. I know I can."

She busted out a full snort. "I highly, highly doubt—ahhhh!" *Smack.* Her mouth became an O as perfect as her pussy—red, swollen, and full of filthy possibilities.

"Your cunt is so ready, Margaux. Give me the words, and I'll fill it with my cock. I'm burning up, sugar. I want to make you come so many times I'll have to carry you out of here. Just give me the—"

"Okay!" she shouted. "Okay! All right!" Her chest heaved in and out, threatening to entrance me again, though not succeeding. That honor went to her eyes, bright with savage desire. "Y-You're the man. Y-You're in charge." A shiver ripped through her. "Oh, God...it's never been this good. Please, Michael...I'll be good too. Just—just—ohhhh!"

Her surrender was my undoing. I'd harnessed the lightning. Tamed the tigress. I was fucking Hercules. And now, I was going to screw her like it.

I widened my stance. Seated myself tighter between her legs. Framed her face with my free hand, forcing her to the perfect angle for the plunge of my lips.

As I lunged up into her wet, waiting body.

Her scream detonated into my mouth and down my throat. Damn good thing since my answering bellow consumed everything from my balls to my brain.

Heat. Softness. Tightness.

Stabbing her. Stretching her. Claiming her.

Losing myself completely...

"Damn!" she cried. "Yessss!"

"There's my princess." It growled out of me, sliding into the drops along her neck as I thrust even deeper. As my mind faded to nothingness, letting my body reign over my consciousness, I wondered if the shower had gotten so hot, we'd simply taken off and were rocketing toward the stratosphere. Maybe that explained the thunder taking over my heart, the swirling vortex replacing my mind.

And maybe I was missing the fucking point. That this had nothing to do with G-forces, rocket boosts, and the speed of sound. This was her. Margaux Stiletto-In-Your-Balls Asher, surrendering to me with complete trust, with absolute passion—and not just in arcing generalities. It was the details, beautiful and unforgettable, all of them. The curl of her fingers around my hand. The clamp of her walls around my cock. Her panting breaths against my shoulder. Her heels sliding against my back.

Her whole body, taking everything I could give. Then demanding—

"More." It began as the huskiest, sexiest rasp I'd ever heard from her before crumbling into a mewl that grabbed hard at my balls. "More... Please, Michael...harder! More!"

Well, that fucking did it. My new status—unhinged. She tore off the door of my control, making me fling it to some distant mental corner as I clutched her waist and yanked her in, angling her for the most ruthless penetration I could give. Before I finished my next thrust, her head knifed back, another shriek ripped from her lips, and her jaw stiffened in something between agony and ecstasy. I let a bellow tear free too, even while struggling between the victory of invading her and the fear of hurting her. But God help me, if she begged me to stop... freight train, meet act of God. I was consumed, blinded to everything but the fire of her beauty, the blaze of her pussy, the frenzy of my lust.

"Yes," she got out between gasps. "So good. So good!"

I bent my head to study the tension on her face. "Hurting... you?"

"Yes." Her eyes flew open, as if she knew I needed to see them dilated nearly black with arousal. "Yes. Need. More." She pushed her face forward, snatching my lip between her own. "Don't. Stop. Don't you dare fucking stop. Hurt me, Michael. Fuck me!"

Pressure built, intense and unyielding.

My balls pounded.

My thighs clenched.

My senses raced...wondering what the fuck she was doing to them. How the hell she was consuming them, incinerating them—only to stir them into something wholly new. I could only moan from the overwhelming force.

Until I realized...

The force was us.

Passion given flight. Connection given purpose. Force given form.

Tension granted release.

She screamed in the throes of her climax seconds before the flood of liquid fire rushed up my cock and burst, dizzying in its delirium. I let the flow carry me, both heads consumed with ecstasy, until I opened my eyes—to the best damn moment of this morning so far. Beholding her, still lost to the depths of her passion...damn. She was exquisite. With her head still arched back and her breasts pushed forward, she induced comparisons to a sacrificial maiden, offered up to a lascivious pagan god.

If that was the case, then this god was mightily appeased. I wouldn't be razing the village today. Alternate plans for my maiden hostage, on the other hand...

Those could also wait. Right now, all I wanted to do was savor her. And I did. Still balls-deep, I rocked into her for countless minutes, treasuring the press of her skin, the warmth of her breaths, the clutch of her body. When the water began to cool, I pulled out in order to turn it off and ditch the condom. Margaux shivered and wiggled, preparing to scoot off the ledge, but I yanked her up against me instead. True to my pledge, I carried her out of the bathroom and into the guest room, gently setting her on the chaise at the foot of the bed. A quick double-back, and I returned with towels, wrapping one around her shoulders while using the other to dry her body.

"You're still soaked." Thanks to all her shrieking, her voice was sexy-as-fuck raspy. Unbelievably, my cock reacted with a hopeful jerk.

"And your teeth are knocking like castanets." Okay, that ought to keep the fucker subdued—for at least a minute. Wasn't passing up the excuse to get my hands all over her again though. While she was still sex-hazed and oblivious, I took full advantage of swiping at her curves to openly gawk at every one of them. "My God, you have a beautiful ass."

She canted saucy eyes over her shoulder. "You making plans for it, stud?"

The towel fell from my hands. "Fuck."

On a throaty laugh, she whirled back around and slinked right onto the bed, all the while swaying those golden curves in open invitation. "Come on. Help me get the sheets...wet."

"Fuck." It bore repeating. Maybe a few more times after this.

"What? You know where the spare sets are, right? We'll clean up after we're done. Mama won't know a thing."

I had no idea how I managed my answering chuckle. "I'm about three seconds from taking you up on that—"

"One, two, three. *Ding ding ding!*"

"—but I have some other plans for us today."

She bolted upright, a smile twitching her lips—dropping a surprise on me equal to the one I'd given her. I'd expected a petulant pout at thwarting her seduction. On the other hand, the woman might get her way after all. She didn't make a single move to wrap back up in the sheets, just sat there looking like some classic erotic painting from hundreds of years ago, smiling and decadent, naked and damn proud of it.

And I'd made her look that way.

Her hair, tangled from my tugs. Her wrists, still a little red from my grip. Her nipples, engorged from my bites. And the strip of tawny curls between her thighs, such a soft deception for the fierce things I'd done there...

I could get used to looking at you like this, sugar.

Dangerous thoughts. Very, very dangerous. Though we weren't asleep, this all still wasn't reality. I'd all but zip-tied her and wrestled her ass up here. The fact that she delighted so much in the dream was no stand-in for the dark secrets she'd left behind in the city...the demons that'd driven her back into her tower again. The enemies she wouldn't tell me about, let alone seek my help in fighting.

But maybe getting her this far from them was the key to unlocking her trust about revealing them. Maybe just a little.

And maybe today was the day she would.

I had to try.

Damn it...I had to try.

Giving up on her, especially after the last two days, was not a goddamn option anymore.

★ ★ ★ ★

"Michael!"

The moment instantly made me wish I'd recorded it—not that any playback would be able to duplicate the magic of it. The delight in her smile. The awe in her eyes. Her cute little jump against me, threatening to knock the picnic basket out of my grip. It was the only incentive my body needed to spring to life. Well, more life. I was pretty invigorated already...

"You like it?"

"Are you fucking kidding me?" she countered, just before taking off at a run into the ankle-deep grass of the forest clearing. Unlike when I'd been here last, tiny summer wildflowers sprang from the green expanse, yellow and white and pink looking like dessert sprinkles across the area. They thinned closer to the tree line, where pines and oaks tangled to form protective walls on three sides of the hideaway. The fourth was bordered by a mass of rocks, majestic as a huge wedding cake at the end of the sprinkles runner.

I laughed and pulled out the blanket as she plucked flowers and began tying them into a chain. "I found it by accident one day." *When I was out walking, trying to forget about you and ended up in the orchard...where I did what I normally went to the orchard to do...*

"Come." I made it a command. "You haven't had anything but coffee all day."

"And your point is?" She inclined her head in challenge while strolling back over.

"That, contrary to popular belief, coffee isn't one of the main food groups."

"Well, it should be." A deeper argument brewed in her brain, I could all but read it across her face—until she looked down at the spread I'd brought for us. "Ohmigod. You brought brie. And something that stinks even worse!"

"Only way to do cheese."

"Why can't the rest of the world agree with that?"

A grin threatened to split my face open while we lowered to either side of the picnic spread I'd brought. I poured a glass of German riesling for us both. "The apples are ours, of course. It's off-season so they're small. Wait until you see them in about three months. The bread is from the bakery down the hill. Dudley's. Mom and a few other folks in town carry their stuff. It'll make you—" I chuckled when she bit into a slice and moaned in rapture. "Sound a lot like that."

"Damn you," she teased. "I'll be paying for this with my trainer on Monday."

"Unless you burn it off in more creative ways."

She gave me a scorching look over the rim of her wineglass. "There is that."

I almost hurled my wine into the trees and took out the food as collateral damage with my reaction. God damn, when she gazed at me like that...and now that I had full freedom to return those kinds of looks, with no worries about behavioral editing anymore...

And I thought yesterday had been the best day of my life.

I loaded up her plate with everything from the feast—tuna steak sandwiches fixed nicoise style, marinated vegetables, seasoned olives, and custard tarts—and handed it over, admitting to a stab of nervousness as I did. Even after countless business trips, even more crazy happy hours, one unforgettable Independence Day, and two mind-exploding trips to sexual heaven with the woman, this moment carried all the trappings of first-date uncertainty.

I kind of liked it.

And thoroughly hated it.

"You look really pretty today."

Seriously?

I'll take Lamest Flirt Lines for six hundred, Alex.

Pretty was just the start of it, anyhow. She'd opted for a Daisy Mae sort of look, with a black flippy skirt, a black-and-white gingham blouse, and those sexy boots again. No accessories besides her pinkie ring—and now, the delicate flower chain she'd connected and then donned as a crown.

My princess.

So fucking perfect.

"Thanks," she murmured—only to giggle at herself. Or me. I wasn't sure, and the answer felt all-important. Yep, still cruising through the land of fifteen and dorky.

"What is it?" Did it sound interested, not insecure? Cool guy, not jerk-off?

"I just...well, I realized...I'd been hoping you'd say that."

I set down my glass as confusion surely took over my face. "What? That you're pretty?"

"Well..." She took a fast sip. "Yeah."

"You must get told that all the time, Margaux."

"Never when it mattered."

Something crept across her face before she put aside her own glass and dipped her head. Something I liked seeing there—and needed to see more of. Compelled by that craving, I reached over the food to lift her chin with a finger. And was so damn glad I did. Emerald eyes, bright with the sun. Tremulous lips, turning up to welcome my intrusion...and my kiss.

I didn't plunge or attack. Simply brushed and nipped, stealing just the tip of my tongue inside her, needing to discover what her mouth did to transform the wine and food...and fuck yes, my theory was right...the resulting nectar should've been listed on the state's narcotic substances list.

When we finally dragged apart, I grated, "You matter, princess."

Shit. The word tumbled out so naturally that I didn't think about it. I braced for a retaliatory cold front from her.

Didn't happen.

Huh?

Her smile deepened in response to my frown. "I think I like that one better when it comes from you too."

Her confession flooded a new sensation through me. It blazed in like the sunlight but kept ripping through, like a killer Santa Ana gust. A new kind of arousal? No. Shit. This was better. And worse.

And terrifying.

Which meant it got ignored. Now wasn't a time for terror. It was time for the let's-make-time-stand-still perfection of this place, this woman. The poetry of her movements. The light along her skin. The breeze in her hair, flowing around that delicate crown...

I fingered one of the flower stem knots. "This is pretty good workmanship. If the royalty gig doesn't work out, you could set up shop making these."

She snickered. "Years of practice. Mother shipped me off to camp for a month each summer. When you're the token bitch at Lake Chimetoona, you log in a lot of hours stringing flower chains by yourself."

My back teeth ground together. Then my front. I flat-out disregarded the twist in my chest. "That doesn't sound right."

She shifted away, stretching out to the side, though kept her plate within reach. "All-girls camp, darling. There's no such word as fair. Roles have to be filled. I naturally drew the B card." She looked over and punched a deprecating laugh at me. "Stop it!"

"What?"

"Looking like your Captain America helmet is going to explode."

I wasn't about to argue that the guy technically didn't wear a helmet. There were bigger things right now to get at—

and now that she'd cracked the door to this room in the ivory tower, like hell was I passing it up.

"No explosions," I stated. "But I don't think I'm the only one wanting to call out your mother on some bullshit these days."

On the surface, my assertion didn't ruffle her by a single feather. But I knew what to watch for now. The tightness of her lips, battling how her stomach led the charge in combatting her anxiety. The trembles of her fingers as she reached for more bread to calm it. The swing of her gaze, anywhere but back at me.

"Why don't we just sing some camp songs? You know the 'Moose Song,' right? 'Bazooka Bubble Gum'?"

"Not letting you run there, sugar."

"Do I look like I'm running, Pearson?" That kick-started little bobs of her feet—another evasion tactic disguised as nonchalance. I battled not to seethe. She'd actually gone there. With me.

"You don't look or sound like you're addressing my question." In an easy sweep, I repositioned myself at her feet, grabbing both her ankles, earning me a new pierce of attention. "Margaux...what's going on?" I slipped my hands around her calves, coaxing with fingertips, letting my words sink into her tension. "It started a while ago, didn't it? Whatever's gone down with you and your mom...it happened last year, when we were all in Chicago to put out that fire for Trey Stone."

A few rounds of warm-warm-hot, anyone? It seemed so—and I'd just taken a giant step toward hot. The tension through her whole body, even her calves, spoke it as loudly as if she had.

"Trey Stone has nothing to do with this."

"Didn't say he did." Though I highlighted her comment

before stowing it into the Coincidence or Not file for deeper examination. "I'm talking about you and your mom. And what happened that ripped you apart in Chicago."

She let out a tight huff. "Nothing happened in Chicago, Michael."

"And your shoulders just got heavier for no fucking reason." I pressed forward, hoping it came off as concerned and not furious. Because right now, I was a lot of both. "Hiding the burden is going to be damn impossible with me, sugar."

She swallowed hard but didn't look away—yet didn't appear any more ready to open to me either. "Says the one who hid up here for six months?" She nodded at the treetops. "Though now I'm beginning to understand why."

"I was a goddamn idiot." Time to mean business. I freed my hands from her legs and simply sat on them instead. "I think we've been over that already."

"Yeah, but it's so much fun to hear you say it again."

"Nice try. But I'm not biting that hook today." Keeping her pinned, I leaned over once more. "No bantering. Just the truth. I'm not going to insult you with the obvious either. You know life, Margaux. You know people even better. So you've already figured out that my six months of stupidity were tied into you—but not because I was afraid of our attraction, our passion—"

"Which is pretty fucking good."

"Which is pretty fucking good."

I conceded the point to her because it was a) true and b) a great instigation for her smile. Damn it, I didn't want this to be hard for her. It shouldn't be hard. With Andrea obviously out of her life's landscape, she had no one to truly pour shit out to. I wasn't sure Andrea had ever been that person, but the necessity for someone like that was clear now. Though she'd mellowed a lot since getting here, I still caught her starting at shadows like they'd grown claws and were coming for her.

"So what...were you afraid of?"

Her whisper, so uncertain, tore at my soul—bringing a whole new slew of bafflement, since it was exactly what I wanted her to ask. If I could loosen her truth by giving her mine and show her I wasn't scared of it anymore...

"You stripped me naked in other ways, Margaux." I shook my head. "So many other ways. It's been more than bizarre to comprehend. Just a year ago, we talked to each other for business only. When we started taking things to other places, I admit, I was pretty intrigued..."

Her smile was so deep, her dimples came out to play. "Me too."

"Yeah, well...then you started peeling back new parts of me. Things I hadn't exposed to any person, let alone a woman I was interested in, for—well, a very long time."

"So I wasn't intriguing anymore?"

"You were off the fucking charts intriguing."

"Which was also when I became terrifying. Which was also when you took a page out of the Howard Hughes playbook."

"Gooooal."

I threw up both hands and added a Spanish accent for comedic value. But instead of laughter, Margaux sobered her smile. Sat up straighter. Tilted her head. "So in reality, it wasn't all just me. It was the shit I dug up inside you...the stuff that was hard to look at." When I didn't falter my focus, she went ahead and laser-beamed hers in, openly assessing me. Damn it. Discomfort wiggled in. Though I did trust her, she rarely looked at me like this if we both weren't floating in a martini haze. But a lot had changed since we'd last bellied up to a bar together. A lot.

Finally, I gritted, "Keep going. I can take it."

She bent her head in the other direction. "What was her name?"

I inhaled hard. The question wasn't unexpected. "Laci," I supplied. "We were together three years. I almost proposed. She broke up with me to go live in Tibet and find herself."

"Whoa." Her eyebrows jumped. "Seriously?"

"Yeah. Tibet."

"Whatever. Tibet's nice if you don't miss indoor plumbing. I was referring to the rest. Three years?"

I laughed. Loud. It felt good, lifting my face into the sun along with it. When I realized Margaux wasn't joining the party, I cut it short, looking back down. "Breathe, sugar. It's not unheard of. Three years is a blip when you're in love."

Her gaze, deep and green and penetrating, roamed my face and took in so much. Too much. Discomfort corkscrewed into get-me-the-hell-out-of-here. But that wasn't happening either. This was too important. *She* was too important. I was staying put.

"Were you..." she finally asked, "in love? With her?"

I cocked my head in order to meet her gaze completely. "Yes. In the best way I knew how to give love at the time. That was almost six years ago. I've grown. Changed. Learned to deal with lots of things better."

"Like the asshole who gave your mom the black eye?"

Hell.

So it was my turn to look away. Natural reaction when someone came swinging with an emotional mallet to a guy's gut—not that I'd expected her to deliver anything less. Not when she'd noticed Mom's injury before I had the night we'd arrived. Not when I'd fucking ordered her to keep going at me.

But, most importantly, not when I knew she truly cared about the answer.

And there it was. The final splash of paint that sealed off the corner I'd trapped myself in. Why the hell hadn't I envisioned it more clearly? Telling her the ugly details about Declan meant the possibility of the cocksucker catching her in his crosshairs too. Just the idea of Dec sniffing anywhere near Margaux was a match on kindling through my brain. My gut, the unfortunate backdraft zone, burned with bile to the goddamn boiling point. When I envisioned Mom's face once more, mottled as it hadn't been since I was twelve, walls began to slam up inside. Big ones.

"Did he hurt you too, Michael?" She shifted upward, bending her knees, reaching over them at me. I was conscious of the movement but didn't equate it to how jarring her touch would be, alighting over my face but searing to my mind. As if she could see all the shit that invaded it now too...

No.

Princesses weren't supposed to see the ugliness.

I was supposed to be saving her.

No. Have to...stop this. She doesn't save you, dick. She doesn't save you!

I managed to lift both hands. Grab hers. Jerk her away. "Some things are best left in the past, Margaux."

She smiled softly. Not gloating, though she had every right to—for as our gazes locked again, it was with the understanding of what I'd just given her with the words. Victory. Instead, she curled her fingers out and around mine, tugging them in to bring us closer together, before whispering, "Yes, Mr. Pearson.

Sometimes they are."

Wind picked up through the trees, scattering sunlight across us both. I watched the gold and green dapples scatter over her legs, up her torso, and finally into her eyes, transforming her gaze from somber forest into dazzling meadow inside a couple of seconds. And why did that astound me? Why did the hues of this woman, as changing and fascinating as the depths of the ocean, continue to stun me with their newest beauty?

A beauty broadcasting only one message to me now.

She wanted to kiss me.

For the first time in the last fifteen minutes—it had felt like fifteen hours—we were finally on the same page.

I untangled our fingers in order to flow my hands up her arms, delighting in the little shivers I gave as I went, until framing both edges of her jaw with the length of my forefingers. Her eyes pulled me in deeper, so many facets and lights, my personal, sensual Emerald City.

I tugged her closer. "Come here."

I kept the kiss sweet—for all of ten seconds. The moment our lips formed tighter and I began to taste her, pulling in the tang of the wine and the balm of the sunshine, I was demolished. I slid my grip to her neck and yanked her tightly as I pushed inside and ravaged her tongue, her teeth, her pliant, perfect softness. And Margaux, my passionate, magnificent Margaux, gave exactly as she received. With a husky moan, she raked hands into my hair too. Seared my scalp with the force of her torque while blazing my tongue with the sweet savagery of her surrender.

Surrender?

Careful what you assume out of the gate, tough guy—especially when Ms. Asher is coming to the soiree.

A lesson I was taught in breath-halting detail—when she pulled a hand out of my hair and dropped it directly to my zipper.

Yeah. That zipper.

"Margaux!"

"Hmmm?"

Was she kidding? With the Strawberry Shortcake innocence and the My Little Pony eyes?

"What the—?" My own choke cut me off as she reached in, palming me past my balls. Shit. She wasn't kidding. And I wasn't sure I wanted her to be. Just kissing her had woken everything up down there—duh—but her unabashed move was the ideal jolt of rise-and-shine for everything between my thighs. As she stroked down my length, trailing fingers over the veins with appreciative languor, I hissed and then bucked farther up into her touch.

She flashed a grin, razing my defenses even more, shoving down my khaki shorts and pushing up my T-shirt. As she did, I winced for a second. Christ. She had me so amped, even the abrasion of the cotton against my nipples acted as another crank on my cock—and damn if the playful little princess didn't know it. She bit her lip as more of my length came surging out, so impish and eager, my naughty little minx.

"Damn!"

It burst between my gritted teeth as she stroked over and over, including little squeezes at my sack each time she got to the base. I'd never understood all the hype about hand jobs. Now I realized I'd just never been treated to a great one. Great? This wasn't great. This was a fucking spiritual experience. As I fell back on my haunches, supporting myself with my elbows in order to watch every steady glide of her fingers over my flesh, I wondered if I'd start spewing prayer tongues next. Her nails were painted in a lush, deep red. Maybe I had to switch up this fantasy and turn my princess into Little Red...coerced to service the big bad wolf in the woods for his private pleasure. And maybe I had to think about getting my affairs in order, because I was surely going to hell for tapping prayer and sexual penitence into the same line of thought.

But damn, would the fall be worth it.

Especially now.

She'd found a way to go psychic on me, surely discovering my fixation about her nails the second I had it, because she tucked her fingers in enough that they began to scrape my balls along with the squeezes. With every new graze, my hips shot up a couple of inches. Dark grunts and hisses ripped past my lips, making me wonder if that prayer-language thing was coming to fruition.

Until she suddenly stopped.

"Fuck!" I bellowed. "Margaux—Jesus!"

I slashed my gaze up to hers. Unbelievably, my minx had left the meadow. So had Red Riding Hood. Correction—they'd likely been sent off by the goddess who'd remained in their wake, quirking a grin so gorgeous at me, I was tempted to lift up, kiss her senseless, and then flip the fucking tables on her impudent little ass. If only I didn't love what she was doing so much...

"Forgive me...Sir"—she flung out the word as a deliberate taunt—"but I simply want to respect—what's the word they use?—proper protocol? After all, you are in charge here, Mr. P. I'd never think of seizing the upper hand. Ummm, pardon the pun."

"Not pardoned." I growled the words but smirked, making

sure I focused long enough on her face to lock her stare to mine. "And believe me, little brat, you'll pay handsomely for it."

"Oh, no." She pushed out a mock gasp. "Not payment for the pun!"

I chuckled harder. God damn, what a handful she could be. And would I want it any other way? Or her?

The question answered itself—with stunning brilliance. Had someone asked me to sit down and write a wish list for my ideal woman, I doubted half of the descriptors for Miss Margaux Asher would make the list. But I couldn't imagine my life now without any of them.

Headstrong. Histrionic.

Unstoppable. Unapologetic.

Astonishing. Amazing.

And utterly, totally the new guiding beacon of my heart.

"I think your payment will begin right now," I drawled, pulling at her hair. "Suck me, sugar. Let me feel your lips tight around my cock."

Her eyes glittered brightly with her approval of that plan—right before she lowered her beautiful mouth over my erection.

Heaven. Hell. And everything in between.

I groaned as she started by simply kissing my swollen head. Choked and bucked as precome shot up the shaft, promptly sipped off with her delighted little mewls. She kept lapping at the tip, rolling her tongue in unhurried little circles, until I swore I'd discovered the true meaning of losing my mind.

"Margaux!"

"Hmmm?"

Damnable little wench. She hummed it like I'd merely asked her the time—making sure the sound vibrated through my head and then rained reverberations down my whole length.

I didn't know whether to laugh or cry. Ended up choosing neither, instead obeying deeper instincts by gripping the back of her head—and ramming her down on me completely.

Her hum erupted into a startled moan. Then a high little sigh. Then a succession of passionate slurps as she went to work on my dick like no other ever had. I groaned in return—or thought I did. Awareness of anything past the contact of her mouth along my flesh grew more impossible by the minute. My thighs quaked. My chest pounded. I didn't blink for fear of losing a second of this incredible sight. My hand twisted in her hair, plunging her onto me again and again. My groin synced in savage stabs, fucking up into her mouth. The peaceful idyll of nature around us, twittering and breezing in oblivion of our passion.

With a tormented yell, I finally pulled her off. She flashed up a stare full of shock. "Michael? What's—?"

"Condom," I ordered. "Back right pock—back left pocket." Perfect proof of why I tasked her with retrieving the thing. Remembering my own name right now felt more difficult than taking the bar all over again.

I grunted my appreciation when she slid the latex on in seconds, her movements fevered but controlled. As I fell fully to my back, she pushed off her skirt and panties. Then, damn her, took her very sweet time moving back over me, spreading her pussy lips with one hand while balancing on my abdomen with the other.

With her fingers splayed over my stomach, her eyes grew heavy and heated. "Look at you," she murmured, pushing up my shirt to caress over my stomach and chest. "You are so damn beautiful."

A strained laugh spilled out. "You know how much of this

'beauty' comes from looking at you spreading yourself like that?"

"It's all for you," she whispered. "Every last drop."

My cock visibly jerked. "And every inch of that is going to take full advantage of that."

"Hmmm." She smiled, wetting her lips. "So what do you want me to do with it, stud?"

Deep growl. "You know exactly what I want you to do with it."

"But the words, sugar. I need the words."

I snarled. Then laughed again. "Vixen!"

"Scoundrel."

The moment had come to turn the tables. I ensured her punctuation took form in a scream as I rolled us both over in one motion, off the blanket and into the grass. It was warm from the sun and smelled like wildflowers—the perfect setting for letting our animals out of their cages again.

"Look at this," I murmured before slamming a hard, fast kiss down on her. "I've found a sweet little flower to pluck." With a flick, I jerked the ribbons free from the neck of her blouse—only then realizing she wore no bra underneath. "And look at this. She's got some delicious nectar to feed me too."

Her grin grew, betraying how she searched for saucy words to zing in return. So not happening. She didn't need to be coy, charming, or entertaining right now. She only needed to be filled, pleasured, fucked into bliss beyond words.

She only needed to be mine.

The goal burned into obsession. Nothing would stand in my way now. No more hesitations. No more delays.

I possessed her in the space of one urgent thrust.

"Ohhhh!" Her breasts jutted skyward as her body arched

up. I leaned over, already breathing hard, fitting one erect strawberry into my mouth. Reveling in the moan I elicited for that, I slid to the other, sucking with carnal abandon.

Perfect in so many ways, even the timing. Concentrating on her tits forced my attention away from how magnificent her sex felt, gripping every inch of mine, as our bodies began surging and retreating against each other. That surreal feeling swirled again, as if the world were yanked away and the universe sealed us into a bubble of hyperawareness. The brush of the wind on my ass...the grind of the grass beneath my knees...every sigh she let go against my neck... All of it was tossed into a sensory blender and then switched on high, until I growled long and hard from the erotic overload.

When she joined me, a keen splitting off her lips, I grabbed both sides of her face, goring her with my gaze. "Not yet, sugar. Stay with me."

She swung her head from side to side. Her hair, fanned in the grass, grew tangled with flowers from her efforts at control. "It's so good. This is so good, Michael!"

"Look at me. Look at me. It'll be even better. Hang on. Hold it back."

"Bastard!"

"Minx." I smiled it against her lips while lifting one of her hips, curling her knee all the way over my shoulder. "Clamp me, Margaux. Squeeze me tight with your sweet pussy and don't let go." I hissed with the bliss of her compliance. "Fuck, that's good. Yeah, princess, just like that."

I made sure she'd have every reason to echo the sentiment, angling my body so every stroke of my cock also caressed her most sensitive nub. Since she'd already been so helpful in unsheathing her clit, it took very little time to feel that moist little ridge tremor from my fucking. Soon, she started gasping in time to the same rhythm. "Holy—shit—Michael—Michael—Michael!"

I rolled my hips before the next thrust, increasing contact even more—before freezing like that.

We both held our breaths.

Deep inside her body, violent convulsions started.

Deep inside my balls, white-hot molecules detonated.

"Now, Margaux. Let it all go, sugar!"

Her tunnel softened around me. The next moment, clenched tight again. Tighter. Tighter. As I pumped faster, faster—

"Michael! Oh, my God!"

Faster still.

Riding her through the torrent of her orgasm. Then the explosion of mine. Then a second for her. Still she reared against me, clenching me more ruthlessly than one of those Chinese finger puzzles. She tore giant tufts from the grass, teeth clenched and eyes squeezed, as a third wave clearly crept its way closer to her breaking point.

I had become Hercules.

And I loved every fucking minute of it.

"Come on, sexy girl." If I'd learned anything about properly revving this woman to her fullest sensual joy, it was the value of talking dirty to her. And that was just fine by me. "You have another one for me, don't you? I'm not going to stop fucking your naughty little cunt until you give it up. Feel that, Margaux? I've already blown my wad, but you still make me that hard, that huge, inside your tight little body. I'm not leaving until you cream again all over me. Until you make me want to come all over again myself..."

She swallowed hard. Roped a hand around, over my ass, urging me even deeper. "Holy—hell!"

I barely suppressed a smile. We were holy something, all right. She took me to heaven by getting to watch her heaven, drenching her face over and over again in waves of gripping ecstasy. But even if this was a clever disguise for the tunnel to hell...well, it bore repeating—the fall would be worth it.

"You're so close, princess."

"Yes! Yessss!"

She was on the verge of hiking that into a scream—

When her phone rang.

"Ignore it," she panted. No need for repeating that one. I gladly obliged and kept on plunging—until it rang again. "Shit! Damn telemarketers!"

When the device went off for the third time, I peeled back, but not before ordering, "Stay. We aren't done." I dug in her purse—thank God it was one of those Barbie-tiny ones and not a fucking suitcase—and retrieved her phone. "Good afternoon. Miss Asher's—errmm—office."

Silence. A long one. Then a click.

Strange. Telemarketers usually lived for the moment somebody picked up the line.

By now, Margaux had pushed up to her elbows. "What?" she pressed, gazing at my frown.

"Huh?" Yeah, this was me. Yeah, completely distracted. Christ, maybe that thwarted marketer had been my secret blessing. Now that I'd pulled back, I took in the bigger picture. Her well-used body. The glistening curls at its apex. The thought that they'd look even better if I spread her now, making her take a long, teasing tongue fuck before I penetrated her with the real thing again. There were two more rubbers in my pocket—and a sampler packet of lube. Captain America came prepared.

"Michael? Who was it?"

I shrugged. "Scared them off, I guess. Silence and then a hang-up." I glanced at the phone's screen. "Hmm. Chicago number. Did you break a heart out there while we weren't looking, missy?"

My joke...apparently wasn't one. She jackknifed up. Despite the heat of the afternoon, the color drained from her face.

Right before she stared at the device in my hand the same way she'd peered at the corners of her condo.

"Margaux? Hey. What the hell?"

She didn't answer me. Her phone now rang a fourth time. With the same Chicago-based number.

Before I could process any theories about that, she snatched the thing out of my grip. Yanked her top back up as she stood and muttered a terse "What?" as greeting—if one could call it that—to the party—if one could call them that—who'd yanked her back to spooked-shitless mode in the space of thirty seconds.

Who the fuck was doing this to her? And why?

I back-burnered the need to start lining up the clues in hopes that a few fit together, focusing instead on any new evidence to cull from her side of the exchange.

"I told you it'll happen, so it'll happen," she snapped. "Because I said so, that's why." As if she sensed me inching closer, she glanced over her shoulder, flashed me eyes full of alarm, and paced farther away. A few lines went by of furious hisses I couldn't make out and shouted profanities that I could, before she jabbed a finger at the air as if the caller herself—

himself?—had materialized in front of her. "No, damn it," she yelled. "I think you're the one who'd better watch their 'little footsteps.' And you know what they say about men and their little feet, darling."

So the caller was a him. Yeah, and inflation was on the rise. But only one of those statements made me feel like tearing one of the trees out of the ground and going battering ram with it against the boulder wall.

And she still wasn't done. Oddly, she did turn back toward me to finish off the conversation. Necessary or unnecessary? I couldn't tell shit from studying her face. Within a minute, she'd gone from coming undone in my arms to throwing up walls in my face.

Who the hell was on the other end of that phone call?

"We're done here," she bit at him. The savagery in her tone did nothing to loosen the fist in my chest. Him. "I said we're done."

A shaking breath left her as she disconnected the call. As she looked around for her purse, she wrapped both arms against herself like a prisoner at mealtime. Her stance gutted me. I hated it—but if I moved even a step toward her, I knew I'd cave to the need to crush her close again. I was locked in the same prison, scanning the area for enemies I didn't know about, couldn't see.

And if this whole episode had taken place in her condo... I'd be scouring the corners for demons too.

Fuck.

I stood motionless as she jerked back into her underwear and skirt. When she dragged a hand through her hair, revealing eyes so dark I wondered who'd died, I finally snapped to action. It was surprising but not shocking that she jumped from the brush of my hand on her shoulder.

"Whoa. Hey." How quickly old habits came back. Three years of hell beneath Declan's thumb meant perfecting the art of keeping a gentle tone when one's temper raged. It helped that I was upset for her, not at her. "Hi. It's just me."

Why that agitated her deeper, I couldn't fathom. "Michael."

I slipped my hand around, running it from her shoulder to her elbow. "That's me. At least last time I checked."

She blinked. Stared around the clearing as if it had turned into a prison yard. "I-I have to leave."

"All right. Let me just pack up—"

"No. Now."

"Something urgent at the office?" Okay, so it was a massive straw grasp. But working for Asher and Associates had taught me that the most desperate straws were often the ones that worked the best. "Mom has a laptop upstairs and a few PCs in the office. Her internet is lightning fast. I'll get you set up—"

"No. No, damn it. I have to get out of here, Michael. Out of Julian. Back to town." She moved the wine and glasses off the blanket before wrapping the rest of the spread up in it, hobo-knapsack-on-crack-style, and then shoved the bundle at me. "Here. We're packed."

"Margaux—"

"This wasn't a great idea. How could I even think it was?"

"What the hell?" I cut in. "You squealed when you came down and saw the picnic basket." Then jumped on me, locked her legs around my waist, and jammed her tongue down my throat, if I remembered correctly.

"Not this idea." She slashed a hand up. "This entire idea. Coming here. Running away. Hiding out."

My frown was so deep, it screwed down through my jaw. "'Hiding out'?"

"So messed up. So stupid. How could I even think I could—?"

"How you could what?" I went ahead and growled it. Surprise, surprise. Something about having an armful of ruined picnic in my arms brought out my real big, bad wolf. "How you could enjoy yourself for once? Have a little—oh shit, wait for it—fun? Not have to race back to the city on the whim of some irate client?" And who the hell was I still trying to fool with the business call excuse? Even on her worst days on Andrea's team, I'd never heard the woman sound like that with a client. Taut. Desperate.

And, damn it...scared.

The same fear that crawled through the underpinning of her rejoinder. "I don't expect you to understand, okay?"

Well, that did it. My last damn straw snapped. As it did, I let the knapsack drop to my feet with an angry clatter. "Try me."

Her mouth trembled on a manic laugh. "Let me get back to you on that."

"Try. Me."

She stumbled back as I cleared the knapsack in one stride. But then she planted her stance, summoning the bitch on wheels I knew and adored—only this time, I was on the wrong damn side too. She welcomed my approach by shoving at my chest—with strength that was, pretty honestly, astounding. "I thought you walked your talk, Pearson."

Forget the punch of her fists. There was a wallop I couldn't forget. "Excuse the fuck out of—"

"The past?" she countered. "And shit being best left in it?"

"Right. Sure." I folded my arms. "When it's in the past! Not when it's calling you in the middle of a pretty damn hot date, panicking you to the point of full-body shakes—"

"I'm not panicked!"

"Okay. Sure." Her evasion wore me down. I was so pissed off, I'd come full circle back to being lethally calm about it again. "You stick with that, princess, and the rest of us will be waiting outside your door—in the land of reality."

"Reality?" she shot back, slamming her arms back in. They fell to her sides a second later, one still fisted around her phone, the other snatching up her purse. "How's this for reality?" She flung her bag over her shoulder, heading for the path we'd taken to get here. "I'm texting Andre to come and take me home, so you no longer have to be concerned with my carriage, 'kaysies?"

"No. No 'kaysies. Shit. Princ—"

"And don't call me princess anymore."

"Margaux! Damn it!"

She tossed up a hand, full of attitude, but I didn't believe a goddamn inch of it. I wasn't the reason for this. Neither was anything or anyone in Julian. The mystery asshole who'd called her from the city was responsible for this.

Whatever the hell this was.

"Fuck!" I snarled. Then again. Helplessness wasn't just my hot button. It was my red-pill-turns-you-into-a-goddamn-cretin button. As if those minutes in Mom's room Tuesday night hadn't served as a disgusting enough reminder, I stumbled through the same torture chamber of frustration now, thankful the knapsack was there for grabbing up and curling my fists into. Still couldn't guarantee I'd make it out of here without dropping the shit and going to town on a tree, though.

Maybe it was best she had her space. For now.

I gave her that berth while we walked in silence back to the gate to the orchard and then through the apple trees. During our walk out here, I'd stopped to point out the different trees to her, also explaining what kind of fruit they'd bear in a little over a month. Red Delicious, Jonathan, Gala, Fiesta, Liberty. She'd listened with genuine interest, giving me hope that she drew the same parallel as I did, that over the last couple of days, we'd planted the seed of something damn good—and that perhaps, with a lot of care, the tree of us would grow healthy, strong, enduring.

Now, our sapling was dying. Because of some fucked-up root rot I couldn't even identify, let alone target.

So I worked with what I did have. As we approached the house, I strapped on a mental watering can, preparing to douse her with what I'd stocked inside it—respect and kindness as the base for a hell of a lot of direct questions. I didn't care if it took us hours. I'd get inside that shell of hers if it took flooding her out of the damn thing.

Or so I'd thought.

Like the fucking fool that I was.

Before fate chose the most ideal moment to boot me in the balls.

We'd barely stepped inside the house before the sound of a car on gravel echoed from the kitchen. When I looked out and spied the black 750i, with one disgruntled Jamaican unfolding himself out of the front seat, I dropped my jaw—and the watering can.

She'd done it. I'd taken her words on the trail as desperate ramblings, not actual promises for action, but as stated, I was a fucking fool.

A fool who watched, stunned into furious silence, as she handed her hastily packed bag off to Andre and then turned for the open backseat door. I went with the word loss, not trusting myself to say anything remotely diplomatic at this point. No way in hell would I approach her about staying now. Clearly, whatever had gone down on that phone call was more important to her. Wait. No. Withholding it from me was more important.

Trees couldn't grow on secrets and shadows. I saw nothing except the combination, consuming her whole face, as she hesitated before entering the car and suddenly spun back toward me. Her body jerked a little, as if she sought clearance to come closer, but benevolence wasn't mine to grant right now. I'd probably regret it later, but right now, even the thought of her back in my arms was too brutal a kick in the center of my gut.

She was leaving our tree to die before it had gotten a chance to live.

But who was the idiot who'd let his heart twine into those roots too?

That was the shittiest thing to grasp as I turned and reentered the house, forcing myself to keep eyes forward and mind numb. The first goal was a success, at least until I heard the car start up again and pull away. The second? My pounding head and screaming senses bore evidence to that massive fail.

You're just as much to blame for this pain as she is, dumb fuck. Let yourself believe that two days without drama could grow into a lifetime of Ozzie and Harriet. Let yourself believe in her, period.

Lesson learned.

The ugly, agonizing, hard-as-shit way.

Only guaranteeing I'd never let it happen again.

CHAPTER FIFTEEN

Margaux

I knew it was going to be a bad day by the size of the rejected pile of outfits lying on the floor of my dressing room. The fashion dilemma was usually an accurate barometer of the direction my day would take, and from the looks of things, it could only get better from here. There were at least six—or eleven—ensembles down there. Thank God Sorrelle treated the care of my wardrobe as a spiritual calling. Still, I'd make sure he received a little extra in his next paycheck to say thanks for the additional effort.

Wait. A little extra? To say thanks?

This wouldn't do. At all. Where was my page torn from the playbooks of Alexis Carrington and Miranda Priestly? Screw that. Those bitches could take notes from mine, if they dared.

You believe that as much as a fucking fairy tale.

The fairy tale my life was never meant to be.

I looked at my reflection, eyeing the woman who now stood in head-to-toe Stella McCartney. The pantsuit won by default, since it best hid the pooch from the turtle pie I'd shoveled in last night. Further, the slim black pants with a matching tuxedo jacket, paired with a white blouse and subdued accessories, were the ideal meeting-at-the-boss's-house attire. On my feet were a pair of my favorite Cole Haans, lending the classic base—and hopefully, the confidence I was so desperately lacking.

So, alert the damn press. Yes, I was having a confidence problem.

Could have had something to do with the new sign hanging over most of my mind now.

Pearsonville. The place that never lets you sleep.

Pathetic much? God, it was true. I was unable to think about anyone else—even when he was the last damn thing I wanted to be thinking about.

Do you really believe that?

Not one fucking bit.

That afternoon in the meadow had been one of the best moments of my life—followed by one of the worst. Ugh...that fight. Messy was a good description. Ugly wasn't half bad either. But re-engaging the Margaux ice queen had been my only, desperate defense. Without all the frozen walls back in place, he would've inched right under my defenses again—and God only knew how many secrets he'd find waiting in the shadows.

So yeah, I'd speared him with a few icicles instead. And yeah, the blows had probably stung. But at least he was safe.

Safe...from me.

I'd tried to tell him that—in several desperate ways—but he'd seen through the ice princess and matched her by one angry ogre. He was too furious to see the conflict I went through before leaving with Andre, too hell-bent on brooding to notice the tears I'd blinked back. How could he have thought it was a decision I liked making?

Ass. Hole.

And that was why I couldn't stop thinking about him, right? Or block out his face every time I closed my eyes. Or stop hearing his voice in every brush of wind across the penthouse's patio. And, damn it, the songs on the radio... Every stupid tune with sugary-sweet lyrics and an earworm melody taunted me all with memories of touching him, kissing him, squeezing my body around him...

Damn it.

I had it bad for Michael Pearson.

Bad.

Groundhog Day, anyone? Hadn't I visited this exact moment before? And I was in no better of a situation right now than I was then, despite all those tingling, amazing memories. It was worse at night. Sleep had become a cold and restless battle, calmed only by the hope he was suffering the same fate. But that only eased the ache a little—because ultimately, it didn't touch the true issue.

The whole mess with Michael was the mess I couldn't share with Michael.

Trey.

I'd met his demand by only two million dollars so far, siphoning off a combination of my own bank account plus the funds I had access to at SGC. Every day that passed had me wadded in a huger ball of tension, certain someone would catch the missing money and I'd have some 'splaining to do worse than Lucy Ricardo with a mouthful of chocolate. But hopefully I'd be able to chop through the legal red tape on my trust fund soon and replace the funds before they were missed.

In the meantime, Trey was getting impatient. He'd been back for another visit already, once more sneaking into my apartment, lying in wait for me after work one night. Fortunately, he didn't leave any more souvenirs on my face and the stupid sexual innuendos were left out of the conversation too. He was all about the cash now, period. It was a little relief but not much. The sooner this was all over, the better.

One thing in all this was crystal clear. It had been a damn good move to lock Michael out of this equation. Now that I'd seen more of his rampaging lion side, there was no doubt how he'd react to Trey's bullshit. There wouldn't be a corner of the world safe enough for Trey to hide in.

That didn't assuage my guilt though. Yes, damn it—for the first time in my life, guilt was eating me alive. It was such an unfamiliar feeling I'd first thought it was bad sushi, but the shit persisted for days, especially every time I got near Claire or Kil. My stomach churned, my head spun, my whole body eventually wanted to bolt from the room. Neither of them wore sickening scents, so that wasn't it.

It was me.

And it was hateful.

I was hateful.

I'd stolen from them.

Of course, I tried telling myself that it was all a bit silly. Even if I wasn't a biological Stone and due some of the company's wealth anyway, Killian had enough money to wallpaper every room in the Rancho Santa Fe house three times over. And if I had the true balls, I'd have come clean from the start, informing him what was going on with his dickhead brother. But I wasn't just having the guilts. I was battling the holy shits. Trey was getting desperate, and often times, that meant dangerous. I didn't have the guts to drag Claire and Kil into this, not after everything they'd already suffered at the hands of Trey—and frankly, me, before I'd gotten a clue that the way to a man's heart wasn't necessarily through entrapment.

I'd decided then and there to go see my brother and

stepsister-slash-sister-in-law after work. While sending Kil a message via interoffice chat to make sure they were still free, I'd noticed Claire was out sick again. Hmmmm. This was at least the third time since they'd returned from their honeymoon. Was something up in terms of buns in ovens?

I rolled my own eyes at myself. *How's the trampoline holding up, jumping to those conclusions, girlfriend?*

Besides, she was out—but not slacking. Our latest marketing partner had turned into a giant pain in the ass, meaning she had a lot of on-site handholding with their company president. That was likely where she was. Claire wasn't the best at inputting details in her shared calendar.

The sun was long gone by the time Andre pulled up the drive of their monster house. I'd called during the journey and received a thorough chew-out from Big Brother about my nasty habit of working past hours. I'd promptly replied with creative new vernacular. Had his workaholic ass really tried that? Besides, what the hell did I have to go home to except another piece of turtle pie that was literally the size of a turtle? My point exactly.

Kil's valet, Alfred, welcomed me with a warm smile and showed me to the family room. Killian and Claire had made some great changes to the home's décor since they moved in, warming up the rooms with lighted crown molding, some new area carpets, and a breathtaking shot from their wedding day centered over the mantle.

After I walked in to embrace Claire, I sat with her on the plush leather couch, exclaiming. "Sister mine, the place looks magni—" I stopped myself while catching a new look at her. "But, whoa, you don't."

She lifted a wan laugh. "That bad, huh?"

"Don't take this the wrong way, but you know the paste that the gross kid in third grade always made a small meal out of?"

She raised a hand. "Stop. Please. I can't."

Shit. She really couldn't. Now that guilt and I were on close personal terms, a wave of it hit when her complexion turned from white to green. "Oh, little bear." I clasped her hand. "I didn't know you were this bad. Why didn't Killian just cancel with me?"

"Be—because I wanted to see you."

"Gutsy girl," I quipped. "Even when you look this shitty."

"Thanks, Mare. You have such a way with words." She suddenly rose. "Excuse me. I'll be just one second." She dashed by me to hit the bathroom just in time. When I tried to follow, she slammed the door in my face.

Left with little choice but to stand sentry, I leaned against the wall until Alfred reappeared. "She may be a while, Miss Asher."

"A while?" I punched back. "Well, how long has she been as bad as this?"

"A while."

I couldn't help but fume. "What? And Kil hasn't taken her to a doctor?"

"Oh, a doctor's following up with her."

I pivoted and advanced on the man. Don't fuck with a girl in the four-inch shoes. "Okay, listen, man. You want to elaborate on—" I lowered to the couch again.

Claire came back and quickly curled up on the sofa again, pulling a luxurious faux-fur throw around her.

I pulled her feet into my lap and started rubbing, a tradition from our girls' nights together. "Okay, out with it.

What the hell's going on with you? Did you catch Ebola on the honeymoon?" I bolted upright with mock panic. "Shit. Do I need a hazmat suit?"

Claire gave another weak laugh. "Knock it off, you crazy bitch." After I made a point of visibly sobering—and giving her the spill-it-or-face-my-wrath glare—she took a deep breath and murmured, "I'm pregnant."

I shrieked and hugged her. "Bun in the hot Stone oven! I knew it!"

She looked a little alarmed. Clearly, she and Kil were waiting on springing the news on the rest of the world. "You did?"

"Well, I wasn't sure, sure. Okay, pretty sure. But I know you better than a lot of people, so..." I shook my head, dazed and excited. This was so the twist my life needed. "I'm going to be an auntie! Fuck me sideways."

"Well, it wasn't sideways," Claire returned. "Hmm. Maybe it was. He's pretty creative..."

"Stop!" I held up both hands. There were things about Killian Jamison Stone that no longer interested me. After Claire indulged a real giggle, I hugged her again. "Congratulations, Claire! I'm so thrilled for you both!" I glanced down at her slender frame. "It must be pretty early though, yeah?"

She nodded. "Just six weeks or so. But hell's damn bells. I can't keep anything down. It's been awful."

"So where's that asshole brother of mine?" I peered around, even listening for the telltale signs of Kil-is-in-the-house. "Why isn't he here watching over you?"

"Because I ordered him out." She snorted and pinched the bridge of her nose, a move borrowed directly from her husband. "He just makes it worse sometimes. He...hovers."

She smacked me with a pillow when I answered that with a snicker. "Not funny. He hovers, Margaux. It's bad." She waved her hand when I didn't relent. "Go see him. He'll be glad you know at last. I refuse to make an official announcement until I'm further along. It's been eating him alive, not having anyone to share the excitement with."

I rose. "You'll be all right?"

"Sure. Alfred's right around the corner."

"Where?"

"Upstairs in the second guest room, if I have to bet. He's been spending every free moment in there. Dog with a damn bone."

I gently tucked the throw around her so she was nice and snug. It probably drove her crazy, but she was too sick to do anything about it, so I really fussed.

After laughing my way out of the room, I climbed the slightly curved staircase, affording a sweeping view of their new home.

Thumping music pulled me forward. The room it came from was where I'd find Killian. He always had music blaring if he wasn't too deep in thought.

After passing several closed doors, I arrived at the one throbbing with an old Hall and Oates classic, "Private Eyes"—accompanied by an off-key warble that made me damn glad Kil hadn't pursued a singing career.

I opened the door and popped my head in.

And blinked. Then again.

Best blackmail moment ever. Either that, or a hallucination nobody would ever believe.

Mr. CEO.

Mr. Billionaire.

My big brother.

Spread out on the floor like a toddler himself, surrounded by every piece of conceivable baby gear on the market—and probably a few that weren't.

"Picture worth a million words." I shouted over the music.

His head jerked up, reading glasses perched on the end of his nose and befuddlement ruling his eyes. Both sleeves of his Ledbury Royal Twill Worker were rolled to the elbow as he spread an instruction sheet out, its five languages a mish-mash of words. When he saw me, a dazzling grin split his lips. He grabbed the remote and lowered the volume with a fast jab.

"She told you."

"She sure did. Congrats, Papa Bear."

He lunged, catching me in his arms and twirling me around at least three times. I was squealing too hard to keep accurate count. By the time he set me back down, I was laughing pretty hard at his excitement. "Well, what a sight you are to behold, Mr. Stone."

"Thank you very much, Miss Stone."

I dignified that with a hard whack to his shoulder and nothing else. Back to the important subject in the room. "I had no idea you wanted a baby so soon."

"Neither did I. But when Claire told me, I couldn't believe we weren't on it sooner."

"On it sooner? As in, less than a month after your damn honeymoon?"

He let me laugh and even joined in. "This shit is so much fun already. You have no idea."

"No, I don't. Let's keep it that way. Especially because you're so goddamn adorable right now, I may go join Claire for her next puke-out."

"Bitch," he teased.

"Butthead," I countered.

I swiveled before placing a careful step to my left, praying not to hear the crunch of plastic beneath my toe. "Okay, seriously, Kil. You need to pace yourself here. It's really early." I raised my eyebrows, circling around again. Bouncers. Play swings. Bottle warmers. Safety gates. Stuffed animals. And a train set? That wasn't all of it. The crib and a half dozen other items were still in boxes.

Kil kept grinning. "Cool, huh? I one-clicked all of it. Do you know how much shit you have to get for a baby?"

I spied the little remote to his stereo and clicked the music completely off. "Killian. You need to leave this shit alone for a few months."

He frowned, the kid who'd just had the puppy taken away. "But why?"

"Because you won't have anything left to do when Claire gets closer to delivering. Then you'll really hover."

He hit me with a full glower. "I don't hover."

"Hmmm, yeah...I bet you hover. But if you hover in the third trimester, Claire will likely shiv you. And I will cry. Then I will throw all this crap into your cold, dark grave with you."

His eyes narrowed. "You would, wouldn't you?"

"In a heartbeat." I inhaled deep, showing him I was going for the real version of serious now. "Have you been downstairs lately?"

Kil winced. "Nausea's back?"

"Is that what it means when her skin's the color of clam chowder?"

He didn't hesitate to turn for the door. "Let's go."

He offered me his arm, ready to escort me downstairs. I

smiled and took it. Why was it that my nonbiological brother was the sane, classy one? I shuddered to think I shared half the same gene pool with Trey.

"Maybe we can distract her with a movie or something," I suggested. "You know, all three of us, like we used to."

Killian grinned. "Great idea. We've both missed you, honey."

"Awwww." I swallowed, hoping to alleviate the heaviness in my chest...and failing. Was this the shit people referenced when they spoke of lumps in the throat? It didn't suck. But no way in hell was it the greatest. "I've missed...hanging with you guys too." Maybe I could open up to him—a little—and not spill everything. "To be honest, I could use the company." Perhaps there was one more ulterior motive. Easing my guilt about the Trey mess was a perfect build-in for all this.

"So maybe I've been a little carried away," he admitted as we walked.

"First step to recovery is admitting you have a problem, brother."

"Shut up."

"You shut up."

We laughed again. "I'm so goddamn excited," he said then. "Can you imagine our little mini Claire running around here?"

"Not a little mini Kil?"

He pretended like I hadn't spoken. "She's going to have her mama's red hair and fiery attitude. And that adorable little nose that I can kiss good night after I read her a story..."

I swore to God, my brother had stars in his eyes. Just looking at him...

Oof.

There was my damn, nagging stomach ache again. No use

trying to mask the cause. Jealousy. Fucking jealousy. It swirled in my stomach, dark and debilitating, making me want to hurl the latte I'd declared as nectar from heaven just thirty minutes ago.

I wanted a man to look like that when he talked about me.

Seriously, girlfriend? You had your chance—right before you kicked him to the curb.

When we reentered the family room, the sofa was empty and the fur throw tossed hastily on the floor, giving me a pretty good idea where Claire was. My clueless brother scowled in confusion. "Alfred, where's Mrs. Stone?"

"She's in the washroom, sir."

"Shit." I interjected it with a huff. The bigger picture was clearer now. "Okay, reality check. Alfred? The sweet little fibs you and Mrs. Stone are perpetuating on Mr. Stone? That shit stops. Now."

"Y-Yes, Miss Asher."

"You can cut that shit too. I'm just Margaux, okay?"

"Yes, Miss Margaux."

I turned up the frost another notch. "Just Margaux," seethed between my teeth.

"Wait," Killian growled. "What sweet little fibs? What the hell?"

I grabbed his elbow. "Time to cut Bob the Builder loose, brother. He can come back to play when Mr. Hover Board isn't needed anymore."

As he nodded, I pivoted back to Alfred. "Why don't you hustle to the kitchen and grab Claire something with ginger in it? Ginger ale? Tea? If you have peppermint, that's even better. And bring back a few cool, wet hand towels too. And some saltines."

Alfred ping-ponged his stare between Killian and me.

"She scares the fuck out of me too, man," Killian blurted. "Just do it."

Alfred rushed out, passing Claire on the way. Her complexion wasn't green anymore.

It was light blue.

"Holy hell." Killian rushed to her. "Fairy...my God." He scooped her up into his arms like she was the baby herself. "When did you get this bad?"

Claire swung a glare at me. "Tattletale."

I held up both hands. "Guilty as charged. Now handcuff me. Oh, wait. You're too damn weak for that, aren't you? Bad guys go free. That's what you get for being stupid."

I didn't examine that one too closely.

"Psssshh."

"Margaux's completely right," Kil snarled. "No more sucking this shit up. I'm not leaving your side now."

"Crap," she muttered.

"Hush," he chided.

"It's just morning sickness." She batted uselessly at his chest while he completed their trip to the sofa. "I've been reading up on it. It just hits some women harder than others. Margaux, stop glaring."

"She cares." Kil perched himself on the cushion, leaning over her.

"She sure as hell does," I added. "You need to stay hydrated, woman. And talk to your husband more. And you"—I jammed a finger at Killian—"need to cut the Tim Taylor and stay glued to her for a while. You're the fucker who did this to her, so take care of her."

Kil smiled and saluted. "I'm all over it."

"Oh, God," Claire groaned.

I nodded, satisfied. "Okay, I'm going to get out of your hair so you can rest. But you can expect my text later."

After they nodded in unison, I grabbed my coat and bag and then leaned in to press a soft kiss on the crown of her cute red head. Killian rose to walk me to the front door, helping me with my coat as we walked.

When we got to the door, I turned and flashed him a grin. "You did good, Mr. Baby-Maker-Daddy-Man."

"Thanks, princess."

I groaned. "Not you too."

"Huh?"

"Forget it. Just get in there and make sure she drinks, okay? She's barfed at least three times while I've been here. If that keeps up, you'd better call one of the doctors you own, stat."

Before he could say anything, I kissed his cheek and slipped out into the balmy night. And sucked in the first real breath I'd had in an hour.

Until his shout yanked me back around. "Margaux!"

When I turned, he smiled again. The man radiated so much happiness, I was certain the moon simply chose to reflect him tonight.

"You know she wanted to tell you first."

I followed my initial instinct to swing my middle finger high.

"Yeah, yeah. We love you too."

Shit.

Just...shit.

Andre already had the door open. I slipped inside the car without my usual smartass line. I didn't have any more smartass left in me.

I had nothing left in me.

And yet...I had everything.

And had no damn idea what to do with it.

The confusion hit at full force, making me shamelessly grab at the proper white handkerchief that appeared in my line of sight. "Damn it!" I rasped. These fucking people were thawing me, no matter how hard I fought it. I tried to dab daintily at my eyes, but the dark eyes assessing me from the front...they knew better. Had already dissected me like a disgusting science project.

"Just...drive," I croaked out.

These were the times I was most grateful for Andre. He didn't ask where. He didn't ask why. He just did it. He'd been with me almost four years now, surviving longer than any staff member of mine. And yes, surviving was the right verb. In more ways than one.

We merged onto the 5 south at a decent pace, the freeway lights lulling me into a trance as they zoomed past the tinted windows. After tucking his handkerchief into the pocket of my jacket, I took a long, heavy breath—before surprising him as much as myself with my next words.

"Will you take me to Mr. Pearson's, please?"

His eyebrows bounced up but quickly resumed position again. Wasn't often he got a sincere version of the p-word from me. "Yes, ma'am."

He put his blinker on and merged into the fast lane, apparently wanting to get there before I changed my mind. Smart man.

"I'll have Sorrelle return your handkerchief after he does the laundry."

"No rush, ma'am." Thank God his snarky side had taken the night off. After getting exposed to the nuclear reactor core of peace, love, and adoration at Kil and Claire's, I was a bundle of raw emotions. Not only did Andre have a straight link to all those feelings, he seemed to know what I needed now, in the shaky aftermath. Before I could even think to ask for it, soft music filled the car's back seat. Mozart. My favorite. And very few people knew that, Andre being one of them.

I rested my head back and listened to the music, absorbing every lush note, willing their beauty to center me like a tight embrace. But I never got there. Remembering Kil and Claire and all the love they'd found with each other just magnified the emptiness of what I couldn't seem to feel...of what I'd never have.

By the time Andre drove into the La Jolla neighborhood where Michael rented, my teeth were clenched, my heart was racing, and my throat constricted, fighting the temptation to order that the car be turned around.

I trembled through several breaths, fighting for the courage to get out. What the hell was I even doing here? I hadn't called. I hadn't texted. For all I knew, I'd get to the door and he'd slam it in my face. This wasn't how I did things. I always ran my game clean and clear. Seeing the destination first always meant it was reached. Anticipating the victory always meant it was achieved.

The door opened, and Andre appeared. "Do you want me to see if he's in?"

I forced as much of a smile as I could. The gentle giant had as deep a protective streak as Michael. Maybe that was why they dug each other. "No," I finally replied. "I have to do this one on my own. I made a big mess of things in Julian. It's time for me to pay the piper. If I'm lucky, I won't need a ride home. If I don't come back out in thirty minutes or so, go ahead and call it a night. He can take me downtown if I don't stay."

"Are you sure? I don't mind waiting."

His concern was so sincere, but after the mush-fest in Rancho Santa Fe, I was reaching my saturation point. "Yes," I snapped. "Just do as I ask, okay?"

"Yes, Miss Asher."

We traded glares as I exited the car. He knew I was over that fucking name months ago, and when he was trying to piss me off, he used it.

He slammed the door. The whump made me jump a little—but shot my ass into gear up Michael's walkway.

After I rang his old-man doorbell, I pulled back a maniacal need to laugh. *Ding dong, the witch is dead.* Maybe not literally, but close enough. That was certainly the gig I'd just signed up for. Pangs of sympathy sickness for Claire pierced my stomach—and their only cure was the person about to answer this door. For a moment, I allowed myself a blissful vision. Me, ensconced in those huge arms and pressed against the tattooed planes of his chest, letting the world fall away...

He could do that. Oh God, could he do that. I'd been there, done that, worn the T-shirt. The thing fit so fucking well, there were moments I never wanted to take it off—not even for washings.

You are so damn pathetic.

Finally, the light came to life above my head. At the same time, the door was pulled open. This was it. Do or die. Sink or swim. Visualize the victory.

"Hey." Well, that was fucking original. Nice play, Miss Asher. Stone. Whatever.

"Hey."

"Mind if I come in?"

"Do I have a choice?"

"I asked the damn question, didn't I?"

"You ask a lot of questions." An exhalation flared his nostrils. "You just don't like the answering part."

I matched his harsh breath. "Michael..."

"What?"

"I'm trying here."

He finally pulled back to move aside, opening the entrance for me. I battled not to stare as I passed. Thank God he wasn't just wearing boxers this time, although his black workout pants weren't much better. Apparently the guy didn't believe in shirts unless he was leaving the house. Hallelujah.

"Not *Ice Road Truckers* again." I couldn't help but tease him. It was familiar ground for us, and it felt good. He smiled a little—but I could see he was still pissed. His whole body was tight as a spring—not that it was a bad look for him. At all.

Since he wasn't playing host tonight, I took my own jacket off and laid it over the back of the sofa. Before he could close the door and walk back to my spot, I sucked up my courage and dove right in. "I know you might want to tell me to go fuck myself right now. I wouldn't blame you. But I just—" Damn it. I hadn't rehearsed anything past this point, expecting he'd cut in and help steer by now. "Well, I just—it's just..."

"It's just what?" All right, it was official. His fury made him hotter. Much hotter. As he approached, his gait commanding and sure, his sweats rode a little lower on his hips. His wonder V came out to play in full glory, every ridge toned, every line perfect. I let my stare wander all the way down and then back up to confront the deep fires in his eyes.

I swallowed. Then again. "I– I needed to see you. It's just been a confusing, terrible day and...well...confusing overall lately–"

"You don't say." The mirth disappeared from his lips.

"Don't be that way."

He stopped, hanging back on the other side of the couch. "Don't be–" He laughed, but the sound wasn't pleasant. "This is good," he muttered. "So good."

"Michael."

He fanned his arms and gave me a mock bow. "Right. Okay. Where are my manners? You have something to say. Please proceed."

His mocking tone was grating–but hell if I was going to let him triumph with that. He knew it too. The bastard smirked, knowing he could push. He had the upper hand here and relished it. Trouble was, he knew it secretly turned me on too.

I shook my head to try to clear it. He stepped a little closer. Near but still too far. But I could smell him now, his skin so rich with pinc and wind and soap. Memories instantly flooded because of it. Kisses in the water. Caresses in the barn. Feasting on our picnic...

"I just...needed to see you." Okay, this was good. A complete sentence, even if it was in parts. "I had–to tell you–that what I meant–Jesus, I can't even think straight–"

He just stared at me, expecting me to say more. Shit. This wasn't good after all. I'd gone inside out at just the sight of him again. I ached, needing to feel his arms around me, his body against me. I ached...

"Since...since the day I left Julian–"

Why didn't he move? At all? Couldn't he see how I was

struggling here?

"It was a shitty thing to do, but I had no choice. And ever since then, I— Well, I've thought about you. A lot. And...I..."

Couldn't he just have mercy on me? Take me in his arms, make it all better? His eyes softened. The breath he pulled in was resigned, perhaps forgiving.

"Everything we shared was—well, it was good, damn good and—"

What the fuck was he waiting for?

The moment the question blazed, so did its answer.

He needed me to ask for it.

To prove to him that I still wanted it.

Wanted him.

No games, no ploys. Straight-up feelings, out on the table.

Okay. I could do that.

Maybe.

"I— I need you." I croaked out the words while desperately inspecting my pedi.

"Pardon me?" He seemed baffled. Did I read this wrong too?

"I need you, okay? Is that what you want to hear?" I snapped my head up. Lurched toward him on legs that wobbled thanks to nerves that raced. Keeping my hands off him was like being tied down to a rock and being forced to gaze at Icarus in all his beautiful, burning fire. "I need you, Michael. I'm unraveling, and only you can help...can make me feel safe again, like you did in the mountains. I need it again. I— I need you again."

I closed the rest of the space between us, sliding my hands up the ripples of his bare chest. He didn't rear back, thank God, but he did go still as a statue. A golden, flawless one.

He finally spoke again. An uneasy grate. "Margaux..."

"Please don't say no."

And please don't try to look through me or decipher me, because what you see won't be beautiful. And right now, I need beautiful.

"Please." The word wasn't easy for me, but I was sure I'd never meant it more. "I can't be alone tonight. I need you. Please." It ceased being a plea, moving into the realm of pure need, basic instinct. The fire of Icarus burned through me now too, leading my lips to little kisses up his neck, toward his ear. Michael still didn't move—either direction. I refused to take that as a bad sign.

"Put your hands on me." I was nearly whispering, my voice husky and pleading. "Touch me as only you can, Michael. Revive me. Reveal me. Arouse me..."

"Margaux."

His head fell back. A moan ripped out of him. The sound ripped at me, drawing spiritual blood. He ached, really ached, and I'd done it to him. I hated what that felt like, an agony as strange as it was new, but I wasn't giving up. Somehow, I couldn't.

"I can't keep playing these games with you." The words vibrated up his throat. "I can't..."

"No games. I swear. This is my reality, okay? Things are complicated for me." I grimaced. "They're...ugly. But you... you're my beauty. My safety." I took one of his hands in mine. When he allowed the contact, I reached for the other one. His eyes glittered like weathered copper—tinged with brilliant green, beckoning my gaze to his face. I met his stare with the full brutality he gave me and whispered, "Take me to your bed, Michael. Take me *in* your bed. No more hay lofts or showers or meadows. I want to go to bed with you. Explore you, taste you, worship you...lose track of time with you."

Silence screamed between us as the man seemed to take my words literally. His stare shackled me forever...for a second? For eons...or just minutes? The answers didn't matter. All my fucked-up feelings didn't matter. He was all that mattered. The moment of him. The now of him. The wonder of him.

And the power of him as he swooped me off my feet and against his strength.

Was this real? And once more, did I care? I didn't want to dissect it. Only wanted to grasp the magic of it. This was happening—to me. For once, I was being carried like a treasure. Taken to the bed of the one and only man who'd ever truly mattered to me.

A lump rose in my throat, but I smashed it down by grabbing his head and kissing the hell out of him. There was no way I was going to let emotions fuck up the most amazing night of my life.

CHAPTER SIXTEEN

Michael

What the hell are you doing?

It was stuck on repeat in my mind, which obviously hoped something else in my body would get the message. A dim corner of my consciousness fist-pumped in agreement. Christ. What the hell was I doing? This was the behavior of a desperate pussy, not a man who'd gone balls out—literally—for a woman and then left with same balls swinging in the wind—literally—because of a phone call more cryptic than a summons from Tony fucking Soprano.

Even crazier thing? I'd added a mafia plot to the list of possibilities about Margaux's trip to the cryptic. A mafia plot. What else was my imagination supposed to do but go there, when the woman gave me nothing but one-eighty behavior, lame excuses, and a getaway so fast, it was like a movie spliced on fast edits.

Even then, I'd expected her to call and apologize. Or explain. Or yell at me about taking her to Julian to begin with. She'd dealt a blow even worse. She pounded down the giant Mute button between us again.

This time, I hadn't bothered with calls to banter with Sorrelle. Or the stalker-boy visit to her condo. I'd been in pure existence mode, one foot in front of the other, pausing every few days between work-sleep-food to let Keir beat the crap out of me on the beach again. I'd avoided any extended trips to my head or heart, terrified of what I'd find there.

Petrified of finding out what I knew the second she stood in my doorway again.

Somehow, in some idiotic, beyond-logical way, I'd tumbled far over the cliff of crazy for Margaux Asher.

A fact not helping the current lose-lose I faced.

Ease her ache, though I had no idea what I was easing—or cut this shit short right now and mitigate the pain while I could?

The answer came as soon as I swept her into the bedroom and then lowered us both to the bed—and our stares twined deep as rainforest vines again.

Mitigate the pain? Who the hell was I kidding? If I let her walk out now, two hours or twelve hours from now, it would hurt. Like a motherfucker. So what was the difference—except that getting her naked again might, *might*, be the right key to unlocking her at last? Yeah, I know, stupid desperation at its finest—but never had I seen her so shaky and unsure, almost as if she wanted me to find that portal and blast it open now.

There was a damn good chance I'd be miserable after this.

Like I'd been Buddy the fucking joy-joy elf before?

Some rides were worth the terror of the first drop.

I slanted my lips over hers, closed my eyes...and let the zero gravity take over.

Beneath me, Margaux whimpered. Then moaned. Fuck. She tasted better than I remembered. Felt even more incredible, with her legs tangling with mine, her body fitting against me as if there was a lovers' version of bespoke tailoring. When a growl left my own throat beyond my cognizance or control, I gave over to the heady haze of discovering her once more.

"You smell so good," I rasped into her hair. "You taste so good." As I licked her neck. "You feel so good..." As I slipped the buttons free on her lacy summer blouse and curved fingers around her breast—

Until moisture from her face seeped through my stubble.

"Sugar?" I jerked away a little. "Hey. What's—?"

"I'm not good," she blurted.

"Huh?"

"Stop telling me I'm good!" She snapped her head and flung a hand across her face, as if ashamed I was even looking at her. "I'm not good, Michael. Nothing's good right now."

Damn. This was better than I'd expected. And worse. Her fissures were more unstable than I'd assumed. I braced myself for her next exposure, unable to do much else. I had no idea what exactly I was preparing for.

"Can't we—" she stammered, "just do this—like—?"

"Like what?" I kissed her as I asked it, firm but gentle. Instead of soothing her, it worsened her agitation.

She snapped her face back, staring hard. "Like we're animals again." Her eyes went pure tigress. "The way you know I need it." So did her lips, reaching for mine, pulling me down in savage bites. "Hard and sweaty and filthy. Make me wet and needy...totally yours to control...before you fuck me until I can't see."

I groaned. The sound was as tormented as I felt. While every instinct in my blood roared to life, ordering me to just oblige the little she-cat and give her the hard pounding she begged for, a shocking percentage of my brain cells were still present and accounted for—shouting a different message entirely.

What she wanted wasn't what she needed.

And damn it, if she was going to walk away into silence again after this, she'd do it with her needs met.

I began by kissing her again—though purposely kept the dance of our tongues to a minimum. As I expected, Margaux was all for a solid veto on that choice, desperately trying to deepen the contact with every sweep I made inside her mouth. When I sensed her ramping up toward a full growl, I dragged completely away.

"Mich—"

Two fingers across her lips, along with the dagger of my frown, sliced her into silence. Her chest immediately pumped, signaling she was actually willing about it. Damn. Her compliant side was such a beautiful sight. For all the hiss and swagger she threw down at the world, it amazed me that no man had figured out how much she needed the tables turned when the lights were lowered and the sheets turned down.

"Take off your clothes, sugar. Slowly. While I watch."

Her face bathed in a deep flush. As it descended over her neck and the cleavage I'd exposed, I hoped to God it didn't stop there. I pushed up, leaning against the headboard for better sightlines as she unveiled her graceful curves, inch by breathtaking inch.

When she finally sat before me in just her lacy bra and matching thong—red, of course, and fitted to her like a flawless paint job—she lifted a quiet, serene smile. If I was still smiling at all, it was wiped clean now—as my tongue hit my throat. Dear fuck. This wasn't the woman's normal come-hither smirk, practiced on a hundred other lovers. This was a smile just for me, timid yet eloquent, beaming from her eyes as well as her lips, sucking my breath out in ways I could've never imagined.

Thank God I'd made a pact with myself already. Needs. Needs. Remember her needs.

"Now the rest." It serrated up my dry throat and came out a little hoarse. That was going to have to be okay. Nothing wrong with the woman having a clearer understanding of exactly what her beauty did to me.

As she unhitched her bra, I pulled off my shirt.

As she slipped off her panties, I unzipped my fly.

"Damn." Much worse than the first croak. Like I gave half a fuck. My verbosity seemed to touch off a secret amusement in Margaux. She shook her hair, letting it tumble over her breasts, teasing at the dusky perfection of her nipples. Her gaze slinked to the swell beating at the opening in my jeans. Thank God they were old jeans, worn to softness, lending pliancy to my aching erection.

"Like what you see?" The coy slant of her words was as clear as the emerald glints in her eyes. Yeah, the come-hither Margaux was back, working an angle at guiding the situation back to what she'd come here for. Wham and then stir—thank you, sir. As soon as she got my cock out of my pants, that was going to be a lot easier for her—a fact fully backed when said penis ignored orders from my big head and visibly jerked beneath my briefs, inspiring her to lean forward, hand stretching for the big brass ring, and—

I clinched a hand around her wrist.

With careful command, lowered it.

"I like everything I see." I pulled her in for the briefest, lightest kiss, finishing by licking along her top lip and then her bottom. "But now I'm going to see more."

Her brow crunched in an adorable scowl. "*Qué, Señor*

Pearson?"

I smiled indulgently. She could cling to the coy—for now. I actually looked forward to the process of prying her from it.

"Lie back," I directed, banishing the frog from my tone now. "Right here, in front of me. Knees up. Legs spread. Don't hide an inch of yourself from me."

Not a peep fell from her now. With a little gobsmacked expression on her face, she quickly checked mine. I arched a sharp brow. *What the hell are you waiting for?*

Inside the next minute, she was in position as I'd asked, fully on display for my gaze. The well-trimmed strip over her mound glistened with dew already. I gave her an approving growl.

She giggled and squirmed a little. "So happy to know you approve."

"Sshhh." I swung forward and lightly smacked her mons. "No more words now. No more shielding yourself behind the banter and the snark. Just listen...and comply."

A tiny huff. "You expecting a 'Yes, Sir' now? Because it's not—ahhhh!"

She cried it as I swatted her again. *Yeah, right there. Yeah, a little harder.*

"Listen."

She simply nodded. I kissed the tops of both her knees in appreciation before rocking back on my haunches.

"You have no idea how much I love gazing at your pussy. It's all the right shades, all the right textures. You know how badly I want to stretch it right now, sugar? How bad my cock is screaming at me to sheath up and screw the pigment out of your eyes?"

Her moan, long and high and gorgeous, was her only

answer. Her hands, now at her sides, twisted into the comforter. Her gaze, heavy-lidded and hot, dropped to the V of my jeans again.

"You're wet, Margaux." I curled a one-sided grin. "You thought about me inside you, and your wicked little mind turned your pussy into a soaked mess for me. Your desire twisted deep inside your body and wrung out this little stream of wetness, so shiny for me." I leaned back a little more, appraising her like a billionaire bidding on a car, pushing a thumb at my lips before dictating, "Show me more. I want to see exactly where my cock is going...that you're soaked everywhere."

As if there was a serious doubt in my mind about that—but the effects of my imperious tone on her were unmistakable. I watched her buttocks contract, her hips rock. This was exactly what she needed tonight. Complete surrender. *Make me feel safe, Michael.* That meant taking every decision from her. All of it. And oh shit, was I willing.

"Do it, Margaux. Slip your hand there. Spread yourself for me."

As she complied, bucking her body higher, she unsheathed her clit. The dark-red ridge was a shimmering gem for my gaze, matched by the stunning sight of her deeper tunnel, moist and tight in readiness.

"Perfect," I growled. "So fucking perfect."

She mewled in reply. Her fingers trembled against her flesh.

"You want to touch your wicked little clit, Margaux?" When she intensified her cry in a wordless yes, I commanded, "Thank you for being so sweet about the request. But you may not stroke your clit. Use those nasty fingers on your cunt instead. Fuck yourself, beautiful girl. Show me exactly what you want my cock to do to you."

Her eyes squeezed shut and her mouth opened wide, sucking in air to her straining, stunning body. With her thighs constricting and her free hand kneading the comforter, she was a mesmerizing sight of banked sexual heat.

"Christ," I rasped. "Look at how beautiful you are. Use two fingers now, sugar. Get them in deep." I pushed forward again, needing to marvel at the light on her flesh as she creamed harder over her fingers. "So incredible. I could paint you like this." Except that I was a shitty painter and wouldn't get past the base sketch before wanting to slide her fingers from her body and suck them into mine.

Not a bad idea at all.

She groaned as I pulled in her flesh, licking down to the sensitive skin between her fingers.

Again.

Again.

Again.

"Fucking delicious," I praised, unable to get enough of her. The smell of her on my skin heightened the perfume of her pussy in the air, swirling sweetly through my senses... and around my cock. I groaned from the siren temptation of it—as it transformed my erection from a tolerable pound to a deafening thunder.

It was time.

Fuck, yes.

Instead of releasing her hand in order to get free from my pants, I guided it beneath my briefs. Not a single word escaped Margaux's lips, bewitching me further with the magic of her obedience, especially as it took the form of sighs, moans, and erotic little-girl growls as she squeezed the precome from my pulsing head. My locked teeth and flattened lips surrendered deep grunts as she worked the length of my shaft, proving herself, hands down—pardon the pun—a damn artisan in how to stroke a man right.

A lead I wasn't going to let her take tonight.

This was about her surrender. Her letting go.

"Enough," I issued, pushing her back. "Position again. Just like before. But spread your thighs wider."

She gave me a fresh version of our private smile before complying completely. That meant I had the VIP upgrade view before even reaching into the nightstand for the condom. While rolling it on, I reveled again in how perfect she was—in how lucky I was—before instructing, "Arms up high, beautiful. Over your head. Make them comfy. This is going to be...quite a ride."

She sighed harder while positioning her hands just as I asked. Her fingers twisted into her hair, now a gorgeous mess on the duvet and getting more so with her impatient writhing. I simply watched her for a moment, pretty damn proud of her. This was taking more courage than she let on, the control freak ice princess giving in to the blaze of pure surrender, but she was doing it. Goddamn, how she was doing it...

My cock bloomed with more precome, a not-so-subtle reminder that the time to get poetic was far past. About fucking time.

I pressed in, seating myself between her legs, fitting my cock to her entrance...locking my hands atop her wrists. Her face was the precious prize before mine, and I kissed her with deep languor while probing her sex with my own. Then a scraping bite. Another easy thrust. A thorough roll of tongues. Another teasing push.

Though Margaux moaned and shuddered every time I entered her again, her breasts were soon heaving from frantic breaths and her heels dug into my back. "Ahhh," she groaned. "Ahhh, God. M-M-Michael!"

"Ssshh." I captured her lips in another long tongue tangle. "Take your fucking like a good girl."

"But—but I need to—"

"I know what you need. Soften for me, Margaux. Surrender to me. Take my cock in whatever way I give it to you."

She pulled in air deeply through her nose. "I— I trust you."

"Then let go for me too. Know that I'll make this good." I plunged in a little deeper and then swiveled. Retreated and entered, swiveled again. I saw what it did for her and smiled. Just because she liked the tempo all hard and fast didn't mean she couldn't see the beauty in slow and steady.

Beauty summed this shit up pretty damn good too...at least with the effect it had on her incredible, classic face. I was spellbound by how different she looked when she wasn't trying to make a point or prove something. Softer, lovelier—yet never more brilliant and full of life, as she grew fuller and fuller with me.

For maybe the first time in her life, she wasn't obsessed with fighting a thing.

Which meant she was free to embrace everything.

"Michael!"

When she burst with the scream, my spirit soared in victory. I meshed our hands while finally increasing the tempo to help her ride out the orgasm—and push mine to its final detonation temperature.

"Yeah, princess. I know. I— I—"

My groan made the rest impossible. I came with brutal intensity, white dots bursting behind my eyelids as I emptied myself with shattering completion.

Completion.

Holy. Shit.

Margaux Asher...

Completed me.

I didn't know whether to laugh out loud or puke my guts out. Neither was the right call, considering that my dick still pulsed against her walls and I'd barely relented my lock on her wrists. *Afterglow, asshole. Remember? The minutes you have to cuddle her and kiss her or at least high-five her. In this woman's case, maybe all three.*

But I couldn't look at her without thinking it. Without knowing it.

Without wanting it.

Damn it.

"Hey." Her breathy little summons was another twist to my mental torture rack. "You still here?" At my nod, she persisted, "Really? Because you look like you're walking to the damn guillotine."

I shook my head. "Princess, one shouldn't even joke about off with his head when you've got a guy in this position."

She gave up a snort, but it never erupted into the laugh I expected. "Okay...seriously. Give it up. You just looked a thousand miles away, with your neck under a blade. Penny for your thoughts?"

"Penny for yours?" It rolled out before I could temper the how-does-that-feel delivery—and instantly could've knifed myself in the balls, were they not still pressed against her ass.

Who else has completely killed the afterglow—while still

buried inside her? Anyone?

But proving yet again that this was a night for the unexpected, the knee in my gut and the squirming escape never came. Her hands along my back, though? Her touch against my nape? Her seeking, soft gaze?

“All I was thinking about...was how good this was. How good we are.” She knew I wouldn’t argue with that, so she plunged on, “And I know things have been...weird...”

Okay, so the laugh got to be mine instead. “Weird? You mean how you went from going wild thing with me to hopping in the car with Andre, inside one hour?”

“I had to.” Her voice broke. Suddenly, I wondered how much rehearsal that had taken. “I had to, Michael.”

“Right. Because of that phone call you also can’t talk to me about.”

“Do you think I enjoyed doing that? I love”—she stopped herself, clenching her teeth and punching out another huff—“Julian. And your mom. And being there—with you.” She broke into a little cry as I pushed up and out, hiking to her knees while I tore off the condom and slammed it into the bathroom waste can. “Michael—damn it! There’s nobody but you, okay? The call—it was business—and—”

“Right,” I growled. Clawed a hand back through my hair. “Business—that required you to call Andre for a pickup instead of asking me to take you—”

“Because you would have?” She spread her arms. Christ, why did she have to be so delectable, even doing that? Why did her hair have to cloud like that and her breasts have to be so rosy and her face have to be so captivating? An angel playing the devil’s game...

We glared each other down for at least a minute while I

wrestled with a fucking answer. Finally, convinced I did mean it, I muttered, "Yes. I would have taken you."

She let her arms drop. Tilted her head, making the light from the living room halo around her head again. "Without asking me a thousand questions about the phone call?"

Busted. And this time, not in a cute way. "Not a thousand. But...enough."

"Enough," she echoed, "to qualify as the same kind of grill job you're firing up now."

A savage sound ripped up from my gut. I tore another hand through my hair. I'd be a goddamn cue ball if this kept up. "You came pounding on my door, princess, remember? And I held you, welcomed you—without getting any more of a half-ass explanation than you had for me back in the meadow."

"And you took that condition. Carried me in here—"

"Because you needed it!"

She bounded off the bed—using the other side. "I think needs were met on both sides, Mr. Pearson."

"Yay. We both get a gold fucking star." I zipped up my shorts—beating her to the angry cover-back-up act by two fabulous seconds. I didn't bother with my shirt, taking advantage of the moment she had to deal with hers to grate, "So what happens with all this now, Margaux? What's the next step? When are you going to let me in?"

She pulled her hair out from her shirt. Went for flipping it all into some fancy braid to the side, using a hair tie she pulled from her pocket—and actually attempted an eye roll to match the teen-scene 'do. "Okay, seriously, Michael. It's not that big of—"

"Stop. Stop." I stabbed a thumb at my chest. "The guy standing next to you when you got that call in the meadow, remember? *Not that big of a deal* isn't the kind of thing that pales you by three shades and makes you shake like a permanent brain freeze just hit."

She scooted around and parked herself on the end of the bed. "Fine. So it's heavy shit. But it's not heavy shit that you need to know. It's—it's just best that you don't."

I didn't sit with her. I knew she wanted me to, but sheer shock clamped my whole body, leaving me locked in place.

This wasn't going to change. She wasn't going to change. But I'd made the massive, moronic mistake of banking on the belief that she would...of thinking that everything we'd shared until now wasn't just the stuff of hot sexual memories but of mutual communication, affection, and trust. I'd even told myself not to do it, including the blatant self-motivational speech after carrying her in here, and still fallen into the trap. Assumed our mind-blowing sex had to be due to something else working right between us too...

Holy shit.

I'd turned into a chick.

I walked across the room. I had to get away from the bed—and the reminder it now served as my beyond-belief stupidity. "So let me get this straight," I said, bracing arms to the doorframe. "You want me to stay signed on for sexual relief from the heavy shit, but it's just best that I don't know what any of that is."

Margaux rose. Her arms were ramrod stiff, her hands working as rotating fists. "The last time I checked, the sexual relief thing was a perk for both sides here."

"Which all sounds real good, if this was a business partnership. Is that what it is to you, Margaux?"

She blinked. "Excuse me?"

"Because that's what I'm beginning to feel." I ground my own fists, crunching knuckles into the wood. "But maybe that was my mistake, right? The whole feeling thing. Because if this was just a business merger for you, supply and demand meeting at opportune moments, I could've saved you a little time and effort." I went full-in for the conclusion, spearing her with my stare to drive it in. "I'm simply not for sale."

She stiffened. Glared. "That's disgusting."

Instead of replying—and probably saying more that was wrong, rash, or both—I pushed off the jambs, spun, and marched through the living room to my office. In the middle of my desk was the sheaf of papers I'd been staring at, off and on, for the last week. Had even tossed in the trash a couple of times before fishing back out, torn about whether I was looking at them through the right lenses of logic. Then wholly convinced that letting my heart weigh in on decisions might not be such a bad thing.

Until now.

Following your heart? That shit worked for knights fighting windmills, lost clown fish, and little girls stuck over the rainbow.

Bad, bad choice for dumb fucks like me.

As I picked up the stack again, running a thumb over the expensive vellum paper, Margaux appeared in the office doorway. Not-so-mild shocker. She wasn't one to stick around when anyone pulled what she called an extreme asshat, and I was sure I'd just qualified. But right now, I was too spun-out to care.

"What are you doing?" she asked. Her sneer was gone, in its place a voice closing in on a whisper. Did she already sense what I was about to reveal? Did it even matter?

The speculation led to my own quiet query. "Damn. I care for you so much, Margaux. But you're not ever going to let go and care the same way...are you?"

"Mich—"

I gashed the air with a hand. "That field's not worth stomping again. We'll just ride the merry-go-round and end up back at the same place, probably more torqued than we are now. I know you can't let me in. I know it's for my own good. I'm a grown man, not a six-year-old who needs to be led through it again."

"I never thought you were—" Her face contorted as if I'd stabbed her. I refused to feel shitty about it. Apparently, neither did she. Her queen bee mask snapped back on, so seamlessly fitted that most people wouldn't have recognized the transition. "Fine. No merry-go-round. You got it, boss. Far be it from me to hold you back from the pity party you're set on instead."

I didn't jump at the bait. Not out of anger but of exhaustion. I couldn't do this with her anymore, and if I hung around here, I would—over and over and over again, like an adrenaline junkie swearing he'd only bungee it off the bridge one more time.

How many more times before the rubber band snapped?

With the thought of my head bashing into a riverbed, I held up the sheaf. "These papers are from a law firm called Hayden and Hutton. They're one of the finest outfits in Atlanta. Client list includes Mercedes, Mohawk, and Rubbermaid. Met them at a USD Law School career day. A couple of weeks ago, they reached out—with this."

She blinked. "With...what?"

"It's a job offer, Margaux."

She blinked harder. "So they're expanding to San Diego

or something?"

"No. It's an offer with their offices in Atlanta."

She lowered herself into a chair, gripping both armrests during the jerky movement. "Oh."

Every goddamn bone in my body wanted to go to her. To kneel before her like the knight I yearned to be for her, begging her to let me protect her, cherish her, be the completion she needed too. Instead, I lowered into the chair behind the desk. "I've already talked to some friends about it." When they weren't turning my body to mush up and down Coronado Beach. "And Mom, of course."

"And she's supportive?" She scowled a little, seeming surprised.

"Yeah. Weepy but supportive. Things have stabilized at home. Carlo's started to go a little growly watchdog about her, which I don't mind in the least." I shrugged. "She wants me to be happy."

"And you're not?"

Screw wanting to kneel for her. "Margaux," I snarled. "Damn it." Lurched to my feet, opting to pound the desk. When that jerked her stare to mine, I didn't stall about taking full advantage. "Tell me not to go." Every syllable shot from between my teeth, viciously pleading. "Tell me I have a reason to stay. Look at me now. Tell me. Mean it. Tell me—and I'll shred all of this with my bare hands, right now."

A moment. Another.

Her silence, like spikes of steel, twisting between my ribs, up my torso, into my heart.

Her tears were the acid poured into those wounds.

"Yeah," I finally muttered. "That's what I thought."

I'd taken one last bungee jump—and survived. Barely.

★ ★ ★ ★

It was the butt-crack of morning, but after Margaux left, I gave up on sleep. Now that I'd really made the decision to burn the bridge, I wanted to strike the match and be done with the whole thing.

At exactly five thirty-two a.m., I slid my key card across the pad next to the designer glass entry doors of Asher and Associates and entered the building for the last time. At a place like Asher, used to dealing with scandals that broke at the speed of light and had to be contained even faster, two-week notices were more a nuisance than a help. Besides, I imagined Andrea being more relieved by my departure than anything, especially if she guessed a commoner like me was sniffing at her princess. Whatever rift had gone down between her and Margaux, blood was still blood. A mother still loved her daughter. Now the two of them could hunt for a suitable prince together.

Resignation letter in hand, I walked down the silent halls toward boss lady's office. The document was brief, to the point, and somewhat edited, though I'd not poured a lot of stress into it. The woman wouldn't read past the first paragraph.

I only hoped my departure might wake up Chad now too. He needed to get out of here just as much as I did. In reality, just about everyone on the staff did. Lately, it felt like Andrea checked in her Gucci-clad ass to the office but simply phoned in her brain—with a line that had serious disconnection problems. Her distracted behavior was becoming the source of more and more coffee room in-jokes.

Not my problem anymore.

Thank fuck.

I repeated the words while placing my sealed letter on

Andrea's space-age desk, its chrome and Plexiglas surfaces beginning to glow with the orange tones of the sunrise. I turned and took in the bay and the Embarcadero, both golden and glimmering in the early morning light, before gazing across the water to the shore at the Naval Base, where SEAL recruits practiced maneuvers with their Zodiacs. While turning for my own office, I promised myself to ping Keir for one last torture session before I left to get fat on peach cobbler, cornbread, and full-sugar Coke.

I took the long way home, so to speak, in order to duck into the mail room for a box to dump my personal things into. When I emerged, I frowned. I was sure I'd turned the light off after leaving boss lady's domain, but I'd also been up all night. Functioning memory cells were at a premium right now.

I was halfway back to Andrea's office before being stopped by the sound of laughter. Andrea's laugh wasn't what pushed my brakes. She worked at all hours, especially if a client crisis had just hit. But she wasn't the only one in there. A masculine timbre rumbled through the air.

Colin. Of course. I vaguely remembered Andrea telling everyone she'd be in Cabo over the weekend—since she'd returned early, he must have accompanied her straight from the airport.

I heaved a soft sigh. Twirled the box on my finger a few times, basketball style—like that added to the productive output of the moment.

Just go get it over with.

Since she was here in the office and would soon know I was too, the decent action would be a short visit to tell her about the contents of the letter. Sooner was better, since Colin was still here. The man balanced Andrea, filling in the places she was weak—like smiling, remembering names, and not treating everyone in the world like the help.

Yep. Best to get my ass in there while the air was still palatable.

Whoa.

I froze in my tracks again. Immediately backed away on ninja steps before tucking into the alcove near the water cooler, pressing my back to the wall and controlling my breathing.

What the hell? Few too many episodes of Jack Bauer, man?

If what I'd just seen was right, I was allowed the bizarre action. It completely fit the mind-blower of a twist to the morning.

Colin wasn't the guy at Andrea's side for the breakfast-hour view. And the you-got-a-fine-ass-girl embrace. And the dual glasses of champagne, sloshing over as she returned the sentiment.

Trey Stone was.

I risked another glance, taking advantage of the abnormal angle on Andrea's double office doors, to confirm my eyes hadn't just fucked over my head.

They sure as hell hadn't.

Damn it.

"What the hell?" I fired beneath my breath—applying it to both aspects of this craziness. This nod to my inner Jack Bauer? In a word, bizarre. But Andrea Asher, my married boss, getting on with the feels—with Trey fucking Stone? Bizarre didn't cover a second of it.

Whop.

The *smack* of a champagne cork escaping its bottle snapped my stare back up. Foam dribbled over Trey's hand.

Andrea leaned in and licked it off.

As Margaux would say, ew. I dealt with a less polite reaction from my throat, swallowing hard against the invasion of bile.

"Easy, Barbarella," Trey drawled out. "Time for that later."

Andrea perched herself better on the desk—scooting her ass right over my letter—and then crossed her legs, leaned back on one hand, and arched her back a little. "You mean after your brilliance makes us five million dollars richer?"

Koo-koo-ka-choo, Mrs. Robinson.

"Oh, I don't know if I'd call it 'brilliance'—or maybe I would." Trey sipped his fresh bubbly with one hand and ran his fingertips over her knee with the other. "But it was a team effort."

Andrea lifted her flute. "Here's to great minds, then."

"And knowing how to yank the chains you want."

"When you want."

They clinked glasses, opening a damn good moment for me to move again, but I was riveted in place. This wasn't like watching a train wreck or a car chase. This was like walking through a murder scene and feeling like shit for the person whose body lay on the floor.

Andrea slid to her feet, encased in high-heeled ankle boots on top of black fishnets, and paced to the window. Trey followed like a smitten puppy, shoving aside her hair to nuzzle her neck. She laughed softly. "Now who's the one who needs an 'easy Barbarella'?"

Trey growled. "Don't tease me, Dre."

Dre?

"No teasing, my sexy big boy. You know that. As soon as the circle's complete, it'll be just you, me, and the Caribbean

Sea."

He pushed a little closer, caging her between the glass and his body, shoving at her ass like—well, a mutt.

"Gah." I spat it softly toward the floor. Some things just couldn't be erased, no matter how much brain bleach you wished for.

Fido wasn't getting the message. "I hate meeting like this."

"I know. But it was the only way to get free. If he calls me from Cabo, I have to pick up the phone."

I guessed that the he was Colin. Poor, trusting idiot.

"You're right." Trey pushed away, chugged his champagne, and then poured himself some more. "What's a few more days to wait, when we have years of pleasure ahead?"

Andrea drained her glass a little more carefully. "Do you think anyone's caught on?" she asked. "At Stone Global?"

"Like I fucking care. If they do, it's not traceable back to me or you." He chugged again. "SGC. Fuck them. Stands for Shitty Goddamn Cocksuckers, you know. They can all smooch my brilliant, tight butthole."

Andrea erupted in laughter. When Trey joined in with a snicker more obnoxious than Beavis and Butthead, I knew I'd heard enough—in more ways than one.

The shit in my office wasn't worth hanging out for. I left the building via the back stairs and then doubled back to the lot, jumping into the Denali with the urgency of fucking Batman headed for the bowels of Arkham. But I was headed for a destination possibly more dangerous for me than that.

Margaux's place.

CHAPTER SEVENTEEN

Margaux

"We need to talk."

Nothing good ever came from a conversation that started that way. This time was no different, even if the words emanated from the golden god of a man I was still half-peeved with. Atlanta job offer, my ass. He belonged in Atlanta as much as I belonged in a Barstow fast-food joint.

"Michael." I peered across the living room, checking the time. I hadn't even looked when first buzzing him up, but now, even looking at twenty-four-inch-high numbers on the wall, I found the truth hard to believe. "It's a quarter past six."

"I know." He awkwardly pecked the top of my head. "Sorry."

Despite my half-conscious state, I instantly wanted more than the kiss. I hated the way things were now—and now was only a little more than eight hours old. I wanted to slap him and mack on him at the same time. Sounded like the stuff of a very hot fuck to me. But he wanted more than—how had he phrased it?—*supply and demand meeting at opportune moments.*

In short, he wanted what I couldn't give. Hearts, flowers, date nights, a drawer at his place. Everything a girl dreamed of from a guy. Everything I dreamed of from *this* guy.

Everything I'd fuck up in major, awful ways. Especially

now.

So, I'd pulled the classic Margaux. Walked out of the door first—even if it had split my heart cleanly in two. And, very likely, his too.

"You missing something?" I muttered. "Did you leave something here?" It seemed the only explanation that made sense—except that maybe he just wanted a closure fuck. *I'm open to the suggestion, stud.* I'd never turn down the chance to have him in my bed. The man rocked my senses like nobody else—and if required, I could park all the emotions right outside the door.

For the most part.

"I was just at the office," he said.

"Mutant," I countered. "You're worse than me. If I go in on a Sunday, at least I wait until the sun is up."

"I went in to submit my resignation letter and get my shit packed."

Well, now I was awake. "Oh." What the hell?

"But something strange happened while I was there. I can't put it all together, and I'm hoping you can shed some light on it."

Something strange. He seemed sincerely troubled by that, but I was beyond confused. A ploy for the closure fuck still made more sense. But turning in his resignation letter—if he was playing this straight up—meant he was serious about Atlanta. Shit.

This was a lot to handle before caffeine. "Look, Michael... I'm not sure what any kind of drama at your office has to do with me." I licked my lips and tested out a little step forward, pulling at the collar of his jacket. He'd showered recently. Hell, it smelled nice. Soap and shampoo and his untamed scent...

ohhh, yes. "I would've been happy to just meet up again. You didn't have to make up some weird story about—"

"Stop." He cut me off so vehemently, my teeth audibly crashed from my jaw closure. Though he didn't push off my hands, he didn't touch anything else, either. "Just stop and let me finish, Margaux."

As he dragged a hand through his hair, I looked at him. Really looked. Shit. His eyes were bloodshot and his skin sallow.

"Go on," I encouraged softly. "I'm listening now. I really am."

He shook his head, and I tried not to notice how ridiculously sexy he still was. "I dropped my letter onto Andrea's desk and was in the mail room, hunting for a box for my stuff. That was when I heard voices—back in Andrea's office."

"Where you'd just been." After he nodded, I pressed, "So was one of them Andrea?"

"Yeah."

"Not shocking yet." Or having a damn thing to do with me.

"Of course not. And I wasn't stunned either. I was just bummed, knowing the polite thing to do was go face her in person and explain the contents of my letter."

"Captain America."

My mutter didn't detract him. "I headed straight for her office. Figured facing her would be easier with Claire's dad there."

"Colin's was the other voice you heard?"

"I assumed so, since the other voice was a dude."

Slow burn. "That man was the one good move my mother ever made. It'll be a damn wonder if he stays around much longer, though. I can already see the dull glaze in his eyes."

"Well, this will be another nail in her coffin."

I scowled. "Shit."

"About sums it up." Now that he was relaying the details, he loosened a little. *A little.* "When I rounded the corner and got a good view of her office, our favorite Irishman wasn't in the office with her. It was Trey Stone. And they were already going for some hands-on training—as in hands on ass."

I needed to say something. But a person needed a functioning brain to do that. Mine froze solid. Everything froze. My tongue, my throat, my arms, my legs. I was suddenly sucked down a black tunnel, surrounded by echoes of one awful question.

Why was my personal Satan keeping frisky time with my cheating tramp of a mother?

Oxygen. I needed oxygen.

I whirled and dashed toward the patio but only got as far as the couch, where Michael caught me and forced me to sit. "Whoa, whoa, whoa, sugar. Easy. Put your head between your knees. Don't argue."

Somewhere, through my horrified haze, I heard somebody approaching hyperventilation. Dear God, it was me. I didn't argue with Michael, letting him push my head between my kneecaps. Finally, the humming in my ears lessened. The tunnel got shorter. I wiggled my toes just to make sure I could. I liked black on my toes. I bet Michael would end up with a girl who painted her toes pink all the time.

"Better?" he finally asked. I nodded slowly, and he growled, "So do you want to tell me what the hell just happened?"

I pulled upright again, to find Michael staring at me with real concern etched into his face. Damn, he was handsome.

As in, whiplash-inducing handsome. His features were mesmerizing but rugged, his smile reminiscent of the boy next door—who'd take you to his room and show you his naughtiest comics. I never got bored of gazing at him.

Fuck, I was going to miss him.

Was he really going to do the damn Atlanta thing?

But if he didn't, would it change anything?

Snap out of it, girlfriend.

"What?" I retorted at him. "Sheez-uss, Michael. This isn't a big mystery. The two people I hate the most show up in the same place with the person I care about the most. So yeah, I freaked out a little bit."

He canted his head. Actually tilted up one side of his mouth, but not without a price for the look. Naughty comics. "To quote a stunning blonde I know—bullshit."

"What bullshit?" I spread my arms. "The entire world knows what Trey did to Killian and Claire last year. Hell, you were there to help clean up the mess. Why are you acting like an ass about this?"

"I'm not calling bullshit about that and you know it." He caught my hands, encased them in his own, and then brought them together between us. "Stop skirting the issue and level with me, Margaux. How is it going to hurt you at this point?"

I ducked my head. *It isn't me I'm worried about hurting. At least any further.*

"Damn it, you are one stubborn woman. Talk to me. Please. Look at it this way—soon, I'll be out of your hair for good and you can stop worrying about anyone getting close to you ever again. Hell, if you're lucky, maybe forever!"

Ouch.

I gaped at him. No one had ever pulled cojones like this

with me, exercising the right to just call me on my shit like this. I didn't know whether to kick him in those damn balls or just kick him out of my house.

Or weep and beg him to stay forever.

"There are days I hate you," I whispered. "You know that?"

"Yes, ma'am." As if on cue, there was that damn crooked grin of his again. I wanted to slap it hard off his face—and lick the red mark I'd leave behind.

I arched an eyebrow. "Okay, first of all, that was a low blow—even in my book. And now, just so we're clear, I've wanted to tell you things about my world for a long time. But damn it, Michael, I'm trying to protect you."

That erased the grin. "You're trying to protect me?"

"Yes. It's a lot of a mess, okay? I've dreaded the idea of you getting dragged into all of it—not because I don't trust you, or because you're leaving, or whatever other jackass reasons you've made up." I twisted my fingers through his. "You've come to mean...so much to me, Michael. You probably don't believe it, but the day you leave is going to be very hard. Only for you would I risk the world's cheesiest line, okay?"

He eyed me warily. "That being...?"

"I— I hope we'll still be friends."

Michael groaned. "You're right. That's awful."

"Come on. We were before, and I can't imagine my life without you in it." A winch twisted in my throat again. Ugh. I'd fought back more tears in the last three months than I'd shed my whole life before. "I've never...cared...about someone before, the way I do you. I'm going to miss this. I'm going to miss us." When he answered my whisper by leaning in closer, I pulled a hand free and pushed at his chest. "Let's not make it worse now." Yes, that just happened. This was me, turning down a pass from him. "You've made your choice, so let's move on. Let's talk about the weirdness"—understatement gold medal—"you saw at the office. And I'll really try to give you as much truth as I can in return."

The man didn't miss much, and this moment was no exception. My statement jerked his brows up. "Maybe you should tell me about the scene at the office, sugar. Sounds like you're uniquely qualified." He jabbed his chin. "Go ahead. Take a stab. What were they talking about?"

I took a deep breath. Another. Shoved my hands between my knees now. It was so hard to decide where to start. It was so hard to be doing this, period. I'd been hiding so much of my private life for so long.

"Do you remember the night I spent at your house after Claire and Killian's wedding?"

His lips turned up, soft and sincere. "Won't ever forget it."

"When I came home that morning, I was still hungover—"

"To say the least?"

I shoulder-whacked him. Then went on. "I was also flying pretty high on the memories of what happened with us that night." Glad I hadn't let my hand stay, I pushed at the self-satisfied turn of his smirk. "Whoa there, Mr. Modesty. The pretty's about to get ugly." Hands between the knees again. Helped to hide the shaking. "When I got home, the alarm wasn't set. Should've panicked but didn't. By the time it clicked that something was wrong, it was too late. Trey Stone was sitting at my kitchen island."

As I'd anticipated, Michael tensed. I waited through the long second it took for him to absorb all of it.

As stupid a move as waiting for a fuse to a bomb to burn

down.

"I'm going to kill him."

"Michael." The censure sounded like Di. I didn't regret it. "Calm—"

"I will kill that loser motherfucker."

"—down! Now."

He lurched to his feet. Also not a surprise, given the chest beating he'd clearly gone all in on now. I'd known he'd go ooga-booga ape man... I just hadn't pegged to what degree. "Did he hurt you? Did he touch you? So help me God, if he laid one finger on you, I will kill him."

It was all I could do to keep my ass on the couch. Wouldn't do for two of us to be tearing up the carpet. "This was exactly why you didn't know about this sooner. Until I had things taken care of—"

"Taken care of?" He started pacing. Hard. "You don't take care of a rich-boy psychopath like Trey Stone, Margaux. People like him refuse to be *taken care of* until they've sucked you dry. Have you forgotten everything he put us through last year—and we were a team of six people. He still had his cars, his women, and his swagger rep then. God only knows what fuckery he's up to now—and he's involved you?"

I kept my shoulders back and my face calm. I'd dealt with this before... It was just usually some politician or rap star caught with their pants down in the wrong place. And as alluring as the idea was of Michael Pearson with his pants down right now...

Focus.

"You need to take a breath, Pearson. The world doesn't need saving at the moment."

He lowered to an ottoman near the window. Braced

his hands on his knees. In lethally low punches of sound, he charged, "What the hell did he do to you, Margaux?"

"Not until you're more calm."

"I'm not five years old, damn it."

"And neither am I! Look at me, Michael. I'm fine. I don't need rescuing."

"The fuck you don't." Back up to his feet, stalking the room worse than before. "You already did. And I failed you. I failed you, Margaux!"

I sprang to my feet. Rushed to where he was and grabbed his hands again. "Listen to me. And look at me, damn it! You need to hear my words." I waited, trying to catch my breath, as he swung his brilliant gaze to mine. "I've lived for twenty-seven years, nearly on my own, in a privileged circle of people who don't always play nice. Contrary to what you believe or the dynamic we share—shared—in the bedroom, I don't need rescuing. I really want to share some of this with you, but I can't if you keep freaking out. People are creepy sometimes. Not everything is sweet and gentle and neighborly and kind like up in the land of the Apple Dumpling Gang. You have to deal with that fact right now if you want to hear the rest of this story, because it's not for the faint of heart."

I ran my hands up to his elbows. Yearned to do more, to press myself to him and take away some of the torment that glittered in his eyes. And while I'd hoped my pep talk would bolster him a little, it only made matters worse. He put on a great performance of calm, but only on the surface. I saw right through him. I felt right through him. His whole body was poised and ready to pop like a cork in a shaken champagne bottle. His jaw ticked like a high-energy dance beat. Yay, a self-contained party in one hot hunk of a package—only the deep jade of his eyes didn't promise a very festive conclusion to the celebration.

"Shit," I stammered. "You're starting to scare me."

His gaze darkened, intensifying his menacing appearance. "I'm just a little tense."

"You think?"

"Just keep talking. I'll be okay. If that piss bucket Trey was in the room right now, it'd be a different story."

"And now you want me to tell you more?"

"I can handle it. I'm just enraged that I wasn't here to watch over you. And yeah, I know you don't need watching. I heard you, loud and clear."

His bitter tone was transparent. My speech had hurt him. But he'd needed to hear it, so I wasn't apologizing.

I sucked in a big breath and went on with the story.

"Trey confronted me with some information—okay, some dirt—about me, from an awful period in my life about two years after graduating college." Blinding lightbulb in the brain. "Wait. Whoa."

"What?"

"The secret Trey had...well, it's a mind-blower—and was supposed to have been sealed in the records at Scripps Mercy. I'd been racking my brain trying to figure out how Trey got his paws on those files, especially because he didn't necessarily have the money to pay a bunch of people off. But if he and Andrea are"—I winced and shuddered—"together, then that explains a lot of things." Knees gone to mush again, I dropped to the couch. "Holy shit. A lot of things. He didn't pay anyone off for the information. He got it straight from the person who originally had the records sealed."

"Your mother."

She's not my mother. Thank fucking God.

I whipped a stare out of the window, thoughts spinning wildly. "But why would she do this to me? Does she really hate me that much?"

My senses were a messy web, spiders of hurt and anger crawling everywhere. Andrea Asher, who'd maintained how she'd loved me exactly like a daughter, had sold me out like a gutter-level hooker—to Trey Stone.

Was there any way to even a score like this, short of pulling a trigger? There had to be. And I was damn well going to find it—and implement it. But those thoughts only reinforced my stand. These were dirty waters, not worthy of Michael even dipping his pinkie toe into.

I snapped my gaze back around, drawn by an uncanny sense of his. Sure enough, he was waiting with his I-miss-nothing scrutiny, helping me process all this with his silent, firm strength.

She'd signed my report cards.

Attended my lousy clarinet recitals.

Set up the *Hello Kitty* humidifier when I had a cold.

She'd been pretending.

A sob formed out of the nausea in my gut. I refused to let it take form. I refused to waste a second of my sadness on that woman. My fist clenched as I vowed it myself, over and over and over.

"Hey."

I jerked my head up again. Wound my hand into his once more. Needing it this time. "Hey."

"You all right?"

I nodded fast. Concentrated on the beautiful power of his fingers. "I want to tell you the rest."

He pressed his grip tighter. "Then I want to hear it."

Well, that was fine and dandy. Pushing the words out my lips? Another story.

"Need a bookmark?" he asked. "You said something about being out of college a few years...?"

"Right," I said, nodding again. "Right. I don't know if you remember or not, but I dated a professional baseball player for a while. Doug Simcox."

"From the Yankees?" He jolted a little. "Sure, I remember him. Who doesn't? Never cared about his personal shit, though. I was deep into school back in those days. I had no clue about the gossip lines or the entertainment shows until Andrea hired me."

I actually grinned for a split second. "Unreal. I've actually found one of the three people on the planet who has no idea about DougMar."

"DougMar?" His eyes sprang wide. "Oh, say it wasn't so."

"It was so."

"Agghhh."

"Right? Anyway, fast forward by a year, to the day Doug broke it off with me."

"He didn't pull the hoke move and just text, did he?"

My grin sprang into a laugh. "No. He was a little classier than that—but it was still pretty ugly. It was all over the tabloids and social media within hours, and I was devastated. I was so worried about my social standing back then, trying to figure out what they all wanted me to be and hounding Doug to fit into the same mold. I think he'd just had enough."

Michael chuffed. "Sounds like he was just a pussy."

I spurted. "Is that so?"

His upper lip curled. So sexy. "Yeah, that's so. Why didn't

he just put his foot down with you and work it out?"

There were so many variables to filling in that blank, I didn't start. Doug was part of my past—and, though a meaningful part, wasn't worth talking about right now. "That's a lot of shit, for a different day. The DL is this—I did something desperate to try to get Doug back. In a nutshell, I was young and foolish and crying out for attention. Lots of therapy and years of maturity and I can finally say that."

Naturally, I'd started twisting the hell out of my pinkie ring. Hawkeyes Pearson zeroed right in on that again and moved in, lifting one hand to the side of my face. I leaned into his touch for a tiny moment. How could I resist? His hold was so warm, so calming. Safe. I was safe once more.

God, I was going to miss this. Miss him.

"Tell me what you did to yourself, Margaux."

I couldn't deny his request any more than my own breath. He'd made it okay to do so. "I took a bunch of pills my mother—Andrea—had in her medicine cabinet. She'd had a nose job. Or maybe it was her boobs?"

"Irrelevant."

"True."

"So what was the shit?"

"Vicodin. I took...a lot. I don't really remember how many. It certainly doesn't matter at this point. I just wanted to escape it all, you know? Anyway, I was an idiot."

Michael inhaled hard. Exhaled with twice the intensity. "But an idiot who survived."

"Thanks to Andre." I nodded at his widened eyes. "Oh, yes. He'd just started working for me and looked for me in the house when I was more than fashionably late to the car. He found me lying on my bed in my favorite black Zac Posen gown, beyond revival. He called nine-one-one and followed the ambulance to the hospital. Held my hand while they pumped my stomach in the ER." I shrugged. "The rest, as they say, is history."

His face hadn't given up its frown. "Andre was there for it all? But...where was Andrea?"

"Barbados. Handling a client. She handled me via phone calls to the office—and, of course, to me directly at the hospital too. She wanted to be sure my words dovetailed with the press releases." I smoothed a hand over the fist he'd curled. "In her mind, that was good mothering, Michael. Andrea was never the apple-pie-and-Independence-Day-parade type. She handled the spin for me, made sure the world saw my crisis as only exhaustion. They even floated the story that I'd broken it off with Doug, that it was his insane schedule that put me in the hospital."

I watched him battle to let the fury go. After a minute, he looked up, piercing me with every gold and green facet of his gaze. He brushed strands of hair back from my face, the tiny pieces that always seemed to get in my eyes, before tucking them behind my ear.

"I'm glad you didn't succeed," he murmured. "My life would've been so incomplete without you."

I just rolled my eyes. *And that's why you're leaving.*

"I'm not feeding you corn chowder platitudes, sugar. I mean it." His stare glittered deeper. "I've never met a woman like you—and I know I never will again." A wistful smile dusted his lips. "The rest pale in comparison to you, Margaux."

His fingers lingered on my face. I meshed mine with them, unsure what to say. I had comeback lines for every insult people could dream up, but responding eloquently to his adoration and kindness? I was lost worse than the Galactica.

"Michael—"

"Sshhh. Not done," he insisted. "I need to let you know... I'm so sorry you were alone back then. That you were in a situation that led you to hurt yourself as the only way out. That things were so desperate, you wanted to end your life. I'm sorry Andrea left you all alone to deal with the aftermath from Doug. That woman isn't fit to be called a mother. And I hope you know now, that no matter what goes on between us, you can always come to me."

Okay...lost? Try thrust out of the damn universe. My comfort zone was blasted behind three galaxies ago. He couldn't keep doing this to me. Not when he was about to be living on the other side of the damn country!

"Stop," I bit out. "Just...stop. Cut the twelve-step bullshit, Michael. Doug was eons ago. That was all another lifetime ago. I wasn't half the woman then that I am now. How do you think I got here? This version of me rose from those ashes."

He smiled. "A real phoenix."

"Whatever." Why was he always so poetic? And why did it always make my chest flip over my stomach and then back again?

"All right." he finally relented. "Let me circle this all around again to—God help me—Trey Stone."

Did we have to? Just hearing that asshole's name forced bile up my throat. But Michael had a point. We'd digressed, and it hadn't been pretty. "Trey came here...to blackmail me."

Michael's eyes darkened to that same violent green shade. "And that doesn't surprise me...why?"

"He knew every detail—the real ones—about my suicide attempt. Clearly, Andrea either gave him the scoop about it or told him where to find it. But he had all the dirty details down and told me if I didn't give him a small mountain of money, he would go to the media with my whole story."

"So what happened?" He almost answered his own question by keeping his scrutiny fixed on my face. "No," he blurted. "Ahhh, no, Margaux. Don't tell me—"

"Okay, I won't." I pulled my hand back, folding both arms in. "I told you this wasn't going to be fun."

"You gave him the damn money?"

I ignored his thunderous glare. "Not all, but enough—for now. I drained my savings and skimmed some more off an account at SGC until my lawyers can get into my trust fund. After that, I'm going to replace what I took. At least it's holding him over."

"Wait a minute."

If I cracked his skull open, there'd certainly be a hundred gears whirling inside. Damn it. For being raised in the land of seed spreaders and boot stores, the man was damn smart. But at the moment, the lawyer in him had clearly kicked in.

Exactly what I was afraid of.

"How did you have access to an SGC account?" he demanded. "That's not a normal perk for an employee, even in the milk and honey clouds of Stone Global. I mean, Claire probably doesn't even have access to the corporate bank accounts."

Shit.

In for a penny, in for a pound, right?

I lifted my shoulders. Leveled my head. "Because I'm a Stone."

Stare. Stare. Head shake. Stare.

"Michael?"

"Huh? What did you just say?"

"You once asked me what kind of shit went down between Andrea and me during the trip to Chicago last summer. Well, that's the shit. I learned that my last name is rightfully Stone. And while we're having so much fun with the mindfuck, my first name is actually Mary."

"Jesus Christ."

"No relation. Whatsoever."

The chuckle I hoped for? Not happening. "Wh-When did you find this out?" he stammered.

"Right before Josiah Stone died. From his deathbed, he spilled the beans about being my rightful baby daddy."

He peered around the room, his jaw slack. Shock had overtaken him. I sat quietly, giving him time to process it all, careful about overloading him with facts he didn't ask for.

"So Andrea..."

"Is not actually my mother. She adopted me after Josiah knocked up a secretary. There was going to be a pretty huge scandal, so they agreed that Andrea could adopt me. Everyone had the win—until Josiah decided to clear his conscience before taking the final train home. The scene in his hospital room was very soap opera dramatic."

To his credit, Michael didn't bolt to his feet again. But an entertaining string of profanity later, he turned toward me with full upper body attention, bracing one arm to the cushion behind my butt. His focus was almost overpowering. "So how are you doing with all this?"

Thunderbolt of awkwardness. If he expected me to crumple on impact, I was about to disappoint him. "No worse for the wear. I actually lost about ten pounds when it first happened, so I might even tag it another win."

He grimaced. "I'm serious. This is some crazy shit."

I bugged my eyes at him. "Welcome to my so-called life." Really, what else does one say after dropping a bomb like that on someone? It was a lot to digest, and I'd lived through all of it already. "Hey, how about a drink? I know this is a broadside."

He pulled his what-what-what face. "At seven in the morning?"

"But in Lahore, Pakistan, it's seven at night. Happy hour!"

"I don't think they have happy hour in Lahore, sugar." A revelation seemed to cross his face before he relented, "You're right. Fuck it. A beer does sound good."

"I think Sorrelle actually got that sissy microbrewery shit you like," I joked on the way to the kitchen. "And now that you won't be around anymore, I'll just be throwing it out."

"Ha fucking ha." He teased, but the shadows in his eyes betrayed how my comment struck home. He had a lot to deal with right now, and I'd just added to the pile, despite the fact that he'd asked for it.

My own pile deepened too. Saying the words somehow made them true. He really wouldn't be coming around anymore.

My chest was heavy. My stomach was a hollow pit. Screw it. For once, I wanted a Honey-Cinnamon Pale Ale Brewer's Select too.

I grabbed two bottles from the stainless-steel monster in my kitchen, battling not to consider all the Michael-sized fingerprints that wouldn't smudge it anymore either. Why the hell had I told Sorrelle to wipe the last set off? Maybe I could get Michael to smear it up one more time, for old time's sake.

"So you're Claire's stepsister—"

"And her sister-in-law." I knew where he was going, so I cut him off while handing over his beer. "Yep, it was funny for a micro-second to us too."

He chuckled and chugged. "Oh, hell. I'll bet!"

I gave him a halfhearted smile, but just as quickly, it fell.

Now that you won't be around anymore...

I couldn't do this. Couldn't face this.

He was leaving.

He was leaving.

My heart shoved itself inside out. Then leapt to my throat and set up camp there.

"I– I think you should go now."

Michael set down his beer. "What?" Glowered hard. "Why? What the fuck? I thought we–"

"I don't know what you thought, but it was wrong. You got the information you came for, right? So...I just need you to go now." I stood up, smoothed my skinny jeans down my legs, and waited for him to follow suit. For some reason, he didn't budge. What? Like the beer was a temporary parking pass for his ass?

"Please, Michael. Let's not make this harder than it already is, or has been, for both of us. I just think it would be best if–"

"If what?" Now he decided to move, approaching me like a lion newly out of its cage. Slow. Stealthy. Steady. "If we ignore the feelings that are sitting in this room like an elephant?"

"Well..." My return volley of flippancy came out better than I'd hoped. "Yes, actually. So sorry you didn't get more beer, but it is seven a.m. Bye, now. Thanks for coming."

I walked toward the foyer with him hot on my trail. Finally.

A short-lived triumph.

He grabbed my arm, forcing me back around. "That may be your game, beautiful, but it's sure as hell not mine."

I shook him off but only because he let me. "Good thing I

have the home field advantage, then, huh?"

He slammed his hands to his hips—making me guess premeditated distraction. The way his jeans rode his endless legs...and the blatant bulge of his biceps against his T-shirt... Damn.

But my lust only reinforced what needed to happen here. Right now. If he stayed, everything between us would get sexier. Hotter. And much messier.

So I matched his pose. And steeled my tone too. "Actually, I'm pretty sure we've covered all the major ground, Mr. Pearson. You said all you needed to say already with that awesome ultimatum you threw down at your place. And now, you know the whole story of me, including the ins and outs of why I've kept you off this fucked-up train wreck I call my life. Maybe someday I'll write a memoir, and you can read it all as many times as you want. But seriously, right now? I think we're done."

I pulled the door open, treasuring the cool air that gusted in from the hallway. Another short-lived relief from the stifling heat of my grief. In a flash of motion that really was superhero-like, Michael slammed the panel shut and then blocked it with his strong body.

"You seem to forget there are two parts to a conversation, blondie." He folded his arms over, intensifying the muscled glory of his chest. "One part is talking. The other part is listening. Guess what? You're really behind on that last one today. So get your fantasy-fine ass back on that yacht you call a sofa and get ready to listen for a change. Don't even think of getting pissy with me about this—or that I won't sling you over my shoulder and carry you."

I whooshed out a heavy breath of air. Was unable to

decide if his high-handedness was ass-hot or just asswipe. "You. Wouldn't. Dare."

"I would."

Deciding this was not a key battle I wanted to fight, I whipped my ponytail over my shoulder and started toward the sofa. When I abruptly stopped, Michael ran right into the back of me. Grinding my ass into his crotch purposefully, I said over my shoulder, "You really think this ass is fantasy-fine?"

He snarled into my ear. "Fucking walk or so help me..."

"Oooo, so bossy."

"Don't push it, sugar."

I huffed and plopped down on the far end of the sofa. Right now, distance was going to be my best friend. When he was in this prowling Simba mood, fires flared deep inside me, extinguishable only by the lion's bites. And sure, I'd put a closure fuck on the possibilities list, but second thoughts weren't against the law. Considering another round with him now felt like a very dangerous game, in a shitload of terrifying ways.

He settled on the other end of the couch—and then stiffened into a long, contemplative silence. Probably collecting words for whatever speech he'd deemed it necessary for me to hear, but that didn't stop my imagination from taking his sternness and running with it.

Mmmmm-hmmmm...

"Hey! Are you listening to a word I'm saying?"

I straightened. "Yeah! Of course. Totally."

"Margaux. I'm being serious."

"Yes, sir. I know."

He lifted an eyebrow and slanted his jaw. "Not going to work, sugar. I'm the one who's watched you weave this spell over other guys when they wanted to actually talk about—oh my God, I'm going to say it—feelings."

"Oh, please," I volleyed. "You want to be serious? I'm here, aren't I? I haven't called security on your ass, have I?" I reclined a little, watching him absorb that undeniable truth. But could I stop there? Of course not. More of the shit spilled out, though I battled to thread as much face-saving snark through it as possible. "Look, I've never had this many conversations with the same person in my entire life, man or woman, let alone about fucking feelings."

"You think you have it all figured out, don't you, little girl?" His stare bore back down on me. Though I'd returned to admiring my pedi, I felt the unmistakable bulk of it. "You think you know everything about me, don't you? That I had it easy growing up, in the land of sweet, gentle, and neighborly, but guess what? You don't know shit, Margaux. Not about my childhood, not about me, not even about that perfect farm life, which isn't what it seems at all. Forgive me for sounding confused that somehow you don't get that. Maybe I thought you, of all people, would understand that things are rarely what they appear to be. They're just what people want you to think. The big show, the Instagram filter, the Facebook edit. But everyone's hiding behind those façades. Everyone has secrets. Some are tiny, and some are huge as an eight-foot teddy bear. Some people cover their secrets up with makeup, while others mask them with press releases."

Shit.

My pedicure wasn't so fascinating anymore. As if I could see it through the stinging haze of my vision.

Michael huffed softly. "Your poker face needs a little work, princess. Looks like the lightbulb just turned on. Too bad you're so self-absorbed that sometimes you need someone to point out the simple things—like the fact that you, my precious city mouse, aren't so different from this humble country mouse. Trouble is trouble, no matter where you live, what the balance is in your bank account, or how important you think you are."

I swallowed, feeling as tall as the mouse he'd compared me to. Every word of his statement was true. I'd forgotten about Di's troubles, which had been literally stamped across her face the night we first met. And if my instincts were right, I was certain I'd felt scar tissue beneath a number of Michael's own tattoos. No wonder my confession about Trey had turned him ballistic. He felt helpless, just as he had that night when I pointed out his mom's bruise. Clearly, there had been more than one occasion in his life for that shit too.

But all of that had flown the proverbial coop of my selfish bitch of a mind.

I failed you, Margaux.

Oh, God. His hero complex wasn't just a Captain-America-Save-the-World thing. It was a deep-rooted, fight-or-be-destroyed thing. It was his survival, woven into his blood—as much an essential truth to him as my pride was to me.

He didn't wait long to confirm exactly that.

"Do you have any idea how long I've wanted to be your savior?" He'd turned to the mantle, braced his hands on it, and then dropped his head between them. This strong, giving, gorgeous, virile man looked...defeated. Because of my actions. "I've watched you from afar. I've watched you from close up. You've become a part of me, Margaux." He turned around, revealing a face grooved in taut, agonized lines. "I'm not sure... how I'll ever separate you out now. When I started at Asher, you were always there by Andrea's side, like an elusive golden dream. I was one of the few people who looked forward to our big morning meeting—and it sure as hell wasn't because of her."

"Really?" I laughed, weak and watery, giving up on any possibility of damming the drops that flowed past my defenses. My savior was now my destroyer, tearing down every brick of my soul. I hated him. I cherished him. I'd never, ever, forget the imprint of him on my life.

"Yeah," he murmured. "Really. I could smell your perfume the minute you came in the building. Coco Chanel. It's my favorite now, you know." He smiled and closed his eyes, seeming as if he drifted into a dream. "I suffered in silence, figuring you'd never give a guy like me a second look."

"Whaaat?" I hurled a pillow at him.

"It was okay, blondie. It was all fine. I just liked being around you. I knew how you took your coffee and that your favorite afternoon snack was Skittles. I could tell when you were a little under the weather and how that differed from when your allergies were acting up." He laughed again, louder this time. "Shit. Now I sound like a stalker. Maybe you really should have thrown me out when you had the chance."

"No way," I whispered. "No fucking way."

He lifted a smile—though it inched nowhere near his eyes. "I wasn't a stalker," he grated. "I was just a fool, Margaux. A fool caught in your spell. And now? A fool in love."

I slammed my eyes shut. Rammed the heels of my palms into them. Oh, God. Please, no.

The L word. Why did he have to go and ruin everything with the damn L word?

"Michael—"

"How many people know how many laughs you have?"

"Three." I barely whispered it.

"That's right. Three." His voice was quiet now too. "One is completely fake. It says *get away, I have no interest in this, walls are fully up*. The second one is polite, like when something is funny but you're holding back and trying to be a lady. And the third is the only one that reaches your eyes and makes my chest tight—right here." He put his flat palm and long fingers over his heart. "Like when I tickle your knee, or tell you bad jokes, or—"

"Michael."

"What?"

"I really need to ask you to leave, please." My bawling, blubbery ugliness was not the parting snapshot I wanted him to have before he moved nearly two thousand miles away. No man needed such a burden. And the shit was only getting messier from here.

"Baby, come here."

I batted at his outstretched arms. There was no point prolonging this misery. "No, Michael. Stop. I want you to leave. I'm not going to fall apart in your arms. I won't be the subject of some fucking mopey love song that makes me sob every time it plays in the elevator. I'm not the sobber in the elevator, damn it!"

"And I don't want you to be."

The idiot tried tugging on one of my ankles next. I yanked it back in, along with the other, as tight as I could against my chest. All the better to hide the disgusting display I was making of myself. "Please, Michael. Please. I just need you to leave!"

"But...I love you, Margaux. And I don't want to take that fucking plane ride. I want to stay here, beautiful, and make you happy. I want us to make each other happy. We can do this, Margaux. I know we—"

"Christ! Do you hear yourself? Have you heard a word I've said today at all? Are you listening? Oh my God, Michael. Don't you see the truth? Look at me. Look at me. I'm a broken, fucked-up mess." I was reaching hysterics and didn't give a flying shit. Maybe somebody would call security on my ass and they'd drag me off to Scripps again. I'd liked it there once... "I'm selfish and cruel and undeserving of love. I'm undeserving of your love." The sobs shook me now. Fucking great. And yes, he still tried to get closer. And I still kicked and scratched and fought. "I'm broken, Michael. Just accept it. You need to find a good woman, one who will make you happy, treat you right, and be completely present for you. And that woman...isn't me."

Oddly, that truth filled me with a new peace. I slumped forward and looked up at him, sure I possessed demon raccoon eyes by now, thanks to my haphazard makeup removal job between bites of cherry pie.

"I'm going to ask you nicely one more time to leave, Michael—and then I'll call Andre to come remove you. And, trust me, I've seen him lift heavier things than you." With that, I rose. On my way to the front door, I grabbed a tissue from the hall table, took a fortifying breath, and then swung the door wide again, standing next to it.

He took at least a minute of consideration, maybe longer. Halfway through, I resorted to studying my toes again. I couldn't look at him any longer and risk caving to the damn waterworks again—at least not while he was still here.

My heart felt like a mosaic of chipped tiles. Piece by piece, the squares crumbled and fell, until the whole thing was nothing more than a pile of rubble at my feet.

Finally, thank God, he took a step toward the door. Another.

But stopped before he cleared the portal.

"Broken can be fixed, Margaux. Incinerated can't."

Three steps later, he had walked out of my life for the last time.

★ ★ ★ ★

Time both flew and stood still. Only a week had passed since that agony of a scene at my place, but it felt like a hundred years. Real life was an effort, every step a chore. But at home, I could dive into bed and lose myself in memories and fantasy—and time raced.

For the first time since starting at SGC, I took some time off work. Nothing needed my immediate attention, though there was one element I missed about being at the office. Seeing my sister.

The day Michael was scheduled to leave for Atlanta seemed perfectly scheduled for a little Claire time.

As the car wound through the streets of Rancho Santa Fe, I considered telling Andre to turn around. I really should've called first. Monster Dearest had raised me better, especially in light of the fact that Claire and Kil's oldest was doing his or her best to kick their asses twelve years before puberty. At least the last time we spoke, she told me she was feeling a lot better, making fewer sacrifices to the porcelain god. She and Killian were cautiously optimistic.

Then there was the other monkey on my back. I didn't dare delay telling Claire about the breakup—if it could technically even be called that—any longer. My sister card would be revoked if she learned about everything from Michael instead of me.

Andre pulled up in front of Palais de le Steecks and Stones, as I'd started to jokingly call it, and leapt to get the door for me. He was starting to piss me off with the doting big brother vibe this week, but I forced a patient hand, remembering he was the default first responder to the carnage from the last heartbroken sob-fest fallout. Guys could be so warped.

"Hey, big guy." I put my hand on his arm as he held the door open.

"Ma'am?"

I raised my eyebrow.

"Sorry, Miss Margaux?"

"Nothing crazy is going to happen, okay? He's leaving today, and I'm fine with that. We're moving on. That's all."

"If you insist."

"What's that supposed to mean?"

"Nothing. Nothing at all. Will you be a while? I'd like to go get some gas in the car."

"Nice change of subject."

He just chuckled deep in his belly, which always made me grin too.

"That'll be fine."

I watched as he smirked and motioned his hand to the front door, indicating he would wait until I got inside before he left. Basically dismissing me.

I was just dismissed by my own driver.

Not the hill I wanted to die on. It was my new motto. I didn't have the energy to fight every fight right now, and if Andre wanted to imagine more was going to happen from this breakup, I certainly wasn't going to be the voice convincing him otherwise.

I trudged up the walk and was just about to press the bell

when Alfred opened the door.

"Good afternoon, Miss Margaux. How are you?"

"Peachy and perfect." I gave him a thumbs-up and a cheeky wink. "How are you today, Alfred?"

My tone was off even to my own ears, so I wasn't surprised when the older man responded with nothing but a quirked eyebrow, as if calling me on my shit. We were all good, but still—had all the service staffers been drinking the same water? They were all too astute for their own good today.

"Is my sister around? I know I should've called, but I wanted to stop by for just a few minutes."

"It's fine," Alfred replied. "We were expecting you. Mr. Andre sent me a text and said you were on your way."

"Did he, now?"

"Begging your pardon, Miss Asher. Don't blame him. I simply thought you might be coming and—"

"Did you, now?" Oh, yeah. Definitely the water.

"Well, in light of Mrs. Stone's delicate situation, it's been a little touchy around here. I took the liberty of texting him to coordinate. If you're cross, be so with me, not him."

"Cross?" I held up a hand. "Alfred, I grew out of Laura Ingalls Wilder a while ago." When I'd learned it was uncool to root for Nellie instead of Laura. "I'm not pissed. And, really, I should have called, so if Claire isn't up for a visitor..." My voice surrendered to curiosity. Why were we still standing in the foyer? Alfred hadn't taken another step. A weird shiver skittered down my spine.

"Mare? I'm in here."

My sister's voice emanated from the family room, but I could barely hear her. I stepped around Alfred, who might have actually tried to intercept me for a second, until I met his stare in a blatant don't-fuck-with-me face-off. Man, could Alfred bring the Killian Junior act.

Not helping the weirdness up and down my spine.

I found Claire on the couch again, wrapped once more in the faux-fur throw. "Hey, baby cakes. How we doing?" I leaned down and kissed her forehead. She managed a small smile, but her color was no better at all. "Yikes. Is the morning sickness back? Is that why Freddie went all stern-man Sergeant Pepper on me?" I perched on the edge of the overstuffed chair near the sofa. "In that case, I really, really should've called—but apparently, my rat of a driver is now BFFs with him, so we've got full cahoots."

"It's all good, M. I'm glad you came over. I've been wanting to call you myself, actually."

"Hey! It's Mare Bear." My brother strode into the room, greeting me with a warm smile and bending to kiss my cheek before nearly attaching himself to Claire's side. "Can I get you anything, Fairy?"

"No, thank you."

The shiver down my spine turned into a full freeze.

What the hell? Since when did the two of them talk to each other like Charles and Camilla at Sunday tea? And why was Claire speaking in the smallest voice I'd ever heard from her? I couldn't imagine they'd had a huge fight, but I wasn't here to take the temperature on things between them. I'm sure things hadn't been easy with her having the Technicolor yawns every hour...

"Do... Do you guys want me to leave? I can come back later."

"Maybe that would be better," Killian answered.

"Please stay," Claire said at the same time.

I looked between the two of them like a spectator at a tennis match. Yeeeahhh, something was up, and not in a good way. When Claire's big brown eyes spilled over with tears, Killian sank fully to the couch with her, gathering her into his arms.

"I'm going. You two clearly need some—"

"I lost the baby." Claire blurted it out and then burst into tears. Killian stroked her back while she cried. He handed her the handkerchief from his back pocket.

"Mother. Fucker." It just slipped out, but it was exactly how I felt. Margaux Asher, self-absorbed extraordinaire, had struck again. Had I actually come here to cry on her shoulder about my pissant boy problem when she was dealing with this? The loss of a human life? I wanted to curl up in a ball of shame and roll out the front door.

I did the next best thing. Dropped to my knees next to the couch. "Oh, my God. When did it happen? No, wait—it doesn't even matter. I'm so...sorry, you guys. I wish I could take all the pain away. I would do it in an instant."

"We know that." Killian gave me a brave but wobbly smile. Clearly, he was falling apart inside. The strain I'd sensed was likely his ongoing offer to God to take away every ounce of his wife's agony. "The doctor can't give us an explanation. He said it just happens sometimes. It doesn't mean we can't try again"—he rubbed Claire's shoulder, still papa bear protective—"when we're feeling up to it. Doesn't mean there's something wrong or that it will happen again."

Suddenly, Claire yanked back from him. "Okay, just stop."

The Charles and Camilla formality fell between them again. And what do you know, Kil rose and said, "I'll go get you some tea, baby. You need to have more fluid." He glanced at me, his eyes all but screaming *help me*. "And maybe some girl time."

As soon as he left, tears welled in Claire's eyes again. I scooted up, filling the spot Killian had just vacated next to her. "Hey, listen. It's still so early, baby. Just give it time." What was the other shit I always heard them say on dorky TV movies? "You and Kil love each other so much, and—"

"Have you ever had a miscarriage, Margaux?"

I reared but then almost grinned. Well, this was more like it. If she'd gone back to the Luna Lovegood whisper and all its forced politeness, I'd be out to cut up some of this fancy new room décor. This was sharp and sad and hurting and real. And if she thought it would get me off her back, she had another think coming. Her sister was the queen of spouting shitty in times of deep hurt.

I hiked my head up and studied her closely. She sure as hell knew it too. Back in the day, when we were still in mortal enemies territory, she'd seen this look from me a lot. I knew she wasn't fond of it. "No, Claire, I haven't. Nor do I know the exact thing to say to you right now. I do know that I love you and that I'd lasso the moon for you right now if that helped you feel better." I stroked the hair hanging listlessly against her cheek. "But, baby, I think the only thing that's going to help this is time. And I can help hold you through that. So can that incredible guy you're married to. And all you have to do is let us."

Well, shit. Now the waterworks came on—for both of us. I looked up to see Killian standing in the doorway to the kitchen, clear in my sightline but not hers.

"I— I don't want time, Margaux." Her voice tremored. She pushed the back of a hand over her forehead. "I just want to be whole again. Make me not a failure...please. Make it so I'm not broken."

I hugged her to me, meeting my brother's destroyed stare. "Stop this," I whispered. "What's this you're saying about failure? Why would you say something like that? What the hell gives you the idea that a miscarriage makes you a failure?"

"Oh God, Margaux. Isn't it obvious?" Claire pulled back to push a heavy sob into the handkerchief. "Having babies is what a woman's body is meant to do—but mine can't even do that. I'm so screwed up, Margaux. I'm so...broken. How will he want to stay with me like this? He's going to leave me. He's going to be just like his father and go find another woman to make babies with. One who isn't broken."

"Enough." I grabbed her by both shoulders. "I will not let you do this anymore, Claire. You will stop this bullshit right now. You are not broken. You are amazing and perfect and beautiful, just the way you are. Did you hear a word Killian said? Nature's timing simply wasn't right this go around. It had nothing to do with you or your body." I swung my head toward the kitchen. "And that man in there? He loves you, adores you, and worships you with a power that defies reason. You know how he looks at you, right? Like you have fucking fairy dust coming out of your ass? It's true." I stressed it in the face of her incredulous, soppy smile. "Aha. There she is!"

"Shut up." She giggled but sobbed again.

"Not how I roll, honey. I'm going to keep hammering this in until you hear it. You're stronger than this, Claire. You lived through the crucible of Asher and Associates, damn it. You're better than this *poor me* bullshit. Claire Allyn Stone doesn't cry and say she's broken. Claire Allyn Stone doesn't give up after the first try. And I know that Claire Allyn Stone does not hand her sexy-as-sin husband over to other women to make babies with."

She yanked me into a fierce hug. I held her tightly in return while she broke down anew. "I'm—I'm so heartbroken, Margaux."

"I know, honey."

"I already wanted it so much. I tried not to get into all of it, tried to stay unattached, but I already was thinking about it all the time. We heard the heartbeat last time we were at the doctor's office. It was so fast and so strong. I don't know how this could've happened. I did everything right. I swear I did."

"Of course you did. So know that it just wasn't meant to be. That sweet little bean wasn't strong enough after all, but it wasn't his fault or your fault. You have to stop blaming yourself. Yeah, I know that's easier for me to say, that this has never happened to me. But you are young and healthy, and so is Kil. When you've both recovered, you'll try again." I growled because she'd already started shaking her head before I finished. "I said when you're ready. Maybe that's next week, maybe that's next month. Maybe your doctor can give you some advice on how to best get through this."

I exchanged a look with Killian—his nod told me he was already on top of it—before he reentered the room. "Here's your tea, Fairy Queen. Just the way you like it."

Claire wiped her eyes again with his handkerchief. She took the tea and smiled up at him, sliding over a little so he could join us. His black eyebrows jumped a little at the gesture, but he quickly took advantage of it. I guessed she'd been icing him out since the miscarriage, so I hoped my little lecture was already setting in.

With a small sigh, I rose. "Now I'm really going to get out

of your hair." It was clear the two of them needed to reconnect, and talking was going to be square one.

"Nooo, sister. Please stay." Claire sipped at her tea, but Kil stabbed me with his ink-dark stare, pleading for some time alone now that she'd warmed a little.

I didn't need a second hint. "How about if I promise to come running the moment you call me in the next day or two?" I offered to Claire. "After you've had some proper rest. I could use a little alone time too. Life's been a little crazy lately." Said the queen of irony. "I'll just text Andre, make sure he's back from his errands, and then be on my way."

Claire reached and squeezed my hand. "Fair deal. You can catch me up on things at the office too. I need to get back in the groove anyway. I'll probably be ready to roll in a few days."

"Easy, tiger," Killian chimed in. "There's no hurry. Let's just play it by ear and see how you feel, okay?"

"Yes, Master."

Kil grinned, even at her mockery. "I kind of like the sound of that."

"Forget it," Claire rejoined.

I chuckled as I made my way back to the front door. Alfred appeared to see me out.

"Thank you for cheering Mrs. Stone up. She's been inconsolable." It was no secret how much the old guy had cared for Claire since the start of her romance with Killian.

"She'll come around, Fred. She just needs some time." I bumped my shoulder into him, throwing him off balance a little before heading out the door, to where Andre and the car were waiting for me.

I slid into the back of the car—and made a request that was beyond bizarre, even for me. "Take me to Torrey Pines, please."

Andre stabbed a stare at me via the rearview. "The golf club, right? You have a meeting at the clubhouse or something?"

"No. The beach." Silence. Dark eyes still in the mirror, now narrowed. "Am I speaking French?"

"Close to it."

I turned my look into a glare. "What the fuck is the problem, Andre?"

"First? You said please."

"And your point?"

"I can count on both hands how many times you've used the word in the last four years."

"So I'm using it today. Mark it with a gold star."

"And the beach? You? Willingly?"

"Oh, for—" I rolled my eyes and shot him a fresh glower. "Can you just do it, for chrisssake?"

He let out one of his barrel laughs while we rolled out of Kil and Claire's neighborhood. "Aaahhh, there's my girl!"

I had no idea why the beach called today. Maybe it was just the combination of great weather and a head badly in need of clearing. People always went on about the peace they found at the ocean, so it bore some checking out on my own. Full disclosure—it was second on the destination choices list. Normally, I'd just head to Saks, but I was too afraid of committing a felony if I was around too many idiots today. The beach got its win over South Coast Plaza.

I rested my head back and closed my eyes, working to absorb everything that had just happened. Had only half a day gone by? I felt like I'd run a marathon already and could easily fall into bed.

I decided to ignore the obvious crap about Michael and

concentrate on Claire for now. I was devastated for her and my brother. The look on Killian's face, as he'd looked on while she cried in my arms, would be seared on my soul forever. He was bereft. Barren. Broken.

No.

I refused to use that word one more time. No one in this situation was broken. They were grieving and sad for the little life that couldn't fight hard enough to term. I understood that. But everything happens for a reason. I was smart enough to keep that gem to myself today, but they'd soon see that light too. They'd come out on the other side of this stronger and deeper in love than they were when speaking their I dos.

I just wish it hadn't hurt so much to watch them suffer. Did this mean I was going soft around the edges? And if it did, who cared? Fuck it. Those two people were all I had now. They'd sneaked their way so far into my heart there was no chance in hell of ever getting them out. Not that I ever wanted to.

A heavy sigh escaped me. If I looked up, I knew Andre would be quizzing me about it in the rearview. Damn it. He knew me too bloody well, and it was starting to get on my nerves. But to the man's credit, he never pried.

"Andre?"

"Hmmm?"

"Where is your family?" I had no idea what made me ask. The words simply slipped out, and I realized I was deeply interested in the answer.

His forehead furrowed. "What do you mean?"

"*Tu familia?*"

He barked out a laugh. Of course I knew he wasn't Hispanic, but I loved teasing him that way—to which he usually responded in thick Patois, making me laugh.

No Patois today. Just very quiet, serious words.

"I don't have any living relatives."

Okay, then. I respected him enough not to snoop. He had done me the same favor more times than I could count.

We took the exit for Torrey Pines State Beach, the place Claire told me Killian had proposed to her. Michael had threatened to bring me hiking here one time, but when I threatened harm to his boy parts if he did, he'd backed off. He'd never pressed me again, simply understanding that those refreshing physical activities weren't my thing. Unless shopping was in that category—in which case, I was all in for daily training.

"Do you want me to come with you?" Andre queried. "I can follow and just give you your space."

"Thanks, but I'm fine." I smirked. "I won't last long out there in the elements. We both know it."

Andre answered with a chuckle but had the good sense not to say anything as I kicked off my heels and headed for one of the easier-marked trailheads.

After wandering my way down toward the water, watching the crazy-ass people running through the crevices in the cliffs, I shook my head and concentrated on staying upright. The sand was a warm, soothing scratch between my toes. I dug in a little deeper and made my way down to the beach in no time but already discerned the trip back up was going to be a suck-fest.

Later.

Scoping out a nice dry spot on the shore, I sat and watched the waves break over and over. Before long, the water's rhythm lulled me. The tension in my shoulders eased, and the dull ache between my eyes vanished.

On tentative mental tiptoe, I entered the emotional muck that I'd come to figure out.

Michael.

Waves or not, here came the tension again.

Breathe. Slow. Easy. Go step by step, and maybe you won't drown.

The last time we'd been together, he'd said some pretty harsh things. And though I'd kicked him out, one hideous fact remained.

I'd deserved every one of them.

I still did.

He was exactly right—and that was where everything turned to sludge again. Would I ever admit it out loud? Probably not, even to him—not that I'd ever be given the chance now.

But did I want to be given the chance?

Damn good question. Maybe I'd have to come back to that.

He'd accused me of being self-centered. Well...guilty as charged. Had it hurt, hearing it come from his mouth? Not so much, until I thought about the reasoning he'd used for it. And? Yeah. Ouch.

But it was pain I'd brought on myself. A tower I'd locked myself into.

That bore looking at again.

When I was self-centered about things like my lifestyle? Not guilty. My ridiculously comfortable car choice and giving a man a solid job because of it? Not guilty. The latte I drank instead of a plain coffee? Not guilty. My designer handbag instead of—gasp—off-the-rack? Not guilty.

But when he accused me of being selfish, of not

understanding his protectiveness of me over the ugliness with Trey and Andrea? *Ding ding ding*. Guilty as charged, officer. Lock me up.

I owed him an apology. A big one. I'd been pissy and petulant instead of seeing the bigger picture about what had obviously happened to his mom at the hands of an abuser. Shitty thing was, I'd probably have to do it via email, which rankled but was the only choice. If I called, God only knew how much farther I'd be able to shove my foot up in mouth.

I'd also have to address the rest of my ugliness—my unfair jibes about his small-town upbringing. Cheap shots. I knew it then like I knew it now. Truth of the matter was, though I was raised on marble floors in America's Finest City, I was jealous of what he'd enjoyed in Julian. People who knew and admired him. A community much like a huge family. And those meadows...

Damn. I was turning out to be an awesomely mature adult. I was drafting an apology email to my jilted lover on my smartphone on the beach. See? I could grow as a human. Miracles were possible.

Who the fuck was I kidding?

None of this was me! I didn't want to send a goddamn apology email! I didn't want to be—

The completion to that sucked the air from my lungs. Stung my eyes with a thousand needles. Turned my legs as mushy as the wet sand out on the berm.

I didn't want to send an email to Michael...because I didn't want to be apart from Michael.

I wanted to throw myself at his feet and beg him to stay in San Diego and never think of leaving me again. God, he'd hate Atlanta. What the humidity alone would do to his thick hair...

I shot to my feet.

"Ohhh, shit!"

Now what did I do? How did I tell him? Could I tell him? Was there time? What was it going to take? I was so far out of my league. Ruined politician? Action plan for that. Besmirched pop starlet? Action plan for that. Movie god caught with his dick in the wrong place? Had that action plan on autopilot. But there was no action plan for this. I didn't have a damn clue what to do. I couldn't ask Claire. I couldn't ask Killian. Shit, I couldn't even ask Andre.

Could I call Di? If I told her what was going on, would she shed some light on the amazing puzzle that was her son? And what if she told me to go grovel? And if I did, would Michael still tell me to go fuck myself? Could I take that sort of humiliation? That heartbreak?

I had to try.

Damn it, I had to try.

I couldn't imagine my life without him. When I spun my mind back through the last two years, every major event had his gorgeous face stamped on the memory too. He thought he'd gone unnoticed? World's hugest joke. He was woven through my life's tapestry as thickly as Claire and Killian at this point.

Crazy—and perfect. I'd reached this decision before realizing it had to be made, hadn't I? He'd been right in front of my eyes all this time...just waiting for me to wake up and see him. I'd made up excuses. Told him I was broken. But the word was just as ridiculous on my lips as it'd been on Claire's. Why was I selling myself short and not allowing myself the love of a stunning man as amazing as him? He kept insisting he loved me. Who was I to tell him he didn't?

I was done with excuses. With blaming my pain and my

childhood and especially my "mother." Andrea didn't get to dictate my life anymore—or my heart. I'd given too much of myself to the bitch already. Not anymore.

I wasn't broken.

I was whole and worthy and good, and I deserved Michael's love just as he did mine. And oh God, I did love him. I didn't just believe that I might be able to. My heart was one hundred and fifty percent in on this deal.

"Shit!" I blurted again.

I had to find him. Had his flight left yet? Well, tough Margaux titties if it had. I'd buy a ticket for the next flight out to Georgia and have to race in the terminal at Hartsfield-Jackson to kiss the living hell out of him.

I didn't want to wait. I'd been such an idiot. The sooner I proclaimed that to him, the better.

Speaking of me and idiot in the same sentence...

What the fuck was I thinking, coming to a beach that required a steep hike to reach the sand?

The walk back to Andre was going to suck big, hairy balls. No other way around it. But there was no other way back to my phone—and the information I desperately needed about Michael's flight.

That was it. I'd consider the trip my pilgrimage back to Michael.

Riiiight.

By the time I made it back to the top, I was sure I'd sprained both ankles and was likely dehydrated. Andre bolted out of the car and approached like a frantic father. It would've been adorable if I wasn't near death.

"Jeeez-usss, woman! What are you trying to prove?"

"I had to get back up. Fast. Water. Please."

He thrust an opened bottle into my hand. "I'll pull the car over. Just stand there."

Good plan.

As soon as he had the door open, I tumbled inside. Damn. I smelled like a platoon of Marines—perhaps skinny jeans hadn't been the right wardrobe choice for the beach—but at the moment, I didn't care. The only goal burning in my mind was finding Michael. Now.

I scooped up my phone and began tapping at the screen. First stop was a search for Pearson's Apple Farm. Di would be the fastest source about his flight status.

An incoming call blared in, interrupting my outgoing one.

A thousand daggers of dread gored my gut—

Until I realized that Trey Stone no longer dictated my life either.

This was going to be fun.

"*Hola, mi hermano.* What the fuck do you want?"

"Shit. Are you ever not a bitch?"

"It's rare, but it happens. Kind of like a unicorn sighting."

"You're such a cunt."

"Mmmm, there's that family love. So what do you want, asshole? I gave you all the money you're going to be getting from me, so go find another tree to go piss up."

"Do I need to remind you of the stakes of our little game, sister?"

"See, that's just the thing. I'm done playing, Trey. You can go fuck yourself. Or maybe just my mother. Guess she doesn't mind catching a disease or five."

He had the grace to hiss when I dropped the bomb about my knowledge of his and Andrea's alliance. But like a bull that didn't know when to stop, he charged right in again. "You'd be smart to shut up while you're still ahead, bitch. I'm getting really angry. You won't like me when I'm angry."

"That would imply that I like you now. Or at all."

"I want the rest of my money, Margaux. You know what I'll do if that doesn't happen."

"Tell you what, Trey... Let's play a new game. It's called chicken. You go right ahead and do what you need to do, because you won't be getting one more dollar of my money. Just know that I'll be simultaneously filling in a few people in about your little blackmail attempt." I couldn't resist giggling a little. "Hope you've put a deposit down on that deep, dark hole you'll need to hide in, scumsucker—because things aren't going to be pretty when they find you this time."

Surprise, surprise... The conversation was ended with a click.

Trey would make good on his threat, of that I was certain—but it didn't matter anymore. Michael loved me regardless of a mistake I made when I was young and wrapped up in what I thought was heartbreak.

Now I knew the difference.

What I'd suffered with Doug was a flesh wound compared to the carnage of my heart if Michael wouldn't take me back. But that was the proverbial bridge I'd jump from when I came to it.

I exhaled hard when the public line at Pearson's was picked up on the third ring. The receptionist quickly patched me through to the right extension.

"Hello, Di?" I was suddenly nervous. Like that was going to stop me. "It's Margaux. I really need your help. I'm in love with your son—and I need help in doing something about it."

CHAPTER EIGHTEEN

Michael

"Have a safe and pleasant flight, Mr. Pearson."

"Thanks."

I managed a smile out of habit, knowing that if I didn't, Mom would somehow find out I'd been rude to the woman at Lindbergh Field TSA and drag me in here to apologize. The second I grabbed my carry-on and stepped away from security, the black cloud assumed its rightful place over my head. Right where I wanted it.

I'd helped the movers load the last of my shit into their truck yesterday afternoon and then confirmed they'd meet me at the storage facility in Atlanta in three days. The rest of my life was contained in one suitcase and the bag slung over my shoulder, meaning the Hyatt had the privilege of hosting my morose ass last night. I'd hit the hotel gym hard, parked my sorry self in the whirlpool, and scowled down flirty glances from three models working the convention center's car show before heading back upstairs for three hours of semimeaningful sleep. But that was my way of aiming for the positive today. I dared fate to ask for more, because it'd be damn fun to answer that bastard with what I really thought of his latest turn my life had taken.

Seriously? This is fate's fault now? You made this decision, asshole. Nobody forced you to make that call to Atlanta—not even the woman who kicked you to the curb. You climbed your way back up from that muck. Grew a pair and decided to take a chance on a new start. Now buy yourself a beer and force yourself to remember that.

I grabbed a seat in the corner of the Terminal Two bar and ordered an Alpine IPA. Bumping my head back against the wall, I tried out a little more self-bolstering, courtesy of the Di Pearson book of cheesy quotes. I'd been treated to enough of them during our phone conversation last night, her last motherly rah-rah before I officially left the state—for the benefit of us both. She'd definitely pulled out the stops on this one.

Sometimes the right decision isn't the easy decision.

The best thing about the story of life is that there's always a new chapter.

Changing is growing—and growing is the key to living.

Pain is inevitable, Michael. Suffering is optional.

There were more, but the minor buzz from the beer kicked in, bringing a welcome gauze to the wound I'd once called a chest. At least on the surface. Deep down, where the real blood still flowed and the real ache still throbbed, I'd be a mess for a while. Thank fuck Hayden and Hutton had both already promised I wouldn't see my desk or bed for months after signing the contract. Now if I could only think of work therapy without memories of a certain gaze full of green mischief or a pair of legs to rival JLo and the Queen Bey...

If I could think of any damn thing without associating it with her.

I snarled but managed to confine it to my throat. The rest of the world didn't need to deal with the noise of a man repeatedly booting himself in the gut.

Maybe another beer was in order. I had all the time in the world for wallowing.

Before I could catch the waitress's attention, my phone let out a text bing. I retrieved it from my pocket, expecting a classic Mom text like *safe flight—text the minute you are on ground!* With the requisite string of smileys, of course.

"Goddamnit." No way to control this growl. But there was no way I expected the boot in my crotch to be replaced with one woman's perfectly aimed stiletto.

Hey.

I wiped my thumb over the delete key. Proud as hell of myself, I nodded at the waitress for another Alpine. Maybe I'd ask for a tequila chaser—unconventional, yes—understandable, huger yes—maybe the extra, golden prod I needed to go ahead and wipe her from my phone.

Have you boarded yet?

Delete.

Don't board that plane. I need to talk to you.

Delete.

"Because that went so well last time?" I muttered.

Michael, please tell me you're still in San Diego.

Delete. Although any second, she was going to remember the app I'd installed for her that morning before our Buffalo Bill's breakfast, giving her access to my location at the touch of a button.

I know you're still here.

"Faster than I thought, princess." I hadn't fallen in love with a stupid one.

Rephrase. Hadn't fallen over the damn cliff, beyond ridiculous, I-will-die-in-the-dragon's-mouth-for-you, love.

Who was truly the stupid one here?

Apparently the one who dashed his thumbs over the keys in one of the most juvenile moves invented for the modern age.

Who is this?

Before I could talk myself out of it, I stabbed the Send button. Within seconds, I envisioned her slow, pissy burn, lips all twisty and cheeks all flushed—all but demanding a kiss to bring her down to earth and back in line. Yeah. I'd do exactly that if I were anywhere near her too. Dig my fingers into her scalp, thrust my tongue down her throat, and—

Goddamnit.

A soft giggle tugged my head up. The waitress, named Roxy, if her name badge was correct, added a little grin. "Get her, tiger. Grrrr."

"What?"

"Whoever you're telling off."

My eyebrows crunched. "How do you know—?"

"Oh, I just do." She set my fresh beer down. "Three years doing this, a girl gets good at the reads. From your first step in, you had brokenhearted written all over you."

"I'm not..." I shifted against the leather seat. Wasn't polite to make a friend stand, and my new bestie, Unnerved, was ready for a long visit.

Just like that, Margaux filled my mind again. This time, she wasn't pissed. She was tear-streaked, near-hysterical, defeated—

And breaking my heart.

I'm broken, Michael. Just accept it.

Then shattering my soul.

Broken can be fixed, Margaux. Incinerated can't.

Was this what incinerated felt like? Was I there yet?

I knew the answer before the phone buzzed with an incoming call. I didn't have to look at the screen to know the image filling it. It was a shot I'd taken of her during our trek to the meadow, sunshine spilling over her hair and highlighting her adorable freckles...

Nope. Not incinerated. Because if I was, thinking about that picture wouldn't feel like a goddamn cleaver through my heart—and a bucket of acid behind my eyes.

Every second felt like an hour until the damn thing stopped vibrating. I only had three seconds to suck in a new breath before her redial connected through. By the time she'd done it a dozen more times, I turned off the phone. That, of course, meant looking at her picture on the screen again. New cleavers. More acid.

"Fuck."

I framed my head in both hands and leaned over the table. Across the room, a group of Brits whooped in victory. Their man was likely going to clinch the Tour de France. At least someone in the world was reaching for the sun and not getting fried.

I was suddenly very thirsty.

Alpine number two went down without a pause.

Though I muffled my belch in my elbow, it still tripped

Roxy's call button. She was right—the magic people reader was permanently installed on her hard drive.

"Three's the charm?" she asked, tilting her head so her black bob swayed. "Or are you leveling up? Some Señor Patrón? Mr. J. Daniels, maybe? Maybe a handshake with Jim Beam?"

Yes, yes, and yes. "No." I thanked her with my eyes. "Close me out before I do something stupid."

Well...something else stupid.

After settling up with Roxy, I made my way to the gate. They'd just started boarding. Along the way, I turned my phone back on. Scrolled down the list, too many to count, of all the calls Margaux had attempted. My gut lurched, and my jaw clenched. She'd tried really hard to contact me...

For what?

Logic crashed in like an eighteen-wheeler falling through ice. The force was warranted, considering what I'd contemplated doing for one treacherous second.

Don't. Go. There. What is tapping back at her digits going to get you—except a shit ton more of all this? She told you to leave. Threatened to call her henchman on your ass if you didn't beat it.

You need a shrink, asshole. Or a lobotomy. Or a castration. Or all three.

Hell. Maybe I should've taken Roxy up on that offer of the big boys' booze. I wasn't buzzed enough for the reality of this.

Pulling out my ticket. And hating it.

Staring out of the windows at the sailboats on the bay, with the understanding it'd be Thanksgiving before I returned for a visit.

Hating. It.

Forcing a smile at the gate agent while she scanned me in.

Hating. Every. Fucking. Second.

"Goodbye, princess."

A shriek ripped through the terminal.

Everybody froze.

Another scream.

People hit the floor.

What the hell was...?

"Sweetie, get your nasty Playtex Living gloves off me unless you want those returned on bloody stumps."

The gate agent burst out a giggle. I would have joined her but was too busy trying to heft my jaw off the floor. "Holy shit."

As I managed that, another banshee war cry peeled through the air. "I will not leave, and I will not get in line. I already told you, this is an emergency!"

The gate agent laughed again. "I guess it is."

I choked because my throat had gone dry from not breathing. It succeeded in convincing me this was really happening. If I needed more proof, the terminal-wide PA was activated.

"Michael Pearson. Paging Mr. Michael Pearson at once to the Terminal Two security checkpoint."

"Hey." The agent gaped at me. "That's you."

"Thanks." I think I meant it. I really wasn't sure I remembered who I was. This felt like one of those loopy after-death scenes in B movies, where the dearly departed floats over their body and watches life in a mix of wonder and horror. I told myself to stay up there, certain full inhabitation of my body—and my thundering heartbeat, laboring lungs, and misfiring nervous system—might not carry me all the way to the checkpoint where an army of bright-blue shirts raced around as if a bomb had just been detonated.

I stumbled a few more steps. Then found my voice enough to mutter, "Oh, holy hell."

An explosion had rocked the Lindbergh Field terminal, and its name was Margaux Asher.

I swallowed on a paper-bag throat again. Edged closer, baffled and wary, until I saw her in full. Hair blown and wild. Eyes bright and wilder. Plain T-shirt, black leather pants, danger zone heels that dangled from one hand as she squirmed in the grips of at least four burly TSA officers.

Funny about that danger zone. My psyche fired into an F-18 on overdrive.

"Hey!" I surged forward. "The lady's right. Get your hands off her!" Since two out of the four complied right away, it was clear they'd already patted her down in full. Just formulating the conclusion made me see darker red.

I zeroed in on the other two but should've remembered the force of nature they attempted to contain. Margaux flung them free like a diva doffing a mink, ditching her shoes between them. Holy fuck, she was amazing—but also distressed, emphasis on the stressed. More of the protective burners fired, despite how I rammed all the buttons to order them otherwise.

"Marg— Oof."

She leapt on me like a tree frog, her grip like suction cups, her breaths at hyperventilation status. "Thank God," she rasped. "Thank God you're not on that plane. Oh, Michael. I'm sorry. I'm sorry. I'm sorry!"

She stepped down but grabbed my face on both sides, her own a crazy compilation of angles. I quickly connected the cause. *I'm sorry.* She usually only spouted it as part of a snarky takedown, never in this frantic form. She was actually seeking confirmation that she'd done it right. I gave it to her in a firm squeeze at her nape before forcing her to move on.

"What is it?" I charged. "Has something happened? Are you okay?"

"No!" Her face contorted—right before she slapped me. Not hard but sure as hell not a playful tap. The fuck? She clenched back a sob and then slammed her lips to the cheek she'd just smacked. "No," she repeated. "I'm not okay. Okay?"

"Okay." I wrapped both hands around hers but still didn't dare believe what all this hinted at. "So what's going on?"

She winced again. "I— I—"

"What?"

"You know all that stuff you mentioned? A couple of days ago? At my place?"

I didn't want to laugh, but I did. I didn't want to be enchanted by her all over again, but I was. I didn't want to get up any hopes...but I did that too. "Sugar, I said a lot of stuff at your place. Can you be more specific?"

"Do I have to?"

"Well, yeah. I still have no damn idea what—"

"Okay, okay!" She twisted her hands in, around my jacket's collar, before locking her gaze on my Adam's apple. "The stuff about...how you love me," she whispered. "And want to make me happy."

Buh-bye, lungs. Breathing's overrated anyway.

"Yeah." I pushed closer to her. And closed my eyes, ecstatic, as she did the same. "I do remember all that stuff."

She lifted her head. Fuck. Here was the bomb they'd all been freaking out about. But this catastrophe was all mine, with the green fires of her gaze, the sweet strawberry of her smile, the shimmering tear tracks on her cheeks...the perfect warmth of her embrace. My dazzling little disaster.

"I mean all of it too, Michael. I mean, if you still want me to." Her brow furrowed. "I suppose even if you don't want me to. Oh, shit. How the hell would that work if—"

I sliced her short in the best way I knew how. When her lips fell prey to mine, opening beneath my assault, I let the beast out in full, letting him take her senses down like a hapless gazelle. "I want you to," I finally said. "Fuck, how I want you to."

And that was the moment the shittiest day of my life turned into the best goddamn day in the history of man.

"I love you, Michael. I do. I really do."

I tugged at the back of her head, exactly like I'd been fantasizing back in the bar, and took her in a kiss that sealed the deal before she could think of taking it back. "As I love you, Margaux-Mary-who-the-hell-cares."

Coincidentally, that was the same moment a flurry of whispers erupted in the security line. Before a camera flashed at us. Another. A dozen more.

"You sure you don't care?" She grinned, full of her old sass, though mixing something new in with it. A sweet adoration, glowing from the depths of her eyes, flipping my chest on itself. "Because we're about to go viral, stud."

"I'm down with viral." I winked, purely wicked about it. "As long as it's a little contagious and I can share it with you."

"Ew." She threatened to smack me again, but I was ready this time. I easily caught her hand, jammed it over my ass, and moaned deep as she squeezed hard, giving the shutterbugs something else to tweet about. "Errr...that reminds me," she murmured. "I have a thing about germs."

I pressed my lips, holding in a snicker. "You don't say."

"You'll have to be okay with that. And my shoe closet. And my crappy morning moods. And my nighttime TV-drama addictions. But I'll give the *Ice Road* guys a try for you, okay?"

It was more than okay. It was my fantasy come true. She loved me. She loved me. And she didn't just want me in the ivory tower as a boy-toy. She wanted me in her life, in her mornings, in her germ phobias...in her heart.

"Keep talking. I sure like your terms, princess."

"Don't call me—" She figure-eighted her head before grousing, "Ohhhh, fine. If you're going to try *Empire* and pedicures for me, then I'll let you keep princess."

"Wait. Pedicures? The hell?"

The brat threw her head back and laughed, supremely pleased with herself for the sneak. I growled and snapped her back in against me, swooping my head low to crash her lips with a let's-review-who's-in-charge ravishment. As our mouths melded deeper, I poured every drop of my joy and passion into her, promising her a greater flood where that came from. Praying I'd be drenching her for a lifetime.

As our tongues started to dance, the crowd broke out in wild applause.

Seriously...the best day in the history of mankind.

CHAPTER NINETEEN

Margaux

Was it possible the sun was higher in the sky? The sky bluer? That the bird twitters in the trees now sounded like the coolest conversations ever—and I was tempted to join in? Words weren't necessary when the language of happiness was spoken.

Or was it just that I was seeing everything through rose-colored glasses, courtesy of the amazingly hot man next to me?

Yeah, that sounded more like it.

And shit, was he beautiful arm candy. I could ditch every single Chanel, Louis Vuitton, and Hermès bag I had and just strut around with this heartthrob on my arm. My other accessories would be jealous, but I'd traded up and there was no going back now. Ever.

Michael's luggage would have to be reclaimed tomorrow since it was checked through to Atlanta. In the meantime, we'd have to make do with simply the clothes on his back—a concept full of wonderful possibilities. If the luggage didn't make it back safely, I'd replace everything anyway. Hmmm, styling one's own perfectly sized Ken doll...and this one had every correct part included. I might even let him have some say in the matter. A few times.

No, I hadn't lost my mind.

I was in love. That's right, world. I, Margaux Corina Asher, was madly, completely in love with Michael Pearson. And the sooner I could find a private, horizontal surface to fully prove that fact, the happier this princess would be.

Unfortunately, that plan would have to wait. The minute we came downstairs into the baggage claim area, a throng of rabid reporters were ready to swarm. Clearly Trey had made good on his promise to go public. Stir in a few tweets from bystanders about Michael's and my PDA back in the terminal, and boom. Showtime, kids.

"Brace yourself, baby." I leaned into Michael, using the sweet gesture as an excuse to whisper in his ear. "The ride's about to get a little bumpy."

"What the—?" was all he could manage to me before the reporters advanced, shouting questions and shoving every portable recording device invented into our faces. Cell phones, smart pads, even old-fashioned mini tape recorders. The gang was all here.

I raised an arm, consumed with the sudden need to beat them all back from Michael. So this was how that ooga-booga protective gorilla thing felt. "Back up, people! I'll make one statement, and then you can all go fuck off."

Voices sprang from the crowd.

"Ohhhh, she's back!"

"There's our Margaux!"

"The ice princess reigns!"

Michael seemed to pale when he heard that comment. Maybe it hit home why it took me a while to warm up to his version of the endearment.

The media fools finally cleared a small semicircle. Didn't stop them all from getting their pictures and video. Michael tightened his clutch on my waist by increasing degrees, sending a very clear message about where he stood in my life at the moment.

When the roar died a little, one voice rose above the rest. "Margaux, have you seen Trey Stone's tweet?"

"Nope," I quipped. "Did he spell my name right? Because really, nothing else that tampon says is worth wasting my time on."

"Then there was no suicide attempt over a split with a boyfriend?"

"Did I say that?"

"So it's true? Is this the boyfriend? Looks like you've made up to me."

I slashed up my arm again. "Okay, hold up there, sparky. Let's set this record straight, once and for all. First of all, Trey Stone is a world-class loser, and we all know it." Mumbles of agreement rippled through the herd. "It makes me sick that we have to even address anything he says, but I want you all to hear this from me." I jogged up my chin as Michael squeezed me close in support. "The story is true. Years ago, when I dated Doug Simcox and he broke up with me, I thought I was devastated. I was young and dramatic"—I laughed as they all did—"okay, more dramatic—and screaming for attention. I took some pills, thinking I would glamorously end it all. Doug would see the error of his ways and mourn me forever. Well, nothing about it was glamorous. I ended up in the emergency room with a tube down my throat, getting my stomach pumped. It was dumb and naïve and expertly covered up from the media." I sucked in a ton of oxygen. "So there you have it. I wasn't exhausted. I was an idiot. Now everyone knows the real story and we can move on."

A bunch of the reporters shouted more questions about

the Doug-clysm, but as soon as I raised my hand again, they quieted.

"Listen. I just told you the facts. That's all there is to the story, kids. It happened a long time ago. The news is as yesterday as Kim Kardashian's ass."

They all chuckled and time-stamped their devices. Bow to the queen of sound bites, ladies and gentlemen. Kim's camp would have an equally awesome zinger for me tomorrow, and I couldn't wait to hear it.

A reporter I recognized from the *Huffington Post* stepped to the front of the crowd. "So do we get to know who this handsome hunk is?" He motioned to Michael, all but eye fucking him in the process. Yeeeaaah...not going there today, Marc!

The question sparked a new buzz through the crowd. I glanced up at Michael, who squeezed me again and smiled. I tucked myself tighter to him, realizing I grinned like a total fool. For once in my life, I didn't care. I wanted the entire world to see how happy I was.

"This very fine man is my boyfriend, Michael Pearson."

"Is it serious?" someone in the back shouted.

"I hope so." I all but giggled it. Giggled? Jesus wept.

"Do we hear wedding bells already, Margaux? Maybe another event up at the Stone estate in Rancho Santa Fe? Can we actually come to this one?" The remark was a pissy punch at their lockout from Killian and Claire's nuptials.

"Don't be stupid. We just started this thing." I waved a finger between Michael and me, indicating the thing.

Entertainment Weekly spoke up this time. "Just love, then?"

"Just love?" I volleyed. "Just love? Christ, Bill."

The reporter smirked. "Excellent point. Forgot who I was talking to. So this is a big step, huh?"

"In full, five-inch glory, baby."

"Reserve the marquee," somebody else quipped.

"Not a bad idea." As I laughed it out, I beamed my smile back out over the crowd. Then did a double take. A woman caught my eye, standing quietly toward the back of the throng. Not another reporter but definitely interested in all the dazzle. Our gazes met. I smiled a little wider, feeling a bizarre urge to wave. The woman lifted a hesitant smile. Why did she seem so familiar? Sure, most of the people in this were familiar—I'd frequently worked with all of them over the years—but something was different about this woman. Something was off...but not in a disturbing way. I knew her from a different place, maybe even a different time...

But when I looked back for a second read, she was gone.

And there was the not-so-small distraction of the beautiful beast next to me.

I sighed as Michael yanked me closer. Mine. He was all mine. The joy of it burst through me again as he pulled me in for a long, slow, tongue-twisting kiss, inciting cheers and wolf whistles not only from the press but the small crowd of travelers who'd gathered now.

Once he released me, our stares remained riveted. We were locked, a couple of stars who'd collided and fused, floating through a firmament of flashes and shouts and chaos. He was my safety from it all. The match to my soul. The farmer boy with the devil inside. The love of my life.

I finally swung back toward the throng. "Show's over, gang. Get the fuck out of here, you little monkeys."

They all laughed, but I wasn't kidding. Imagining the troop

of them swinging through the trees and nibbling at peanuts was wholly plausible—and another reason to giggle, right before I turned, reached up, and pulled Michael into another kiss. He tasted so good. So right. So much like the anchor in this storm...my best and luckiest break. Oh, God...if he'd boarded that plane a second sooner or those bozos manhandled me three seconds longer, I would've missed him.

"Mr. Pearson?"

"Yes, princess?"

"As long as I'm spilling my guts for everyone to see, I'm going to lay something else out."

His golden eyebrows pulled together. Slowly, he drawled, "Okay..."

"Don't leave me again. Please. Just so we're clear. Okay?"

"Okay." His face relaxed. A smile warmed his lips. "Hmmm. I kind of like you all mushy like this, princess."

"Oh, I'm sure you do. But don't get used to it, mister." We kissed again. Then again. "I'm really just trying to get in your pants. You know that, right?"

He threw his head back on a laugh. It was my favorite laugh of all, when his eyes glistened like the sun was shining right into them, even if we were in the dark. And they did—just before he leaned down to issue an intimate rasp into my ear.

"Sweet words or not, my pants are good as gone the minute we clear your front door."

"Front door?" I narrowed a teasing glare. "Who said anything about that? Have you seen the size of my car's back seat?"

He growled.

I mewled.

More tongue dancing.

Holy shit. At this rate, we were going to get arrested for public indecency before reaching the car.

"You should've decided you loved me a long time ago, Ms. Asher. It's a damn good look for you." He kept me pulled in tight, our hips fitted against each other, even when shock took over his face. "Well, hell."

"Uh-oh," I muttered. "What is it?" I could work with anything except second thoughts. Or the revelation of a secret pet iguana.

"Hrrrmmm. I've terminated the lease on my house."

I was still waiting on the stunner. "And...?"

"And all of my furniture is in a truck on its way to Atlanta. The moving company can bring it all back, but for now, your boyfriend is homeless."

I wound my arm back and decked him in the shoulder. "Idiot."

"Hey! Ow!"

"You're staying with me. As long as you want. And as long as there's no iguana coming back on that truck."

"Huh?"

"We can discuss a dog, though I'd prefer a cat. But no igua—" I frowned, catching the new glint in his eyes—like he was actually contemplating payback for the punch I'd landed. "Michael?" When he made his full intention clear by ducking his shoulder and eyeing my pelvis, I screamed. A few straggling reporters dashed over, ecstatic they'd lingered. "Michael! Stop! Stop!" But I laughed too hard to resist as he barreled in, hauling me up in one easy motion. Inside two seconds, he hung me over his shoulder like a sack of potatoes.

I shrieked and took a smack at his amazing ass—before realizing there were much better things to be doing while back here. When opportunity knocked...

Without hesitation, I slid my hands beneath his jeans and briefs, rewarded with tight, Michael-muscled glory.

"Hey," he yelled. "Behave yourself!" But then he landed his own shot to my ass. Let me tell you, a spank on the ass in leather pants stung worse than one might think. But, hell, was every second worth it.

When we got to the car, he flipped me over and plopped me inside and then turned to Andre, who was beaming like the Rasta Cheshire cat. "Damn good to see you again, Andre."

They did some variation on the guy greeting, bumping fists and shaking hands and slamming shoulders in a language more mysterious than dogs sniffing each other's butts. Andre's booming laugh practically shook the car. "I had no doubt in my mind, Michael Pearson. No doubt at all."

Michael climbed in, still grinning, as Andre slid behind the wheel.

"Take us to the El Cortez, please."

"Right away, Miss Margaux."

Michael stared at me in mock agony, still rubbing his shoulder. "Who the hell taught you to punch like that? Wait... Maybe I don't want to know. Think I've heard enough about ex-boyfriends for one day."

I scowled. "Oh, don't get all weird on me now. The past sneaks up on us sometimes, Pearson. We both know that."

"Yeah." His gaze sobered. "We do."

I had no doubt his mind had kicked back different memories than mine. So many things still to know about him... but I'd do my best to give him space. A lifetime's worth, if he'd let me.

For now, I had to brace us both for more bumpy roads

ahead. "You know Trey won't leave this all alone with one measly tweet. He didn't get everything he wanted, so we haven't seen the last of him. And..." Deep inhale. "I have to come clean to Killian about what I did with that account at SGC. Fuck. He's going to be furious with me."

He reached to caress my nape. "Don't worry about Killian. I'm sure it'll be fine."

"Have you forgotten what he's like when he's mad?" I countered. "I mean really mad? Sometimes, even I'm scared—but you're sworn to secrecy on that part."

He flashed my favorite version of his lopsided smile. The expression hit his lips but turned into something very naughty on its way to his golden-green eyes. "My silence isn't free, Miss Asher."

I unbuckled my seat belt and slid over to him. Into his ear, I breathed more than spoke, "Name your price. I'll pay anything."

He pulled back enough to stare at me, gaze turning dark and lusty, before he whispered back, "Get back over there and put your seat belt back on...or I may have to think of punishment."

I obeyed but wasn't happy about it—and let it show. Michael leaned over, grabbed my chin, and then turned my face up to meet his. Silently, I begged him to tighten his grip. He slowly grinned, reading my mind as always, while torqueing his fingers harder. Harder. Ohhh, yes...

"You're so beautiful, even when you pout."

"I'm not pouting."

"Uh-huh."

Good thing the drive to my place was short. I spent every one of those five minutes debating whether to snap my seat belt free, rip off my shirt, and kiss my way into some payback. I settled for keeping my fingers or toes on him any way I could.

As soon as Andre pulled the car up to the El Cortez, I sprang out of the back seat. Michael was only half a step behind. Great minds lusted alike.

I waved the key for the elevator to open and let us up to the penthouse, making a mental note to have Sorrelle call management regarding a new key for Michael. They would probably raise a little hell, but Sorrelle could be a charmer when he wanted.

As soon as the lift doors closed, Michael moved into action. He pushed over me, pinning me into the corner quicker than I could spot a fake fur from a real one. His knee nudged between my thighs, and he grabbed my wrists, slamming them both against the walls that formed the corner at my back. My breathing instantly quickened, meshing with the same passionate huffs of his.

"Wh-What's going on here, Pearson?" I rasped.

"Very good question, Asher," he growled. "Now let me answer." He jerked his knee up a little. Every nerve in my core cried out in joy and agony at once. "This is me showing beautiful you how things are going to be once we lock ourselves in at your place. And this is you agreeing to it...because you want it that way too." He dipped his head, trailing the heat of his lips down the side of my face. "Say you do, pretty princess."

I could barely breathe. Holy hell, he turned me on—like nobody else ever had. Or would. "I...I do."

"Look how easy that was." He turned his head a little, biting into the side of my neck. As he soothed the throb with firm strokes of his tongue, my pussy began pulsing in time with the pain. Oh, dear God...

The elevator slowed.

I let out an aching moan as he pushed away, allowing my hands to fall to my sides. I stayed slumped into the corner, certain I'd be on the floor, a heap of horny goodness, without support.

He turned just as the elevator dinged, sliding open at my floor. How the fuck he timed that so perfectly, I'd never know. It made every minute that much hotter now. The bastard was killing it at this game. He was killing me. But what a way to go.

After wobbling out of the elevator, I made it to my door. Mr. Ridiculously Sexy was waiting, naughty grin in place.

I glared.

"Is that any way to treat your houseguest, sugar?"

He barked out a laugh when I added a raised eyebrow. "Houseguest? Is that what you are now? In that case, you'll be staying in the guest room on the other side of the penthouse—downstairs and far, far away from my boudoir."

He stopped after closing the door. "Boudoir?"

Point regained, Asher. His what-the-hell expression gave it up loud and clear.

"Of course." I breezed past him, walking toward the guest area around the corner from the staircase. "Come, come now. I'll show you to your room."

I covered only two steps more. After that, I was spun around, smashed against him, consumed again by the hot domination of his kiss.

Oh...this kiss...

It felt so different than anything else we'd shared. So new. So raw. So hot. Untamed passion was our blazing reality, dry timber mated to burning brush, promising to ignite the whole forest. Screw the tanker planes. Forget the fire crews. We don't need no water... Let the motherfucker burn.

"Michael," I managed to croak out.

"Yeah, baby?" His voice, just as needy, sent a thrill straight to my sex.

"Stop fucking around. Take me to bed."

He jerked back, making me growl. I tamped the sound just as fast, simply hoping he saw the ache building through me.

A corner of his mouth lifted in quiet command. "Ask nicely."

"Oh, my God. Are you ser—?"

Yeah. He was serious. His perfectly arched eyebrow said so.

Very well, Mr. Pearson. Two could play this game. I'd proved it to him before with a hell of a lot less incentive.

Without a pause to give him warning, I lowered to my knees in front of him. When his breath hitched, I bit back my grin. I was eye level with the beautiful bulge in his pants. Perfect. I leaned in, letting him feel the warmth of my breath through his jeans before climbing my gaze all the way back up his body. He stopped the air in my lungs, even with all his clothes still on, especially as his abdomen started heaving in and out with the excitement of beholding me like this before him. I loved his reaction. Fed on the pure power of it. What I wouldn't give to flick open the button in front of me and then slide the zipper beneath. I looked up again, letting that fantasy play out through the slow, dramatic process.

When I finally tilted my head up all the way, I found his hooded gaze waiting for me. His breaths were harsh rasps, in and out through his nose. Even more perfect.

"Please," I finally whispered. A softer, sweeter tone hadn't left my throat since I was a girl practicing fashion show etiquette with my dolls. “Please, please take me to bed and fuck me into tomorrow. Please.” I added that one with an over-the-top blink. Not a flutter, just one blink.

It worked.

Michael jerked me to my feet. Slammed me with another kiss. No tongue, no fuss, pure demand. “Upstairs. In your room. On the bed. Naked. Two minutes. Go.”

I already knew how this one worked.

As of right now, I had one minute, fifty-eight seconds and counting.

CHAPTER TWENTY

Michael

One Mississippi. Two Mississippi. Three.

Fuck. I was never going to make it to ten seconds, let alone a hundred-twenty. My cock begged for an escape route from my jeans with every step I climbed toward her bedroom, burning for the sneaky little minx who'd turned the tables on me—and was going to pay for it with several screaming orgasms.

That gave me a smile. Oh, the ways I could define punishment...

Thoughts that fled as soon as I beheld her again.

"Fuck. Me." It escaped on a grate as I walked in. Stopped. Took another step. Stopped again.

I didn't know whether to grin or groan.

The sun spilled into her bedroom through a high window in the corner, casting brilliant light across the bottom third of her enormous bed. She was on all fours in the center of that beam, taking perfect advantage of nature's spotlight. Her hair seemed streaked with gold, her skin infused with crushed pearls.

But her beauty was only the first source of my astonishment.

How the hell had she accomplished this—in two minutes?

And why was I fixating on logistics—when she looked like

this?

That tiny leopard print thong. That matching nothing of a bra. Those black thigh highs. The black patent pumps, heels so high and skinny they were only good for one purpose—and it wasn't strutting.

And the final, fierce tug on my cock?

She topped off the outfit with little fur kitty ears.

Holy shit, they were cute. I assumed the things were attached to a headband, now lost in the voluptuous mane of her hair, making me wonder how hard she'd have to be fucked until they fell off.

Logistics again?

Not so shockingly, my dick forgave me for this one.

She lifted her head a little. "Meow?"

Ohhh, damn. Her voice was already husky and low. I felt every note in the center of both balls. "Christ, woman," I bit. "You're going to be the death of me."

"Why?" She pouted a little. Minx. "Are you allergic to kitties?"

"Hmmm. Clever." I whipped my shirt over my head, enjoying the reaction she tried to cover. Her eyes never left mine as I walked to the side of her bed. With slow purpose, I pulled out my wallet and set it on the nightstand—removing the condom from inside and leaving that on top.

That's right, princess kitty. Stare at that rubber and think about my cock sheathed inside your hot...pussy.

I unbuttoned the top of my pants but thought better of taking them down myself. It seemed my little kitty needed some busy work. When frustration grooved her face, I knew I'd made the right call. I kicked off my shoes and pulled off my socks, savoring the coolness of the polished floor beneath my feet. The woman had jacked my body temperature into overheat mode.

"So, kitty...do you know any tricks?"

She smiled and purred, all Eartha Kitt coy, and then murmured, "Come closer, and I'll show you."

I shook my head. "Kitties don't speak." I couldn't help but chuckle when she realized the tables—the cat box?—had been flipped on her yet again. I leaned over to press a gentle finger to her scrunched nose. "Kitties don't pout, either."

She burst into a sharp hiss—before lashing out with a hand curled up like a claw. Crazily, her playacting move caught a lucky break, resulting in a long scratch on the inside of my forearm. The sting spiked my adrenaline—and arousal. Kitty wanted to play fierce? I could do that. With her wrist grabbed in my hand, I hunkered in, nose-to-nose with her.

"Naughty, naughty kitty. Now you have to be punished."

"Mmmm," she whimpered. "Meow?"

"Too late for nice kitty. Let's go." I maintained my grip while sitting on the edge of her bed. Didn't stop her from attempting the play nice again, so fucking adorable as she licked her wrist and then rubbed it behind her costume ear, but I refused to cave. With one yank, I pulled her facedown, across my lap.

And dealt with instant retaliation from my cock.

Holy. Hell.

Just looking at the perfect swells of her ass like this, completely at my mercy, turned my senses again to the surreal. Was I really going to do this? I'd never spanked a woman—not in a formal production like this, at least—though Margaux had always taken delight in my little foreplay smacks. We were both about to learn what all the fuss was about—if I could get on with things. Staring at the spheres below my hand, bisected by that trail of wicked lace, was enough to make me jizz already. Plus column or minus column? I went for plus. The idea of watching that flesh bloom beneath my discipline? Plus column. Her obeying me regarding anything? Definitely one more plus.

She trembled a little as I rubbed both globes. The reaction was so pure, unadulterated. She was scared and thrilled at the same time. She wanted this but wanted to deny that she did.

"It's okay, princess. We'll do this together." I said it as command instead of consolation, affirming I'd made the right call as I pulled her back up against me. Her face was flushed, her gaze a shade of dreamy spring green, her lips parted a little. I fixated on them, knowing I had to have more. I dug my fingers into her hair, compelling her face to mine. This time when I kissed her, a thought embedded itself in my brain.

This is for keeps, Margaux. This is for forever.

It was the truth. She was my forever. The fire of my heart. The sun of my future. The woman of my dreams. I'd spend the rest of my days proving it to her...showing her she would always be safe with me. Safe because of me. I would always be there for her and for us. I needed her soul to know it as thoroughly as her mind and heart did.

So I went for broke.

My lips started gently but didn't stay that way for long. I plunged my tongue in against hers, twirling around it, tasting and teasing in and out, and then back for more.

When I finally pulled back, I had to channel my inner Hercules for the will to press her back over my knees, directing her to drop her head toward the floor. Though she mewled as if in protest, there wasn't a single wiggle or squirm from the creamy flesh now filling my hungry vision again. She wasn't restrained in any way. If she really wanted to tell me to fuck off while she sashayed this gorgeous ass out of the door, she could.

Time to take things to the next level.

I growled, low and menacing, while caressing her ass again. I'd roughened my voice and now did the same with my strokes, digging fingers in a little at the end of each swipe. "You scratched me, little brat. How many swats do you think that's worth?"

I left her to be creative about the answer—and was damn glad I did. "Meow?" she rasped from near the floor. "Meow, meow?" She pawed at my foot. "Meow, meow?"

"Five, eh? Okay, we'll do ten and call it forgiven."

She stiffened—for about three seconds. Instantly, her shoulders slumped and her body went slack again.

Ohhhh yeah, did she want this.

And I so wanted to give it to her.

"Well. You learn quickly for a naughty kitty. Too bad I still have to punish you."

Now she squirmed—though hardly in protest. Damn, I was going to enjoy this—and had a strong feeling she would too.

Smack. Smack.

"Ohhh! Meow!"

I dropped my gaze, letting it feast fully on her ass. "Holy shit. This already looks so good, sugar girl."

Smack. Smack.

"Mmmmmm!"

"Fuck. Fuck. You're perfect. These sexy little globes are so firm and round...and now blooming so perfectly for me."

Smack. Smack.

"I could do this for hours. Touch you all day and night,

Margaux. Do you feel what you're doing to me? Do you feel my cock, surging for you? Sweet, sexy creature. And now I can say you belong to me."

I rubbed her roughly, pressing the warmth of the blows in but coaxing fresh blood to the surface of her skin, warming her for the rest of the count. She was limp and relaxed, damn near purring like the kitty she pretended to be. So I switched things up a little, raising my hand a little higher, raining the last four spanks in hard succession.

She yelped and nearly fell off my legs. I caught her and started caressing again. "Easy, beautiful. That wasn't so bad, was it?" My cock surged when she answered with another mewl, soft and sexy and lusty. "And now for the good part, kitty. Spread your legs for me."

"Meow?"

"Ssshhh. Trust me." I slid my hand between her legs, starting at her knees. As I worked my way higher, her legs parted wider. Inches before arriving at her core, I could feel the warm, wet heat of her arousal.

"Mmmmm." She wriggled a little, battling to entice me farther.

"Well, what's going on here?" I dipped two fingers under her soaked thong. The sweetness of her pussy was too damn tempting to pass up. As I pressed them in, I was rewarded with a moan as lush as any favorite melody. Though I pumped slowly, Margaux squirmed with mounting urgency. To tame her, I had to wrap my free arm around her waist.

"Kitty." I drew out both halves in censure. "I stop if you can't be still. Understood?"

"Meow," she grumbled.

"Such a good kitty."

I pumped my fingers in again, faster now. Despite her little fume, she didn't squirm anymore. Instead, she contained her lust by flexing her thighs and clenching her ass—twisting the winch on my torture rack now.

"Time for a change," I growled, pulling her back up. "On your back, sweet kitty. Every good pussy needs to be properly tasted."

As she maneuvered to obey, I caught the sides of her thong and slid it down her thighs. Over my shoulder it went, followed by my jeans and underwear. Thank fuck. My cock was about to declare mutiny from that prison.

But now, nirvana was spread in front of me. How had I gotten this woman's freak on so many times and not made contact with this heaven yet? A mystery not worth solving in the bliss of now. I hooked my arms up under her thighs and pulled her to me, all but diving into her pussy at the same time.

"God! Michael!"

"Same rule," I ordered. "You squirm too much, I stop."

"Are you fucking serious?"

"I don't joke about your pussy." I chuckled as she flopped back, appearing as if she had to take the hardest exam ever given. "You can do it, kitty. I know you can."

My breaths brushed her well-trimmed strip. "Not helping."

"Just think about how hard you're going to come."

"Not. Helping. Ohhhhh!"

She screamed as I sucked in again.

Best. Meal. Ever.

I wanted to do it for the rest of the night. No—for the rest of my life. I quickly learned all her delicious nuances—what made her crazy and made her moan, what drove her to the brink—and how I could pull back once there, just enough to make her insane. I slid my fingers in and toyed with her from the inside too, curling up against the sensitive spot inside that made her hips buck off the bed and her lips burst my name like a plea to a pagan god.

"More, beautiful?"

"Yes. No. I don't know!" Her fists twisted into the sheets. "Holy hell, Michael. Fuck me or finish me. I'm going to explode. Please, please, do something!"

"But we have all day."

"No! We don't!"

"You're so breathtaking."

"You're such a scoundrel."

I chuckled before dipping in again. Licking her. Sucking her. Biting her clit. Finger-fucking her tunnel. Then again and again and again, until she screamed out her orgasm, drenching my tongue in the tart nectar of her fulfillment.

"Fuck. Jesus. Fuck. Damn it. Michael. Fuck. Christ."

My girl's version of sweet postcoital nothings. It was as uniquely her as the taste on my lips, and it made me grin like—well, Captain America. I rose up to kiss her, plunging deep so she'd taste her own elixir, hoping it'd get her as high as I was. No way was I letting her come down from the trip, either—not until my cock visited her heaven too.

I scooped the condom off the nightstand. The moment I took to suit up was the opening Margaux needed for a little payback of her own. By the time I looked up again, she'd popped back up to her hands and knees, swerving her rosy-red ass in blatant enticement.

"Hell. Yes."

I scrambled over, quickly lining myself up behind her,

fingering through her wetness again. Her clit was swollen and wet from all the attention I had given it. Just one glance at the swollen nub, and my cock strained at the confines of the rubber.

"You. Lady doctor. Birth control. ASAP," I snarled. "I want to fuck you without these as soon as possible. But for now"—I spread my fingers against her scalp and twisted her head to the side—"put your head on the mattress like this. Your shoulders flat too. Yeah. Oh yeah, kitty." With her backside raised like this, I could stretch her pussy, staring into the tight depths she was ready to welcome me with. "Now reach back like you're grabbing the soles of your feet. Holy fuck, that's good."

I was really tempted to give her a few more spanks just for fun, but my dick had bigger, better plans. I prayed they didn't include getting inside her and finishing off in three pumps.

I lined up at her entrance and closed my eyes, thinking about anything and everything other than how amazing this woman's body felt around my engorged cock. She was so warm. So tight. So right.

Time for the big guns.

ABCs. Backward. Now!

Z, Y, X...

So wet.

W, V, U...

So good.

Fuck it. She defied distractions.

I rubbed her ass, kneading the flesh, still so red and warm from my swats. "Sexy kitten," I grated. "So, so good. You ready to try for another one? Try for me. Reach between your legs and rub your clit."

"Wha...?" she mumbled. "M-Michael. I-I don't know—"

"Do it!"

Smack. My fresh handprint bloomed red on her ass. Temporary diversion. So temporary—especially as her slender fingers moved up through her glistening folds. When she gathered moisture from where we were joined and worked it over her clit, it was like live-action porn. Fuck, no. Better.

"Shit," I rasped. "Holy. Shit. Don't stop."

She rubbed slow, large circles around it at first, but soon they were smaller and faster, concentrating right over her perfect cherry bud.

"It's coming on soon, sugar. I feel you quivering. I have a front-row seat too. So gorgeous. Do it. Come all over me. Cover me in your juices. I'll be right behind you, love, I promise."

"Michael! Ohhhh!"

"What, princess? What do you need?"

"More," she insisted. "Deeper. Harder!"

"Then get up. Get up and take more of my dick. I'm straining for you, Margaux. I'll fuck your cunt as hard as you need it."

The minute snapping her neck was no longer a concern, I let loose. Bam-bam-bam. The bed frame smacked the wall, a brutal echo of my body against hers. I grabbed her hips, pulling her back to me, until even that didn't work. With an arm around her waist, I slammed into her like the rocket my cock had turned into.

Five, four, three...

It was time.

"Margaux. Now!"

"Fuck! Yeesss! Goooddd! Michael!"

The exact words I needed to hear. When she collapsed to her stomach, I followed her down, rutting on her, emptying my seed as deep into her as I could get. I buried my face into the juncture of her neck and shoulder, sinking my teeth into her skin. I wanted to bite so much harder, but there was a difference between passion and marking your woman like a fifteen-year-old. Not that I felt a lot different than one. In a few minutes, I'd probably be ready to go again. As it was, my hips didn't want to stop. I kept pumping, forcing myself to remember that the woman beneath me was probably crushed and needing air.

Damn it.

I pulled out and scrambled off the bed, not wanting to make a mess on her gazillion-dollar bedding. I found the bathroom connected by her lavish closet and trashed the nasty, washing my hands before tucking back into bed behind my adorable little kitty.

"Come here." I pulled her close.

She sighed. "Oh, God."

"What?"

"You don't want to spoon again, do you?"

I tugged harder. "Come here." And gently nipped her neck again. "I'll spoon you whenever I goddamn want to, woman."

"Fine, fine."

Her lips might have groused, but another tremble claimed her. I knew a frisson of happiness when I felt one. After a few minutes, I resumed the nips. Under her ear, down her neck, along her shoulder...she smelled so good. Tasted so good.

Sure enough, my dick rose to half-mast again. If she wiggled right just a few more times, we'd be looking for a second condom.

"I'm in love with you, Michael Pearson."

"So I've heard."

"I just want to keep saying it."

"Don't let me stop you. Please, go right ahead. But for the record? I love you too." I braced up onto one elbow. I'd been wanting to ask her a question, and this seemed the right time to broach it. "So...do you ever want me to call you Mary?"

"Not if you want to keep your balls."

"Okay, then." I chuckled. "But now that I've been thinking about all of it in a new light, Killian and Claire's nickname for you...it makes sense. Mare Bear, right?"

She tensed but only a little. "Whoa. Nothing slips by you, does it, Pearson? Maybe you should be a private dick instead of a lawyer. Key word being dick."

"Do you need another spanking?"

"Couldn't hurt." She wiggled that naughty ass into me. Shit.

Change of subject. Now.

I pulled at her shoulder, a wordless request for her to turn so I could fully see her face. "Okay, so talk to me. Did you... enjoy this? What we just did? What're your thoughts?"

"Thoughts?" She spat it like I'd asked her to discuss lancing a boil. "Fuck, Michael. You and all this talking."

I starched my jaw. "Not an answer."

"Ugh. Fine. It was hot as hell, okay? Good answer from the therapy couch?"

I smirked. *I'm a fucking stud.* "That's what I figured. I wanted to be sure."

"Here, let me beat you over the head with the obvious. So...ummmm...what did you think of my kitty outfit?"

"I didn't really like it. I mean, it was okay."

She jacked up. "What? *Okay?* Are you serious?"

"Not in the least. But how else would you have known if we didn't talk about things? Do you see my point?" I shot up a hand, snatching her wrist before it descended into the new smack she intended for my chest. "No. Don't try to deal with this by fighting your way from it. You're stronger than that, Margaux."

Her shoulders slumped. I relented my hold. She yanked back her hand as if I'd fried it, curling it against her upper chest.

"But I'm good at fighting."

"I know."

I felt shitty for harshing our afterglow, but only for a minute. We needed to do this, even if it irked and twisted and felt uncomfortable. Little by little, we were finding our way.

"I don't know how to do things in a lot of other ways."

"I know that too, princess. But we'll both learn."

She peered at me, eyes huge. "But you've got so much more of it figured out."

"Not true. At all." I shook my head. "I've got weak spots too, sugar. Lots of them." Wasn't that the fucking truth?

Her eyes pooled and glimmered. "I'm sorry, Michael. So sorry."

I gathered her into my arms. "Whoa. What's all this? Tears?"

"I'm so fucked up, Michael! I don't know how to do all this. This girlfriend thing, you know? I'm going to make mistakes. A bunch. I have issues, more than the quick T-shirt slogan kind. Mommy issues. Hell, probably daddy issues too. Maybe you were smart to have run when you did."

I yanked her chin up with a fierce tug. "I love you, Margaux. You. I wasn't searching for perfect, okay? I was searching...for you."

She sniffed. "I don't deserve you."

"Now that's fucking funny, because right now, I feel like

the luckiest man on earth. And for the record, anytime you want to play kitty, I'm game."

"What about schoolgirl?"

I gulped. Could she have asked that in any sexier a voice? "Well, that isn't my chalk stick popping up in approval, sugar."

The next moment, she looked like she wanted to get started on that one right away. "Ohmigosh." She jerked up in my lap like a fifteen-year-old who'd scored Comic-Con passes. "As long as we're doing the honesty thing, I have to tell you something."

I sighed. "It's all right. I already know you snore." I'd known since the red eye we'd been on to Tokyo last year, actually.

"I do not snore."

"So that wasn't what you needed to tell me?"

"I do not snore!"

"Margaux?"

"What?"

"Want to spit out what you were going to tell me?"

She blinked. "Right. Okay. I told you I wasn't good at this shit, didn't I?"

I hauled her in for a fast but mushy kiss. "You're doing just fine. Breathe and take it easy."

She complied with a long, soft sigh. "All right. This may sound a little crazy."

Not any crazier than how she'd strong-armed past TSA this afternoon. Lovable little loon.

"Something weird happened at the press attack this afternoon."

I sat up a little. Now she had my attention. And the full alert of my ape man protective mode. "Oh?"

"I...saw someone."

"Trey?" I seethed. A possibly worse answer stabbed. "Doug?"

"No, no. A woman. A stranger, actually...but not."

I stroked her shoulder with my knuckles. "How do you mean?"

"I was answering a question and made eye contact with her. She smiled at me, and I wanted to look longer, but when I scanned the crowd again, she was gone."

"So how is that weird? The airport is a very busy place. San Diego is the eighth largest city in the country. It's an international airport."

She rolled her eyes. "Okay, Mr. President of the Tourism Authority. That was kind of creepy."

"But sexy."

"Kind of."

"But this woman...she resonated with you. Why? Can you peg the connection?"

She licked her lips. Took my hand. "She looked exactly like Carolinc."

My eyebrows shot up. "Whoa."

"Yeah. Whoa."

"Are you certain?"

"Of course I'm not certain. It's also been over fifteen years. But here's the stranger part. I'm pretty sure I've seen that woman before. Every few years, she shows up at the same event as me. Press conferences, society parties, client events... It's random, just out of the blue. I never know when or where, but I catch a glimpse of her in the crowd, and when I look again, she's gone."

"Well, have you ever tried to find Caroline? Like, hiring

someone to track her down?"

Now she gaped like I was the crazy one. "Duh. But like my birth mother, she's disappeared off the face of the earth. I'm sure Andrea had her erased too."

My gut clenched. "Bitch." I cupped her face, brushing a thumb across her cheek. "But you still don't have closure, and that sucks."

She surprised me with her reply. A brightened smile and an aha look came before her exclamation. "Hey. Maybe Killian has some different resources for this than I do. I wonder if he'd help? After he's over wanting to disown me about this whole Trey mess."

I growled. Hard. "Killian is going to understand, okay? Just explain to him how you tried to screech the brakes on the Trey train by yourself. Which, by the way, was the dumbest thing you ever—"

A flying cat cut me off. More accurately, a blonde kitty bombshell launching herself at me all over again, filling my arms like the fiery, feisty little feline I knew—and loved. Ohhh yeah, how I loved her.

"I'm not perfect, Michael, remember?"

I tangled my hands in her hair, filled my senses with her amber scent, and curled her tight against my body. "Yeah. I remember."

"But I am yours."

"Mmmm. Now that I really remember."

I held her even tighter. Like bottling lightning? Grabbing fire? Pinning down a cloud? Perhaps. Probably. But I had to believe that finally, fate—and love—were on our side. What other explanation was there for how this apple farmer's son had finally found the other half of his soul in the world's highest ivory tower, in the heart of a magnificent, maddening, magical, not-so-perfect princess?

I'd spend the rest of my days fighting for that love. Telling her, each and every day, how I'd never take it for granted or stop working to make it better. To make us better.

We wouldn't always get it perfect.

But we'd always make it right.

And, for now, that was all that mattered.

Continue Secrets of Stone with Book Four

No Magic Moment

Available Now

Keep reading for an excerpt!

EXCERPT FROM *NO MAGIC MOMENT*

BOOK FOUR IN THE SECRETS OF STONE SERIES

CHAPTER ONE

Michael

If any moment proved I was hopelessly in love with Margaux Asher, this was it.

Dirty water dripped down my face—technically, up my face, toward my hair—as I watched a water beetle scurry along the wall of the drain sewer off 5th and G in downtown San Diego. Yeah, the sewer I'd dived down headfirst, in the full suit I'd worn to dinner, still half-buzzed from the martinis I'd enjoyed at said dinner.

Thank fuck for those martinis. In some strange way, they helped with my inverted equilibrium. They sure as hell didn't hurt.

This was about as low as I went.

Literally.

Laughing at my private joke wasn't an option. I settled for grunting. Good compromise between breathing and passing out from the stench. America's Finest City was a different world below the surface.

"What? What is it? Do you see it, Michael? Do you see it?"

In an instant, I forgot about the smell and the wet—and the fact that if Andre's hold on my ankles slipped at all, I'd be reenacting the *Star Wars* trash compactor scene, minus the blasters and the Dianoga. Or so I hoped. But even facing a giant sewer snake would be worth it to banish the dread in my woman's voice.

"Andre," I barked at the burly Jamaican, "don't let go."

"I got you, boss."

Now wasn't the time to tell him I hated that "boss" crap—and the laugh he surely intended as reassuring.

"Michael!"

Margaux's cry was shrill. She'd been in this panic for at least ten minutes now, when our after-dinner walk had gone from relaxing to horrifying in the space of five seconds. Instead of gunshots, our black moment had been delivered in five pings—the sound of a small gold ring falling to the pavement and then disappearing through the hole in the sewer cover.

"Do you see it?" She choked it out this time. Hell. My girl did not like bawling, despite how much she'd softened in the three months since our relationship began. She fought the tears with everything she had. Her conflict echoed down the sewer, shattering my heart and steeling my resolve. Find the damn ring. The jewelry represented a huge chunk of her past, the only part that had meant emotional safety for her. She wasn't strong enough to lose it yet.

I knew it. She knew it. I just prayed Andre knew it too.

"Michael. Talk to me!"

I grimaced. "Not in a position to chat right now, sugar."

"Just tell me if you see it." Her breath caught again. "Please. Please tell me you—" A car horn cut her off, something sporty by the tenor of it. "Hey! The translation of Maserati isn't *license to be an asshole*!"

Andre's grip tremored from the force of his chuckle. I grimaced and then swore. "Not funny, man."

Margaux backed it up with a gritty girl-growl, a sound curling straight to my cock, which apparently didn't care about its current setting. "Drop him, and your testicles are mine."

"Not until you've dealt with other testicles first," I muttered.

"What?" she shouted.

"You mentioned testicles," Andre explained.

"Oh, for—" She snorted. "You two want to focus with your big heads for once?"

Andre snickered again. I wanted to bark at him but was busy smirking myself. God damn it if my princess wasn't more irresistible with a pissy bee under her figurative crown. On top of that, envisioning her in the middle of the street above me, leaning over the manhole in the slinky dress and pumps she'd worn to dinner, still unsure whether to play out her stress with sass or penitence...

Yep, it was official. Even hanging upside down in a sewer, I had a hard-on for the woman.

The sooner I found the damn ring, the—

"Bingo."

"What?" she shouted.

"Bingo," I yelled back, curling fingers around the small gold circle that had, by a pure miracle, caught on a steel peg to my right. Miracle was putting it lightly. The band, not fancy, was sized for a child of nine—the age Margaux had been when she first received it. It never left her pinkie finger now—except, as we'd learned the hard way, on cold nights when her fingers contracted. It had become just as important to me once I knew the story about who had given it to her. I'd never forget the night she'd dug so deeply into her past and all its pain to give me the confession. It had been the start of our journey from friendship to passion...and finally love. The trust she'd handed over to me that night still blew me away at times. It was a gift I'd never take for granted and a responsibility I'd never diminish.

She meant so damn much to me.

More than I could screw up the courage to admit.

But somewhere, somehow, I was going to have to do just that.

She'd put the secrets of her past into my care. It was about damn time I gave the same to her.

I'd start with giving her something more pleasant.

"Dre," I shouted. "Let's roll it up, man."

"Oh, my God," Margaux exclaimed. As soon as I emerged, brandishing the gold band, she screamed, "Oh, my God!"

Before I could remind her I'd just been down a hole dripping with slime and runoff water, she mashed herself against me. As her body and lips molded to mine, the ecstasy of her yelp hummed through me. "I love you, Mr. Pearson," she declared against my mouth.

I chuckled, ordering myself to enjoy the moment—and for the time being, leave my morose thoughts from the sewer in the sewer. "I love you too, sugar."

"No shit!" As she slipped the ring back on, I literally watched her reconnect with that part of herself. Joy flowed from her, but it wasn't the only thing. She was grounded again.

Solid.

I didn't know if that recognition was heartening or disconcerting.

She muted the conflict by kissing me once more. *Whoa.* This time, there was tongue—the kind of tongue I loved. Pulling at mine, as if needing my mouth deeper inside hers... usually her fun little way of asking to have other parts inside her too. She emitted a kittenish mewl and waited for me to give back the Captain America version, before dragging away with a lust-heavy gaze.

"The knight who saved me."

I smiled. "The princess who saved me."

"Take me home, stud. This princess aches to reward your bravery."

Andre had already pulled up in the BMW, waiting for us to finish the PDA as he yanked open the door to the back seat. With his other hand, he extended a small silo of baby wipes. "Not saying you smell worse than a baby's batty, but..."

I chuckled at his Jamaican slang. "But you're thinking it."

"Never said that, either." His lips twitched as he kept the hand extended, waiting to take the cloths I scraped from fingers to elbows.

"Thanks, man." I made sure our gazes met. "And not just for the cleanup."

As I expected, the big guy just rolled his eyes. "Not a worry, brother."

When he shut the door and sealed us in, I swept toward Margaux in one lunge, lowering for another kiss. Now that we weren't in the middle of the street, I attacked her with deeper passion and growing need.

"What if I don't want to wait for my reward?"

Her eyes flared at the husk in my tone. As she nudged her head up and bit into my bottom lip, she replied, "You still smell, Sir Knight."

"Exactly how you like me."

"We'll get the car dirty."

"Exactly how you like it."

I watched my edicts curl through her, making her writhe with renewed arousal. Yeah, I was in love with a woman who reveled in orgasms on silk sheets, beneath gold showerheads, and in marble elevators—but my princess also craved being taken like a peasant, her passion just accepted and enjoyed, as raw and raunchy as she could get it. Getting her to admit that? Another thing entirely—which was why I yanked the decision from her sometimes. Told her exactly how hard she'd take it from me and love it as I did.

"You want me to get you dirty." I hovered my mouth over hers, tempting but not giving, while pushing a hand beneath her dress and bra. We both moaned as the bud inside stiffened. "You want me to put my naughty hands all over you...to make your body as filthy as your mind."

She cupped a hand to the back of my neck. Tried to drag me down for another kiss. I held fast where I was, pinching her nipple at the same time. "Say it, Margaux. Tell me you want it—and exactly how."

This story continues in

No Magic Moment***: Secrets of Stone Book Four!***

ALSO BY ANGEL PAYNE

Secrets of Stone Series:
No Prince Charming
No More Masquerade
No Perfect Princess
No Magic Moment
No Lucky Number
No Simple Sacrifice
No Broken Bond
No White Knight

Honor Bound:
Saved
Cuffed
Seduced
Wild
Wet
Hot
Masked
Mastered (May 15, 2018)
Conquered (Coming Soon)
Ruled (Coming Soon)

The Bolt Saga:
Bolt (Summer 2018)
Ignite (Summer 2018)
Pulse (Summer 2018)
Fuse
Surge
Light

For a full list of Angel's other titles, visit her at angelpayne.com

ABOUT ANGEL PAYNE

USA Today bestselling romance author Angel Payne loves to focus on high-heat romance starring memorable alpha men and the women who love them. She has numerous book series to her credit, including the Suited for Sin series, the Cimarron Saga, the Temptation Court series, the Secrets of Stone series, the Lords of Sin historicals, and the popular Honor Bound series, as well as several standalone titles.

Angel is a native Southern Californian, leading to her love of being in the outdoors, where she often reads and writes. She still lives in Southern California with her soul-mate husband and beautiful daughter, to whom she is a proud cosplay/culture con mom. Her passions also include whisky tasting, shoe shopping, and travel.

Visit her here:
angelpayne.com

ABOUT VICTORIA BLUE

International bestselling author Victoria Blue lives in her own portion of the galaxy known as Southern California. There, she finds the love and life–sustaining power of one amazing sun, two unique and awe-inspiring planets, and four indifferent yet comforting moons. Life is fantastic and challenging and every day brings new adventures to be discovered. She looks forward to seeing what's next!

Visit her here:
victoriablue.com